DEAL ME A CARD

by

Mary Penelope Young

March 2019

Terri —

Best Wishes !

Mary Penelope Young

Cover Image:
by
Mary Penelope Young
and
USA Photo Tallahassee, Florida

ISBN 978-0-578-11343-2

ACKNOWLEDGEMENTS

I thank my editor, Judy Gross, for her relentlessly honest and gentle assistance. To the hundreds of my friends from Mexico, Central and South America I offer my gratitude. Your *joie de vivre* and hope, often in the face of great odds, have inspired me over the years.

Si se puede. Yes, it's possible.

DEAL ME A CARD

CHAPTER 1

"MOTHER RAISED ME to never need a man. But close encounters of the male kind are a fifty percent probability if you want to exist beyond a vegetable state."

Emma read the sentences aloud, added a period. She set down her pen. Her listener uttered not a word, sitting sphinx-like on the cushioned chair with her limbs neatly aligned and her golden eyes unblinking. Emma looked at her with an amused smile,

"What do you think? You want nothing to do with males, do you? Never did, except for that one time. You had the three babies and then, no more! Well, me, I've loved too widely and not well! "

Her audience of one still remained silent, indifferent to the tentative plea for empathy. So Emma reached out and massaged her between her jet black ears. The cat made a sound now, a low satisfied rumbling. "Go ahead; purr your heart out my little Mamasan!" She kept stroking her pet until its eyes, and slowly all of its body, sank into the twenty-third nap of the day.

Emma stood up and stretched, legs wide apart, fingers reaching to the ceiling, her five foot three and a half inch frame erect, her back ramrod straight, to get the full benefit of circulation. She rotated her hips five times to the left, then five times to the right. Her nano-exercise set complete, she sank back on the soft pillow. Twirling her right index finger around a strand of hair that hung loose on her shoulder, Emma slowly closed lids over grey-green eyes. Her olive drab tank-top and roomy khaki capris, a change from her workday suit, gave her room for a comfortable wriggle. A jolly little tune rose softly in her throat.

Yes, she could amuse herself.

From the second-story window of her townhouse she overlooked the Chatsworth hills rosy after a day's exposure to the heat. Early summer breezes sweeping up the San

Fernando Valley, still keeping the Los Angeles smog at bay. The Wednesday evening sky with its streaks of red and magenta was spectacular.

Sunflowers in a tall cylindrical vase at the corner of her escritoire pulled her gaze away from the outside world. The merry yellow made her eyes dance. Those petals would radiate their brilliance long after darkness arrived. A careless bunch of week-old fading pink, cream and crimson roses, splayed in a mason jar on the bookshelf, still exuded a faint perfume.

Meanwhile, the journal in front of her was on fire, ablaze from the last flaming ray of the sunset filling the little alcove. Emma stared at it for a second, reached over, realigned the purple satin marker, shut the book. There, she was done with self-analysis for the day.

Absently, her fingers wound through Mamasan's thick fur. The animal heaved a sigh, oblivious to her owner's musings.

"All well and good for you, kitty. You have nine lives to try again. Me, I've used up half my life. Four decades. Two of them spent in a dysfunctional union from which I had to escape, or perish.

It's nineteen eight-nine, there's a millennium looming, ten years and six months from now. And I'm still alone."

Mamasan continued to lie languidly comatose, so Emma turned to dinner and television for distraction. Someone had doused her spicy turkey and avocado sandwich with too much oil and vinegar. Countless well-mannered Chinese protesters seemed doggedly intent on marching to their deaths as they infuriated their stony-faced leaders in Beijing. Mangled remains of the freight train that had derailed in San Bernardino were still puzzling the officials, good grief that was right here in our own back yard. The puppet-like pundits' prattle about Ollie North's conviction droned on and on. Nothing lightened her mood.

Beethoven's piano sonata made her feel slightly less pathetic. Afterwards, she fell asleep early under a light cover.

Deal Me a Card

CHAPTER 2

PERHAPS IN CONTRAST to her blues of the night before, or in anticipation of the evening ahead, the next day was copacetic.

Emma met weekly with Doctor Schwarzman in her cocoon-like office. The room, always cool, smelled of books well-read, lined up on polished cherry-wood shelves, and occasionally of orange jasmine blossom or lavender bouquets spilling carelessly out of a rotund urn standing in the corner. A hot-house spray of orchids perpetually bloomed on the doctor's desk. Sometimes Emma would sink into the overstuffed armchair and curl up on the cool smooth fabric. Deceptively cozy, *with the subtle intention of inducing thoughts of childhood traumas?* No matter.

She looked forward to each intimate fifty-minute hour with the psychologist who was Freud personified, backed up by the philosophies of such greats as Shakespeare, the four evangelists, Jung, and Donne, and infused with Carl Rogers' unconditional compassion. Somehow, her sessions had sprung the lock on Emma's journal writing and each Thursday evening was a time of revelation.

****

Up at seven, she was soon donning jaunty *sure-happy-it's-Thursday* attire, a swinging skirt with tinges of mauve on indigo, splashed with crimson, and an off-white silk blouse, complemented with a Nehru collar and short sleeves. The cool morning air stroked her bare arms as she watered the frilly lace of potted geraniums surrounding her handkerchief-sized balcony.

By eight thirty she was careening southeast on Rinaldi Street. The artery zoomed through suburban sprawls where she noted, as always, that homes were unable to shake off the

4

dust of the Southern Californian semi-desert, though the masses of purple, salmon and pink bougainvilleas still flaunted their colors. Soon she was weaving through more closely-knit clusters of modest wood and stucco houses where recent immigrants from Central America bivouacked alongside houses of those who had moved in shortly after the Franciscans arrived in 1797.

Next she hit the industry row of Van Nuys Boulevard. There, early-morning accordion mouths yawning, auto body shops lined up haphazardly, rubbing corners with small manufacturers, a *panaderia*, a clothing enterprise, a *supermercado*. Street vendors, hawking toys, *tortas* and tamarind drinks, were colorful splotches on the cracked sidewalks.

Stopped at a red light, Emma dared to beckon to a figure holding out a plastic bag of oranges on the edge of the curb. The saleswoman took the two dollars and handed over the fruit. Her cheery smile displayed too many gaps among teeth and too many wrinkles around the eyes for one so young. Imperfections could not mar her Mayan beauty. Vivid blue, white and scarlet embroidery on her navy skirt and the sheen of her black braids pledged allegiance to Guatemala, or perhaps Mexico.

One transaction complete, with seconds to spare, the entrepreneur astutely dug two golden mangoes out of the depths of her voluminous skirt and, thrust them at her customer. Another dollar changed hands. The light turned green. The woman stepped back onto the pavement. Emma drove on.

If the Jetta had not turned right two blocks later, into the Jones and Guerrero Construction Company lot, but had turned left, the automobile would have begun an ascent up the San Gabriel foothills sloping beyond the freeway.

Honking horns, noxious diesel fumes and clanging machinery were announcing the nine o'clock hour as Emma parked.

Deal Me a Card

First, she piled eleven oranges on a tray in the lunchroom for general consumption. Then she checked on the status of lumber and roofing shipments. Just as yesterday, the loads were making satisfactory progress from the Cascade Mountains to Pacoima.

Mr. Jones and Mr. Guerrero remained obediently focused on her agenda during the morning staff meeting. Emma presented her reports on the growth and glitches of their housing and remodeling projects in the surrounding communities and burgeoning valleys beyond.

An hour later in her office, some workers from the warehouse had questions about the English classes available in nearby San Benitez. She made a phone call for clarification, and distributed copies of the educational center's fax. A couple of faculty members from St. Anselmo High School met her for lunch at Sierra's in the adjoining neighborhood of La Coloma, to apprise her of their hectic end-of-the-semester schedule and vacation plans.

The call from Edward Lopez was the proverbial fly in the soothing ointment of the day's simplicity, interrupting her as she was preparing invoices. As soon as she picked it up, the sound of his wheedling hit Emma's ear.

"Hello, Senorita Emma Hazelton, my sweet one. It's Eddy. You haven't forgot, have you? I need that letter real bad! Come on, when is it ready for me?"

"Hi. No, Edward, I have not forgotten. I realize the urgency, but I need a few days. These things take time."

"Friday, right? Tomorrow is okay. Friday. That's my girl."

"Yes, I believe Friday is a good target day. It'll be done. Have a good afternoon."

"Hey, wait, can I come over tonight. We could have some fun."

"I'm busy this evening. We'll talk later. Goodbye."

She heard his 'adios' as she hung up with a less than gentle slam. And felt the beginnings of a migraine chew at

6

her temples. The implications, of her rash promise made to Edward some weeks ago, stabbed her forehead. His spotty employment history benevolence she offered to furnish a referral from the company, requiring some sleight of hand.

But the timing was not right to tackle this hurdle. She shoved any anxiety out of her mind, cleared her desk, and left for the day.

Emma headed for the Encino Hills in her search for self.

CHAPTER 3

WITH HER DIARY IN HAND, and her train of thought still chugging from the previous evening's brooding, Emma plunked herself down on a chair in her therapist's office and got to work. After the pleasantries, she plunged right in selecting words and phrases she had recorded,

"My relationships have run the whole gamut of slime to sorrowful to sublime, Doctor Schwarzman.

"I look back; reflect on the past, on the present. Often recollections ooze to the surface of my consciousness like bile on my tongue from a meal better not indulged. Memories and dreams flood my mind, slippery and sudsy like a backed-up bathtub.

"When that happens, doctor, I am sucked to the brink of seductive vortex of self-recrimination. Then, except for a cynical sense of humor, and a balance of truly fine men on the scale of remembrance, I'd be squeezed dry."

The psychologist spoke soothingly, "You're too hard on yourself. An attractive, intelligent woman like you knows your attributes. Your education, your broad experiences, the way you draw people to you. There's no need to deny it or to indulge in false modesty, Emma.

"We both recognize that a failed marriage or other unfulfilling liaisons can be festering cankers on the soul. To approach another commitment is to scratch up the raw and bleeding past. It's daunting to the strongest spirit. I understand your fears."

"Of course I want to make another commitment. I yearn to marry again, Doctor Schwarzman. But I need to meet the right man. Just look at my current beau! Edward, the loser of my life. His lack of class in every instance leaves me breathless.... I've got to clean out the sludge before I can start over."

Deal Me a Card

Her counselor nodded, "I think we both agree you're ready. Let's do it. We can make some inroads today."

Deal Me a Card

CHAPTER 4

WRIGGLING HER BODY, Emma relaxed into the oversized patient's chair, leaned her head back, and relaxed her arms. Drawing a deep breath, in almost a child-like voice, Emma started from the beginning.

"Blinking away the mist of drowsiness, I grapple the knob of my bedroom door with my right hand. It creaks open slowly. I peep through the widening crack. The afternoon is still, napping.

I hear the house breathing very quietly. It is sleeping. Empty, except for me.

I am alone, all, all alone. A little girl, just five years old. My brothers and my sister are in school. No one else is in our great, big house.

Leaving the door slightly ajar behind me, I pad across the hallway.

I pause at the arched entry into the living room, peer inside, and glance around. Four steps forward. I stand in the middle of the living room.

Toby, our part bulldog with no tail, is not snoring in his favorite spot on the carpet.

A ceiling fan whir-whirs, the grandfather clock tick-tocks, tick-tocks.

Otherwise silence in every available space. Daddy's lumpy armchair, crooked stacks of his books on the table, ferocious Chinese dragons etched in the lamp stand, all sag under its slumbering weight. Hushed shadows lurk in the corners, lying in wait.

The sharp edge of a sunbeam cuts across the curtained darkness.

I clasp my arms across my chest, a slight coolness stirring the air. My left hand moves up and down slowly smoothing the creases in my sleep-crinkled blue gingham.

Deal Me a Card

The dress, a little damp, rubs against my tummy, feels cool on my fingertips.

I raise my left thumb to my lips, quickly lower it. Mother told me I was a big girl. Big girls don't suck thumbs. I frown, pout, remembering, then take my other favorite stance. Grasping a strand of hair at the crown of my head with my right index finger, twirl it round and round until it tangles, then release it and start again. My breath makes a low whistle through my barely-parted lips as my finger swirls in my thick, very straight hair.

I breathe in and out through my mouth. To me the sound is like wind in the trees.

But only those mute shadows stand around me, beckoning from the sofa.

I back out, stumbling, to search for more lively companions.

When I tiptoe through the dim bedrooms, where my brothers and my mommy and Daddy sleep, nobody shushes me.

I creep away.

Sunshine beckons through the French doors. So I step outside, scamper across the porch. It is a long distance. My bare feet slap on the warm tiles. My toes tingle.

Panting, I reach the kitchen.

Go in slowly, preparing a giggle of surprise, opening my mouth to shout, "Here I am!"

I stop.

The refrigerator hums.

Smells circle around pots of boiled rice and a bubbling chicken stew putt-putting on the stove. But no welcoming granny, chopping vegetables at the kitchen table, looks up,

"Darling, awake already? Want a drink of water, a biscuit?"

Now I am scared and shivery, lonely. I am so small, and there is nobody to take care of me, to play with.

I call out, "Granny? Mamananny?"

11

The room resounds with my mewling.

I look around, first turning my head slowly, then looking back quickly when air brushes my shoulder. Only emptiness stares into my eyes.

My legs stiffen. But I keep walking, padding through the passage away from the kitchen.

I dare not look to the left into the dark ice-cold pantry.

Sometimes I help mother stack away the groceries. So I know they're just cans of baked beans, Campbell's soup, evaporated milk squatting on the shelves, merely rice and flour bins propped up stiffly on the red- tiled floor and stiff brooms with sturdy handles leaning idle against the wall.

But a big spider lives in the corner, and once I saw a tail sticking out from under a sack of potatoes. Adam said it was" just a lizard. Silly."

I'm almost running when I reach the dining room.

Mustardy yellow plates, cups, there're seven, and silverware are sitting primly on the table, patiently waiting. The baby's not born yet, so he doesn't have a place.

Then I'm back in the sitting room.

Maybe I'll go jump back into bed.

No.

I want someone to hug. Where is everyone?

A sound pierces my ears, a faraway reedy wailing. Smooth zigzag lilts of a pipe sweep away the silence.

I hear it spreading up the driveway, spreading over the car porch. The sound slithers under the front door, wafts through the half-open shuttered windows into the living room. A pulling tune, weaving around me from the top of my head to my toes, in and out my ears.

My lobes are pulsing. My hands drop to my side, heavy like lead, my fingers gripping my skirt. Elbows glue, maybe with sweat, to my sides. The soles and toes of both my feet are frozen, cemented to the floor.

The spidery thread-like strains tighten around me. I heard that song last week at the market.

Deal Me a Card

The music had attracted a crowd. Shoppers had veered out of the stream of people flowing to the bazaar, elbowing for a space as they craned their necks. I was pulled like a magnet to the front of the gaping, shuffling circle. I dragged granny with me, insistently,

"Come on, come on, Mamagranny. Let's watch."

In the center sat the fifer.

I took him in, my eyes and mouth wide open.

His sarong and singlet were blinding-white. Meringue swirls of a turban hugged his head. In yogi pose, his dark-chocolate ropy muscled legs twisted, ankles crossed, knees grazing the earth. Twig-like elbows and arms branched out, jutted back and forth. Fingers, too fast to count, were a centipede running up and down a carved ebony flute. Wisps of black hair straggled on his chin.

A pair of alert jet black orbs moving from side to side drinking in the crowd's fascination. Until they settled on me.

The dark circles stopped their swivel, fixed on my face. The eyes spoke to me.

"Welcome, welcome, little one. Listen, listen, hear my call, the siren that wakes the king."

Eerie notes from the instrument filled my skull. They forced me to look down at the open basket.

From atop a grubby rag, a snake uncoiled, swaying upward. Mesmerized, it slowly rocked from side to side. The hooded cobra's tongue flicked the air, smelling, tasting for prey. The eyes of its hood surveyed its subjects.

In my mind, they gestured to me.

I leaned forward, fixated. Suddenly I stiffened, drew back.

Repulsed.

My five fingers are tiny claws, scraping frantically at my granny's hand. She patted my head, she tried to reassure me.

Deal Me a Card

My mouth shut tight, I was scared a wail would come out, how shameful. I screwed my eyelids closed, as I buried my face in the safe folds of the older woman's batik sarong.

"It's all right, it's all right. Don't be afraid, child. We're safe. The snake will not harm us. Only if we disturb its rhythm. The man has it trained with the music. Ssh, ssh. Hush."

But I persisted. I stamped my feet so the sandals thumped up dust. My "Let's go, let's go," escalated to a plaintive distraction.

Granny sighed, shrugged. Tsk-tsked.

Frantic, I whimpered some more.

We left. Pushed through the milling spectators. They were indifferent, rapt in what they were seeing. I took one furtive backward glance.

The charmer stared at me still, while playing his pipe. Gradually the notes faded. But his glance still seared my sweat-drenched blouse.

At last I crouched safe in the shelter of the rickshaw, pulling granny's arms to encircle me tight.

Now, he was walking up the road toward me. I know because the enticing sound soared and wove louder and louder."

14

CHAPTER 5

MOVING UNEASILY in the psychologist's couch, Emma sank back as she dredged up her childhood panic. "Thirty years ago, well more like thirty-five years ago, Doctor, and you see I remember every detail like it was this morning."

Emma glanced at her watch. Before she concluded her soul-searching for the day, she wanted to delve more deeply into her love-hate encounter with the snake charmer. The dial said she had ten minutes. "We have time?"

Doctor Schwarzman nodded.

Emma went on...

I know that sound. It is the dreadful call of the snake charmer. He is not too close. He is far away at the end of the long lane that comes up to the front door. It's a long way to walk. But the winding, whining notes are growing clearer. I know he is getting nearer, and nearer.

He's an Indian man. He'll wear a turban, have a beard, and a sarong drawn up between his legs, The basket slung on his side, the snake curled inside, drowsing, waiting. The man keeps playing the pipe.

My stomach is churning.

The sunlight wavering in the heat catches a shadow. It darkens as he nears. The silhouette, a hooked nose with a slim lively saw-toothed stick protruding from the lips, dances on the inner wall. I scream silently at the profile,

Why have you come here? Don't you know I am afraid? I'm little and I'm small, and I'm frightened of snakes. Like that one in your basket!

Deal Me a Card

But only the pipe's slow trilling answers, weaving notes, penetrate me with the spells of the snake charmer. Singing to me,

I'm coming. I'm coming. I'm here. I want to show you my dancing snake. I won't hurt you. He'll just dance.

Stay away from me, I'm all alone! I'm afraid. Mum says not to let anyone in. Go away.

He keeps coming, luring me. The writhing tune is very loud now, right outside the locked front door. Plays on, inviting.

I'm still. Like a statue in the church. I'm frozen, too petrified to move a finger or foot, hardly breathing. If I move, he will see me through the glass window, know I am there. Come close. Knock. Enter and surround me with the coiling rhythm of his pipe.

The music plays. Mesmerizing. Hypnotic.

If I stifle my breath any more I will die. Will the music play forever? Will I always be paralyzed?

My feet are numb. My arms are all locked muscles. My jaws are clenched. They ache. When my teeth chatter, once, I grit them tight, desperately stifling the whimper that is rising in my throat.

He does not see me. The snake does not dance.

I see his shadow. I do not see him.

I do not see his snake dance.

The scales start their retreat, recede down the long pathway. Notes drift, swaying lazily into the air. Widening zigzags vanishing, gone.

The snake charmer departs.

I am safe.

Silence.

The house is quiet once more.

But I dare not move a muscle.

Suddenly it is peace no longer.

Deal Me a Card

Car pulls up in the driveway. Doors open. Doors slam.

Front door bursts open.

My body melts. It's as if I release springs in my arms and legs and in my throat. I shriek, delighted.

Sister's and brothers' and father's laughing voices chattered about school, homework, me being good, the marigolds I planted in the front yard are brilliant. Everyone hugs me, the baby sister.

Then it was time for biscuits, milk, a cold drink…

"Our time is up." The words though softly uttered, halted recall, rudely stemmed the flow. Emma's shoulders jerked to attention.

"We're making progress. I'll see you next week at the same time on Thursday?"

"Of course, Doctor Schwarzman."

Deal Me a Card

CHAPTER 6

EMMA WALKED SLOWLY to the elevator. Her strappy navy high heels soundlessly stabbed the beige and turquoise dots that splotched the burgundy wall-to-wall carpet. Deep mauve flowers swayed on her indigo flared skirt as she hit the Down button.

The doors grumbled apart, let her in, slid shut. She stood alone, staring at the floor as the pod whooshed from eleven to one in three seconds. Heavy metal swept apart with a ding to, let her out.

Walking across the atrium, she gave a slight nod and barely glanced at the doorman, and scarcely heard the tap-tappity-tap of her stilettos on the marble. At seven thirty on an evening in May, the parking lot still basked in daylight. The pavement sweltered.

That's California summertime for you, as she bundled into the car, clicked her seat belt and jabbed Classic KCPT to life. A Chopin etude played low, lulling the mood born at her session.

She drove home.

****

Eddy had left a message. Terse, "Call me! For Chrissakes, where are you? I tried to reach you. Three times already."

She knew why. But right now she did not care. First things first.

Mamasan, feline eyes accusing, demanded a greeting and food. Her litter box needed fresh sand. As the two females purred affectionately to each other, abdominal chortles grumbled and rolled in Emma's stomach, insisting on attention. Quickly she dispensed with the chores, pulled off her clothes down to bare skin, threw on a soft tee shirt and loose shorts.

In ten minutes, she was sitting down to dinner, the ingredients piled neatly on her plate. They sported an appetizing splash of color, and provoked a spurt of saliva as she brought the first forkful to her lips.

Her teeth sank into the mandarin orange segment even as they crunched on the mélange, of romaine leaf, a tiny raw onion ring, large gorgonzola crumbs and a walnut half. Quiescent taste buds sprang to life, watered, drenched in raspberry vinaigrette. Emma munched, savoring the salad, chased an evasive cranberry morsel around the plate before she pierced it. She sipped from a tall glass of cold water.

With half an ear, she overheard Dan Rather's earnest continuing commentary on the precarious student demonstrations in Beijing, but her mind was elsewhere, muting her empathy for their pain.

She was still thoughtful as she pulled the two mangoes and three oranges from the paper bag and arranged them in the monkey wood fruit bowl. She stacked the few used dinner dishes in the dishwasher. After filling a second glass of water from a refrigerated bottle, she clicked off the television. Taking her journal out of her leather organizer, Emma set it on her desk, and opened it to a blank page.

The telephone's jangle shattered her resolve. "Where have you been? Why didn't you call?"

The twanging whine needled at her eardrum, whittling away at her soul's serenity.

"Look, Edward, I have a life beyond this tangle you've trapped us in. You'll get what you need, want from me. I'm tired. I worked all day. Saw the doctor. I'm ready for bed."

"Want me to come over. I'll soothe all your memories; make you forget all your pain, your angst."

Emma felt her cheeks flush. Her pulse quickened. Her nipples, unleashed from their size-C cups, grew erect. Her pores opened as heat rose in her body and intensified. *Good*

Deal Me a Card

God, she was way too young for menopause, though she had started her periods when she was ten. No, this was not a hot flash. This was Edward's effect on her.

She insisted on calling him by his real name, even in the throes of passion, though he demurred. "Eddy," she told him haughtily, time and time again, "sounds like a Mafia moniker." Though he was a fast one all right. His demands infuriated her. And lured her.

She surrendered. "Sure, come on over."

"See ya in fifteen minutes." She heard him chuckle as she hung up the receiver.

Emma did the full-body scan in front of the mirror in her bedroom. She noted gratefully, gravity still withheld sentencing. Her breasts pronounced their jutting perkiness. The slight bulge of her tummy was definitely genetic. Thighs, calves and ankles complemented each other, firm and taut. Faint tan lines on her shoulders and hips were visible, but last summer's paint job at the beach was noticeably faded.

Whiffs from almost any perfume set off her alveoli instigating near-asthmatic heaving. But a daub of Shalimar behind each ear never hurt. A quick run of her fingers through her heavy ebony hair gave her that disheveled, slightly slutty look that made up for her abhorrence of cosmetics. Her lips shone deep-pink from a tongue-licking and slight biting.

Emma chose a light, fleece sea-green robe from her closet. The color caught and enriched the shining grey of her eyes. Buttons ran from cleavage to knees. Emma was just unbuttoning the top fastener when the doorbell sounded.

****

Twenty minutes later, they stood naked, stroking belly with belly. No other body parts touched.

Their dance began.

Deal Me a Card

Emma clasped her hands high above her head. Thick hair, glistening silk, flowed from a middle parting over her shoulder blades. Some errant strands toyed with her breasts. They nudged forward, aching. Her feet spread apart, buttocks taut. She inhaled and exhaled slowly through barely-parted lips. Slowly her hips rotated as if oiled. Bare, soft flesh grazed, nibbled at coarse male fur.

Edward stood upright, his penis rigid, buttock muscles tightening and relaxing rhythmically. He forced his expectant fingers to hang loose, stilled his caress-ready hands. Spasmodically, lust triggered the tendons on his shoulders to quiver, exude a tremor.

Air growled from his aquiline nose, mingled with Emma's breath.

"We are the charmer and the charmed," Emma whispered, as she inched her nipples forward to play with his. Her hands continued their circular motion over her head. But his sprang to life, paws jettisoned to mangle and massage.

At last their bodies melded.

Afterwards, when the cries and squeaks, the grunting and the heaving had subsided, Emma snuggled under the sheet.

"Hold me, stroke me to sleep, Edward, Edward?"

Eddy pecked at her forehead, turned on his side, sat up, sated. His hunger glutted, he belched, indulged in the commission of other bodily functions unapologetically. One itch scratched, he now used the fingernail of his index pinkie to soothe his inner ear. He stood, stumbled to the chair, picked up his skivvies, pulled them on, and distractedly tucked in his deflated penis.

"I'm out of here. Gotta be up bright and early tomorrow. Meeting some folk, job prospects. Now remember that letter, you hear. I'll be at the copy shop waiting for your fax. Eleven thirty. Sharp."

Deal Me a Card

He buttoned his shirt, pulled on his jeans and shoes. He walked into the bathroom and peed, leaving the door ajar. As he zipped his pants he walked back towards the bed,

"You're one beautiful lady, y'know. And a great lay. Don't get up. I know the way out. Sweet dreams. Adios."

The door clicked shut behind Edward. Seconds later, he drove away.

Emma lay spread-eagled on the sex-crumpled sheets. Her thoughts lost themselves in recent sensations. She panted feeling the weight of her erstwhile lover's body. Moaned as her legs writhed and her back arched, as if once more under the late deep thrusts of his stabbing phallus. Her palm brushed across her lips painfully bruised from the other's amorous mouth and tongue. She smiled languorously as her hands ineffectually kneaded her breasts. His hands had been so huge and greedily cruel.

Twisting upright to sit at the edge of the bed, she glanced down at the faux three by five foot Persian rug.

The used condom lay there. Shaking her head, Emma contemplated the wilted flower. Seduced into blooming just two short hours ago, now it drooped. The little rubber vial contorted, twisting on the floor as if in agony. It gaped forlorn, empty of that blunt-point dagger, its stamen smeared with unsought, unloved, useless semen.

Grabbing a tissue from the bedside table, she picked up the dejected shield gingerly with thumb and index finger, flushed it away.

CHAPTER 7

STILL NAKED, her body glowing from strokes of love, Emma sat at her piano and trilled 'Fur Elise.' Mamasan, a sleeping ebony comma on the red paisley couch, wheezed gently. The last note rang sweetly. But she was not soothed.

Feeling the chill from the air conditioner, Emma rose and went back to the scene of recent sexual excesses. Found and wound herself in her discarded robe. She walked over and looked out the tall window at the intermingled stars and head lights that at eleven o'clock in the evening continued their firefly dance. Then she settled in the chair at her desk, in the niche which she grandly dubbed her office. Her journal sat ready, opened before Edward's visit.

Now another encounter from her youth nudged through the veils shrouding her memories. Sleep appeared to have targeted only the cat, leaving her mistress wide-eyed and restless. So Emma started to write.

This anonymous, turbaned, white-shirted and saronged, Indian man, exposes himself to my friend Amelia and me.

That early Saturday afternoon in 1959, I'm swinging loose-limbed, lighthearted down the sandy sidewalk. My sandals scuff up small puffs of fine dust. Tiny pebbles crunch, flatten under the siege of my feet.

Every few seconds I glance around. No need really, since the wide street is deserted. At two o'clock, during the weekend in this sleepy new-born suburb of Teluk Anson, spotting a vehicle on this road was almost as rare as not finding splotches of acne on my cheeks since I started my periods two years ago.

Right now I'm feeling virtuous.

Deal Me a Card

My bosom buddy, Amelia, and I, two innocent twelve-year olds are on our weekly trek to clean the parish Church. Our leader has approved the duties. As youthful legionnaires for Mary Mother of God, this is our mission. We set out dutifully and joyfully, to sweep the floors, to stack neatly the hymnals in the pews, to refill the religious literature slots on the wooden shelves in the vestibule. Alleluia!

There isn't much traffic out there.

Most people sit at home, drowsing in the shade or seek the cool, indoors.

After lunch, the men loosen their sarongs, slump bare-torsoed in rattan chairs. Sleep creeps up behind them, shuts their eyes. They nod, snore softly.

The table is clear. Two hours, then it'll be time to cook again. So the queens of the kitchen slack off, take a little rest. They sit barefoot on wooden floors or cool terrazzo, blouses unbuttoned, legs stretched out wide so the air can get up there. Their right wrists, or left, flick up and down wielding palm-frond fans that swish-swish. Fingers of their other hands raise moist silken strands of hair off the nape of their necks. Slow, languid.

Amelia and I, we're the idiots for God out in the heat. Our walk to church from home measures almost a mile.

Sweat tickles down from our armpits to seep into our bras. We're so proud of our rounded AAA-sized mounds of mashed potatoes. Another watery rill bounces salty over our vertebrae. The perspiration meanders from the crease in our bums, across our thighs, gums in the backs of our knees, continues its course over our shins, and muddies on our dusty soles.

We're too absorbed in school gossip of girls' foibles and teacher travails to notice, or too idealistic,

24

to care about our surroundings. Natter flowing like a river, we swipe moisture off our chins with index fingers without skipping a beat, fumble with our knickers bunched up between our cheeks and crotches, break the rhythm of our steps as we run damp digits through lank hair flopping on our foreheads.

Five minutes from our destination, I see him with the corner of my eye.

He's standing, legs apart, on the other side of the street.

Always friendly, I smile, nod, twiddle my fingers, flick a little wave.

Just a glimpse, his sarong seems pulled up a little high on his legs. A swift thought, must be because it's so hot. Legs need cool air.

We keep up the patter of our chatter as we turn the corner to the front entrance.

There he is ahead of us again.

I wonder why he followed us. For a second I feel embarrassed, apologetic. Oh God. He's circled around the other way to pee in the bushes. We surprised him. Yikes, his sarong is still drawn up. We really caught him mid-stream!

Stupid me.

Amelia, more observant, eagle-eyed through her thick glasses, clutches my arm. Whispers a horrified squeak,

"He's showing his thing! Holy Mother of God!"

We turn on our heels like soldiers on parade. We run, troops in retreat, silenced as if under assault.

Running helter-skelter, giggling in gullet-choking shame, more than slightly hysterical.

Almost tripping, we clatter up the ten stairs that lead to the back door of the building. Grabbing the iron handle, Amelia drags open the heavy door.

Deal Me a Card

Through the narrow opening, we stumble into the shelter and safety of the church.

What was he thinking? Where is he now, this weird little fellow who harbored such a need to show two young girls his private parts, sully their eyes, pique their curiosity, this sad clown, who to this day continues to be a vague indelible smear on my memory.

Do I regret that I didn't even stop to stare, to ogle his penis, to react in awe, amazement, fear, revulsion, or shock to his ready-swollen prick?

In dreams, I fall to my knees, cry out, grab his erection submitting in rage or in mockery to his pimping. We satisfy each other. I awake. Pathetic bastard! Naïve child, full of pride and curiosity. Devastated, I never told anyone. I urged Amelia to keep it our dirty little secret, so they wouldn't forbid us to go again. It was almost as if I dared, wanted him to return. Like I wanted the snake charmer to show up and entice me once more.

My body playing with fire even then.

Emma punched in a dot after the last word. She leaned back.

This had been a full day. Now, slumped in the chair, thoroughly exhausted from the earlier physical exertion and the journeys she had taken back in time, she was ready for deep sleep. But she pushed it away for a few more moments.

Her lips twitched. She closed her eyes. *Rub-a-dub-dub, three men in a tub*, she sang silently, tunelessly. It was time to unplug the stopper. She did, watched with her inner eye as they drained out with the bath water.

Just then the wall clock chimed the half hour after midnight. A new day was starting.

26

Deal Me a Card

CHAPTER 8

THE NEXT MORNING, Emma sat at her desk, knees crossed, fingertips clicking relentlessly on the keyboard. Her jaws worked furiously massaging strawberry-flavored gum with her molars. Every inch of her body felt both used and useful.

To celebrate last night's spree and the ensuing decision, she wore a red V-necked sweater and a black mini-skirt. Her silver hoops and bracelet swung and jangled in unison. Black high heels emphasized her runner's calves. Mother would have unblinkingly woven the "whore" label on this outfit. But she knew she looked eye-popping, and said a prayer for mom's peace and rest. She heard a tiny snap.

"Damn, it's broken again," she muttered to herself.

Frowning, still chewing doggedly, she stopped typing. What the heck, it was Edward's deadline, not hers. He could wait a few minutes. After all, I'm the one sticking my neck out.

Holding out her right hand with fingers spread, she grimaced. Then, leaning back in her chair, she gave the finger to nobody in particular as she examined the damage.

Looking down at the slightly-open desk drawer to her left, Emma yanked at the handle. It screeched open. Scanning the muddled - there's-a-method-to-my-madness contents - she spied the nail file in the back left-hand corner half-hidden beneath a dog-eared Post-it pad and a box of paper clips. Her thumb and index finger fumbled around, then dredged the file from its hidey-hole.

She started the repair job.

****

One mile away, Eddy paced back and forth, chewing at the lick of whiskers drooping at the corner of his mouth. A

27

Deal Me a Card

thin line of sweat trickled from his hairline into his sideburns. Its musk threatened to obliterate the sweet scent of his after-shave.

The collar of his pin-striped white shirt was unbuttoned so that the knot of his black twisted tie, with its red-yellow floral design, hung loose and bedraggled. Underarm perspiration had just decided to pick a fight with his deodorant since the odds were in its favor. Any essence absorbed from his soap-on-a-rope during his shower earlier that morning had evaporated.

His hands were thrust deep in the pockets of his jeans to prevent their clenching or slamming something within his reach. He glared at the fax machine. It crouched silent as if anticipating a blow.

In the cramped space of the copy shop, his mincing twirling steps were an agitated water bird's, performing an expectant mating dance. Even his neck jerked up and down, marking rhythm with his wobbling Adam's apple.

He frowned at his watch, heaved a sigh. Then stomped to the entrance and shoved the door open. The glass vibrated, grumbled squeakily in protest. Scowling, his lips in a pout, he stamped to the phone booth a few yards outside the store.

Gritting his teeth, he dialed Emma's office number. He listened for the rings and drummed his fingers on the glass wall. His nails needed trimming. They clicked rhythmically

What's the bitch up to? She was supposed to send me that letter. How can I go to that interview without at least one damn reference?

She picked up, sang the octave, "Jones and Guerrero Construction Company. How may I help you?"

"Broke your nail again?" he sneered. "Where the hell is my letter?"

"As a matter of fact, I did," Emma's voice icy voice held no hint of past passion. "And it's not your letter. It's a recommendation I wrote for you on company letterhead, and signed Mr. G's name to it. And thank God, you son of a

Deal Me a Card

bitch, that there's no one else in the office right now. They've gone to lunch so I can do this, this fake thing for you, so you can maybe get a job and earn your own money for a change, instead of mooching off everyone else. I'm faxing it to you this minute, so go there and wait. Good luck. And, by the way, I never want to see you again, Edward Lopez."

Eddy stared at the dial tone. Stifled a sigh of relief. Emma hadn't given him a chance to thank her. Maybe later. He clattered the phone on its hook and pushed open the door. Slowly he trod the ten steps, entered the copy shop. A piece of paper pushed out of the fax machine.

****

At Jones and Guerrero Construction, Emma wheeled her chair backwards. She sauntered to the water-fountain. Sipping the cool water calmed her down. Tranquil once more, she reproached herself, despising the coarseness of her recent words. Edward brought out the worst in her. *Well, probably the best also in other ways*, she thought, lifting her lips in a tiny smile. But now she had to lose something else.

Back at her desk, she tore into tiny scraps the letter of reference and deleted the original from her computer. Just in the nick of time. Raoul Guerrero came whistling towards her desk,

"Didn't take a lunch break? Thought you might have a date, you're looking so fine."

Guerrero, sixty-five, a youthful great-grandfather and lover of all women, had never read the sexual harassment rules posted prominently on the office wall. He whistled again, rubbed his hands together, and leered at Emma.

"How's about you come over to my place tonight?"

He grinned widely at her raised eyebrows, the gold-filled molars and bicuspids on both sides of his jaws glittering. His brown eyes, deep in the shadow of two black hairy caterpillars, sparkled behind square-rimmed glasses.

29

Emma adored his Groucho-ness. Or was that his Harpo-ness. She could never remember which. He tapped her nose as she twitched her lips.

"No nothing like that, though I can dream. It was your birthday last weekend, right? We're having an eighteenth birthday party for my niece. Everyone will be there. We can enjoy together. Better late than never to celebrate. Bring your boyfriend."

Thank God he doesn't know about Edward.

Mr. Guerrero fired him after the last cancellation. A roofing job. The homeowners had called, screaming, cursing at Emma as though it was her fault. She couldn't blame them. Their interior was ruined, flooded. Edward had forgotten to secure the tarps over the open roof. A storm had swept through. He swore that he had instructed his men, but he was such a liar. He had let the company down more than once.

Great lover. Lousy liar.

Her smiling eyes looked earnestly into Guerrero's, "Thanks. That's really thoughtful. I'll be there. Alone. It's more fun."

"Yeah, who needs a dude like Eddy?"

Oh God, does he know something? Seen them together at Abuelo's or El Ranchero?

"Seen him lately?"

Emma shook her head slightly, "No!" Well, it was over twelve hours since she had seen him, all of him. And she had sent him packing just thirty minutes ago, over the phone.

"Good. Beautiful, educated woman like you can do much better than that no-good wetback. Cost me thousands. Worse.

"Word gets around when there's damage. But, hey, that's all over. Just sorry I introduced you. Remember last New Year's Eve. He was glued to you in five minutes."

Emma shuddered as the vision flashed before her eyes, of her and the recalcitrant Edward glued together the night

30

before. Her shoulders twitched. She folded her arms across her chest to hide the budding nipples.

Guerrero mistaking her tension sighed, "Yeah, too bad. But you saw through him. Anyway, he's not been hanging around for three, four months now. Good riddance."

Emma opened her mouth, choking on words.

Guerrero answered her gurgle, "A woman of good taste. I like that. Well okay, see you tonight, about seven. My brother will be there. Good man, Guillermo. Owns three tax services operations. University degree in Business. Forty-seven, with cojones."

Guerrero chuckled throatily. He patted Emma on the shoulder, picked up the messages from his in-box, and turned to his office. His step was light. It was Friday. There were just a handful of phone calls to answer. Then the weekend would begin.

In four or five hours, this patriarch would be surrounded by people who loved him most. A loving wife of forty-five years, and numerous younger siblings, nine to be exact since two had passed away taken by the cholera when babies and three still lived in Mexico.

Deal Me a Card

CHAPTER 9

THE MILKY WAY WAS ROTATING faster than usual. Soon the stars would be crashing down. Right now they were skating vertiginously among the caverns of the universe, and between her swimming eyeballs. Meteors were on the verge of visibility. *Didn't they start off as stars, then as they cascade nearer and nearer, their tails blaze a trail?* She just knew that at any minute, soon, one would land with a bang.

Emma's giddiness whipped her brain around as another sip of tequila jettisoned the spin cycle. She and the others in the small group were crouched, silent in the darkness. Only crackling gunshots fired by the flames of the campfire startled them now and again. The river rushing over the rocks twenty feet behind them, beat in time to the murmuring mountain breeze. The five companions were savoring nature's sleepy late evening symphony.

Now Emma leaned back on the low canvas chair, closed her eyes and surrendered to the sumptuousness of sensations. Raoul's invitation to the party in May was the best thing that happened to her in years. From the first "Hello, good to meet you," handshake and light cheek kisses, she and his brother Guillermo, set off sparks as if they were flint stones rubbed to red heat.

They had talked all night. Gone to a movie two days later. Dined the following Friday, picking at Joie de Vivre's most garlicky escargots, indulging on succulent scampi and filet mignon, finishing a bottle of merlot. They met for lunch. Went shopping in Westwood. "Oohed" and "aahed" at the Fourth of July fireworks on the Santa Monica pier.

In their conversations, sometimes animated, now and then intimate, the couple began to touch on their relationship like dancers dabbling fingertips. One day, Emma opened up,

"In my life, I've discovered that feelings, yearnings are much, much sweeter than actions. Perhaps I'm just a romantic, like Keats and Wordsworth, reaching out for something 'ever more about to be.' Or maybe I've been hurt once too often."

"I could change your mind. Help you forget the pain," suggested Guillermo

Emma looked straight into his eyes, "Or perhaps I want you for a friend forever."

"To be only a friend. These platonic relationships can only stretch so far."

"Our emotions are so fragile, so delicate really, like flowers. You know, there are some blooms which can only take the heat for one day. Then they fade, droop, die," Emma pensively insisted.

Another afternoon they swam at his home. Emerging from the pool after a vigorous half-hour, they stood face-to-face. The sun's heat soaked up the moisture off their shimmering bodies. Emma knew that the black garment with splashes of red and yellow below her breasts had attracted his frequent, and she noticed, lascivious, glances.

But no, he was gazing at her face. A teeny frown furrowed his brow. The edges of her hair dripped water down the front of her suit. He raised an index finger, wiped a droplet that hung from the lashes of her left eyelid. The digit hovered, a butterfly's wings fluttering.

In a guttural whisper, he said, "I never want to wound you, you dainty little sea lion, you, never, never."

Later that same evening, energized by roast turkey, tomato, guacamole and lettuce sandwiches, they walked. Guillermo had to grasp Emma's hand a few times as they clambered up the loose gravel of the fairly steep incline leading to the peak of the rocky outcropping. Each gulped at a bottle of Evian.

"We have this chemistry, you know, between us," he said.

Deal Me a Card

"And so we are able to talk to each other, really listen and hear," she nodded.

"Touch each other ever so lightly, lightly," he said as he touched her lips with his, ever so lightly.

She let his hands slide from her shoulders to her waist. When they meandered upwards to cup her breasts, she demurely covered them with hers and held them tight. They kissed a little more. Then hand in hand, they descended to the house that glowed in the dusk of this mid-summer day.

On yet another day, she lay at home in her dim bedroom, blinds drawn to darken her surroundings as she nursed a migraine. At times like this, she abhorred all human contact.

Guillermo called to cheer her up. For ten minutes they teased each other deciding on whether he should come over to cuddle or coddle her. They settled on both. After they hung up, Emma snuggled under the cool percale and sank into an invigorating nap.

At six o'clock, after work, he appeared armed with all the ingredients for a light vegetable soup and a fresh-baked baguette. Soothed and nurtured, they reclined comfortably in each other's arms letting Beethoven's sixth and eighth symphonies enrich the blood flowing rhythmically through their veins the whole evening long.

****

In August, Guillermo asked her to go camping. He owned a stretch of property along a river near the Sequoia mountains. Several of Guillermo's friends were going up on Saturday afternoon for a quick weekend of relaxation.

Guillermo and Emma had arrived late the night before.

She held the flashlight while he pitched the dome tent. As a scorpion scurried away in the pitch black, her companion had pooh-poohed her shrieks,

"You're a thousand times bigger than it is!"

Deal Me a Card

Still, she meticulously examined every inch of their sleeping bags, and shone the light on all corners of the tent before she crawled in to sleep.

The morning had been cool when she stuck her head outside the tent-flap.

She needed to pee. The river-bed sand was slightly damp from the nighttime dew. So she wriggled her toes into her blue sandals, looking out for early-morning creepy-crawlies, then headed for the circle of small grey-white rocks about ten feet away.

Squatting behind the largest boulder, about five feet high, she pulled down her black panties. The stream of yellow urine buzzed down, as a curious bee zoomed by on his way to the beckoning morning glories. She swayed, balancing on tiptoe so that no drops splashed on her skin. The liquid would be good for the withered, brown-leafed weeds protruding from beneath the stones. Then she kicked clumps of sand over the puddle, before walking back towards the aroma of early-morning coffee, bacon, and eggs.

Guillermo, in cut-offs and unbuttoned checkered shirt, his hair rumpled on his head and curling sultry on his chest, shook a frying pan over the small gas stove. He told Emma of his affinity for the outdoors, touting his wilderness culinary skills.

"Better than making love," he grinned, adding, "at least when we're camping," as he ladled four crisp golden-edged strips and scooped two steaming mounds of scrambled eggs, onto her plate.

Which was a lie, considering the frolics of the next few hours.

Scout-leader fashion, Guillermo had demanded order on the camping ground. After breakfast they washed the frying pan and cutlery, lugged the sleeping bags out to air, and secured the trash. Each wandered off to use the outdoor toilet. The master camper had dug it in the midst of a ring of bushes and trees that modestly sheltered them. Then he

Deal Me a Card

strolled up to the van to bring down more supplies for the evening.

Emma crawled into the tent, rummaged for the suntan lotion and her book. She pulled a beach towel from her duffel, wrapped it around the other items and went off to explore the stream.

The narrow arm of the river rumbled and splashed behind a curtain of tall, wispy-branched trees. Leaving her flip-flops on the bank at a gap in the shrubs, she poked one foot at the surface. The water was hair-raising icy. Snow melt was still descending from the sequoias towering above the flats.

She dipped her toes cautiously. Then plunged in up to her ankles, tumbling the pebbles with her soles. Teetering, she slithered toward the huge monolith in the middle of the stream. Twice she paused to regain her equilibrium in the swirling current, and scoured her goose bumps with one hand while she clutched her loaded towel with the other. Reaching her destination, she used the smaller stepping stones to clamber onto its flat surface.

Now, she could start her sunbathing regimen. She spread the towel and sat, legs outstretched with her face to the sun. As the sun grew hotter and hotter, Emma shed her shorts and tee-shirt. She applied more lotion to her breasts, shoulders, abdomen, and thighs. Then she dozed, spread-eagle naked on her reclining throne.

Minutes, one hour later, she lost track of the time, her eyelids flickered. Drops of sleet landed on her bare flesh, stung her ribs. Something tickled her inner thighs. She laid still, her sense of touch on red alert.

Solar rays licked her arms, legs and midriff. Drops of water, bounced from the stream dashing on the rock, pierced her deliciously on random spots. Guillermo's fingers untangled the moist hair between her legs. Emma surrendered to the massage.

"I need a softer bed," she murmured.

Deal Me a Card

Given the license, her lover wrapped his arms around her waist and lifted her off the granite surface. For a few minutes, they stood with wavelets sucking politely at their shins. The man's hands were not genteel as they cupped handfuls of melted snow all over his woman's body. Her fingers were not gentle as they dug into his buttocks. Their laughter gurgled and roared, echoing the powerful push of the eddies. Hand in hand they balanced their way to the bank.

They paused just long enough for Guillermo to wriggle out of his swim trunks.

Then they were lying in the warm fine-grained hammock formed across the eons by the fury of storms. She was the larkspur; petals widespread as he sipped her nectar, swallowed her honey. Mother ewe, she suckled her ravenous lamb. Stag, he mounted his doe. They were growling bear cubs cuffing each other, entwining arms, licking each other's body from toe to neck to brow. They were wolves howling out in heat, their passion as searing as the noonday sun.

Limp-limbed, they sauntered down the path back to the waters. There, hands splashed off the musk and perspiration. Every inch aroused once more, they made love to the rhythm of the smashing torrent that pounded their gyrating hips.

****

"Time for bed, sweetheart. You've had a long day, and we're taking Pepe, Vicente, and Walter to the top tomorrow. Moro Rock calls."

Emma tumbled off her nova. She opened her eyes, saw she was sitting with the four other campers around the campfire. It was after dinner, barbecued steak, beans and corn on the cob, and they were sipping tequila. Nearby, the river continued pounding the rocks. The splashing water and cool breeze had lulled the group into silence until Guillermo spoke.

Deal Me a Card

Guillermo's words swept through her. His fingers tangled lightly in her tousled hair. Reaching up into the near-pitch black above her, she touched his teeth with her fingers, her head still wrapped in earlier emotions.

"But first I want to sing," she slurred. The men indulged her whim graciously.

Jumping up, she gave her best tribute to the Righteous Brothers that she could muster under the circumstances,

"I need your love …"Her voice soared to heaven, " … tonight!"

"Bravo, bravo!" Her audience of four clapped raucously.

"Well, that was enough to get the coyotes going."

"That'll keep the scorpions away."

"We'll know why the fish don't bite tomorrow."

Then Guillermo led her gently away, his arm encircling her waist. He kissed her sweetly on the lips. "I love you."

Emma crawled into her sleeping bag.

Guillermo stayed awake a little longer with the other men to polish off the bottle of tequila. They gravely discussed the affairs of the world, especially since the news struck so close to home. But the murmurs were not urgent. Rather, the exchange was relatively mellow, as emotions are wont to be when liberated from suppression by the spell of agave juice.

The next morning quite early, they drove to breakfast at a restaurant that perched on the edge of an ancient avalanche. Emma felt a little fragile. Spooning valiantly through a hearty bowl of oatmeal, she looked askance as her companions ploughed through stacks of pancakes, ham slices and eggs fried easy-over.

"My God you gentlemen must have stomachs of steel," she muttered, munching on her bland, belly-soothing fare, eyes heavy-lidded.

"And you can sing at my wedding anytime," Pepe teased.

Deal Me a Card

She grinned, bobbing her head to acknowledge the mock applause of the four men for her fine singing under the influence. Guillermo stroked her thigh ever so slightly under the table.

Deal Me a Card

CHAPTER 10

AT SCHWARZMAN'S OFFICE FIVE DAYS LATER, Emma smoothed the back of her hands, one with the other, admiring the contrast between her pink nail polish and her tanned skin. The collar of her blue-and-white striped dress gaped enough to show the dark brown of her neck, its short skirt flounced over bronzed thighs.

"I was so happy when Guillermo invited me to the hills. Doctor Schwarzman, Guillermo is what I call a real man. He's sensitive, but he's virile. He just has to look into my eyes and I start to glow. It's like being on fire. And he's thoughtful, always the gentleman who thinks of my needs.

"Like another man once. When I was a student in Paris. Leonid, his name was Leonid. I remember because there were two men with the same name. From the same country.

"The second was such a contrast. I met him when I was a graduate student. He was a fraternity boy at the University of Colorado. All he wanted was to bed me. Chalk me up as a conquest. A feather in his damn cap, a graduate lay. Some sort of hazing ritual. Jerk! I blew him off.

"But the other, earlier on, the older one was a refugee from Hungary. *"Partir, c'est mourir un peu,"* he would whisper to me. I remember, I remember, each time I separate from a lover.

"He and I exchanged those words. 'Parting is dying a little. A little bit each time.' He wrote the thought in my journal. Etched it in my memory, a mantra that haunts my life ever since. Leonid, his last name began with a B. I don't recall it. Just Leonid is enough. We met in Paris in 1964. For a little while we studied the French language together.

"He owned a motorcycle, and we rode all over the city after classes for thrills. One afternoon we roared through the Bois de Boulogne. It was exhilarating. We stopped and

40

bought ice cream cones. He had strawberry and I had chocolate. We shared, licked each other's milky delight. There's nothing to match French ice cream, or Italian gelato for that matter.

"Later in the evening we lay in each other's arms companionably among the trees. Gazed deeply in each other's eyes. Kissed, mingling our tongues. He thumbed my nipples until they ached. I cupped his penis. It stirred, swelled. We had to thrust each other away, we were panting so heavily. He vroomed me back to the women's dormitory.

"During a visit to his apartment once, Leonid cooked some savory dish. Sausages and onions, sprinkled with other Eastern European ingredients. We were ravenous and indulged noisily, smacking lips, sipping wine between mouthfuls of the steaming casserole, kissing after every few bites.

"Afterwards we made love, soaring to the very edge. I tugged at him, leading him into me, yearning that he fill me. I longed for his strength. His courage that had led him to freedom. To become mine. But he grasped my hand, brought it to his lips, kissed my palm.

"There might be a baby", he whispered, his voice hoarse, breathless, "I do not want you to be a mother so young," as he kissed my lips sweetly and hugged me tightly.

Emma gave a small laugh,

"He was a tender, passionate lover, and a perfect, thoughtful gentleman. We met many times in cafes. We were close. And we were intimate, warm friends for those brief three weeks. "Then we parted never to meet again.

"*Partir, c'est mourir un peu,*" he whispered as he kissed me goodbye. Parting is dying, a little. *C'est vrai.* So true."

Bringing her hands together in front of her face, Emma pensively continued,

"I think I love Guillermo. I don't want us to part. It's not all sex, you know. He respects me. And he certainly must

41

appreciate my skills. He offered me a job. He heads the office for processing immigrants. This is happening through that IRCA program, the immigration reform law. The students are learning English so that they can get legal status. I've started to work part-time in the evenings at the educational center he directs. I'm so excited. It's right up my alley. That's more than I could ever ask for - working alongside the love of my life at night and for his doting brother during the day. I'm practically family!

"Oh, and the students I've met, boy, are they dedicated, and so much fun…"

Seeing Doctor Schwarzman close her notepad, she asked, "Is it time? Alright, thank you. Good night. See you next week."

CHAPTER 11

THE NEXT MORNING, an early day in September, was hot. The quivering vibrations rising from the Southern California valleys, reminded one they are deserts, artificially pumped up to oasis status.

Emma loved the air's dry crispness she could almost feel on her skin each time she looked out the window of the Pacoima office. Her nostrils quivered, though she really could not sniff the wild rosemary, anise, and sage. She could see the hills, rocky and dotted with dry brush. Two of the four offices in the small building had no windows and opened out into the clattering company's lumber yard. Such a landscape would destroy her peace of mind. She relished her position.

She had already discussed a quote for a deck and patio with a prospective customer and completed five invoices. The phone rang again.

"Jones and…"

"Ah, so you're still with that outfit? Thought you had left for richer pastures, as they say. Guerrero's girl. That's you. Right, bitch?"

The voice, growling, startled her from her complacency.

"Edward? I thought I told you never …"

"That's right, but I want to see you again. Stroke your beautiful boobs, kiss your…"

Emma squeaked, "Stop that, just stop that. Can't you be a gentleman? Or at least use a modicum of decency?"

She glanced quickly over her shoulder. Nobody was at the copy machine or the water fountain, who might overhear that exchange. Keeping her hiss low, she went on.

"I thought we agreed, no strings attached. When it was time, we would take our bows gracefully and leave."

Deal Me a Card

"You call that nasty tone you used the last time we spoke, graceful? By the way, thanks for the letter. I'm with Santa Clarita Landscapers, Inc. right now.

"Been with them about two months. They love me. And I'm being a good boy. Must have been your influence. Hey, maybe I should come by and thank Mr. Raoul myself. I'm sure he'd love to see me and hear about the impact of his letter."

"You are such a low life. You know?"

"You didn't call me that when we were making out, all lovey-dovey and let's dance to our rhythm, Edward."

She could hear the slur in his tone and realized that he had been drinking.

"Why aren't you at work?" It's ten thirty in the morning? I thought you said.."

"My day off. Mondays. So they can work me on Saturdays keeping the model home lawns looking good for the customers. It's been a good weekend.

"But Irene didn't come close to you. Neither did Joanne, or Katie, or Patti. They just didn't measure up. No way, Jose!"

"And, your point is?"

"Well, I thought we could have lunch today, or perhaps dinner with milady at Joie de Vivre?"

Her jaw tightened. She could see him smirk as he put the twang in his words.

"No, no dinner with you! Sorry."

"Well, let's meet for lunch. Look, I'm just pulling your chain. You're such fun to tweak. Sierra's at twelve, okay?"

"No. It'll be too crowded and there'll be too many...I know too many people. We can meet at the Happy Go Burgers on Davenport Street. At one o'clock. Bye."

The sleeves of her linen blouse itched from the dampness under her arms. A tiny rivulet of sweat tickled her tailbone, soaked her panties. She shrugged. There was no time to think about elegance or comfort. For the next two

44

hours, Emma worked intently at her computer to complete the remaining invoices. Finished with one task, she turned to another. Soon she was scribbling on a yellow legal pad and transcribing her words to her keyboard to fashion a business proposal.

Mr. Jones had dumped the request for a contract on her desk last week after his Friday meeting and wanted it by the end of the day Monday. The company could get a hunk of the big development planned for Lakeview Hills next year.

"Ms. Emma, here, take a look at this. You're our writer. Put together something fresh and smart for us."

She was glad for the pressure of a deadline even as she desperately tried to shove Edward out of her mind. But still his words intruded, gnawed at her temples. *Why did she agree to meet with him?*

****

At five minutes to one, she was sitting in a booth facing the weasel. The joint could seat twelve, and they had chosen seats ten and eleven so as to be as far away from the other humans as possible.

Ted, who couldn't be more than seventeen, bleached hair in a pony-tail under his cocked paper hat and his title "Manager," proudly embroidered on his brick-orange work-shirt, was busy with a drive-through order. In mouth-to-mouth combat with the Beach Boys California Dreaming blaring from a wall-speaker, he repeated the meal request over his shoulder at about a 100 decibel level.

"Double, with onions, tomatoes, lettuce no mayo, mustard. Large fries. I'll handle the super-duper Coke."

Amy, his assistant, who had to be at least five years older than her boss, nodded and grimaced, covering her ears briefly from the cacophony. As if she did not already have enough problems, the most glaring of which being her acute case of acne. Emma had glimpsed her dilemma as she placed her order. Scarcely hidden under a thick layer of pink clay-

Deal Me a Card

textured make-up, the ripe zits seemed close to eruption as her pores sucked up the steaming fumes from the deep fryer. Sweat trickled down the sides of her cheeks, while her never-still fingers worked with robotic efficiency to assemble the sizzling delicacies. Emma might have attempted to commiserate if she herself had felt less put upon.

Three other customers sat munching on their lunch, seemingly caught up in deep roller-coaster thoughts.

Eduardo, Edward, whatever, was a weasel, a pathetic creep, without a doubt, she thought as she ate. In that denim jacket and those ragged jeans. He looked like the laborer that he was.

Why oh why had she been so stupid, so insecure, to let herself be flattered by the attentions of a younger man? She felt her jaws tighten as she bowed her head and lowered her eyes. Then she looked up at the ceiling. Her index finger grabbed a strand of her hair and twirled it round and around.

While his companion did everything she could to avoid eye contact, Edward was swallowing her up even as he gulped down his cheese burger. He ventured, "I'm sorry, honey. You're upset, aren't you?"

She said not a word, just pursed her lips and kept swirling her finger.

He reached over and took her hand, loosening her grip. He was gentle. His breath stroked her nostrils. It smelled of beer vainly disguised with an overlay of Colgate and mint-scented chewing gum.

Her stomach churned, and it was not from the fat winding its way down her gullet as she chewed on her chicken burger. Memories drummed at her brain demanding to be released. She beat them off, scared that the effluvia would gush out in hysterical tears.

"Tell me what you want and let's be done. Yes, I was rude to you over the phone when we talked last time. But it was tense for both of us. You unemployed, and me about to be if they found out."

Deal Me a Card

"Okay, okay. I s'pose I could have asked you all this over the phone. But I wanted to see you. You're beautiful in white y'know, with that suntan. Been lying by the pool at the ranch?"

He felt her stare. Drew back, scorched from its intensity. "Sorry, sorry. No more teasing.

"Look, I want to learn. To speak English, to write. Better than I do right now. I heard your man offers classes. When can I sign up? Where do I go? That's one thing.

"The other is something weird. I'm trying to find a man I knew. It's been a long time. Difficult circumstances."

Edward's face had lost its silly grin. Briefly his brows furrowed. He chewed at the strands of his moustache. He gazed beyond her. His faraway look transformed him. His demeanor seemed much older than his twenty-eight years. Emma caught a glimpse of the softer side of the man's character she had been attracted to those many months ago. His eyes were moist. But of course that could be from the hangover.

"For the classes, go to MacAdam Street, where it intersects with Mission. You can't miss the billboard. I'll be at the center tomorrow evening and I'll help you with registration and enrollment. But you have to promise you don't know me," she said stressing every one of those last nine words. "About the man, what's the deal?"

"We were close, then he disappeared. I thought he was dead. Now I don't know. Some people were talking about someone in town who sounds like him. He walks with a limp. Maybe an accident happened. He's prob'ly changed his name too. Just wondered if he is in your class."

Eddie looked at his watch, squeaked off the canary naugahyde, stood and stretched his arms out wide. "Hey, we're finished here. Got to get you back to work. The boss might ask the wrong questions. I'll come around one evening soon to the school. Maybe next week will be good to sign up and check out my options."

Deal Me a Card

His hand, like a feather, touched her shoulder.

"We could have made it, you know, together."

Her shudder when she felt his caress through the soft material, stung his fingers. He snatched them back, clenched a fist. "Awright, awright. Bye."

Emma sat still until she saw his pick-up turn onto Davenport Street. The meeting had left her feeling indifference, but slightly curious. Edward was Edward, who thought only of himself. But he had mentioned having a friend.

At least he paid for lunch.

****

That evening at the language center, she asked Leticia, the receptionist, to schedule an appointment for Edward Lopez during her office hours, and to give him the placement tests for reading and writing. He would be starting classes in a few days.

She casually surveyed the students as they entered her classroom, but nobody had a discernible limp. *Well, Edward's mystery friend could be attending Isadora's session.*

When she got home, she called Guillermo. And since the temperature still sweltered, she drove over for a swim in his pool. It was just after midnight when she snuggled down between fawn silk sheets in her bed, feeling incredibly loved.

Deal Me a Card

CHAPTER 12

GUILLERMO STOOD on his patio. The Sylmar foothills at the edge of his property rolled up, up, up until the strength of the cerulean blue flattened their rounded breasts. Well, two mounds had escaped and forever stuck out their multiple nipples yearningly, demanding the caress of raindrops. The rest of the troupe sat there looking slightly embarrassed surrounded by their frills of stratified rock. Mostly stolid and stoic, their occasional grumbling hiccough ejected a few small boulders down the slopes. Some crumbling rocks even decorated his fifteen acres of backyard, wearing garlands of purple and white morning glories at dawn and then changing dress in the early afternoon to necklaces of golden poppies.

Behind him, the house basked sleepily under the shadow of a sprawling profusion of salmon, white and purple bougainvillea. Its architect, a pupil of Cliff May, had married the best features of Spanish colonial style to the California ranch house. The offspring was an airy, free-form home. Roughly j-shaped, adobe walls with heavy pinewood accents.

In the foreground, the flagstone courtyard sported a cactus garden, while flaunting bushes of white sage and Conejo buckwheat and hiding its sweat under shady olive trees and a jacaranda. Somehow the sun managed to find wide glass windows below the tiled roof and elicit intermittent paths of light. Overflowing pots of geraniums and fuchsias hung from the eaves.

Inside the house, where the air was cool, the living room, dining area and kitchen flowed one into the other. A huge stone fireplace towered to the wooden beams above. Around the corner, low ceilings created four cozy bedrooms.

Deal Me a Card

The master bedroom, tucked into the tail of the J, stretched to an enclosed spa. A skylight invited in the starry heavens on two hundred cloudless nights each year, and a cultivated wilderness of native plants ensured privacy on the exterior. A rover's eyes could feast on birds of paradise rubbing shoulders with a low-slinging Mexican elderberry while Santa Barbara daisies danced around them, and mint and oregano wound their merry way among their more stately kin.

As he slurped another sip of steaming black coffee, Guillermo looked towards the tennis court. His older son, Richard, in white shorts and light-green tank top, was practicing - lobbying balls against the boards. The regular thump-flub-thump, thump-flub-thump seemed to have annoyed a mocking bird. Otherwise, the only sounds were scuffing sand and rustling weeds. Up among the rocks, a rattler shook its tail at the sun, and then nestled in the intensifying heat.

In jeans, bare-chested, Guillermo sighed, happy, and inhaled the fragrance of jasmine that twisted around the porch's posts. He needed this time, an empty Saturday morning leisurely submersing in its fresh rhythm. He looked over his shoulder, his eyes pleased with a glimpse of his home. His haven and cocoon. Still, it needed completion.

His mind lingered over the memory of last night, when Emma had come over for a swim. They had skinny-dipped in the moonlight. The barely-cool water had blanketed their bodies in ebony-and-silver ripples that soothed and sucked the stresses of the week from their arms and legs. They swam a lap, dog-paddled, letting the fluidity coyly oppose and resist their movement. Afterwards they had dried each other off with thick Turkish towels. Refreshed and eager for bed, they had kissed goodbye.

She was becoming more than a quickening in his heartbeat. The hollow that Mary Lou's death had carved in his soul, while not yet quite filled, seemed less empty.

Deal Me a Card

Despite the brightness of the day and the dazzle of his new interest, memories of his late wife percolated to the surface.

He grimaced to himself as he succumbed. Mental self-flagellation, though less frequent these days, was still one way to deal with his failures. His wife's addictions had not made her early passing more palatable. In fact, they had made him feel all the more helpless. To this day, he wore his guilt like a gag against any anger he might direct at her.

Mary Lou had come to him such as she was, she said. "Take me or leave me," she challenged, emptying her sixth bottle of cerveza at the semester-end party where they first met. He had accepted the dare. He took her, because she was lovely and fair, with blue eyes and pink lips and a degree in sociology. He was just finishing his last course for a business degree, and working two jobs. One as code-breaker of other people's income tax returns, the other as a waiter in his uncle's restaurant, just three years removed from the back-breaking, flesh-scorching orange groves and vineyards of the San Joaquin Valley.

He craved her being, as the next brushstrokes on his life's canvas. Three months later they married before a justice of the peace.

Life changed for him, not for Mary Lou. She was herself.

"And I'll take whatever I want, so I feel however I want," she shrieked over and over again. That time she was pacing their bedroom anxious and agitated, coked up after six months of sobriety.

"And I'll drink whatever I want, so I act however I want," she shrieked over and over again. That other time he had come home late from closing the store and found Richard and Daniel, the younger boy, huddled in their picture-perfect rooms. And there she sat perfectly straight but perfectly mad in the middle of the living room carpet

Deal Me a Card

with a glass of vodka in her hand, and a half-empty bottle on the kitchen counter.

But he gave her everything, and forgave her even more because, even as the flash-flood torrents of her self-destruction eroded their life, she gave him two sons. So, to protect the family and preserve the marriage, he sent the two little boys to their uncle's sheltered home in Los Angeles. The schools were better there, he had argued.

"What's wrong with the nuns in San Jose?" she wept, pouring herself a glass of wine. "Want one?"

"No thanks. Not a thing, they are holy women, but the Carmelite Fathers prepare the students for the university system. Raoul's sons are graduating this year.

So they packed the young ones off, and visited them every other weekend, unless Mary Lou had a bad spell. The migraines, his brother told the little boys, comforting them, "Your mama has terrible headaches and stomach aches. She'll be here next week, for sure."

He missed them as much as they did him, while they grew from children into teenagers. He lived for those Saturdays and Sundays, when he could hold his sons in his arms. He would look into their eyes and ask them,

"Do you remember who I am?" he would ask, with a smile that he knew could not hide the quiver in his lips. Twelve days, sometimes seventeen days were a very long time.

"Of course, Daddy, why would I forget you?" Richard would look puzzled.

"No way, I can't forget you. Uncle Raoul's always saying, 'If you don't do your homework, I'm going to tell your Dad!' So how to forget?" cheekily from Daniel who was the child who loved to laugh.

"And you love me still?"

They hugged him, sensing like children do, his father's pride and adoration, and his need for affirmation. Then they would, all three, run out into the yard with baseball bats and

Deal Me a Card

balls, while Mary Lou watched from the in-laws' window, sipping a glass of soda.

As the boys grew older, the family would go to a movie on Saturday evening, and everyone, even Mary Lou, would stuff themselves with buttered popcorn and cokes. On some visits, she would help Juanita with the dinner, chopping the cilantro and onions, shredding the meat, molding the tortillas.

They became almost a normal family, she a laughing loving mother tweaking Daniel's nose and exclaiming over Richard's grades, as he stood by, the proud father and husband watching with gleeful relief.

God, how he wished he could have saved her. Agghh, there I go again. The minute I think about her, I get maudlin. Damn! She's dead, God rest her soul. She was in no pain. The doctors said, no pain with the morphine. Like she needed more drugs. But with her liver gone. At thirty eight. Darn it. That's it.

He bumped his mug on the wooden table hard enough to startle the mocking bird off its perch on the eave. It squawked at him reproachfully, and then flew to the wall to dive-bomb the tabby dozing innocently in the sun.

Guillermo shook off the depressing memory. He called out, "Richard. Tournament coming up? You're sure hard at it!"

"Yes, Dad. At the Beverly Hills Country Club next week. Starts Friday evening"

"Really. Is Jeff Henderson playing? It's a little soon after what happened, but..," Guillermo walked toward the tennis court.

"I don't know, Dad. Too much sensationalism, excessive furor surrounds those events. That whole scene gives me the creeps. I think the twins, Patrick and Jeff, are off in San Francisco somewhere, keeping a low profile. God only knows what they must be going through!

Deal Me a Card

"I've played against Jeff a couple of times. Nothing much. At invitationals, and two of the men on the UC team belong to the club so they've invited me for games.

There was some talk. I couldn't help hearing the whispers and gossip. No love between him and his grandfather. The man was a hot shot CEO once upon a time, but boy, was he arrogant. Made you cringe, the guys said, the way he tossed his power around. Acted as if he was crown prince of the soap opera production industry still.

"On a sweeter note, take Isadora Rubio, she's one hot Cuban and not at all arrogant, no way!"

"Now, no talking about my staff like that. She's a very lovely lady. Aggressive, though I believe the word is assertive these days. But you're right; she's a fine figure of a woman."

"So you noticed. My old man hasn't lost his eye. She's going to be here this evening?"

"I invited her. She said something about bringing a date. Your girlfriend Sarita is coming, isn't she?"

"She wouldn't miss this celebration for the world. Yes, she's my date. Not just for tonight either. We seem to be hitting it off … caught a couple of concerts, did the 10K AIDS walk with a few friends. Isadora's way too mature for me, anyhow. Divorced, and a mother of two.

"But tell me… is everything ready for the party? I kept the day open so I could run errands if you need me."

"Your aunt and uncle will be here in fifteen minutes and we'll get things moving."

Richard grinned. "I figured with that pig on the spit behind the garage we'd done the main event for food. Man, it smells good, he laughed. "I saw you standing there savoring the scent of barbecued flesh!"

"Right! Nothing like it!." But you know, there's the corn, and the beans, and the tortillas, the salsa, the salads. Your aunt Juanita has it all lined up. She's the consummate party planner, thank God! I can leave all the details to her.

54

Deal Me a Card

She informed me that some people are bringing desserts. For our part, I think we have enough beer and wine and sodas.

"There'll be a few youngsters with their parents. Good way to keep the kids off the streets."

"I hear you. Are Doc and Maricela bringing their gang with them?"

"Please don't say that word around here. Yes, Israel, Abram, Ishmael, Rafe and Mathilde. The whole Velasquez bunch, like the Brady family used to be.

"Big M's bringing his daughter. A couple of the ladies from work will have sons, a niece, a nephew. They'll get to dance, shoot the breeze. Do they use that expression anymore?"

"So Mrs. V. will be here? Great! I really love that lady. I remember when I was in middle school and Daniel was right behind me in sixth grade. Uncle Raoul took us to the boxing ring and we pretended to be Sugar Ray and Ali. Doc would show us a few moves. She'd be watching us, encouraging us 'Go... go.' We were all worked up after thirty minutes, totally worn out using that energy.

"I used to spar with Zachary. Man. I still can't believe what happened. We were kind of like friends. He was cool. Then ... what happened, God, what happened?" Richard stared at the ground.

Putting his hand on his son's shoulder, Guillermo said, "Tragic, all that gang banging, even while his parents were working with the other kids to stop the killing and violence. Life is a quadruple twisted DNA helix for some people. Doesn't matter what you do, how much, how little. An individual has to choose his own way....Or hers."

"I know, Dad. You mentioned Big M's daughter? She's a sophomore at USC, aspiring to graduate studies in the film school. Go figure."

"Big M's been out and clean, what, two years now? The girl hardly knew her father while he was inside. Maybe she's

Deal Me a Card

inspiring him. And it doesn't hurt that he's working with Doc.

"But enough about the guests. We'll have plenty to gab about tonight. Let's go haul some furniture onto the patio. Your aunt and uncle will be here any minute, and the bustling around will start in earnest. Then I'll have to leave you all in charge after three. I'm heading out to the airport to pick up your brother."

The two men looked at each other, grinned, chuckled in satisfaction, embraced. Guillermo's relief was visible in his next words, "He's home at last. That's all the celebration we need!"

Richard drew further back to scrutinize his father. The dark mop of hair always disheveled till after his shower, showed light streaks of white. The widow's peak perked straight up. There were deep grooves around the corners of his mouth and eyes, more pronounced than his infectious grins could generate.

The young man was very conscious of his Dad's ferocity, on a par with a bulldog protecting her whelps. And Daniel's close brush with history occurring thousands of miles away, had taken a toll. The son gripped the older man's shoulder affectionately, "Seven hours more, and we'll be dancing fools!"

CHAPTER 13

AT THIRTY-TWO THOUSAND FEET, somewhere over the Pacific, five hours estimated flight time from Los Angeles, Daniel shifted his weight in his exit aisle seat. He stretched his legs, wiggled his toes shod in the ropey kangaroo-leather sandals he had found in the Australian Outback. The extra space was a luxury for his five-foot eleven-inch frame. As he took another sip of water, he gazed out the window at the infinite calm of blue, ran his left hand through his shaggy black hair that his Dad would half-reproachfully call his "tresses" within minutes of seeing the mop.

The tumult of the past few weeks slowly receded as the Northwest 747 sped down the last lap of his journey then advanced once more like a menacing tsunami as he allowed his thoughts free rein. *People mountain, People sea.* The Chinese phrase rose in his mind as it flitted wildly from event to event, making an inebriated beeline through the profusion of images.

He succumbed once more to the sensation of being towed by a current, the flood that had swept him unresisting down Beijing's Avenue of Peace to Tiananmen Square. He was one drop among a million. The million students and workers who had coalesced to cry out for democracy.

Wrong place, wrong time. It was the worst of times, it was the best of times. Not making a decision is a decision in itself. Man, he would have to lose the clichés if he ever sat down to write about his experiences.

How was he to know last September that this faraway revolution was brewing? He had been acing his Mandarin 101 course at Cal State when he made up his mind to visit China. It would be a part of his delayed high school

Deal Me a Card

graduation gift trip. Two years ago, Richard had chosen Europe. He opted for the Far East.

"It'll be a short detour, Dad. It'll help me decide for sure if I want to spend my junior year in China or in Turkey. You know I'm planning to apply for an internship through the International Studies program."

His father had encouraged his ambition. What he experienced had been completely unexpected. Scary, but intoxicating. His mind flew back to China.

****

Half a day after a fourteen-hour flight in the middle of May, he had landed unwittingly in the midst of overwhelming but wondrously restrained protest marches.

The people's zeal was infectious, enough to overcome his fear of succumbing to a barrage of countless spinning wheels as he tramped through the crush of bodies. Blinkered cyclists converged on him, swarmed towards him, a buzzing army of killer ants, then swerved seconds before they stung him.

Moments later, the human wave lifted him off his feet. Momentum propelled him forward, the press of tens of thousands of pedestrians sporting sedate suits, locked arm-in-arm with tens of thousands of others in more casual student and worker garb.

All moving in the direction of the Square, towards an uncertain destiny. If there was an inkling of a doubt, it was obliterated by the bandanas and banners brazenly flaunting the forbidden. The endless parade of red, the black, the gold and the white gyrated in an ecstasy of longing, for free speech, independent newspapers, fair pay, and human rights.

Desire for change engulfed him.

Having thrown in his lot with them, since it was not difficult to lose himself in the squeeze of bodies, he embraced the demonstrators' vision. And they adopted him.

Deal Me a Card

"Go back and tell the USA what you are seeing, and smelling, and tasting," his new-found comrades urged in their classroom English. "This is the new Chinese revolution. We shall overcome injustice. We are demanding dialogue," they chanted.

That was all well and good when the manifestos were read. And even when the sustained stubbornness and pure weight and volume of Sino-humanity prevented the mobilized troops from setting up a blockade. Especially when the Goddess of Democracy was raised to thunderous roars of triumph.

But when the tanks, blind metal rolling pins, relentlessly flattened hapless blood-gushing bodies in their path, when soldiers opened fire, killing their brothers and sisters on Chairman's Deng Xiaoping's orders, when the vast sea of protesters shrank to a lake, then a pond, then dried up to a trickle, when ring leaders were dragged away for trial, to prison or execution, they knew, and Daniel knew, there would be no dialogue.

Daniel stirred from his reverie, used the lavatory, grabbed another bottle from the stewardess's tray and regained his seat. He resumed his reverie.

Would he one day remove himself far enough from the scenes to describe the mixture of terror and giddiness that propelled him and his five University of Beijing companions through those June days of crushed dreams? Together they navigated the hazardous streams of suppression, avoiding violence, but aware every second of its loaded muzzle aimed at their backs. The keening of an ambulance tugged them here. The chatter of gunfire eliciting shrieks and moans of the wounded dragged them there. Rickshaws dripping the gore of victims urged them one way. The sharp command of a soldier snarling, "Halt," drove them in the other direction.

Still, they survived.

Morning dawned. He had risked his life as a miniscule part of a huge but abortive attempt by China's youth to impact an unyielding ideology. And lived to see another day. He had insinuated himself into China's history as it thrashed in the throes of new birth pangs, bellowed in its raging labor. He reached out and trapped a whiff of a new era.

The aftermath was remarkably peaceful. Or successfully crushed. Authoritarian shushing suppressed democracy in its infancy. He left the Imperial City, splitting from his fellow rebels for safety's sake. His passport and visa opened all the right doors.

Daniel pursued the rest of his journey in a state of surrealism. Shanghai, Xian and small towns he visited as part of his itinerary seemed oblivious to the radical upheaval in the capital. With communications control, they probably knew little, or were fed a pabulum version.

The wonders of the world presented themselves. It was indeed a Great Wall. In their natural habitat, the giant pandas lived up to their reputation. But all the while he felt numb as he wandered through the sights. The stupor was unshakeable.

After he left China, he wended his way through Thailand, Malaysia and Australia. But unforgettable circumstances now bonded him to China forever.

****

A clipped voice broke into Daniel's reverie. His body jerked awake in a spasm, disoriented by the swirl of recent memories that droned through the young traveler's head. Seconds later, he turned his head and flashed a lopsided smile at the solemn, aged Chinese attorney sitting beside him. A moment's hesitation, then she lifted the comers of her mouth in return. Daniel wondered if he had indeed fallen asleep and muttered something incriminating. *Nonsense, he was being paranoid.* He swiped a miniscule drool of saliva from his lower cheek. Then he stretched, and straightened his baggy peasant pants and shirt, listening as the stewardess continued, "Ladies and gentlemen, the captain has turned on the seat-belt sign. We are approximately forty-five minutes from LAX."

CHAPTER 14

EMMA PAUSED, sipped her sangria as she mingled in the conversation. Her azure halter-top sundress, ankle-length, modestly covered her. She moved freely, lithely. The blue-green silkiness fondled her curves as she moved from group to group. Latin-American music whiffed at her ears, mixed with the lilt of voices, a segue to classic Beatles with a touch of Elton John, back to salsa.

Guillermo's celebration of his younger son's homecoming was in full swing. The moon had gone elsewhere, taking the clouds with her. But a thousand stars obligingly pinpricked the sky's inkiness. Lights, indoors and out, in the shrubbery emitted a muted glow. Guests lounged on the patio. Now and again, couples took to the floor in the living room to dance, languidly or with élan, depending on the beat. Some teenagers with younger siblings stood, arms akimbo, on the pool deck, contemplating a late-evening dip.

Emma joined a cluster of women at a table under the jacaranda. As four of them listened, rapt, Carmelita, a clerk at the center, was shuddering in mock horror,

"He's such a dirty old man. About forty, maybe thirty-five, I can't tell. There he is, in church every week. He enters by the side door and makes his way to the back.

"Comes in, looking very earnest, pious. Wavy, grey-streaked hair, very neatly Bryl-cremed. Signs himself, clasps his hands in respect.

"So you're watching this guy in church instead of praying?" Rosalia chimes in. "Just what he hopes you will do. Don't you know that's what these freaks want to happen?"

Undeterred, without missing a beat, Carmelita continued her righteous train of thought, "But then he sees some young woman taking a seat. She's always got long hair, slim, dressed nice, some lipstick, make-up.

"It's mostly different women, but sometimes it's the same one. He strolls up casually. Then he kneels beside her, real innocent-like. You can't help but observe him every Sunday. Same Mass, same man. Does he think nobody notices?"

"Hey, these fellas, they have an obsession, they don't care who witnesses. I don't think they realize it. They're predators. But you're right," Rosalia grimaced. "Yuck!"

"Then he edges closer and closer to the girl. Not too close, just enough to get her scent, I suppose. Really creepy. At the recitation of the Lord's Prayer he takes her hand, very brotherly. Sick! One time, he sat beside this blonde three weeks in a row. She must have sensed something was eerie. The fourth Sunday, she came in with some friends. He didn't go near them. After that, she wasn't in Church. I think he drives the women away."

"Just you wait. He'll kneel next to you tomorrow," Rosalia teased.

"He does, and the Virgin of Guadalupe will be so scared out of her wits by my scream, she'll knock him senseless with her bouquet of roses!"

Emma joined in the laughter, then drifted away to help herself to dinner. Juanita, Guillermo's sister-in-law was leaning on the table, listening to her cousin's daughter, Dulce. Her lips twitched and her head shook or nodding alternately in time to her relative's heated words,

"You think after all we've been through and he's back with us now, he could spend a little time with his kids. He hasn't seen them for what, three years? They put him away for three years, two months and four days. I know I marked off every day on the calendar. Now I am, the children are, we're all happy. The kids start asking for his attention right away, 'Daddy, Daddy we're going to the circus next week. You too!' This is four days after he comes home.

63

"Mark, my youngest, he was newborn when Marco went in, so he's not sure who's this guy. The other two were five and seven so they have some memories. I told them all the good stories about him, and his life and the family in Mexico. I tried. And so they welcomed him back, lots of hugging and kisses and kept telling him about school and showing him their toys. Especially the baby. Markie's so cute. He looks like his Dad. Reaches up with his chubby arms, 'Up, Up. Da-da.' Big toothless smile.

"God, I was so happy. But after awhile I could tell his heart wasn't with the family anymore. Like at the circus. He's under the tent for just twenty minutes, then he's complaining about his butt being sore from the wooden seats. Like he's some Mexican Mafia king with a velvet throne to cushion his backside. Nothing but a farmer from Sinaloa. And now an ex-con. He goes out to sit in the pick-up and doesn't come back. I think he snuck a coupla beers. You tell me, why should I put up with that shit?"

"But he's trying, Dulce. Making an effort. At least he seems to be giving you a break. Minding the house, the children. Like this evening."

"Yeah, Juanita, I know. I was surprised. He offered to stay at home with the kids. Said he'd feel out of place at this party, needed more time to get used to being out."

Juanita sighed, "We can't begin to fathom what prison is like. Give him some leeway. You have to adjust also, no?"

Emma dolloped some guacamole and beans beside the ribs and greens on her plate, and sidled off. She walked by a woman whose mass of black frizzy curls surrounded a heart-shaped face. Worried brown eyes stared from the middle. They looked deep into her listener's widened orbs.

"You ask me, 'Eva, how are you and are the kids doing? Well?' Here this very minute it's calm, peaceful, everyone's mellow. Most of all, it feels safe. They're with me here, Ralph Junior and Patty. But I'm not invited to parties every evening, or even every weekend.

Deal Me a Card

"The rest of the time, every day, it's a whole different story."

Eva reached out a hand and drew Emma into the conversation. Her voice was tremulous,

"Come join us, Ms. Emma. I gotta tell you about these problems too. What we live with all the time. It's hell there in the middle of town. Dangers on every little street of La Coloma. No doves of peace, that's for sure. There's no warning. The cars drive by slowly. And then the devils open fire. We hear gunshots every evening. Any time after dark. It's gotten so bad, we stay in the back of the house and go to bed early.

"My God, do you know, Patty has to study in the bathroom? Sometimes I have to pick her up early from the library, so she can't finish her homework there. At home, she actually sits reading in the bath-tub!

"Naomi, Ms. Emma, we're scared."

Her hand was quivering as she placed it again on Emma's arm, then on Naomi's. Her ample breasts shook beneath a fitting sleeveless sweater, lemon with orange stripes. Emma's shocked 'Good grief' and Naomi's sympathetic tsk-tsk's urged her on,

"We can't sit in the living room anymore. After that one time, when the bullets came through the window smashing the glass. We all dived to the floor. Screaming, crying. My heart almost stopped. I was spread out on top of the children. My hands over their heads. Like it was an earthquake.

"But it's worse. It's actually a war zone. Thank God no one was hurt. Junior was yelling 'Get off me, mom. You're crushing me!' I'm not exactly a lightweight, as you can see. But it was no laughing matter then!

"But why us? Junior is ten years old, turning eleven next month, and Patty is just twelve. Maybe it's those boys in her class. They're young but they join the gangs earlier and earlier these days. She's very quiet, keeps to herself

65

mostly, and only has two real girlfriends, Lorraine and Rosa. But those boys, they tease her and want her to go out. She's too young. Or there are other girls, jealous perhaps. Now maybe they're retaliating?"

"Did you do anything when you were shot at?" Naomi interjected.

"I made a police report. The officers came, took pictures. So what can they do? My house is not the only target. Lots of houses get attacked. It's hard to believe La Coloma is just three miles from this quiet hacienda." Eva paused. Her voice quavered, distraught.

Emma patted her shoulder, vowed to discuss this further and hugged her. Resuming her search, her steps quickened as she spotted the host. Guillermo and Daniel were deep in conversation, between gulps of cerveza. Their locked eyes barely swiveled to greet her.

"After that, Dad, I was ready to kneel down and kiss the ground when I got off that plane today. We just don't appreciate what we have here. It's all so easy, all too easy for us young folk."

"You've grown up, Daniel, my boy. You're a man now. Baptism by fire, baptized by blood. But thank God not your blood."

"And the stink, Dad. I want to vomit when I remember. It's like… it's still in my nose and in my throat. I have to think of it like the smell of martyrs. Or else I'd be totally disgusted. It was horrible, those buses and cars, like hell, like an inferno, and flesh burning. Dead people lying there.

"It was different when Mom was all laid out in her coffin with all those beautiful flowers around her. Their scent was like her lilac perfume. I remember it. I remember her, her skin was so soft even though she was dead, and her lips were pink. She was pretty skinny, right, pretty sick when she passed away. I'm sorry, Dad, to bring up those memories. I shouldn't have. It must hurt. "

Deal Me a Card

Daniel paused. He laid his hand softly on his father's forearm. His eyes were sad under worried brows. Guillermo said nothing, simply nodded for him to continue.

"But those people there, in Tianamen Square, one minute they were running, shouting, challenging their government. Alive, full of energy. Next minute they were dancing fire bombs, writhing in flames. Oh my God, *Papa, Papa*, Dad, the shrieks were like nothing I ever heard before. And the stench of the flesh burning was…was..I can't describe it. It's still in my nose, in my dreams…a nightmare.

"I wake up wanting to throw up. Then they were piles of ashes. Nobody could know them. Nobody dared mourn at their funeral pyres."

His father drew his child closer as he placed his arm around his shoulders. "*Mi hijo,* son, Danny boy, we'll talk more about this later. Come now. See, this is Emma, my very special friend. She works for Uncle Raoul and she's teaching English at the Center. You two will get along great. I know."

Guillermo grasped Emma's hand and joined it to the younger man's, introducing them. His lover could see the moisture in his eyes that pleaded with hers for help. She let go of Daniel's hand, and pulled him gently into a hug.

"Welcome home, traveler. Your father told me that you were in Penang for a few days. I'm all agog. You must tell me all about how that city had changed. That was my birthplace."

Emma's gaze met Guillermo's over his son's shoulder briefly, lovingly. Then she led the younger man into the house, away from the laughter and voices, where the quiet was interrupted only by the staccato sobs of the young voyager.

Guillermo walked off. His shoulders arched, his fingers dug deep in his palms. He nodded to Isadora, and managed an 'All's well' smile when she raised her eyebrows at him. Good host he was, as he queried on the richness of the feast and the delicacy of the wine with a guest here and a friend

67

there. Then welcomed with a few claps of his hands and an easier smile, Paul McCartney's voice insisting that "All you need is love," as it throbbed forcefully through the air.

Deal Me a Card

CHAPTER 15

THAT SAME EVENING in another part of the Valley, the British super-spy nuzzled his latest lover, triumphant and ready for passion after his gory and grueling confrontation with the killer Suarez in the Mexican desert. He had no license to kill but he did. Now unscathed, he was reaping the rewards, wrapped in silken sheets, entwined with his sexy lady.

As the credits rolled, Felipe pulled his torso forward and turned to his date. Brenda's red lip gloss and sparkly sky-blue eye-shadow glittered, just visible in the theatre's still-dim lighting. Long shiny black ringlets bounced on her subtly rouged cheeks. She looked into his eyes as he spoke,

"Some movie, eh, Brenda? Got to hand it to that guy. No matter what, he obliterates his rival every time. Pow, pow, bam, bam. First he survives the crazy plane dives, then he gets it off with his lady. Enjoyed it?"

"Sure. But all that violence and explosives. You think there's anything or anybody left or living in Mexico City?"

"You can't think too deeply. It's all escape from reality."

But even as he uttered the words, his hazel eyes were losing their warmth and turning to marble. Felipe lowered his voice dropping it to a hissing whisper,

"Hey, who's this guy?"

Before his girlfriend could reply, she heard behind her, "Hi, Brenda. Long time no see."

The young woman's head swiveled, a spinning top whipped by the voice. She and her boyfriend jumped quickly to their feet. Before she said a word, it continued,

"Remember, at grandfather's eighty-first party? Last June?"

A lanky man, their age, stood in their faces, halting them in their path. He wore a Tide-bright tee-shirt and hip-hugging blue jeans. Muscles rippled, flaunted the red, blue and yellow sinuous movements of some fire-breathing underworld monsters etched the length of both his arms. The line of his short-cropped hair wandered off his head, down past his ears in finely-etched sideburns, and ended in a neatly-trimmed goatee and wispy moustache. Close-set snake-icy pupils darted back and forth between the two.

Brenda's eyes, wide as a rabbit's at bay before a wolf, stared into the newcomer's. Her strangled voice burbled out words that unraveled like a yo-yo's string, "I remember. That was so much fun! How're things? This is my friend, Felipe. Felipe, he's my cousin, Mauricio.

"Did you like the movie? Not bad, uh? That Brit is always so sexy. But maybe too much violence for my taste. We're on our way home. Where're you off to?"

Her cousin, Mauricio, spoke more slowly and deliberately, "Meeting my homeboys at someone's pad. Where you hail from, Felipe?"

"Pacoima."

Mauricio's response did not hide the threat. "Better take her back to her house, to her family. Now. Or there's some rumbling up ahead."

Mauricio stuck out his hand. Felipe stole a surreptitious glance down as he gripped the proffered fingers, taking in the M, S, 6 6, tattooed on each of the knuckles. He looked up and stared straight into the cold black eyes that lasered his face. Felipe was glad his checkered long-sleeved, buttoned-up shirt hid his arms and most of his neck. The orders kept coming at him,

"Keep her safe. Drive straight home."

"Right. Good to meet you. Later."

"Maybe. Take her home right now, you hear?"

If the atmosphere had been more amicable Felipe might have saluted with a "Yessir" and a grin. Instead, clutching

70

icy hands and pretending nonchalance, he grabbed his girl at her elbow as they exited the cinema quickening their pace, trotting out to the car. They drove off uneasily, the target of a dozen pairs of hostile eyes.

****

The six-pack of cerveza thumped heavily against Marco Ayala's thigh as he slunk across the uneven parking lot. Under the street light, cracks in the asphalt threw black lightning zigzags across its surface. But they barely caught the corner of his eye. Instructions on ways to "diss' your bitch and love your bro'" floated through the open window of a car pulled up in an empty space. Its loose muffler rattled in time with the rapper's flagrant admonitions. Marco's ears were tuned off. The sour smell of stale beery vomit tickled his nostrils. He wriggled his nose indifferently.

He and Dulce had a two-bedroom rental just a one block away, around the corner from the main drag of La Coloma. He could make the return trip like this one in eight minutes flat including the stop for the purchase. He glanced at his watch. Ten fifty-five. His timing was perfect. Four minutes left to get back home to the kids. When he left, baby Markie was asleep. Invincible Mr. Bronson had the other two youngsters transfixed on the couch as the intrepid vigilante fulfilled the death wish of a zillion predatory thugs in some barren New York war zone. Thus cozily nestled, with the front and back doors locked, the three children were safe.

Marco's pace was brisk. His thigh muscles tensed as he strode. The evening was empty of the sound of real men's voices. The time inside had made him antsy around that kind of silence. It boded evil. Noiselessness meant dead air in which creatures were planning or preparing to instigate the unspeakable. He shook off his qualms. But the flick of his head and the shrug of his shoulders turned to a shiver.

He used the brief minutes to conjure up his excuse. Dulce had said not to expect her until around midnight since

71

Deal Me a Card

she was riding home from the party with Juanita Guerrero. He'd pop one can, and tell her Geronimo had brought the six-pack. How could he refuse? That would seem ungrateful, unfriendly. He was trying to reestablish the connections with his long-lost buddies, get back to normal life. Gerry had come over unexpectedly, how could he shut the door on his overtures? Anyway, she was off having fun with the high falutin' crowd, so why couldn't he relax also with an old pal. In her face, but not harshly. They were adjusting, getting along better, little by little. At least, he thought so. Couldn't tell, from her sour expressions.

But, damn, I need to cut her some slack. She's the one kept the kids all this time. While I was rotting inside that hellhole. Maybe we need counseling.

Down the road about a half block away, Tommy's OPEN sign was flickering off for the night. He liked their hot dogs. Some afternoons in the last few weeks since he got home, when Dulce was working late, he took the kids there for dinner. Convenient fast food. Good exercise for the baby. They all liked the burgers and fries. Markie slurped up their milkshake like it was a Bud. *Man, Dulce would slap his face, both cheeks, break his teeth if he made that joke.* Anything related to booze was no laughing matter to her. Well, not to him neither.

A couple left the joint. Kids in their teens, holding hands, whispering and looking into each other's eyes. Ah, young love crossing the road. They were jaywalking, but at this time of night, minus traffic, their sauntering did not seem reckless.

The two disappeared down his street. The car farting offensive lyrics and dirty fumes slid by him. Another, cleaner black Chevy with three passengers, pulled up behind it and followed its path. License plate smudged with dirt NBX 070. Like slick oil the two vehicles slithered down his street also.

Seconds later he heard the two shots.

Deal Me a Card

His heart ejected into his mouth. For one fraction of a minute his feet were mired as if in wet concrete. The petrified father shrieked in his head to his vocal cords to be still.

Then adrenaline shot through his body. It sent him speeding like a bullet down the alley that circled back to the rear of his house. The gate was still closed. *Thank God and His Holy Mother Mary!* The sound as he released the latch was as though someone was reloading a piece. He heard the metal aperture slam shut behind him as his giant strides took him up the three steps to the back porch.

Marco fumbled the key out of his pocket, unlocked the door, and entered. As slowly as he could, he tried to control his scrambling footsteps, though he vainly tried to still the rapidity of his heart beat. He poked his head into the living room and inhaled the cozy odor of buttered popcorn. The two junior babysitters did not remove their fixated eyes from the screen. His daughter murmured, so as not to distract her attention from New York's killing fields,

"Hi, pop!"

"Hi kids. Everything okay?"

"Markie got up. But I gave him a drink of juice and he went back to bed. Can we have more snacks. Maybe some M&Ms?"

"Sure sweetie. Film any good?"

"Yup! Daddy, I think you should check on Markie. He wants mom to kiss him goodnight. I guess you can do it. He likes you a lot now."

His sweetie graced him with a cute smile, as he turned to his baby's bedroom.

Deal Me a Card

CHAPTER 16

A HUNDRED FEET DOWN on the tiny beach, two prone nude figures were pleading with the sun for a more burnished bronze. Guillermo squinted at them thoughtfully,

"Maybe we can do that someday soon."

"Too cold! Don't like goose bumps," Emma murmured, though her gaze was also admiring the tanned sleekness.

"We could run around and chase each other to keep warm. Work up a sweat!" Guillermo, ever the clown, shot back. His companion played along,

"Hold that thought."

Directly below them, rocks rumbled and belched salted spume. Somehow the megaliths maintained their sharp perkiness despite the eternal harassment from the dashing waves. The round steely head of a seal glistered, trapping an occasional ray as it bobbled and ducked for lunch. Blue afternoon sky, stretched for miles and miles then halted, cut deep by the horizon's razor-sharp black edge.

A brown pelican squadron in perfect V-formation glided by on an air current. Above them, gulls circled, squawking derisively. Emma's glance swept to her left. Malibu and Santa Monica and some other distant headland were distinguishable.

"Thank you for last night," Guillermo squeezed her hand. He turned her towards him, kissed her hard on the lips. "My son needed a mother right there, right then."

Emma nodded, as she returned the pleasure. "Glad to help. With all that pent-up pain, sorrow and horror, all mixed up in his heart and his head, he had to get it out. But that was only the beginning of the catharsis. It'll be good for him to talk some more. Not necessarily to me, or to you. An offspring never finds it easy to talk to a father, or a mother or a surrogate mom."

Deal Me a Card

Grasping Guillermo's shoulder she continued wistfully at first,

"I'm reminded of my own son, Thomas. When he was sixteen, two of his soccer teammates were in a head-on crash with a drunk driver. Neither survived. Tommy was in another car following behind them. Saw the whole collision! He was traumatized. One day he running around with them on the field, the next week he was attending their funerals. For days, he was a walking zombie, lost sleep, had nightmares about being in that car and dying. Tried to hide it from me and his father. His grades dropped. He skipped school. Poor boy, even got drunk once during those two weeks."

She spoke sharply, "That did it! Thomas started seeing a psychologist. Psyches are fragile, Guillermo, even male psyches. Perhaps Daniel needs professional counseling."

Emma paused, arrested by Guillermo's glare and quick involuntary scowl. She reached up and stroked away the creases around his lips, "No, don't look like that. He's not crazy. No, no! This is like post-traumatic stress. Actually, he was in a war zone of sorts. The battle was raging, like it or not. And he made the choice. He put himself in the thick of the fray. Became a virtual warrior. Escaped, but witnessed death and disappearance of fellow fighters.

"Interesting, he considers himself a pacifist. So he was, playing with fire. Psychologically and emotionally. You have to deal with it, okay?"

Now Emma pulled back from her listener, one hand firmly on her hip. Her voice waxed earnest as she emphasized each phrase. She sensed Guillermo's incredulity.

Then he grinned. He pulled her back into his embrace. Kissed her lips again as she was about to continue. Stared into her serious grey-green eyes. His brows furrowed, but only for a moment, as he burst into a smile once more. Tapping her nose with his finger,

Deal Me a Card

"You're right. I'll sit down with him in the next couple of days and have a serious heart-to-heart discussion. No distractions.

"But, you had not told me much about your son until now. You mentioned you were divorced and had a child. Where is he?"

"He lives in England now, studying for his bachelor's degree in Political Science at Cambridge University. On a scholarship. We talk to each other on the phone every month or six weeks. I treasure those times. But he's a grown man and has his busy life to lead, with a girlfriend. Still, he and I are very close in spirit. He wants me to be happy. 'I want you to read fairytales to my son and daughter, Mum, so stay healthy and alive.' He reminds me every time we speak.

"I miss him." Emma ended with a tiny sigh.

"He's about Daniel's age, right? I hope they meet one day soon. They would become good friends," Richard said. He held her away from him for a moment, his hands lightly touching her shoulders,

"I love you, you know? You're good for your son, for me, for my boys. Stay with me. Forever."

Before she could respond, he continued, "Shall we walk down to the beach? Then we'll climb back up to the car afterwards. I know, you think I'm a cheap skate 'cause I didn't pay for a parking space down here."

"Am I complaining? Hey, we need the exercise after last night."

The stroll down along the path was easy, with them holding hands. A few poppies lingered brilliant amidst the sage scrub, defiantly upright though the slaps from the wind cruelly snapped their fragile petals and disbursed them at will. When they stepped onto the beach, sand crumbled beneath the lovers' flip flops, crunchy, moist.

As Emma stood barefoot at the edge of the water, she relaxed, let herself sink as the fine granules squelched and tickled between her toes, and the bubbly foam lapped and whispered around her ankles. With Guillermo's encircling arm caressing her waist, she felt safe, far away from the tremors of the night before.

When Guillermo had called her that morning to suggest a ride to the coast she had eagerly thrown on denim shorts and a red polka-dot halter, and was waiting for him in the car park when he pulled up. The drive through the towering rock faces of Malibu Canyon, once they left Calabasas behind them, was a rollicking swoosh that uplifted her spirits. Now the salt in the air scoured her nerves, and smoothed the edginess.

They ran, frolicked like children on a summer outing. Fingers digging, found a few beached pearly clam shells. Noses inhaled the heavy scent of kelp. They spit grit, smacked rumps. Loose-limbed and unrestrained, they laughed aloud and chased sandpipers, who hunted crab morsels, vainly trying to keep their dainty claws beyond the reach of the mischievous waves. At last, spent, they trudged up to the waiting car parked on Cliffside Drive, and headed home.

****

The streets through San Benitez were Sunday-quiet, echoing the stillness of the adjoining La Coloma. The car purred through both dozing communities like a prowling puma. Emma, head lolling against the headrest, drowsy from the sun's pummeling, glanced idly at the passing scenery.

In the distance the local museum's angular rooftop loomed for five seconds then vanished. Idly, a memory from a visit fifteen years ago of a high-ceilinged gilded hall full of shiny antique cars, glided through Emma's mind, *Coddled opulence lording it over a serfdom of immigrants,* was her perplexed thought.

More modest homes plodded into view. Here and there a street would verge into industrial zones, their squared-off

Deal Me a Card

accordion doors tightly shuttered and padlocked. A vacant cinder block enclosed with chain-link dented a street corner.

There was Reynoso's Imports on one street. *Must be where they store all that merchandise they drag up from Mexico to sell at the flea market.* On the next street children were playing in the yard. *Haphazard urban planning,* she mused.

Huge grotesque murals, splayed on every inch of a brick wall, hit her eyeballs like hisses of mace. She almost gagged from the spew of gangster art festering on underpasses, billboards, posts. Her heart shriveled before the terrible beauty hurled from the hands of twentieth century wannabe Michelangelos who blatantly spattered their depiction of Hell across the San Fernando Valley. Emma's left hand groped and found Guillermo's fingers waiting wordlessly, reassuringly.

"What the...!" Guillermo's exclamation was chopped silent by the honking of sirens as two police cars streaked by.

They each forced themselves to be quiet as they continued up the road leading to the house. Emma's jaws tightened. She crossed and uncrossed her legs, as she leaned forward in the leather that had suddenly become squeakily hot and wet under her thighs. Her index finger picked at the dry spot near her thumbnail. *If I don't stop that soon, I'll start to bleed,* she thought, and kept on picking. Guillermo stared straight ahead. A muscle throbbed so heavily in his temple that it would have screamed from the pain of repeated impact, if it had a voice.

As they entered the driveway, they saw the parked cars that had sped by them seconds ago. Guillermo and Emma scrambled out, slammed doors, and lurched, towards the two uniformed police officers who approached them with stiff strides and firmly squared jaws.

"It's my son?"

The strangled sound was neither a question nor an agonized throat gargle. One of the men responded, his tone clipped and terse,

"Sir, is your son Daniel Guerrero? We received a telephone ten minutes ago. Other officers are present and an ambulance is here on the other side of the house."

His voice changed as his listener reacted, "Easy now, sir, easy, easy," as Guillermo slumped into Emma.

The other policeman stepped forward to assist the one speaking. He addressed the woman, "Let me assist you, ma'am. Here I've got him."

Emma had hold of Guillermo by his waist. Her helper held him by the shoulders. Firmly, looking Guillermo in the eye, the first officer to speak, continued, "Mr. Guerrero, that's Daniel Guerrero, called because of what he discovered earlier this afternoon. He and his brother are waiting in the house for us. We instructed them to remain there until we had control of the scene. They are discussing the incident with the detective who arrived just before we got here."

Guillermo, regaining his equilibrium, turned to Emma. They embraced. He covered her head with his right hand. Her arms across his shoulders were a blanket of comfort. They sprinted to the house.

"Let's go in, sir, ma'am. One of the plainclothes personnel is DEA. That's become routine around these parts with all the drug dealing. Homicides and crack sales gone bad tend to pal around.

"The officers will question all the people who live on this property. I suspect we will disrupt your Sunday evening for a few hours. My apologies. Let's not waste any more time. After you, sir, ma'am."

The law enforcer, in total control, stepped to one side as he gestured to the couple to enter the house. Emma answered, as graciously as she could under the circumstances, "Sure, Officer Bateman. And you are...

Deal Me a Card

Officer Olivera. Certainly, it's not a problem. We will do all we can to assist you."

In the living room, the couple and the two brothers greeted one other ecstatic with relief. With an explanation to the law and an escort, they fled to the refrigerator, each one ravenous, craving the comfort of food and drink.

Emma was hungry, after a brunch of only a cup of tea and a slim granola bar hours earlier. She pulled containers of cheese, dips, guacamole, fruit salad from the crammed ice-box, while Daniel fetched drinks. Richard fished out crackers and rolls from the cupboard. Guillermo supervised, asked the men if they could offer them something to eat and accepted their preoccupied refusal. The family ate in a hurry, sating their appetites, while the officers stood by, impatiently waiting within sight.

"Okay. Mr. Guerrero, Daniel. Could you tell us everything that happened? Be as specific as you can. All details are important."

Detective Yow dove right in as the four straggled into the living room and slumped in the sofa and armchairs.

Daniel spoke, deliberately, "I woke up way too early this morning. Even though I really wanted to stay in bed all day and get over jet lag. But I'm on Bali time, or Alice Springs time, whatever, so I was restless all night. And wide-eyed, like I had no lids. Then the darn dogs kept barking as I tossed and turned, and pumped my pillow. I heard a coyote howling.

"At one point I went to my window, it must have been about four o'clock San Benitez time, just to stretch my legs. I saw headlights on the other side of the hill." Gesturing, "Up there on the dirt road. That's when the dogs started yapping again. They were in a frenzy for awhile. I lay back down, fell back to sleep maybe twenty minutes later."

He turned and addressed his family members. "Didn't you two guys hear anything? Emma, you went home?"

"Yes, your Dad drove me home at about two. Guillermo, was there anything unusual happening when you got back? "

"No, I heard nothing. After I left Emma, I arrived back here, probably at about two forty-five. I jumped into bed. Slept like the dead. What about you, Richard?"

"Um, I went home with Sarita and, you'll be happy to know, officers and Dad, I stayed put. Too many beers. Got back here about eleven this morning.

"After a shower, I was working in my room on a paper for my Anthro class. Heard you leave at twelve thirty or one, Dad. Then, I lay down to think about my research in comfort. It was too comfortable I guess, and I fell asleep. We had a busy time yesterday. Then Daniel came in yelling."

"Yeah. I woke up again from my beauty rest about three in the afternoon, for chrissake! I know 'cause I was cursing the dogs in my dreams, then when I opened my eyes I was still swearing at them until I saw what time it was. Okay?" Daniel looked around at his listeners, giving a longer glance to Emma who nodded at him to continue,

"I grabbed a drink of water. Then thought I'd take a run up the hill to see what was riling those crazy animals."

Daniel had his hands clasped between his knees as he spoke, gazing with serious eyes from person to person. Now he lowered his face, covered it with his right palm. Three fingers of his right hand massaged his forehead. Fingers of his left hand drummed an agitated beat on his thigh.

"God, another migraine. I made it to the top of the hill, to that big, osprey rock, you know the one shaped like an eagle. Leaned my hand on its wing to rest. Thought I heard a snake rattle. Looked down.

"There was an army boot sticking out from behind the boulder. He was, is, was wearing Levis, a white tee-shirt. Tattoos all up and down his arms and his neck. And his eyes were open, and there was a bullet hole in his forehead. And I threw up.

81

Deal Me a Card

"No! vomit, no! vomit, not another! vomit, dead man! throw up. Then I turned and ran. Dad, Dad, all of you, forgive me. I turned and fled like the other time. I couldn't save him. I couldn't save any of them! Guys, he was dead, they were dead. There was nothing I could do!

"So I turned and ran to the house and banged on Richard's door and we called the cops."

Daniel's last words were hiccoughing sobs. His breath labored. Guillermo got out of his seat and knelt before his son. He put his arms around him, kissed the crown of his head.

"There, there, son, my Danny boy, my Danny boy."

The young man's anguish held a loaded, cocked pistol to Emma's, Guillermo's and Richard's collected hearts, daring them to do anything less than bathe in the pathos that is born from being in the presence of death's futile discomfiture.

Someone harrumphed. It was the detective, Lieutenant Yow. Emma fetched Daniel a glass of water. Everyone gratefully gulped down the sodas she distributed. A couple of men took a bathroom break. Daniel and Richard sat side by side, quiet, all passion spent. Guillermo described the previous evening's festivities.

"You know, officers, there were about fifty people here, not counting the kids, and some of them walked up the hill a little way. We can give you a list of all the guests.

In fact, Richard, why don't you pull up the names on your computer?"

One of the officers walked with Richard to his room. Watching them, Guillermo observed,

"Emma doesn't know everyone yet so she might not be able to help too much. But, honey, they were all saying good bye to you. So you have a good idea when people started to leave."

"So there were teenagers at the party," Yow interrupted Guillermo's remarks.

Deal Me a Card

"What was that, Lieutenant?

"Who were the kids? You want their names? Sure," Guillermo continued. "They were mostly children of the guests, and their friends. I figured that we'd try to do our good turn for Saturday night. Keep at least fifteen teeny boppers off the streets, out of harm's way. You think some of them may have been involved?"

His glance swept across the jury of law enforcers. "Have you indentified the dead man?"

Yow took the lead. "No. We're working on that. He's been taken to the morgue. They'll check the tats, the records. The database should come up with an ID.

"Doubtless he's another gang-banger. For sure it must have been another Saturday night drive-by shooting. Then his friends, or his killers, dragged him out here and left him." The speaker paused, then shaking his head resumed,

"There'll be a big funeral at church. A Mass for the dead. Crowds will overflow the cemetery on Rinaldi.

"You'll see a parade of black tee-shirts and sweatshirts. With logos, 'In Loving Memory,' on every chest. All those young people will pack together like sardines, with stone faces and ice-cold eyes. Nobody will quiet the mother, screaming and weeping. And the father, he's invisible because he's probably in jail or in El Salvador or Juarez, or Vera Cruz, who knows. Or murdered too.

"Two or three days after the hysteria and grief, the 'homies' of the dead man's gang will retaliate. They have to avenge the killing, you see. The crushing wheel keeps turning. One more week, one more corpse."

Yow stopped. Everyone in the room heard his jagged intake of breath. He sighed, cleared his throat, continued, "I apologize, Mr. Guerrero, Ms Emma, but this is the twenty-seventh homicide I'm investigating this year. Same MO. I feel your son's pain. But those guys out there they just answer hurt with hurt, death with death. For what?

Deal Me a Card

"Because someone walks on the wrong side of the road, someone falls in love with the wrong sister, some dude short-changes his connection. Like West Side Story, but no songs and dancing. Only real blood, wet, red, spilled gut stains on the sidewalk. Eyes staring into the heavens, or maybe down at Hades. And they're all high on crack. That's our Valley!"

"So what we have," interrupted Guillermo, "is a new generation of gangsters.

"I remember a time twenty years ago. My brother, Raoul, you know, he's part owner of the construction company in Pacoima. He fraternized with gang members. When I was visiting from Visalia I'd hang out sometimes. We were the young bloods. There were a lot of memories about the home country, the draft, Vietnam, car talk. Muscling each other out of the way, but nothing like this.

"Some killing, but the perpetrators faced justice. Some of them are still doing time. Others, like Mr. M, paid their dues, and are giving back to the community now.

"I still see the same guys drinking coffee in La Coloma's cafes. Every so often we eat menudo together. We didn't take each other out then, so we can shoot the breeze now. Alive, healthy, most of us. Maybe there're a couple on crutches, someone in a wheelchair. But we all are able to look each other in the eye, or talk things out. No more animosities. Just garrulity."

He looked around at his attentive listeners. Shaking his head slightly, he continued, "You know, some of them have never left the barrio. One mile radius is their world. They're like the salt of this earth. Others, I, we left. We've come back, brought another world with us."

"And," Yow picked up, "the new young have brought their worlds with them.

"Those who grew up here, are growing up here, second, third generation of the men you mentioned, most of them are like your sons. Off to college, graduating, returning to help the family business, getting elected to government.

"But there's unbelievable pressure on the younger kids, children of more recent immigrants, others coming in through Los Angeles from all over South and Central America. They've all got to fit in, find an identity. How? They get jumped into a gang. "Now the MS-66 the Monos de Selvas, is getting a stranglehold, taking over the older groups. Man, they're poison, toxic to the community."

Guillermo spoke again, "Don't you have any leads, some way to stop this?"

For the first time that evening the man called Miller spoke up. "The Department of Drug Enforcement Administration, the DEA, is working twenty-four hours a day connecting data. The information we're collecting points to gang members mostly originating in El Salvador. We have our sights on one of them in particular. His moniker is Lucifer. So true. He got his training back at home in the army, compliments of Uncle Sam. Learned to kill for a trade when he was just a young boy, ten or eleven. His mother sends him up here to save his life, and he's laying waste. Lucifer is bad, bad news.

"He's a killer, that's all he knows how to do. And he's a magnet, a mesmerizing serpent luring the others, the poor ones, the fatherless, kids. And girls too. Of course, there are drugs and connections to the cartels."

Lieutenant Yow spoke, "But this dead body's right under our noses, here and now. The word must be out on the streets about the perps. It's hot. We can't let it get cold. So let me get that list from you. Then I have to high-tail it to the office. A pile of paperwork is accumulating on this one.

"Mr. Guerrero, Ms. Hazelton, we'll be in touch with you to let you know as much as we can. Of course there are some limits; you understand. Legal issues, LAPD policy, the circumstances of the death. But we will communicate. The corpse was found on your property. You have some rights to information. For now, thanks for your cooperation."

Deal Me a Card

CHAPTER 17

MONDAY MORNING'S SLOW MOTION was a soothing balm for Emma's frazzled nerves. Excitement around the office over the Lakeview Hills development contract was like sweet peach nectar. The builders' prompt response to Jones and Guerrero's proposal had set the company abuzz. The back-and-forth staff chatter of negotiations, supplies, new hires, expanded office space, while mundane, forced her thoughts into neutral when her mind involuntarily slithered from the motive to murder, to mayhem, to the madness of the past two days.

She focused her gaze on Mr. Jones, as he outlined immediate plans. "We'll advertise for someone to assist you with inventory and maybe purchasing and invoicing. You'll have to coordinate the suppliers and our new partner's construction schedule with their office manager.

"There'll be numerous meetings - count on at least three a week at the beginning. Check our calendars and yours and block out some times in the mornings and early afternoons."

Al Jones coached soccer and Pop Warner football and liked his days to end at four. This was a boon for Emma. She was taking notes.

"Will do, Mr. Jones. May I check the catalog for a new desk top computer? We'll need some broader capacity and state of the art technology."

"Sure. You take care of that end. Research a more sophisticated accounting program while you're at it. Get Guillermo's input, since his office handles that aspect."

Back at her desk, Emma lost no time burying her nose in a tome of office supply merchandise. Through the door, she could hear the owners' animated discussion. With the warehouse carpenter, they were planning a remodel of the storage area into another office.

"Then, there's that other huge residential zone opening up in Santa Clarita.."

She heard the voices drift off to other rooms. Her mind's eye perused two women who worked part-time in the evenings at the Educational Center, who might qualify as her office assistant. Eva with the curls and house under siege in particular crossed her mind. She made a mental note to ask Guillermo about her credentials that evening.

****

Two miles away, in an otherwise well-disciplined classroom at St Anselmo High School, a young man was making a painful decision, one that would change his life forever.

"Martin, please. Hand over that razor. Get back to your work."

Martin did not look up at Ms. Brooks. He stared as if his eyes were glued to it, at page seventy-three in his English Literature text. His hand jerked up, slapped the tiny sharp-edged implement into her hand. His fist slammed down. "Here, take it. But I better get it back after class."

Some students in the aisles nearby sucked in their collective breaths but kept mum. Martin realized that they had heard the insolent surliness in his low growl, but did not care how they reacted. One uneasy thought flickered. *If he ever tried that tone, one word spat out like that with his mom, he'd feel the back of her hand. Twack, on one cheek. Twack, twack on the other. And he didn't blame her.* The thought died. Another glinted. *Hey, if Ms. B slapped him now, maybe it would be a good thing. He could leap up, cause more noise.*

So what if she sent him to the dean for insolence and defacing school property. The rules were pretty strict about it. Private school, Catholic school they didn't have much

Deal Me a Card

money to replace furniture. But they would replace incorrigible students. That's what he wanted.

Trouble. The more trouble the better.

This morning, Mr. Getson had yelled at him in Algebra class for jeering at George that he was a loser, a loser college student. Then the dude really got mad and wrote a discipline note when he kept on sniggering at Amy. *But everyone knows she's stupid anyway. Doesn't ever get it, couldn't understand the theorems.*

Yesterday afternoon at football practice, boy, Coach Raymond almost killed me when I fouled Gregory. *That felt good slinging him to the ground, kicking him in the gonads.* He was writhing as if a boa was eating them; Martin smiled to himself at the memory. *We were like tigers, going at it!* They had to separate us. But Greg and I made up in the locker-room. We're buddies, go back to grammar school.

While stripping off gym clothes after practice, Gregory had commiserated, "Hey I forgive you. I know about Esmeralda. Bad news, good news. You can make babies, but what about all those plans you made?

"College? Football scholarship? Your head must hurt. Like my balls right now! Don't go for my nuts next time, okay? Man, they ache."

But what do any of them care anyway. It was not their life.

A sweet sound interrupted his brooding, "Martin, what's come over you? Your junior year started so well. We were discussing just last week how you could perhaps move up to the honors English class next semester."

Ms. B was still standing over him, using that gentle voice. Her hands were clasped at her waist. She always wore a cream-color blouse and a beige skirt. Like a nun, or someone pious. A spitting image of those Franciscan ladies his mom chatted with at Church every Sunday. Had that holy look, sad, reproachful. You can tell me, God loves you. That

Deal Me a Card

kind of gaze. Man, he hated it. It made him choke up. But no one would ever see his tears. He'd kill somebody first.

Yeah right. Move up to the honors class. The way he was behaving, he'd be out of school in the next week. And maybe next semester, he'd be moving on to selling oranges at the corner of Van Nuys Boulevard. Maybe she'd come by and buy some, to make him feel good and successful. After all, he'd be a proud father supporting the baby and his woman. Isn't that what they kept telling him in the religion classes, about the sacredness of life and responsibility, and on and on. So what if he'd never finish high school. His fist shuddered on the desk, resisting the urge to pound. Ms. Brooks sensed his growing rage.

"Look, I'm sending you down to Brother Keith. You need to talk to a counselor. Something's not right. You're too good a student to let all your hard work go to waste. Here, here's a note. Why don't you jot down your homework before you leave? I don't think you'll be back. Work on the questions at the end of the story and begin your essay outline for Thursday."

"Thanks, Ms. Brooks," he managed to murmur as he collected his materials, "maybe I'll see you tomorrow, or maybe never."

He saw her wince but did not care.

****

Emma kept entering the numbers on her calculator with her right hand, as she reached for the phone with her left. "Jones and Guerrero Construction. Oh, hello, Brother Keith. Good afternoon. How are you? It's been awhile."

Briefly the speakers chatted about the events of the previous May's graduation ceremonies at St. Anselmo, the last time they had met, Brother Keith's summer sojourn in Italy, and his traipsing through Assisi, Florence and Rome.

Then Emma asked, "Now, how can I help you? Wait. Let me grab a piece of paper."

The school counselor interrupted, "But will your boss mind my intrusion on your day, Ms. Hazelton?"

"No, no. Mr. Guerrero won't mind at all. We've got to keep the kids in school. If someone's in trouble and it's urgent, we have to get on top of it. And call me Emma, please."

The voice at the other end continued. Emma took notes, repeating aloud what the youth advisor was asking of her. She ticked off the main points.

"Okay. So Martin's girlfriend, what's her name, Esmeralda, is pregnant, the baby is due in next April or May, so he wants to drop out of St. Anselmo. She's a sophomore at the public school and has already missed school since the start of the school year. He's been doing everything possible to get expelled so he can go out and work to support them. You say he's an A and B plus student? That figures. The good ones with the minds always have the best hearts."

She paused and checked another day planner that lay next to the day-time schedule. "Let's see. Tell them to come in to the Center this evening. No, we'd better see them on Friday afternoon. There'll be someone to help them with some planning then."

She gave more instructions, "Brother, please tell Martin two things. Esmeralda needs to bring in all copies of her school records including report cards. She has three days to get them together. A staff person at the Center will review them with her. She needs to get working on her GED while she waits for the baby.

"Two, tell the proud father to get his butt back in the classroom and the practice field and stay there. Excuse my French. But I could box his ears. After I wring his neck. But I'll let his mother smack him. Yes, I heard you. Esmeralda's living with her parents and Martin with his. Children having children."

Brother Keith interjected as Emma took a second to breathe. "We all appreciate this, Ms. Hazelton, sorry, Emma.

Martin has so much potential. We can't lose him when he's so near to the goal, and his dream."

"No problem, Brother. You just keep him in his classes. God bless you. And your faculty, for loving their students."

****

"Doctor Schwarzman, back then it was another time, another place. The psyche of the era was completely different. Or was I just fortunate? Babies were not going to enter into our lives to spoil our rhythm. And I mean the rhythm of our goals and our passions. I sure didn't practice any rhythm method. I had some vague idea. But it was just not the right moment. We wanted to have our cake and eat it too. So we did."

Emma was engrossed in her weekly therapy session as she retied the burgundy bow collar that had unraveled around her neck. She uncrossed and re-crossed her legs under her light woolen taupe skirt to get more comfortable. She leaned forward slightly in her chair as she began to recall her student days.

"I've already told you about Leonid, my Hungarian. Leonid was older than me, about seven or eight years wiser.

"Bernard, my German lover, was my age, starting college like me. We met in Paris too, in July 1964, in French class. But we had a more lasting relationship during two summer vacations.

"Leonid had departed on his motorcycle to distant lands. I remained behind, bereft. Then, there he was.

"He always took a seat on the other side of the room. We were the youngest in the group, forever making eyes at each other. Once, we fell into a fit of giggles when a *bonne soeur*, one of those French nuns, with a cumbersome wimple impeded our glances. Bernard had to bob his head up and down in time with its waltz.

"After school, we walked, we talked, lunched on bread and sausage and cheap table wine. Once we climbed to the

Deal Me a Card

second level of the Arc de Triomphe. Being students on a strict budget we couldn't afford the higher panoramic vista.

"Sat for hours in sidewalk cafés, people-watching. Held hands. We'd smooch as we drank espressos; dipping sugar cubes in the coffee, once or twice even in our wine, for the sweetness. Often we'd kiss innocently in the darkness of the cinema while Pathe News ran interminable clips of the Hitler horrors, Bugs Bunny, and other old and eternal favorites.

"As the weeks went by we became more intimate. We kissed each other to distraction. Mauled each other's lips, tongues, throats, until sore and numb. Limp in each other's arms, then tirelessly groping buttocks, arms, legs, fingers, breasts, toes, glued together by warm mingled sweat, teeth sunk into neck flesh, bodies gulping at each other like ravenous slippery sea-creatures, almost but never quite sliding into the deep.

"Coming up for breath just a second before diving into each other's being once more. Passion thrust our melting bodies into the furnace like liquid glass, to emerge from the flames as one fiery heavenly comet shooting weightless to the stars.

"Eternal foreplay. But never penetration, not yet. Only promise.

"Then August arrived and we parted with earnest promises and dreams of everlasting love. For twelve months billets-doux alternately enflamed, or dripping with desire, travelled between London and Germany. Our second tryst was the summer of '65."

Emma twisted her shoulders in a brief episode of discomfiture from the intimate details she was revealing.

"My first experience of sexual intercourse was a mixture of relief, confusion, surrender, delight and chagrin, as I gave myself up to my beloved's persistent, tiresome, wearying pleas. He wanted me so much; he was my only love, destined to be my life's core. Knowledgeable, tall,

Deal Me a Card

Teutonic, the accent and stance of the master race, full of himself. I adored him.

"This was Paris in the summer of '65. A university student, I was sexy, sporting straight shiny shoulder-length hair, fresh face, black tights encasing firm buttocks, black blouson loose over small breasts, dark-brown checkered mini skirt demurely hiding my rump, and nun's laced shoes."

Emma sighed, looking down at her long skirt.

"He had photographed me the previous year, soulful black-and-whites of a virgin wrapped in sullen ripeness. I was ready then. I was ready now. So I said at last,

"Yes. Yes!"

"He grabbed me and almost struck me, told me not to talk like a whore. Then, when he finally thrust into me, it was his release, not mine.

"Awkwardness, tension, anxiety ruined this moment of union yearned for, envisioned in every dream, prayed for in every breath of the last ten thousand hours.

"He pulled out and started fumbling with the condom - even then we were careful -mumbling in his guttural German English that it might be broken. Great.

"I went to the bathroom to relieve my discomfort, and I was bleeding. Told him, weeping, and he's as pleased as Punch. Stroked my cheek tenderly, I'm a feather in his damn cap! I'm bleeding and in pain. And he, laughing at my sadness, left me sitting on the bed alone, while he smoked a cigarette. It's over."

Shaking her head slowly, Emma looked at her therapist.

"We'd do it again and again that summer. After walks in the park or along Boulevard St. Michel. Later, weary from strolling along the Seine and waving to the tourist-packed bateaux mouches. Once when we tottered up to his room intoxicated, from consuming a kilo of liqueur-filled candy on empty stomachs while meandering lost among the colorful prostitutes of Pigalle, who shamelessly stalked Bernard and whispered in his ear *voulez vous me baiser mon chouchou.*

93

Deal Me a Card

As soon as our French classes let out a noon at the Alliance Francaise.

"Always we went back to his room. I stayed in an all-women's dorm so he was verboten. We'd have intercourse many times. Sometimes we made love.

"I was captured and razed into the ground. But depleted, I endured, and escaped.

"I sent the German his bracelet six months later when I was safe back home in London.

"And we did not make a baby."

Dr. Schwarzman glanced at the clock.

"It's time to go home."

"I'll see you next week."

****

"We need a new coffee maker or else a different brand of coffee. This is awful."

"Mr. Guerrero, that's been out on the table since this morning. Let me make a new pot for you this evening."

"Thanks, Carmelita. Bring us more of those cookies too, please.

"All right, you other ladies and gentleman. We have about an hour before the students start to arrive. I called this meeting because I thought we needed to touch base.

"We're so busy, sometimes the message doesn't get to everyone. Like last night, Ms. Isadora, when I walked into your class. What a surprise. A banana dressed in a condom!" Guillermo couldn't quite hide his smirk. One of the women giggled.

"Oh yes, Mr. Guerrero, I invited someone from the County Health office to discuss parenting skills. They include a segment on family planning. There was nobody under eighteen in the classroom. So there's nothing to worry about."

"But condoms and bananas?"

94

Deal Me a Card

"Yes, you figure most of these ladies are fresh from other countries, where birth control education is nonexistent in their out-of-the-way villages. And do you think their men are about to care? No. So we need to provide this instruction in a way they can understand," Isadora answered a bit defensively. "And maybe they'll teach their daughters too."

"Good point," Guillermo answered. "However, this makes it even more important that we let the Center know about such things. We could have invited students from the other classrooms. You can bet they're feeling deprived after they heard about the activity from their friends and neighbors." The twinkle in his eye belied his concern. "They certainly appeared engrossed in the, uh…subject."

"Sounds like it was pretty gross all right," Robin murmured, with a toothy grin. Being the only other man in the room, he was tiptoeing through a minefield.

Isadora swung around, demolished him with one of her glares.

Then, she tossed her head back to their leader, "I think there should be a bulletin board in the reception area for announcements. The receptionist and Carmelita can control what gets posted and answer any queries. I've scheduled three more presentations, scattered through the semester. This was the first. The word will get around so there'll be high interest and strong attendance."

"Good, Isadora. Carmelita, you get that started right away. And truly, I'm not being critical. Just taken aback by that encapsulated fruit."

Emma noticed his sardonic smile as he tried to hide it.

"Talking about fruit and vegetables, here's another activity for our clients. Randy in Food Services at the college wants us to organize a field trip. He's spoken to a number of the women who want to take cooking courses. He and Stanley would show a group around the kitchen one afternoon. They could even get them to enroll in the classes."

Robin pitched in, "Now there's a happy couple. Randy, the manly man, and Stanley who's gay. And do they keep those ovens humming."

Encouraged by his listening colleagues' silence, he continued, "Randy Lothario, that's what they call him. They who know. You can ask his ladies.

"Stanley is devoted to his partner Arnie, who's also totally into food. I mean like eating a lot of it. I've met him, and all that bulk is not muscle. When they step out, the two are pretty spiffy."

He looked around the group, "They were at Universal the other day. We were all walking into the masked crime-fighters block-buster for the same showing. I s'pose they can relate to the intrepid duo."

Robin was on a roll. Even Isadora twitched a smile. Guillermo coughed down a guffaw. Emma pretended to scribble notes. Carmelita deftly picked up the initial thought,

"Mr. Guerrero, I'll pin a notice on the board and students can sign up at my desk. Just give me the days, dates, and times. Perhaps there can be one tour in the morning and another in the evening. So we cover everyone."

"I think we should go on the tours so we can answer any questions later."

"Good idea, Emma. Now, any other news?"

She replied, "It's a delight to have your son here counseling the students. He's especially important for the teenagers. They need to know their options. He's a great role model too. And they respect him. I've heard remarks. He doesn't talk down to them.

"Good. In addition to the full load he's carrying at Cal State, Daniel decided to take a community relations course that includes service hours. And, you know him, all eager for the involvement. He's either going to end up being a politician or a priest," he grinned.

"So, Isadora, Emma, Robin, everyone, if there's someone needing to discuss career plans, or social issues,

Deal Me a Card

that sort of thing, he's available. Nothing too deep. No neurotics, or psychos, we have referrals for that. But if one of them shows up, he can begin the process and move the person on quickly." The father's pride was evident.

Emma said, "It was so convenient that he was here last Friday. Two young people really needed a reality check, and some guidance. Daniel spent about two and a half hours with them. I think he's a godsend."

"Great! Good to hear, Emma. Okay, it's time to get to your classes. Emma, can I see you a minute?"

"Certainly." She waited for Robin, who was the last one to leave, to close the door behind him. "Something I can help you with?"

"Now that's a loaded question. But, first I wanted to ask you about the status of this fellow, Edward Lopez. I seem to remember that you and Raoul had some trouble with him at the shop."

Emma looked at Guillermo and faced this inevitable moment, her face burning. She swallowed quietly and spoke. "Yes, he called a couple of weeks ago to tell me he had landed a landscaping job. Out in Santa Clarita. Now he wants to improve his English and skills to advance in life. He's even changed the spelling of his name from "Eduardo" to "Edward" to become more anglicized and accepted by the community."

"Hmm. Not putting any pressure on you, is he?"

"No, no, not at all. He was very businesslike. I referred him to the vocational school in Mission Hills for their certificate program. He seems to have found his niche. Maybe he'll take entrepreneur training at the college later on. He's enrolled in English with Robin."

"Well, we'll keep our eye on him. So long as he keeps his distance and gets on with his life. Just that he's such a weasel."

"That he is."

97

Guillermo gave her a long, searching look. His hand came up. She could see that he resisted reaching up to stroke her cheek. Both their breaths came a little quicker.

"Now, about that something you could help me with? Let's talk after class. I'll have dessert lined up."

Emma stroked his face with her eyes.

CHAPTER 18

"EGAD, IT'S ALMOST THE END of the month. Actually it is. Today's Friday the twenty-ninth, then the weekend which doesn't count, and on Monday we're in October. And mercy me, the Santa Anas aren't through yodeling in the canyons. We'll sweat for a few more weeks." Guillermo took a deep breath.

Emma broke in, "But tonight. It's a balmy night. Feel the breeze. Look at the Valley below us. You know, here, on an evening like this, it's as if we're floating above it all. The muck, the gunshots, the crackheads, the wistful wives of disappeared husbands and sons, they've all vanished. We could be on a starship with an unknown, unexplored world of a million fireflies twinkling below us."

"Fantastical. You're such a Pollyanna. So is this what we're celebrating this evening? A make-believe virtual flight to escape reality?" he moved closer to her.

Emma shook her head gently. She enveloped Guillermo's large sinewy half-clenched fist in her ten fingers. His eyes and torso visibly relaxed under her touch, as he savored her roundness under the slinky black dress, the milky pearls that kissed her throat, as he caught a waft of her Shalimar.

"You sound tired. My poor sweetheart. Some days were exhilarating, but September was a pretty rough month all around, huh?"

Emma spoke wistfully, "First the murder, then the funeral. We still can't seem to shake it off. When Father Reilly recited the rites for that young man, I cried and cried. His killing was such a waste.

"He tried to make a clean break, help his mom with his job at the shoe shop, and take classes at the occupational center. Then he finds a girlfriend from the wrong street. Pfft,

99

pfft. Bam, pow. He's dead. Mostly, I keep thinking of his poor mother."

Her listener grew stiff once more. His back bowed back. He sounded impatient, "Honey, all right, all right. Let's stop dwelling on it. I've had enough of the weeping women.

"Sofie Perez comes in after the wake, plops herself down in my office. She pleads, needs to talk. The funeral brought back memories. Would you believe she calls the dead boy's mother a lucky soul. She herself can never weep over her son's or her husband's graves.

"Then she pours her heart out about wandering the streets of her village. Some place in El Salvador. She'd searched for her husband and son for three weeks. Roamed howling, like a ghost she said. A haunted soul in an abyss full of other tormented spirits. She had to pinch herself to be sure she was alive.

"You know how she is, so dramatic, so morbidly eloquent. I thought she sounded like an Irish banshee, the way she was carrying on."

Emma murmured, "Be kind! She's still very close to those days even though they're years past. How many … four, five years ago now. She's fortunate to have escaped. She told me about when the family was still together. One day, she's at home while her son is attending school in the city. The guerrillas and military skirmish in the town. When her son gets off the bus, corpses are strewn in the plaza. He loses his mind, terrified. The poor boy won't leave home, so his studies at the University are cut short. After that, he and his father have to take sides. Before long, they've vanished and she's a mad woman.

"I asked her how she deals with such bad memories? 'I play cards,' she replied, 'poker, *veintiuno*, twenty-one'. Sometimes I see her with the other students gambling for pretzels before classes start in the evening. Always has a pack in her pocket or purse. She said the fun is never

100

Deal Me a Card

knowing the hand you get. 'E*s importante hacer una apuesta*,' she repeats frequently. 'In life you have to take a gamble.' An unschooled pragmatist, that's our Sofie."

Guillermo snorted, "Good grief. Does our work have to consume us during dinner? And this is supposed to be a romantic date! Let's not think. Let's drink!"

"Absolutely."

Emma paused, silently letting the storm pass.

"All right. I've got it. I read this snippet in the papers this morning. Let's toast Cervantes! It's his birthday today. He'd be four hundred and forty-two years old. Without him, we'd never be inspired to tilt at windmills," she grinned.

"And, hey, I have good news and a funny incident. First, amidst all the doom and gloom, we managed to schedule interviews and decided to hire Eva. She started on Monday as my assistant. Your recommendation was right on target. She's efficient, organized, has learned everyone's name and phone numbers and is catching on fast with the computer."

Emma looked up at him. "You and Senor Raoul are her heroes. She's a single parent. Of course you know that. So the salary and benefits are a god-send to her and especially the children. She dotes on that girl and the boy is the apple of her eye!"

"Good for her! But I want to hear the fun stuff, not about the practical things. Tell me. Lighten my mood!"

So Emma switched gears,

"It's from work … no, don't give me that look! No more tragic life stories and feel-good kudos. Christine and I were discussing class lists yesterday evening. She pauses after awhile, looks at me very earnestly and asks me when I left the convent. She said I behaved virginal, very chaste. Am I?"

Guillermo leaned across the table set for two, its off-white linen tablecloth edged with Chinese lace and its wrought-iron curved legs firmly ensconced on the balcony of

101

Deal Me a Card

the Four Winds Haven. The restaurant, favored by wedding parties, business people and courting coupled alike, perched precariously on the side of a stony hill.

He softly raised Emma's hand to his lips,

"I must say , my darling, that the only time I remember you being chaste, is when I was pursuing you around the living room a couple of Saturdays ago. And, well, I recall that we did explore some virgin territory when I caught you. A long delicious journey through the night."

His face was straight as he spoke. But his eyes were twinkling as he looked into hers.

Emma laughed throatily, thinking back to their intimacy. She trailed a finger daintily along one of his eyebrows, then moved it slowly down to his lips. The backs of her fingers, butterfly feathers, brushed them lightly, tracing their bulging outline. His teeth parted. She let the tip of her middle finger nuzzle, tremble as he nibbled.

"Like my kitty cat. Naughty, very naughty. But nice. Very nice," she murmured.

"Let's skip dessert and open that bottle of merlot I have back at my place," she added.

"You read me like a book."

The couple rose from the table. They paused at the railing to look up at the twinkling canopy formed by the stars above and the lights from the buildings below. Guillermo, his arms encircling Emma's waist, murmured,

"We all play the hands dealt us, my dear one. At this moment, I'm holding a royal flush!"

****

"Hello, Emma, good morning. Is Dad here?"

Richard stood at the front door of Emma's townhouse. It was Saturday morning and she had answered the door.

"Yes, he's on his second cup of coffee. I'm having juice. Toast and marmalade are up next. It's a beautiful day in the neighborhood. Come on in, join us!"

The pair had been perusing their favorite sections of the LA Times. Guillermo flipped through the National and International News, and Emma read aloud Calvin's words to Hobbs, after the couple had laughed over Duke's commands to Honey in Doonesbury. Emma led Richard into the breakfast nook.

"Guillermo, it's Richard."

"Good morning, Dad."

"Hi son. I thought you and Sarita were driving up to Santa Barbara this morning for the weekend."

He set the papers down.

"But, here you are…. Good morning to you. What's up?"

"Dad, Emma, The place is in turmoil. Everyone's going crazy. There was a drug bust …"

"Now, Richard, wait a minute, wait a minute. Slow down. Take a deep breath. Here, drink some juice. Emma, pour him a cup of coffee. Thanks."

The couple watched as the young man gulped down the juice, then sipped at the coffee. He breathed in the rich Colombian mix which seemed to mellow his jumpy mood. They settled back in their chairs.

"So there's been a horrendous drug bust. What about it?"

As Richard began his narrative, his voice rose and fell, sing-song in its urgency, not overly intelligible. The coffee had rapidly lost its effect. The two listeners looked at each other, and stood up.

"Let's go relax in the living room," Emma suggested as she placed her hand softly on her lover's son's shoulder.

Richard looking relieved, poured himself another cup of java, then walked over to the recliner and sank into its comfortable cushions. Emma, carrying a glass of juice, sank down on the couch next to Guillermo who said,

Deal Me a Card

"You mentioned that they raided Reynoso's Imports? Damn, that's just down the street from us. About two miles? One and a half, maybe. Shit!"

"Was anyone hurt? Where's Daniel? That's right, I forgot he's up at the river. Thank God!"

His older son stared at Guillermo and his girlfriend perplexedly.

"Didn't you two watch the news last night? It was all over the channels, Dad!"

"No, I didn't listen to the news or watch TV last night. Let's just say I was indulging myself after a mind-wearying week.

"So in the midst of your garbled explanation I gathered there are looters out there now? How do you know all this? Where were you before you came over? Nowhere near the chaos, I hope. You know, crowds can get ugly."

"Dad, that's our turf. We come and go in San Benitez and La Coloma all the time. Some of those guys went to school with me, and attend college with Danny and me right now …"

His father broke in,

"Not everyone knows you or me, or is our pal. Some little old lady thinks you're going to grab the piñata she just ripped off, and you're on the ground in a split second, writhing on your backside."

Richard placated his dad.

"We know this is pretty serious business, involving some very nasty narco-trafficking. But I gotta tell you watching that greedy mob was hilarious. I was OK, Dad, Emma. One of my classmates from tenth grade let me into his house, and we both watched from his upstairs window.

"After awhile it became festive. A pickup piled with ceramic owls, and deer and ollas drove by. The driver was whooping, 'Eeya.' And a little girl who could barely walk was hefting Jesus and a lamb down the street, cheered on by an old, grey-haired woman. I think it was her grandmother!"

104

Deal Me a Card

His father could not help his quipping.

"And someone dressed as the Sacred Heart floated by blessing the spectators and passersby?"

Richard fell in line with his father

"Oh, two boys were waving around those fine art velvet paintings they just picked up for a song!"

Guillermo turned serious.

"Have the police blocked off the area? How did you get out? Can I get in?"

He jumped up from his cozy place beside Emma, took her by the hand and pulled her up.

"Let's go back to the house. We'll use the back road. Just to be on the safe side!"

And I better not see any holy objects hanging on the living room wall when I get there!"

"Dad, Dad, Dad!"

****

On the following Tuesday evening, the educational center was abuzz.

"It was the Colombians and the Mexicans, working together. There were like millions and millions of these one kilo packages of cocaine, enough to fill a bus or two. And the funny thing, there was 'Baby 1' written on some of them."

"So how do you know all this stuff? Maybe you're making it all up so the teacher will think, Oh wow, Marie Jose knows so much. She can't say 'junk' or 'joke,' but she knows all about coke."

"Teresita, I'm not lying. My sister's husband's uncle, he's a sergeant, works for the LAPD Devonshire division and he helped load all this contraband in armored trucks. He told us."

Another student chimed in.

"Yeah it's true. My grandmother and aunt live three streets down from the place, and at dinner on Sunday, they

Deal Me a Card

say to me, 'Ursula, we gotta move from this place. It's a bad situation. We thought everybody got along. The blue-and-whites were patrolling more these last few months so it was calmer. We didn't know'.

"Would you believe, we even bought some things from Reynoso's. Couple of times the door would be open when we walked by coming home from the park or the grocery store, so we would enter.

"You know, my grandmother said on Sunday, 'I always thought that wife looked frightened. She made the sign of the cross a lot, 'Mother of God help us, Jesus Christ save us'. Always. Even when we were just discussing the weather or the sales at Penney's. And that husband of hers. I knew he was evil. Never said hello. Only wanted to know what we were looking at when we went over to check out the new shipments. Last Friday when the police cars came screeching by, like maybe one hundred of them, we just locked our doors and waited for the gunshots. There weren't any. But you never know when a stray bullet could kill you. If it's your time, it's your time!'

"'Ursula, we have to go away' my *abuela* keeps repeating. I hope my aunt can comfort my grandma. She's too old to move again."

Margarita, another student in the huddled group of twelve, chimed in, high-pitched,

"Hey, let me tell you. I know what happened. Everything. Listen to me."

Her loud assertion silenced the room. She began her tale.

"When my brother, Carlos, came home all excited last Friday afternoon, you should have heard my mother yell. You'd think her home was being raided. She's shouting, crazily, 'You see, see, Carlito, you should have stayed in school then you wouldn't be out there in danger of death! At least your sister is trying to better herself'.

Deal Me a Card

"And my brother looks at me like I stabbed him in the back. The he starts talking non-stop. He gets like that when he's nervous or guilty. All his words stumble out so fast he becomes breathless. He tells this long story. But of course he's got to poke at me first.

'Yeah right, I should be like little Margarita Anna, the goodie goodie. So he says, "What was I doing wrong anyway? I was on my morning break.

'Now you sit down mom, Margarita, both of you, take a break and be calm. Okay, where was I …

'This morning, it was about ten thirty, maybe later. I had just fixed the brakes on two cars. One a Camaro. The other a Mustang, all souped up, ebony with orange flames, real fine.

'Anyways, I see this Oldsmobile cruise by. Nothing special. Navy blue '79, coupla dents in the doors. Needs a wash and shine. Some dudes don't know how to take care of their wheels. No pride.

'The driver pulls into Reynoso's Imports. The warehouse is about five doors away from our shop. We see a lot of cars pull up there. Figure they come to select some merchandise to sell on the corners, at Dronfield and maybe Chatsworth. We mind our business. They mind theirs. Everyone's got to make a living.

'Now you see, mom, you don't want me to be like those guys, selling on the streets, right? The money I give you every week, it's clean money. Only grease on the notes is from the car engines.

'But turns out that car must have been a signal for big-time action. Suddenly, that awful wailing begins. You know the kind when you're walking down the street after a romantic dinner with your girl, and then behind you, this nasty sound. Police sirens. All the sweetness gone. God, I hate it.

'Well, about a dozen police cars pull up and block both ends of the road. Then the cops jump out. Pieces, assault weapons in their hands.

'I'm like in a movie. I think should I raise my hands and surrender. They're looking straight at me, coming towards me. Maybe I did something. My whole life flashes though my mind. Like a slow motion movie!

'But only times were when I stole that candy and those cigarettes from the store. And you whopped me anyway, Mom, and I had to take them back. Nice going, Mom. Now it's all in my records. Yeah, and that other time, I almost killed that wimp, Alan, on campus, in eighth grade when he called you a dirty name. And I got suspended for a week.

'There at the shop this morning, it's just me taking a break from work. All I have is a cup of coffee in my hand and dirty brown grease-stains on my brand-new blue overalls. By the way, you gotta do a load of laundry tomorrow, Margarita. Don't forget, just because you're fixing your hair for a date. Where was I? Okay. The cops are coming at me with their guns, and I'm ready to piss myself. I'm so jittery.

'Francisco in the back of the garage yells, "Get out of the way, Carlos. Hey fool, get down before they start shooting."

"No, come up here."

'I jerk my head to the sky, startled. It's Andy upstairs, he was taking a dump, then looked out the window and calls to me. By now I'm Steve Segal directing my destiny. I'm like moving in slow motion in my head. But in reality I'm like a speeding bullet. I ran around the back. Then up the stairs.

'We witness the whole scene. The driver of the Olds has come out of the warehouse and he's trying to shut the trunk, real nonchalant chatting with his buddy, like they're discussing the price of an armful of stuffed gorillas. The police grab them, start searching, and find a stack of plastic

108

bags filled with the white powder. Next thing DEA agents arrived. Must be DEA, the way they acted. Came screeching up, jumped out of their cars. Plainclothes, in dark suits. Preparing for a shoot-out with pistols drawn, crouched, hiding behind their vehicles. They wait. No action. LAPD got it under control. So they put their weapons away. Then they swaggered up to the cops, real cool and in charge.

'A TV van drove up. They actually parked in our lot. This beautiful lady, before she talked to us, I saw her put on make-up, powder her nose, some guy runs a comb through her hair, it's wavy, shoulder-length.

'Mom, that's what I was trying to tell you in the first place when I walked in. So you wouldn't be all bent when we came on television this evening. She interviewed all three of us. '"

Teresita broke in,

"That was Carlos, your brother, on TV on Friday night, Margarita? He's cute."

"Sorry, he's taken."

The conversation cut off as the classroom door squeaked open behind the chatting circle. Margarita spoke first,

"Oh, hi, Mr. Guerrero, Ms. Emma. We were talking about the drug bust. We all have stories."

"Good evening. Ladies, gentlemen. I've been dropping in all the classes this week just to make sure everybody's fine. Seems like some of your families were quite close to the action.

"You're probably all familiar with the news, but this is what the LAPD and DEA have released to the networks. Over twenty tons of cocaine with a street value of six billion dollars and more was confiscated at that warehouse. Nobody was hurt.

"Undercover surveillance had been on-going for months. The merchandise delivery patterns raised questions, some of the goons going back and forth looked suspicious. So a good neighbor mentioned it to the police.

"Best news, the area is clean. For now. Who knows how long that will last. But everyone gets to be more alert, less complacent. So perhaps they'll take their dirty work to another site far away. Worst news. San Benitez at this moment has a rotten reputation for what the DEA is calling the biggest drug discovery on record in this country.

"I ask you, why not wild fires, or maybe an earthquake. Well, on second thoughts, no, I don't think so. We already had one of those in 1971 in Sylmar close by. Check that big moment off the list. Ah well, I suppose we just needed more excitement.

"Okay, back to work. Ms. Emma, you're in charge."

CHAPTER 19

"WELL, HEY, HELLO, Ms. Emma. It's good to see you again. Welcome back to the kitchen on this lovely Friday afternoon!"

Chef Randy Sanchez looked up from the large pot of creamy orange liquid simmering on the stove. He glanced down quickly and adjusted the gas dial. He called out to a student shredding lettuce.

"Miss Sofie, could you help me out with this potage? Wash your hands and come over here."

"Coming up, chef."

"Now, stir occasionally, let it simmer very slightly. The heat is just right, but you want to be sure the bottom of the pot doesn't scorch. As Mr. Stanley would say this pumpkin soup is to die for. It's that soupcon of curry powder that clinches it."

Emma looked around the culinary arts kitchen, a highlight of the little community college that snuggled in the foothills. The walls, ovens and stoves sparkled, stainless steel equipment gleamed. Enticing scents from cumin, coriander, other exotic herbs wafted to her nostrils. A second-semester student at a stove in the center row sautéed onions, mushrooms and green peppers, preparing a late customer's lunch order of fajitas. Small groups of students, in white jackets, clustered at different counters preparing the evening's specialties. Chef Randy insisted on *haute cuisine* standards.

When he was assured Sofie was giving the bisque her full attention, Randy walked up to Emma. He pulled the cook's bonnet off his head, shaking loose his wavy black hair that curled around his ears. Under the flour-spattered green apron, his white chef's coat was spotless. His muscular body displayed no fat, something he had maintained in the midst of every culinary temptation. The only off-kilter touch was a tattoo, of a heart pierced by a dagger, visible on his neck where it met his shirt-collar. Many were the tales whispered of its origin.

His lips curled in a friendly smile under his moustache as Emma greeted him,

"Good afternoon, Randy. Thought I'd drop by to see if any of the students responded to your suggestions. By the way, you're great at PR. They needed to see the place so they could relate."

The chef smiled, acknowledging the compliment and nodded his agreement,

"The talk and tour were a terrific idea. Glad we put our heads together on that. We have five new enrollees in the program.

"All of them with food service experience from their countries. But you know what that was like. From their home kitchen to the street. Boil the corn in big pots in their garden, grill the pork on rusted barbecues, pat tortillas with grimy hands. You know, Ms. Emma, most of the time the water is polluted or they never wash their hands or don't use soap. And, oh my God, do you know what kind of germs they have on their fingers and under their nails?

"Here, one of the first things I show them is bacteria growing in the petri dishes from the touch of their fingers. Boy, that's an eye-opener. It literally makes them sick."

Emma grimaced. "Yuck, I saw that once in a chemistry lab. So, they're going to learn everything. The reason why I ask is because the teachers at the Center would like to incorporate the vocabulary in our lessons. Get some special materials for those particular students."

He nodded. "Good plan. I'll give you a textbook to work with."

"We have three women and two men who are taking English classes at the Center too." Gesturing to Sofie, "As you see, Sofie is outstanding. She's learning really fast.

Deal Me a Card

Right now we're concentrating on hygiene and back-of the house skills. She's way ahead of the others," Randy smiled.

"Yeah. She's a go-getter that one. Putting her life back together. Also a good leader."

Emma looked around. "What about the men? I know one of them is a high school drop-out and he's working on his GED. Who's the other?"

"Interesting dude, Alfredo. Wants to be called Alfie. Been in the States about three years. Something about his coming here, there're rumors. Fell into some trouble at the border where a terrible accident happened. Since then he walks with a limp. I'm not sure why, and I haven't asked if it's a wound or a prosthetic. No matter, he's full of energy," Randy observed.

Emma stared intently at Randy as he spoke.

"I'd like to meet him."

"Sure. Let's do it right now.

"Yo, Alfie. Finish dicing that last onion, wash your hands and come over here."

"Be right there."

Alfie finished, then hobbled over to the waiting pair.

"Alfredo Ruiz, this is Ms. Emma Hazelton. Ms. Emma, Alfie."

"Nice to meet you. You're the lady at the Center. You teach. Right?"

"Yes. It's good to know you too. Like it here?"

Alfie half-smiled, "When Mr. Randy let's me cook something real, I will. Now it's just chop, dice, julienne, cut, mince, wash your hands, man, don't ever forget, use that antiseptic soap, now go back and cut these peppers for Samantha and Priscilla, 'cause they're making a Spanish torte for the lunchtime event tomorrow, and the ingredients need to meld overnight. "

Randy laughed, interjected,

"We work as a team, Alfie. You know that. And you hafta know all those techniques for the recipes. Remember?"

Deal Me a Card

"I know, I know. But next week, maybe you'll let me do some boiling and baking. Then I'll really be cooking!"

Alfie grinned at his mentor.

Emma smiled a query,

"Sounds like you're getting into it. What other courses are you taking?"

"Biology One, basic computers and conversational English. They seem like a good fit."

"They surely do. If and when, you have some time, perhaps you could come over and talk to the Center students about your classes. You know, the problems with the language, but also how it's paying off. All your effort."

"Actually, it is. Even though I grouch at Mr. Randy "

"'Randy' is OK, man."

"Randy. I grumble at him, but guess what, I just got hired at Los Caballeros in Chatsworth. A back-of-the house job. Randy taught me all the skills, that's how I knew what they were talking about. They love that I speak the two languages. Still not so good with the English, but people understand what I say.

"Maybe in two, three months, I'll be bussing, waiting on tables. My body is taking it slow. I gotta pace myself. The doctors say 'cause the healing takes time sometimes I ache a lot. Food service is a lot of foot work. But, hey, I have one real leg….

"Anyway, I gotta go now, Ms. Emma, Randy. Have to clean up my area fast. Computer lab in twenty minutes. See you soon, Ms. Emma. Randy, I'll be back at four-thirty to help with tomorrow's set-up."

****

"In the final analysis, we really don't have control over anything that happens in our lives," Emma murmured as she set down her glass.

"Is my baby waxing philosophical after just one glass of her favorite white zin?" Guillermo responded, with a little

Deal Me a Card

laugh in his voice, and the gentleness that she loved in his long, gnarly fingers as he stroked her knuckles.

"No, well, yes. I'm thinking of two things that happened today. The first was a pretty close call."

"What, someone dented the car? You ran the orange light again?"

"No, nothing like that. As it was actually happening, the whole action passed by in slow motion. That's makes it so, so surreal. Let me describe it.

"You know I generally come down Corona Street. But today, just on a whim I turned on Kachina to get to the office.

"I was driving at about twenty miles an hour. There's a school nearby. The wind was blowing, nice, not tornado or hurricane force. Not even as if a storm was approaching. In fact the sky was blue, very blue. I remember thinking that, because I deliberately glanced out my rear window.

"And in that instant a huge branch from a tree snapped off and crashed down to earth! Some of the smaller twiggy branches swiped the back of my car. I could hear the swish and feel the slight impact as they brushed against the trunk. I just kept moving, not speeding up or slowing.

"It was only when I was safely ensconced at my desk that I realized …"

"Oh my God, if you had been driving eighteen miles an hour, just a mile or two slower that branch would have smashed through the roof and killed you. Oh, honey, honey."

"But see, I'm fine. It was not my time."

Emma took a few delicate bites of her grilled fish. Her companion worked on his fajitas. They both chewed in silence. She took another sip of wine, he lifted his Cerveza and took a gulp. He put down the bottle. His hand reached over and brushed away a strand of hair from over her left eye.

Deal Me a Card

"I want to protect you from harm every minute of the day and night. I know I can't, but I would do anything in my power."

"I feel very loved, my darling. But in that instant there was nothing that anyone could have done. It was decided by some other force."

"There is something though that I forbid you to do again."

Emma felt her hackles rise. Nobody, but nobody forbade her to do anything she wanted to do. She realized that her response was not in keeping with the current mood.

"What?"

The one word fell on the table between the couple, like a glob of saliva spat out on the sidewalk.

"I just will not allow you to walk alone from one building to another in the late evening. I've seen you cross the street to get to the counseling office and stroll past that block of stores to reach the other classrooms."

"But there's a reason for my visiting those buildings," Emma insisted. "I need to check on my referrals and make sure the students know where to go. I'm a teacher, remember. And a big girl."

"And you could be a very dead girl. You waltz along as if all those folk passing by on the streets of La Coloma are your friends and neighbors. Like it's Mardi Gras in the French Quarter. But it's not! You've got to realize that this is a war zone.

"Don't you understand? Even the cops cruise by in their cars. You don't see them on foot patrol.

"So you can't, no won't do that alone any longer. No more. If you must go out on the street, I or Jason will accompany you."

"I don't waltz. I walk very quickly and am very watchful."

"Random bullets fall like random branches. Next time your timing may be off. No arguments. I don't want to lose you too.

"Now, what about the other close call? Maybe you shouldn't have gotten out of bed this morning."

"No. This is about a man I met today."

"Ah, another man in your life. You're bent on driving me crazy this evening, aren't you?"

"No, this was a student in Randy's class. He wears a prosthetic leg. If he had not been in the situation where he lost his limb, or like me, was one minute early or one minute late, he may still have both legs."

"Well, how did it happen? Is he diabetic?"

"No, he's in his late twenties, maybe thirty. Lanky, fit. Except for the limp, he looks quite healthy. I didn't ask the cause. It wasn't the right time or place. The two incidents merely spurred my thoughts on the inevitability of things."

"Well, now that I know I'm completely at the mercy of kismet, my nerves need soothing. Let's go get naked in the pool. It's still warm. And tomorrow's Saturday so we can forget sleep and spend the whole night calming each other."

****

At eight o'clock that same Friday evening, Sofie Perez dropped Alfie Ruiz off at his apartment. She had spotted him, as he waited, lopsided and stooped with a plastic bag of textbooks in one hand, at the bus stop across from the college. They had both stayed late to help Chef Randy with table set-up for the Saturday Chamber of Commerce luncheon. Moving furniture, chinaware and cooking utensils from kitchen to dining room was strenuous work, and she had noticed her fellow student's limp becoming increasingly pronounced. Her body ached. Another hour of standing, waiting, walking, would be even more debilitating for him. So she took him home in her VW Beetle that rattled to the

117

tune of his profuse thanks. Then she returned to her duplex and a long shower.

Once inside his studio apartment, Alfie swiftly washed the smell of cooking off his face and arms and hands. Then he grabbed a glass of apple juice and a bowl of Neapolitan ice cream from the ice-box and settled down to indulge his taste buds. He flopped onto his one comfortable chair, with cushions strategically placed at the base of his spine and the point where his leg was no more. The prosthesis lay on the floor nearby.

He thought about his Good Samaritan of the evening. Her kind smile was his last image as he dozed off.

CHAPTER 20

THREE YEARS EARLIER, in the middle of May, 1985, Alfredo Ruiz and Eduardo Lopez crouched behind the granite boulder.

They were dead-tired. Hunger and fear, now familiar companions, gnawed at their stomachs. The hope in their hearts was as parched and raspy as their throats. Grime-splotched fingers gesticulating, words choked through swollen tongues, and blood-shot eyes swiveling to the right and to the left, and then up and down, comprised their conversation. They had reached the point of no return. The arduous trek was in its eleventh hour.

For the last week the two vagabonds had bobbed and woven across a punishing landscape. Stumbled, landing on grazed knees long-since deprived of the protection of denim jeans. Rocks and thorns again and again ripped through the ragged threads. Blood seeped from gummy scabs. Dry winds whipped their thin tee-shirts to shreds. Sun's rays bleached the remnants bone-white. After awhile, who knows how many crashes to the ground later, they felt no pain.

A vulture circled, confidently biding its time. Jackrabbits loped by, mocking their clumsiness. Three nights in a row the howls of an unwelcome guest made each of them take turns as an unwilling but wide-awake sentry. The acrid sap from the red stick tree that the Coyote said would quench a thirst only made them gag and dry heave. But even in the highest heat of the day, even when the two men had sucked the last drop from the nipple of their water bottle, nothing mattered but the faraway horizon.

While the pair tumbled through the Sonoran desert, their minds sometimes caravanned back to the others in the group who were making the same odyssey. If they could

Deal Me a Card

have uttered a prayer for the ones they had abandoned, the two desperate wanderers would have.

****

Eight days earlier the band of thirteen travelers had collapsed. Strength, age, stamina swiftly extorted their toll and left the victims destitute. Two of the children had sunk limp and beaten to the ground, unable to move. The mother and the grandmother, themselves wasted, shook them, shrieked, to no avail. The Coyote landed a few kicks in their butts. One child, a boy of six, got up on hands and knees and crawled away, screaming then circled, a rudderless sailboat in a sea of sand, shrieks gradually lowering to hoarse squeaking sobs. The other child made no move. Only a girl's delirious mewl arose,

"Where are we, Mama? This is not the golden land you promised. Take me home Mama, back to Honduras, take me home. I'm so tired. Let me sleep."

"We must continue, my child, my child, it will get better. Just a few days more. Here, here, eat this candy bar. Drink this water."

The eyes of the parent and her offspring gazed into each other. Love and desperation were a curious mixture, producing dirty squiggly streaks that ran out of dull orbs which could not afford to waste their moisture. The older woman, leaning over the younger crumbled body, looked on the verge of collapse. If she did, two lives would be crushed. But she did not. Instead, she dribbled a trickle of water between her daughter's lips. Then used a palmful of the precious liquid to cleanse the dusty, expressionless face below hers.

Alfredo and Eduardo had looked on at the scene. Their dull eyes wandered over the motley group. Then they looked at each other. Without a word, they pulled their backpacks off their broiling shoulders. Extracting two plastic bottles of water each, they stuck them in their pockets. Handing the

120

Deal Me a Card

remaining contents to the weeping grandmother crouched nearby, they redirected their steps to the Northwest, to the Promised Land. Only one glance backwards,

"Goodbye. God keep you safe."

Twenty minutes after, the stragglers disappeared behind the mesa the two men scaled and conquered on bended knees.

****

Now, days later, they sat within tasting distance of the border.

The night was black, moonless. Stars kept a safe distance, dimming their brilliance as if in concert with the hopeless longing of the border-crossers. Night traffic flowed uninterrupted around them, invisible stalkers, prey and predator, slithered by, padded through, fluttered and hooted, barked and croaked, each heading to its destiny.

Alfie stood up slowly.

"I'll go this way," he pointed left, "and you go that way. Here at this point, separate is safer."

"Okay. We'll meet in Nogales tomorrow morning at eight. We'll find each other there, cousin. No doubt. The way has been long, but we've made it."

The kinsmen clasped hands, embraced. Turned their backs on each other to take the last few steps to a new life.

****

Alfie limped to the left, his eyes peering into the blackness ahead. His sandals flip-flopped, the soles barely hanging on to the straps. They crunched clumsily in the soft sand. Then as his foot came down with his next step, he heard the snap.

Eduardo limped to the right, his eyes straining into the murkiness ahead. His sandals, slip-slapped, the soles barely attached to the straps. They thumped clumsily in the soft sand. Then as he took his next step, he heard the scream.

Deal Me a Card

"Agh, argh. Oh, my God, save me! My leg! My leg can't move. Eddy Eddy, help me, help! ... No, don't come over here. Keep going. Run. Run! I'm trapped. ... You must get there. We'll meet up later. ... Oh God!"

Alfie shrieked. Two minutes and his howls diminished. The night wind resumed its whistling.

Deal Me a Card

CHAPTER 21

EDUARDO STOOD STILL, a mouse facing a hawk at the entrance of its hole. Three trembling minutes passed, in which only a shaky sigh dared to move the air every three seconds.

Then, as if the silence galvanized him, he took off in the direction that Alfie had ordained.

He tripped. He wrenched himself up. Struggled up a pile of rocks. He lost his footing as he slid down an incline. Twisting his body so he was lying on his stomach, he reached up with his hands crazily, vainly clutching at creosote twigs. His teeth bit into his lips to stifle the cry of pain as his midriff connected with sharp projectiles. Don't make a sound. Who knew what waited with gun in hand ready to fire on him?

His feet hit solid ground.

Eduardo stopped, writhed upwards, spread his legs, peed. Was there any water left in his bladder?

Squatting to catch his breath, he looked into the distance and saw flickering lights of a village. Not many. But it was the middle of the night. Upright again, ignoring the smarting scrapes that yelled in agony from his chest begging for attention, he plodded on. He owed this to Alfie. He would make it.

"God save him. Virgin of Guadalupe, protect him."

He could not help the tears that rolled down his cheeks or the sobs rising from deep in his lungs. Or perhaps he did not feel them as he walked on and on. Twice, he thought he heard anguished howls echoing in the thin air then landing to burrow into his ears then fading to faint vibrations as he urged on his tortured body. But it could have been the wind whipping the sand and exhorting the ocotillo cacti to a frenzied arm-waving dance.

Deal Me a Card

As early morning yawned and dawn's refreshed glow made sense of his surroundings, Eduardo espied white, grey, and brown blocks ahead. Nearer and nearer the houses advanced, sentries defending against infiltration by the alien. As they loomed larger, their eyes, some black, others golden, glared at the rag-and-bones stranger. Some even blinked now and again as if in wonderment at the bizarre vision. Either they were stunned by his audacity, or they waited for him to make the first move before they pounced.

Then in front of him rose a gnarled mesh that stretched in both directions for what seemed like a hundred miles as it faded in the still-dim light. The rusty barbed wire towered over him. The barrier separating the trespasser from the village clanged a threatening bell whenever gusts of wind shook the intertwined strands. Metallic thorns protruded from among disheveled coils.

His mother's slight figure drifted before his eyes. He was elated. She was always there as far back as he could remember.

When he was young, she came to the children's room to rouse the five boys and two girls for school and work in the fields. She tiptoed to their beds very early each morning. Sometimes he would already be awake, like now. He would watch her through slit eyes. Candle in hand, she bent over each child, gazed at them for a long minute before shaking them gently.

"Wake up, wake up. My little ones, it is almost morning. The rooster is crowing, calling the sun to shine. Listen. The cows are moving. Do you hear their bells? They are full of milk. Quickly, quickly my darlings, open your eyes wide and greet the day. Off to the fields, off to school you go," her sing-song greeting stroked their ears.

She herself was half-asleep, had not yet smoothed her hair with the tortoiseshell comb that her mother, Abuela, had given her on her wedding-

Deal Me a Card

day. So her tresses, shorter strands awry and frizzled, hung in disarrayed loops, a halo askew around her bony cheeks and adoring mien.

"Mama, mama, I'm awake. Look, I'm ready to go to the fields," Eduardo called out, eager to be ahead of his siblings in his mother's eye. But already she had turned away to the kitchen.

Instead, the twisted steel, now staring him in the face, exuded no love. He swayed, almost toppling as he shook off the vision. He could not allow nostalgia to sabotage his success.

Stiffening his aching frame that cried out to crash to the ground and sink into the treachery of forgiving sand, he turned to his right and resumed his trudging, using the sloping dunes to disguise his advance. The dogs in the village were either asleep or repelled into silence by the putrid odors that he secreted, a jinn's desert stew of toxic sweat, shit, fear and urine that acted like smelling salts on his weariness. He heard scant yelping. After every ten steps, he paused and peeked over the low ridge to take stock of his options.

He had ruled out scrambling over the fence. The six-foot wide barrier would become a barbecue grill in less than a minute, and he the fresh carrion for ferocious beasts. His puny hunting knife was only good to slice into a barrel cactus for its pulp and juice. Its blade would shatter into a million shards against the steely plaits of the barricade.

Finding a way to travel under the wall was his only other choice. He kept walking.

Five minutes later Eduardo stopped, stared, and uttered a prayer of thanksgiving for all creatures great and small, especially those that were the size of bobcats, wolves and adult men. Over the years, they had hollowed a ditch, an animals' entry to the world of homo sapiens, humans' gateway to paradise. He stared at the excavation.

Deal Me a Card

A dark cavity gaped at him from under a tangle of rusted iron alloys. The scuffed hollows in the sand, eroded to unyielding brown earth and obtruding rocks, told him that other men, women, and children had been here. He visualized each body wriggling aching bones, skinny torsos, crippled limbs, through the unaccommodating passageway. His hand reached out to a headless doll with palms outstretched and sunk to its waist in the dirt. Perplexedly he stared at the crushed plastic bottle wrapped in a bloody scrap of rag leaning against a rock. He blessed the unknown fore-runners, murmured a prayer for their travails and followed their path.

Eduardo slipped into the drain. It was dry, as his whole world had been during the last three weeks. This time he praised God again that it was May, still drought season with no deceptive mud puddles. He scuttled, crouching low on hands and knees. Sweat, caked muddy streaks of perspiration liquefied from the exertion, snaked down his jaws. The worn edges of his sandals scudded on the earth. Torn nails of his toes and fingers scratched at the stony soil.

Two years from now, the desperate thought ran through his mind, *this will all be over*. He groveled at the resistant ground some more, clawing at it like a hungry rooster. He saw blood on his fingertips. But Band Aids were not his priority. Just finding light at the end of his tunnel.

****

Three miles away, Pete Evanson cinched his belt. The gleaming gems, which adorned the long horns of the steer on the ornamented buckle, sparkled green and gold. Normally he would pause a moment to admire the hand-made quality of the leatherwork and the carving. He'd marvel aloud,

"You know, Liz, couldn't find anything like this stateside. Workmanship like this just doesn't exist here in the U.S. Gotta admire those Hispanics. Boy, are they good with

Deal Me a Card

their hands. The men and women both. Take that gorgeous lace dress you bought last weekend."

She'd humor him, "I know, I know, my love, and for just for fifteen dollars!"

"Right. You should have bought one for Colleen. After all, they call that style the wedding dress!"

"Good point. It would be perfect for Linda and Donald's marriage in July."

But now, at this early morning hour, Elizabeth did not want any light-hearted banter, as she distractedly shoved his cup of coffee into his hand,

"We have to hurry. It's almost seven. I don't like what I heard last night. It's all because of that trap you set. It's antiquated, cruel."

"Honey, it's barely six thirty. Stay calm. The coyotes' howling was what awakened you. The wolf or the bobcat or whatever, something large, that's in the trap? It's probably dead by now. So why the rush? Yep, that trap was my last resort. Been in the family for years.

"Would always do the job, my father said. Every time. Should have used it sooner. I haven't heard a peep since I got out of bed an hour ago."

"Humor me. Hurry up! Look, I know we've lost some calves, but in the cycle of nature humans and animals will hunt and kill. There's a lot of coming and going out there in the hills.

"But last night there was something or someone in trouble. I feel it. We must go out and search."

Her husband zeroed in on her comment about the cycle of nature. He considered it too flippant, dismissive of his hard work. His dander up, he expressed his indignation,

"But nobody or nothing's gonna kill my livestock, by golly. Those dead calves cost me hundreds. Each. We can't afford that too often. And those wetbacks …"

127

Deal Me a Card

"Don't call them that. You know I abhor it. In case you've forgotten, my great-grandfather was from Hidalgo. Lived in these parts a whole lot longer than your family."

"Okay, okay. It's too early in the morning to argue. We both know those people who are crossing the border are doing it illegally. I was just adding that they're like the wild beasts, they cost me money too. When they tear apart our fences."

Pete saw Elizabeth's lips pursing and hurried on,

"Okay, let's go look. I'm sure it's the puma I've been tracking. She's marked her territory, and nothing else I've put out has deterred her. I swear I heard her roar with laughter when I dragged out the cage you found for me. The one for the humane entrapment of wild beasts. After I set it up, she prowled around it, giggling, and pissing on it. I'm sure of it. And slunk off wagging her damn tail. …This time, I feel lucky."

"And I feel sick to my stomach!" Elizabeth snapped back, distraught.

Without another word, the couple stepped out the back door of their ranch house.

Even at that early hour the Arizona sun was on the offensive glaring in their eyes. As they countered with sunglasses, the promise of rising heat hit the rest of their bodies with warning blows. Preoccupied, they shrugged off this immediate discomfort. The woman grasped her husband's hand, pulling him along, hastening his more leisurely step.

They reached the garage where the Dodge sat in the shade. The pick-up's upholstery felt slippery cold as Peter clambered into the driver's seat. As his wife took her place beside him, he glanced through the rearview mirror at the cargo.

Workers had piled tarps and rope, mallets and sacks of cement on its bed from yesterday's building of a lean-to out

Deal Me a Card

in one of the fields. The plan was to finish the structure today. The crew was scheduled to depart at ten.

The route to the site took them over a rocky lane the battleground of frequent struggles between man and beast, located about a mile from the main house. Peter pulled up five feet from the trap. Before it had come to a complete standstill and seconds before he had turned off the ignition, Elizabeth leapt out the truck. She was screaming as she drew near to the trap and caught her first look of the carnage,

"Oh my God, oh my God!

"It's a man. I think he's dead. Oh God, I pray you, do not let him be dead.

"Peter, Peter, quickly, quick! Get over here. For God's sake, hurry! What have you done!"

Behind her, the man, now agitated, slammed the truck door and scrambled with big strides towards her,

"Hey, take it easy, Liz. Quiet, be quiet!

"His leg got trapped. It must have happened in the middle of the night. Calm down. We've got to act fast!"

For a full minute and a half, shock transfixed the three beings in a tableau. Elizabeth knelt by the body. Pete, hands clenched at his sides, looked down on the lifeless figure. The man lay on his right side. His left leg was drawn up to his waist. His other limb was a bloody mess. The trap's jaws had opened wide and chomped down with a vengeful bite that sank all ten teeth into the thigh with total disregard for the futile protection of the threadbare denim. Slick splatters on the pant leg shone, their sanguineous hue a contrast to the dirty bleached blue. The sand around the wound displayed a dainty, neat pattern of reddish-ochre irregular-sized splotches. Horse flies, gnats and other insect cousins buzzed about, gluttonous with the oozing blood, busy with this chance at life and death. The creature's fingers, nails split, filth encrusted, extended talon-like in a useless effort to loosen the grip of agony.

Deal Me a Card

Elizabeth moved, reached out and placed her hand under the human claw. It did not respond. She sobbed. Withdrawing her hand, she covered her face, rocked, and mouthed a desperate litany to every known saint. Then adrenaline surged through her. Expediency took over. She brushed back her hair. Furiously she flapped away the intrusive gad-flies.

"Shoo, shoo, get away, shoo. Check for a pulse, Peter. Now!

"Please God, he hasn't died from shock or loss of blood. He doesn't look very strong. Probably was weak to begin with.

"Look at his body! Skin and bones. Could have been travelling for days in this heat. No food, little water. Just look at those rags. He might have been dead already. Then to lose all this blood."

His wife's flurry of words slapping at his face, galvanized, Peter got on his knees. His fingers on the scrawny neck felt a tiny flutter. He imagined a faint moan raising him to his feet.

"We have to hurry. I'll get the key to the trap. You lay out the tarps."

Elizabeth ran with her husband to the truck. While he found the key and made his way back to the man clinging to life, she arranged a mattress of plastic on the bed of the vehicle. Then she rushed back.

Pete had released the jaws and eased the mechanism under and away from the body. His mind froze out any questions about the wound reopening. For the moment, there was no sign of renewed bleeding. For the moment. He worked with alacrity, dragging the cumbersome trap to a sprawling manzanita and shoved it among the low-swinging boughs. He would send a couple of farm-hands to retrieve it later. He returned to stare at the body.

"We have to lift and carry him to the truck. This is going to be awkward. It's a blessing, I suppose, that he's unconscious."

Elizabeth glanced at him, chewing her lower lip as she bit back a comment that she knew would be not only superfluous, but vicious, and a waste of precious time and energy. She used her mind more wisely, skittered over their options, seized on a solution.

"The sand is soft. Can't we slide a board under him so the movement is minimal? There's one in the truck"

"Yeah, I see what you mean."

Peter's movements were now not only herculean but rapid as he hauled the two-by-six foot flat of timber from the truck. The husband and wife worked in tandem sliding the length of the plywood under Alfie's head. Then they cautiously wheedled it lower and lower along the length of his body.

Peter took charge.

"Thank goodness he's so light. Be careful now…. Wait. Let me scoop the sand away all around his legs, so there's a hollow. He's going to hurt anyway. But this may lessen the pain slightly. But we have to hurry! "

The delicate maneuvering continued.

The zip-zap of wood on sand, and the man and woman's heavy breathing were the only sounds that matched the intensity of the sun's blistering rays above their heads. The couple was oblivious to the pounding heat, totally absorbed in their struggles against death's onslaught.

Finally the body rested on the board. A resurrected mummy still dribbling sand from tattered rags and sere arms and legs and blood from the open tear in its thigh. They carried the mangled form on the makeshift gurney and laid him on the bed in the truck. His body was ice-cold. Elizabeth unfolded another tarpaulin and spread the stiff crackling blanket over him.

"I'll sit here with him. Keep him still.

131

Deal Me a Card

"Drive carefully. But let's move. I think there's very little time left.

"Quick, now, quickly, get on the CB radio and call the ambulance. They should meet us in fifteen minutes. Please don't stop praying."

****

Eduardo heard the voice massaging him into a groggy awakening. But he still reached deep into the child-memory, touched it.

Mama, Mama that feels so good, so cool.

Hush my darling, my little son, you were ill, very, very ill. Drink. Now lie still, rest.

Sleep.

Mama, mama, I made it. I'm home. I'm sorry I ran away. I had to find my puppy. He was lost, and I love him so much. Then I got lost. And you were so far away, and it was dark. Then I saw the flashlight and there you were. And I will never leave you again…. Mama, hold my hand. Don't let me go. I don't want to be alone again. No. No never again. I'm so afraid. Hold me.

"Ssh, shush now, Mr. Eduardo. I'm here and you are safe."

His one eye stayed closed, gummed shut by a gooey mixture of tears and gritty sand. The other, barely open, saw a round, brown head, two twinkling black eyes supported by rosy-apple cheeks peering down from a foot above him. It was not his mother. He slammed his eye shut.

Unashamedly, he listened to his dry hacking whimpers.

"Here, let me lift your head. Now drink this. It's only water. But it's the best thing now. You need as much of it as your system can hold. There. Now lie back."

Eduardo sank back into oblivion.

****

"They're sending the ambulance from Nogales. Then they'll go to Tucson. The rest is in God's hands," Peter told his wife as he got off the speaker and lowered the volume on the CB radio. He kept driving. But the husband and wife did not speak until the truck pulled onto their property. Then Elizabeth spoke, clearly and slowly,

"Peter, when the paramedics arrive, tell them that this man is a farmhand we hired from Sasabe. We took him on three days ago to help with the branding. Explain that he's our responsibility and we will take care of all medical costs."

"But..."

"No arguments. This will be our story. I'll fill in the details as they come up. I found a scrap of paper in his pocket. There's information I can use. Do I hear the ambulance?

"Please God, it's not too late. Peter, go in and tell the housekeeper to send them back here. Tell her to stand in the front yard, waving a red flag or something, anything to hurry them. So they drive right in. Fast."

As Peter left, Elizabeth crouched beside the still figure. She stared at the death mask before her. Although his face was a deep bronze, his lips were pallid. His cheek bones protruded so sharply that their jut seemed poised to tear apart the transparent skin. The aquiline nose projected like the beak of a proud mountain bird. Long, dark lashes swept down over the hollows beneath his closed lids. One brow was glued to a strand of thick matted black hair. No amount of willing inspired the slightest flicker of life from the waxen countenance.

Ten minutes became an eon.

Sweaty faces, wide eyes, and clenched jaws greeted the two paramedics at the open barn door.

Without a word, they trotted to the ambulance and returned with the gurney and life support apparatus. Smoothly they transferred the motionless being to its new bed. Inserted an IV. With the power and tenderness of

133

angels' wings, the technicians lifted the whole contraption into the waiting van. As one leapt into the vehicle, Elizabeth called after them,

"His name is Alfredo Ruiz. He's our newly hired cowhand. We have power of attorney. We'll follow you to the hospital. Go. Go. Go."

The medical mobile spun swiftly but cautiously down the graveled driveway.

In step, the two rescuers turned on their heels. Wordless, they leapt and ensconced themselves in the Pontiac convertible. Tethered themselves securely.

The tires ground the grumbling rocks mercilessly underfoot as the driver sped away from the farmhouse.

"You don't have to say a word, Peter. We have more money than God, remember. And if you're unwilling, so be it. My trust fund will take care of every expense. Or I'll sell my half of the herd."

"So what does this loser wetback have that none of the others possess?" her husband sneered.

"Nothing. You do what you have to do. You don't think twice driving into that little town and picking out ten or twenty of these men to do your bidding. What do those winners have that the others don't?"

"Luck of the draw, I guess."

"I rest my case…. Turn on to some country and western station. I need to think and plan."

"Ah, my Savior of the world. My Mother Teresa of the Southwest. If it's not a battered woman with three dirty-nosed kids to cook and clean for us, 'we must send the children to school poor things they're six, seven and eight and never seen the inside of a schoolroom. God they're cute when they've had a bath' it's half-starved, chewed up Freddie Ruiz who'll need a new leg for sure."

"Shush. Music, please. I'm thinking."

"I love you, my saintly wife."

Deal Me a Card

Elizabeth's eyes were shut as she turned inward, so she missed the adoring gaze that her husband poured on her.

Deal Me a Card

CHAPTER 22

HE LAY ON THE NARROW COT, afraid to open his eyes to a strange reality. A reality he had dreamed into actuality through a nightmarish course. Now he was uncertain if he could face it alone. He had always pictured himself with someone at his side. Two heroes braving it out through any calamity. This was not happening.

But here he was. Trapped and forced to act. So he willed his eyes open.

"Thank goodness, you're awake. You slept for ten hours. Like a dead man."

"Where am I? Am I alive?" Eduardo rasped at the blurry visage five inches above his.

"Safe. Of course."

The brown oval face with pink lips moving and black eyes wide-open under frowning eyebrows gathered focus. But the weary man shut his eyes once more. His awareness was unprepared to absorb something, or somebody new. Behind his lids, the image of his journey's final steps grew clearer, as if emerging from a dense fog.

****

Earlier that morning, clambering out of the tunnel, Eduardo found himself sheltered behind a thick hedge of oleander bushes. A bell was clanging. Like at home on a Sunday, calling the faithful ones to church. Peering through the leafy branches and pink flowers, he saw a white adobe structure with blackened wood supports on the wall facing him. A wooden cross perched on its tiled roof. Its solid form beckoned, unlike the stretched menace of the feathered shapes that had hovered over him and Alfredo in the desert day after day. The building stood apart from other shacks. Deserted. Nobody had yet heeded the pealing summons.

Deal Me a Card

Opening a gap in the shrubby limbs, Eduardo stepped out and slouched towards the refuge. He hobbled as an aged early-morning worshiper might, partly from persistent stabbing cramps that had seized his calves as he waddle-squatted through the tunnel, partly to appear as if he belonged in the neighborhood.

Stumbling up the two stone-and-concrete steps he creaked open the rough-surfaced fragrant pinyon pine door.

Haloed saints and martyrs stared cold-eyed from the shadowy interior daring his approach. He cringed involuntarily, crossed himself.

Stepping to his right, he took three more paces and halted trembling in front of an icon of the Virgin and Child. Their faces, glowing from the heat of votive candles, were alive with welcoming smiles.

He fell on his knees. His shoulders slumped heavily. Hands felt the smoothness of Mexican tile. Then his body toppled forward, and his head thudded on the kneeler. He lost consciousness.

The voice of his guardian angel roused him.

"We found you lying in the church when we arrived for the morning services. You're in the priest's house now. Is there anyone else? Was another person coming with you? In your delirium you moaned a few times, and you shouted some things, somebody's name. You're not Alfredo, no? We emptied your pockets and one paper said 'Alfredo,' the other 'Eduardo.' Which are you?" The voice was soothing.

"Eduardo. I'm Eduardo. I think Alfredo is dead. We separated. Then there was some terrible screaming. Like someone being attacked and eaten. He must be nothing now."

"God rest his soul," the old woman said as she wiped his face. "But we don't know. There was some news about an ambulance taking a man to Tucson. He was dying. Maybe already… But, praise the Lord. You have survived."

137

"He said we would meet in Nogales. But not after all this. How will I tell his mother back home in Agua Blanca, he is gone?"

The listener heard the trembling hopelessness in his voice and saw the tears of despair slip without shame from under the lids of the broken man's eyes. With the lightness of a sprite, she touched his shoulder,

"I think you should rest some more. But first, you must eat something. You are very weak. I am cooking dinner. You need food. It's simple, just grilled chicken, tortillas, some vegetables. Very simple."

Visions of this feast settled in Eduardo's shrunken gut. His salivary glands spurted a flood.

Swallowing hard, he croaked,

"What time? Now? I haven't eaten for six days, I think."

Light-headed and off-balance, he swayed to his feet off the low cot, then, clinging to her elbow, he limped to the dining room. There, three other heavenly beings, recently descended to earth to succor him, gently sat him down at the table of plenty. They all held hands for the prayer of grace. Mercifully, the two women and the priest had firm restraining grips. When they had set his fingers free, with his head emptied of all thought, Eduardo filled the void in his middle.

****

Now, three years and six months later, Eddy downed the first of many cans of beer in a fruitless bid to quench his real thirst. He knew where he was headed. There would be another glass, then another. Numbness would gradually envelop his brain, but somehow the stabbing ache would persist in his heart.

Deep inside he was convinced that he had walked away from Alfredo, left him to the mercy of wild beasts. It broke his spirit over and over as he obsessed on what he could have

Deal Me a Card

done differently. He had confessed his wrongdoing, many times.

"Father forgive me, for I have sinned. I killed my cousin. I turned and took the other direction," he would murmur.

"Father, forgive me. I have been a coward. I abandoned my best friend. I let him down. Did not show brotherly love."

"Son, our God is a forgiving Father. Be humble and accept His compassion."

But he choked on this absolution, knowing that God would condemn his pride if he dared to be forgiven. No padre could absolve him. The guilt that had taken seed wound tightly, strangling his resolve. The burden stanched any flow of forgiving grace.

In moments of clearer thinking and introspection, he acknowledged he was an emotional cripple. Alfredo would laugh in his face for his self-destructive drunkenness if he was by his side.

Then he popped another can.

"Gotta mend my ways," he slurred.

"You're right honey," Irene, the choice for the night smirked grandiosely, humoring this soon-to-be ex-love-of-her-life.

"You've got to find a cause, find a distraction!"

"You're mocking me, aren't you! Laughing at my pain, at my vulnerability."

Eddy savored that last word. He threw it up often. It gave him space to mope and wallow.

"Hey, you wait and see. One of these days you'll read about me and my doings."

"Right. In the weekly police blotter. Come on, sweetie, cut out the blubbering. Let's dance. No, no, let's eat. We get out there in that itty-bitty circle and we'll crash on our backsides or smash that guitar to smithereens when we make our merengue moves.

Deal Me a Card

"Besides, if we don't get some food in us, we'll both be featured. In the obituaries. Crash victims DUI and DOA! "

The two had been crouched on bar stools for some hours in the cantina, amidst a grumbling of conversation broken by the odd maniacal guffaw. The saloon's ambience, created by one electric bulb shrouded in the sour exhalations of imbibers, did not help to lift the spirits. It might as well have been a candle-lit monastery chapel exuding incense and filled with the droning rise-and-fall of monks chanting their 'Ave Marias" while the abbot served a penitential libation. The couple was oblivious.

Eddy had tossed down beer after beer. His arm raised the can to his mouth as if jerked by an obsessive puppeteer urged on by some doleful dirge. Irene, not nun-like, had matched his rhythm with a running octave of limeades and orange Hay, Hay Spritzers well laced with tequila. The acidic fruitiness stoked her rising gall roiling in tune with each self-pitying monologue twanged out of her companion's lips. Gradually the words had sunk to a gurgling whine flowing out of her date as each pint of Bud flowed into his maw.

She hurried him on, "Let's go to the restaurant. This smoke is making me nauseous. Mixed with the other smells, it's like lots of customers couldn't keep their drinks down in here. Bleah!"

"Just you wait. You'll be sorry you jeered tonight," Eddy followed his own morose train of thought. He saw her narrowed eyes, cold beads in two slits.

"Okay, okay, I apologize. Profusely. You're right, we need to eat." He stumbled out of the cantina, Irene on his heels.

One hour earlier, he had tried to catch the attention of the harried waitress. He had gestured, mouthing his need, 'French fries,' across the room. She only retaliated with a 'Fuck you, too!' after stomping across the room to glower at him then sauntered off to attend to others' orders without

Deal Me a Card

regard to his blood-shot leer and gaping mouth. He allowed himself five seconds to shake his head in disbelief at her rudeness before tossing it back in another swallow of comforting ale.

He muttered, "I could go for a plate of their chicken fajitas. The combination. And a large coke. Yes, a giant coke. Need to sober up. Now that I'm on a search for a mission. A quest!"

Irene grabbed his arm to steady his lurch, as he raised his other hand in a gesture of valiant resolve. She spoke not a word, except to order her burrito supreme. Just listened in sullen silence to his rambling non-sequitur comments until later when she said, firmly,

"Good-bye, Eddy," as he dropped her off.

Neither felt any pain.

Deal Me a Card

CHAPTER 23

EMMA WALKED SLOWLY from her car to the offices of Jones and Guerrero. She drew the high collar of her brown suede jacket more tightly around her neck against the cold gusts of wind. Her hair would just have to endure the whipping until she got indoors. This was perfect weather for the holidays. After a while the sun would scorch away the sharp edges of the early morning chill and leave a crisp fall day crackling with clean air.

A smile lit up her face as she thought of the last three days. The atmosphere in San Diego had enhanced every minute of the wedding ceremony that had been enjoyed by all. The drive South and back was always grueling, but the weekend delights that she and Guillermo had shared, served only to energize her for the weeks ahead. Thanksgiving and other holiday festivities were just around the corner.

Inside, the building was Monday quiet. The atmosphere of calm, before the flurry of projects being resumed after the weekend, felt oddly subdued and laden with foreboding. A folded newspaper sat on the table at the entryway. Emma picked it up, then swept down the short, narrow hallway, eager to burst into Eva's room with a bouncy greeting to disperse the heavy ions. In spite of its overflowing cornucopia display, the shut door looked dispirited. Unusual, since the new assistant was always on time, all smiles, and hard at work by seven-thirty every day. Perhaps one of the children had a doctor's appointment, though she had not mentioned it last Thursday when she and Emma had last spoken.

Emma opened her door and placed her briefcase on the chair beside her desk. The newspaper lay beside it. She hung her jacket behind the door, then opened the blinds. Now the sun's rays brightened her cubby hole, touching in particular

Deal Me a Card

the wall shelf, where flourished the miniature palm and the phaleanopsis that still flaunted its white and fuchsia striped blooms, thanks to some secret ingredients that Doctor Schwarzman had given her. She let the pearly tip of her fingernail brush a petal with butterfly gentleness. Sitting down, she was about to peruse her week-at-a-glance, when a headline caught her eye. 'Nine-year-old Boy Needs Blood Donors!'

Even as Emma grabbed the daily, the phone rang and Raoul Guerrero walked into her office. She decided no action was action enough, so she sat still. The phone stopped its buzzing after five rings. In the silence hung the never-absent dread that threatened to cloud every sunny day in La Coloma. Her boss glanced at the newspaper dangling from her hand, then looked up at Emma's horror-stricken face.

"So, you know about Ralphie, Eva's boy. I had a message on the answering machine from Father Reilly when we got home yesterday afternoon. A drive-by took him down. He's in intensive care at Holy Redeemer."

The direction of the next few days took an urgent one hundred and eighty degree shift in focus. Daily work duties at the construction company and the educational center were summarily and efficiently completed. Emma paid particular attention to Eva's tasks, stacking completed files, and compiling one-page reports to bring to her at the hospital. Emma and Guillermo, hardly able to lift their own spirits, met with huddled groups of students, tearful friends of Eva, mostly women, at the Center. Since Emma was coordinating the insurance paperwork, she was able to meet with Eva on the ICU floor and glean some information. Ralphie was in a critical condition after five hours of surgery had removed bullets, two lodged close to his spinal cord and another that had nicked his spleen. Another bullet was embedded near to his aorta too close to be extracted. He was on life support, including twenty-four-hour care of nurses and medical specialists. Father Reilly from the parish and Father

Deal Me a Card

MacGregor the hospital chaplain, were at all times solicitous and prayerful. The little boy was alive, but barely.

Tuesday evening a call went out for blood donations when the doctors determined that Ralphie had to undergo additional procedures. His was not a common blood type. Carmelita posted announcements in every classroom, drove to the college and tacked them on all available bulletin boards. Emma made a trip to St Anselmo High School to attend a meeting on Wednesday morning with Brother Keith and the administration. At the special rally held that afternoon for the home football game and the annual pre-Thanksgiving blood drive, she coached Patty, Ralphie's sister, to deliver a tremulous but mostly impassioned plea for teenage blood. The girl, suddenly matured by her immersion in near-tragedy and loss, begged her audience to give blood to save a life, as an in-your-face response to those who shed blood to destroy life. The next day, the Red Cross rosters indicated an uptick in the number of football players who donated their plasma. At least two dozen residents of La Coloma and San Benitez were listed as off-site donors. Ralphie's condition appeared to stabilize.

The trail to the gunmen was cold. Undercover of the night, the predatory hunters had slithered away into the jungle.

****

On Thursday, Emma poured her heart out to her therapist in a release of tears that had hovered, trapped at the brim of her eyes all week long. If not for the clergy in the community and at St. Anselmo, she would have dissolved into a pathetic pool of salt water many, many hours earlier. Her therapist subtly led her away from moribund event to probe other relationships. Emma, to her own surprise relieved, complied,

"Dr. Schwarzman, priests have always played a role in my life. They were a big part of my youth and young adult

144

Deal Me a Card

years. When I was at the university, one of these consecrated men and I became very close, intimate friends. But that's for another day.

"When I observe the priests here in La Coloma and San Benitez, especially in the last few days, I am overcome with admiration for them, and filled with gratitude to the Lord.

"There are the stories, you know the scandals about a priest here and there succumbing to his needs for companionship and for children of his own flesh and blood. But you and I know also, that the tales are so often about loneliness, about human weaknesses. And too often stories of the goodness are left in the shadows.

"The men I recall from my childhood and teenage years were, are, still my unsung heroes. They molded me, like surrogate fathers. Especially they filled the void the death of my father hollowed out of my heart. You remember, I told you, I was only ten.

"Here's another chapter from my diary. May I share?"

Emma pulled out the ever-present miniscule tome, now somewhat dog-eared.

"Of course. Go ahead. This is significant that you are drawing a light from the darkness that you and others are currently experiencing. Please…read."

"These holy men enveloped me with avuncular warmth, filled me with a sense of familial camaraderie. I recall two, a Father Perriseau, and Father Maurie. French missionaries, rotund, stocky with beards flowing from their chins to the tops of tummies.

'When they hugged me, I was such a little person then, my nose would smash up against those stomachs. Roundness bulging through white soutanes, those long everyday robes like what the Arabs wear, sometimes black, that covered everything. Except the well-polished shoes peeking from underneath. That's how I knew that they had feet and weren't saints or angels hovering above the ground.

145

Deal Me a Card

"And always they were kind-eyed, deep throaty chuckles rising from their midriffs, talking to the other grown-ups above my head, with thick accents, and exuding this sweet smell of briar pipe tobacco.

"Then I'd see them in Church and I was never sure who they were. They'd be solemn strangers, barely recognizable in vestments, surrounded by clusters of lighted wax candles, gleaming crucifix and altar boys. They'd wave the thurible, the incense holder, to and fro, the long chain would swing, swish-swish, clang-clang. Clouds of heady blessed smoke would shroud them, rise to the ceiling, and make my nose itch. Then they'd call out at different times to their Lord to watch over me,

Angus Dei qui tollis peccata mundi,
miserere nobis,
Gloria in excelsis Deo
Pater Noster qui est in coelis
Lamb of God who takes away the sins of the world
Have mercy on us,
Glory to God in the highest
Our Father who art in heaven.'

"When I grew into adolescence Father Eduard and Father DeCroix entered my life. They came from faraway Switzerland to suffer persecution. They were jailed, tortured in China for the love of God. What fascinated me was they spoke Chinese and English with melodious French tonality.

"After their exile, they found respite in Malaya, and began more missionary work. That's how my family became their friends. I was one of their fortunate disciples. They were ever cheerful. Even though I was relatively young, they taught me the meaning of all those admonitions of Christ in the New Testament. Like in the Bible, their voices cried out in the wilderness, they were the true laborers in the vineyard, the fishers of men and women in strange lands far from home. They taught me their prayer, 'I am the clay, the work of your hands'.

Deal Me a Card

"I remember Father DeCroix visiting our classroom. He was a short, muscular man, ruddy, with blond hair cut to razor's edge length. His body was never still, his face never without a wide smile with eyes bright as diamonds. He personified élan.

"We'd beg him politely, since we were well-raised Catholic school girls dressed neatly in blue pinafores and white blouses and sitting primly with our legs together,

"Father, father, tell us about saying mass in prison, again.

"And he would break away from reading a story from St Luke's gospel and return to a tortuous time, just to indulge us.

"I saved crumbs of bread that our jailers gave us, under my fingernails, a bit under each nail", he said. "There was no problem as they did not give us much water to wash or clean ourselves, nor scissors to trim our claws. I saved the crumbs until I had a small lump about the size of a marble that the other prisoners could see.

"We spoke with slight hand movements, fingers to show the time for the celebration five minutes before the guards were changing their post, we hoped. We were forbidden to speak to each other.

"All eyes would look in my direction. Most of the prisoners could barely see me, just a small part of my body if I stood right up against the cell bars. I clutched those bars as though longing desperately for freedom. The guards liked that, smiled, and laughed, and jeered.

"Silently sliding my hand up the bar I raised the ball of rancid bread above my head, made a quick Sign of the Cross, like waving away the ever-present persistent buzzing flies, to bless the others. They swiped away the flies also. I lowered my hand, bowed my head over the balled-up crumbs. This is the consecration, bread changed into God-flesh, the essence of the Sacrifice.

147

Deal Me a Card

"The other prisoners receive the Body in their souls. All this in seconds, because we walked in the valley of death.

"How often did we do this, every month or so, who knows, how do we tell time in the dim light and darkness? We could not know who was a spy or a turncoat so the celebration of Mass could not be regular.

"All right, now back to Luke's gospel. I promised your Reverend Mother that I would explain the parable of the loaves and fishes to you today."

Emma shifted in her chair.

"Father Eduard was the other priest. His looks were so different. He was the heart-throb, especially of all the young ladies in secondary school. Tall, burly, with jowls, handsome, prone to crinkly-eyed smiles, dark brunette hair swept back in a wave from his broad forehead. But he was not strong. He had lost a lung in China from tuberculosis. We whispered behind our hands about it because he was reticent about his medical treatment.

"I do not like to talk of China, and my experience. Let's say that they were neither very nice nor comfortable."

"Pere Eduard and I developed a deep affection for each other. He was truly my father, earthly and spiritual, guiding me through my pimply, self-conscious gawkiness.

"Sometimes he was rough.

"You will be the Angel Gabriel in the Christmas play, you are younger, your sister will be the Blessed Virgin Mary. She has lovely hair and is so beautiful."

"Meaning that I was not!

"Always he was frank with keen paternal observations and subtle warnings,

"Child, child, why do you not sing? I saw you at the ten o'clock Mass and you were asleep. Because you are a teenager now. You were out late last night dancing with your friends, eh! What does your mother think?" he'd admonish in that Yves Montand voice dripping with reproach.

"He was forever patient.

"Bless me father I have sinned, it's been a week since my last confession."

"No, no that is not adultery, dear child, not even fornication when you have pleasure in yourself, you must try to resist the temptation. For your penance say three Our Fathers and three Hail Marys, and three Glory Be's. Now go in peace and pray for me."

"Pere Eduard was my father speaking for the Son, for the Father, and for my father deceased. Imbued with the spirit. My surrogate Dad.

"Even now my nostrils tingle with scents from his study in the rectory, mingled aroma of incense, pipe tobacco, Palmolive soap, tropical flowers. Thirty years later.

"He kept a promise we made to each other. We met in Europe, when I was a university student, and together we traveled with his two nieces and a male friend in a compact Renault Quatre L driving through Switzerland, France, Spain, and little Andorra.

"In June 1964, after a long train ride from Cologne and through the Rhine Valley, we gathered on a farm high in the Swiss mountains, Pere Eduard's brother's home. We spent the night there and woke to the clanging of cowbells, baaing lambs. Then we sat down to breakfast, tastes of creamy fresh-churned butter, and oven-warm crisp-crusted loaves. Amber-golden-sweet honey on the comb and farm-cured ham for lunch, and a dinner of rich fondue, home-made cheeses, sun-ripened vegetables.

"*Camaraderie, generosite, bonne cuisine.*

"Then two mornings later we loaded on the luggage and piled in the car. *Merci bien, merci, au revoir, adieu, adieu.*"

Emma's smiled, remembering.

"Pere Eduard's wicked laughter echoed and reechoed as we stood on the lowest slopes of the Matterhorn, under the hot summer sun glistening on the crispy snow, and he whispered of the fabulously rich women sunbathing nude in their lofty chalet mansions high above us. Then we savored in unison, fresh raspberries and cream. Tart, mouth-watering, puckering sweetness wrapped in smooth, soft tongue-strokes.

"A well-knit team, we shrugged off the discomfort of spending one night in a railway depot. No vacant banquette was available in the waiting room and the car was too tiny, crammed, so we napped uncomfortably on the floor reeking of urine. Sighing heavily, sleepy moans, uneasy groans, wriggling shoulders, aching muscles, twitching lips, early-morning spit, quick water swipe in the toilette. *Tant pis!* Too bad! We laughed at life's little woes, and drove on at sunrise."

She leaned her head on her right hand and continued,

"One night, Pere Eduard very late found us an auberge, a country inn, heavy wooden-beamed, with huge shadows flickering on candle-lit walls as though electricity had scorned this petite ville deep in French country. We snuggled in two huge beds, one for the men, and one for the women, that filled a single room. Then in the morning, the troupe thanked profusely the ancient landlady who had made us welcome, and gave us everything including that hearty breakfast. She called it *petit dejeuner for le bon pere*, the little meal for the good father.

"On we rode on our grand European tour, to historic churches, bridges and castles. We fingered Le Puy lace, danced and photographed each other *sur le pont d'Avignon.*

"We basked and bronzed on a Mediterranean beach, then we smacked our lips through an enormous bowl of succulent spicy paella, downed with bottles of Madeira one late night on the Costa del Sol.

"Headily inebriated from Andorran wine on another late evening, Pere Eduard and I collapsed in a fit of giggles, as, with conspiratorial sniggers, we stuffed his niece's brassiere with two small watermelons. Tomorrow's snack, tonight's caper. And exchanged a kiss that went just beyond fatherly and childlike.

'*Mon Dieu, ne nous sommet pas a la tentation*! Oh, my God, don't lead us into temptation!'

"I glimpsed his tear-streaked face as we stood by the waters of Lourdes, watching the faithful sick and crippled bringing their wounded twisted beings to the miraculous flow.

"Together all five of us merged with a thousand other pilgrims, and turned to witness, in an awe-filled shimmering moment, a long, long, seemingly endless line of candles, joined with myriad voices from across the universe, singing Ave Maria as we wound down the hill to the Virgin's meeting place with Bernadette. Brothers all are we.

"He was *mon pere, mon ami*, my father, my friend. We shared love, agape sprinkled with just a dab of sensuality, offered with a Swiss-French accent.

"To be young, it was heaven,

"*C'est vrai, c'etait formidable*. That's true, that's wonderful.

"Bless me Father."

Emma looked at her therapist.

"One day years later, I heard Father Eduard died old, retired, and happy on his brother's farm. By chance, by design, here and there an ocean and a continent away, I still catch a whiff, the sweetness of his pipe tobacco. Forty years later.

"Doctor Schwarzman, I'm so glad I told you of my priestly encounters. They are a comforting, comfortable part of my life's tapestry. I needed to slip away to that happier time. Now it's time to go. I'll see you in two weeks. Enjoy your family and Thanksgiving. I'll dare to ask you. Say a prayer for Ralphie."

"Of course, dear Emma. We must believe that the situation will improve."

****

151

Deal Me a Card

The Saturday before Thanksgiving, a disconsolate couple sat in Emma's living room under a dim lamplight that struggled in a vain effort to soothe downcast spirits. Emma drew as close as she could into the circle of Guillermo's embrace as she spoke. Her voice sounded to her like a mouse squeak, helpless as she cringed in the face of fate.

"Really there's nothing more we can do, is there? Except pray to the Almighty. It's in His hands now."

"True, true. At the same time, we give Eva all the support we can muster. That's how communities work. Me, I'm thanking Him for the spiritual leadership and guidance. And for those padres who aren't showy or pushy, just doing their duty. Father Macgregor, Father Reilly, they're the stalwarts, always there, the pillars that hold us up.

"I'm going to change the subject just slightly. Okay with you? This should lift our spirits, take us beyond ourselves. It's still about priests. Well, about one good man."

As his companion nodded, Guillermo pulled a folded envelope from his trouser pocket.

"Here, Emma, read this. It's from Father William. You don't know him.

"When we lived in Fresno, he was my savior in some of my darkest hours. He didn't have a parish. Belonged to one of those groups that send its members all over the world to save souls. Do-gooders. Social justice promoters. Well, he was all heart. I guess his family lived in the Stockton area, some little burg nearby, and he'd visit different churches to help with pastoral duties and to raise money for his missions at the same time."

"Did Mary Lou know him?"

"Yes. She loved to flaunt her total disregard for sobriety in his face and dare him to see Christ in her drunkenness. And he did."

"My poor sweetheart."

"He was my shoulder to cry on, I have to admit. Anyway, he's back home to celebrate the twenty-fifth anniversary of his ordination this month. It says here,

'I'm back from a stint in Guatemala. Any gifts that you may kindly think to send to honor me will be used in the missionary work of the Order, to love our neighbors as ourselves. At present, I have a very concrete project in mind that needs five thousand dollars funding. It will provide homes and save lives by raising the quality of life at its most basic level. May the Lord continue to shower every blessing on you and your loved ones. Yours in Christ's name, etc, etc.'

"We must send him something. Who would not! What's his address?"

Guillermo set the letter on the kitchen counter and turned back to the business of loving his favorite neighbor.

CHAPTER 24

THE FAMILY AND GUESTS were seated around Guillermo's dining table. They all agreed tacitly and privately that there was much to be thankful for. For just a few hours the group would dwell on the positives of life.

Swallowing a mouthful of turkey, Guillermo leaned back in his chair. His smile sweeping around the table he offered praise,

"This was delicious. So American, just right. All the trimmings, turkey roasted to perfection, succulent. I carved it like I knew what I was doing. Thank you kindly, my sweet Emma, for preparing our Thanksgiving dinner."

"And my thanks to Sarita and Betty for the centerpiece and table setting. You all know, I love to cook. Especially when I have a family to feed. I'd like to think of all of you as my family."

Daniel grinned as he set down his wineglass,

"Who else could we be, Mom?"

"Daniel!"

"Well, she practically lives here. She works for Uncle Raoul, and at the Educational Center which is your operation, so…"

Richard ended the thought,

"Right, Dad, and we're just waiting for you to announce the date."

"Now you young men are moving a little too fast for us. Right, Emma? Look, you guys. You're making her blush. Pass that eggplant. I love that stuff. Why haven't you made it for me before?"

"Because if I did, you wouldn't be smacking your lips over it now. There have to be some special dishes exclusively for feast days."

Sarita chimed in.

"And you know, this stuffing, dressing, whatever they call it, it's different. It's not that soggy bread. It's rice, right? But speaking about weddings ..."

She paused as Emma grimaced.

"No, no. I'm not going there. All in good time.

"I'm thinking of Maribel and George Madison. You two attended the ceremony in San Diego? That was two weeks ago?"

Emma exclaimed,

"What a beautiful fall wedding it was! Very traditional, and elaborate."

Then she continued as the two younger women leaned forward to listen.

"At the start of the Mass, the padre had a rope that he wound around the necks of the couple, loosely of course, to symbolize their eternal love, in a figure eight to signify eternity. He explained carefully, in detail.

"And the flower girl, the bride's niece, was, oh, so adorable. Her dress was a replica of the bride's. She carried a rosary of fresh roses, tiny red blossoms. She presented it to her aunt at the end of the service. I think it was to symbolize her heart full of love also."

Guillermo piped in, "Yes, lots of declarations of love. What I liked was the white money bag of thirteen gold coins that George offered to his new wife just before he kissed her and they walked down the aisle. That's the commitment that made her glow."

Emma mused, "Yes, you could say her smile widened. Nope, that's being cynical. They are very much in love."

Richard chimed in, "Trouble is, Dad, you anglicized us. Brought us up gringo, so we don't know the meaning of these things. Why thirteen coins? Why not one hundred? She might love him even better and longer."

Guillermo explained, "Well, I didn't know what was going with any wedding traditions for many years. I left Mexico when I was so young, no thoughts of marrying or

155

Deal Me a Card

having a wife at the time. Then your mother and I married in a Lutheran Church.

"I think it was only about three ceremonies ago that somebody's aunt explained it. The number thirteen represents Jesus Christ and His twelve apostles. It's a symbol of the trust and loyalty the couple promise to each other. And that the husband will provide for his wife."

Emma returned to her recollection of details.

"Truly, it was a splendidly rich affair. She and her mother and aunts made all the table decorations, and wedding guest favors. You'd think they were professionals. Graceful swans filled with *koufeta* almond candies meticulously wrapped in tulle at each place setting. Rounded bowls of fresh blooms, sterling silver hybrid roses no less, for centerpieces. Even the money bag. The material was lace and satin to match her gown. Let me tell you about the dress and the bridesmaid and…"

Guillermo interjected, "Why don't you ladies go to the living room and Emma can give you all the very finest specifications. She sounds like a writer of those gossipy social columns in the LA Times.

"We men will clean up and bring you some pie. C'mon, Daniel, Richard. Let's leave the women to their favorite pastime."

Emma and her two guests shook their heads laughing as they left the table. Daniel walked into the kitchen and checked out the desserts sitting on the counter and called out,

"Emma, you baked pumpkin and pecan? Who are you anyway? Randy Sanchez from the college or Martha Stewart?"

"A marriage of the two. I strive for perfection in all things. But those pies? I must confess I baked just the two pumpkin pies. The other two are from the ovens of Nicola's in Northwood. They're famous throughout the Valley. I had to order ahead and line up with at least a hundred other customers. Not a waste of time, you'll see. Every bite will make that wait worthwhile," Emma replied from the living room.

Betty returned to their previous topic of conversation, "But tell us about the dresses and the tuxedos, everything," she said, eagerly, as the three settled on the sofa and in one of the overstuffed armchairs. She giggled, "Don't let me doze off though. This is one of those settees where you just sink in and fall asleep, especially after a repast like that one. That word 'repast' sounds grand. It fits the occasion.

"Shake me if I nod off, or as soon as the pie arrives, whichever comes first. If anyone asks, I'd like the pumpkin."

Emma pretended dismay, "All that standing in line for nothing? I know, I know. Damned if you do and damned if you don't. I'd opt for a sliver of each."

Betty agreed, "Hmm, on second thoughts, I'd like that too. Now at the wedding that was …"

Emma returned to her reminiscing. "The bride's gown had a dropped waist. The bodice wasn't fitted. Skirt flared in the back but fell straight to the floor in the front. You know how small her breasts are…"

"Hey, I heard that! I thought you were describing the bride not assessing her vital statistics."

"Guillermo, just keep loading the dishwasher," Emma giggled. With scarcely a breath, she went on, "She looked so lissome, so fragile. With the scooped scalloped neckline, the satin with the lace overlay continuing just barely over her shoulders. To show off her tan on her neck, and on her chest. Gosh, she has such poise, the way she holds her head. The sleeves were short, mid-upper-arm."

"How did she wear her hair?" Sarita asked.

"Piled high in ringlets to hold the mantilla. Parted in the middle. The train flowed very naturally. Made of some lacy material to match the mantilla. It wasn't a cloud of tulle like you see sometimes, but a light sweep of fabric. Extremely elegant.

"She told me she looked at old pictures of her grandmother so she could get the same effect."

"What about the bridesmaids? There were four, including the maid of honor?" Sarita asked.

"Yes. I thought the dresses were very practical."

"Now, how's that for a put down. The bridesmaids were not dressed glamorously, or in haute couture. See I know all the jargon. Their clothes were practical," Richard interjected from the kitchen, above the metallic rustle of aluminum foil.

"Boy, we'll be eating turkey until New Year's," he added, in a non sequitur.

"Guys, what I mean is, sometimes you see attendants at wedding in dresses they'll give to Goodwill the next day, or hand down to their younger sisters, or hide in the back of their closet.

"At this wedding, the color scheme was deep Prussian blue and silver. Classy, classic. It slims the figures. One of the maids was a mite on the heavy side."

"Oh, that's Olga. She claims she has big bones," Sarita muttered, then called out to the chuckling Richard and Daniel,

"Hey, no snide remarks from the peanut gallery," as Daniel winked at her.

"The groomsmen's tuxedos echoed the same colors. They strutted around looking very dashing," Emma continued.

"The dresses were A-line with long straight skirts. Silvery gemstones were inset on the shoulder straps. We couldn't see them in the church, so I thought at first the dresses were strapless. They all wore silver waist-length boleros. What I loved was the two slim strands of silver ribbon that fluttered down from the center of their necklines. A delicate touch. Very dainty, and could be removed. Those frocks are perfect for other occasions."

"Frocks? I didn't know people used such words any longer," was Daniel's subtle input as he leaned against the kitchen doorway.

Guillermo looked at Emma quizzically, "How do you ladies do that? Absorb all that minutiae. Me, I was so glad everybody was wearing clothes and nobody spilled champagne or salad dressing down the front of their wedding garments and that Maribel's dad decided not to wear his sombrero.

"You know, he actually asked me if he should," he grinned.

"Gutsy man, that Abram. And I'm not talking about his wanting to wear the headgear. That was one bulging tux. Er...substantial figure. How's that for tact, Emma?"

Silverware tinkled against dessert plates as Guillermo sliced the pies and joined in the conversation. He went on,

"But that man, he's the salt of the earth. Ask your Uncle Raoul sometime to tell you the stories. Abram'd die for you, and I've heard, would kill for you.

"Dessert coming up. Who wants what?"

"Dad, who are these people? Are we related?" Daniel queried.

"In-laws. Twice removed. Or close to that. Maribel's father, Abram, the man with big bones... how do you like that Emma?"

"Well put. Very tactful. You're a quick study," she returned his wide smile.

"The heavy dude. He's your aunt's step-brother."

"Yeah. I remember when we were younger living with Uncle Raoul, we'd call him 'Uncle Abe' also. How come we didn't get an invitation? We're family. I thought Latinos are big on family," Daniel asked.

"Well, the two kids wanted to pay at least half of the wedding expenses and so they had to scrimp a little and limit the guest list. As it was, there were at least one hundred and twenty attendees. His parents are well-connected. Hotel

159

Deal Me a Card

business, land developers. That's how the happy couple met. Maribel was managing their Little Abaco in Santa Monica. You might have heard of it. Small, four-star. The restaurant is easily five hats. The guest list had to be negotiated among the various parties. Sometimes it makes sense to elope.

"You should have seen the groom's mother dance with the bride's Dad. Sweaty palms, sweaty armpits, sweaty necks. A breeze was blowing in from the bay. With all that food, the wine, the confitures, the cool touch didn't matter. The place was sweltering. So much so that all the boutonnières were wilting. The wedding photos should tell all."

Emma added, "I could go on and on about the menu and the cake. We'll let Maribel give you another blow-by-blow account when she gets back from the honeymoon. You'll see her week after next at the Chamber of Commerce Christmas dance, and she'll surely want to regale you with all the intimate details."

Richard spoke as he came over to join the group.

"Ah, ha. That's women's talk. The big night, the masseur, moonlit passion. Forget it. We'll have to invite them to our holiday event so Georgie can tell us about the snorkeling in Hawaii. And the golf course. They began their life of wedded bliss in Maui, right?"

His father came up behind him, and wriggled his body into the empty space beside Emma. While performing a remarkable balancing act with his full plate of pie, watched by the admiring eyes of all. He looked around at the beloved faces of his lover, his sons, and their guests.

"Yes! Enough about other people. I want to hear about your lives."

Guillermo turned to Daniel's date.

"Betty, how's the family? Daniel tells me your mother and some your siblings have remained in Guatemala, and you have a brother and two sisters here?"

Guillermo had just swallowed an amazingly tasty morsel of pumpkin pie and was between bites. Betty dispensed with her mouthful of pecan pie.

"I hope they're doing better now. In Guatemala, I mean. You know, my father, he was a tailor, had a weak heart and died unexpectedly five years ago."

Emma leaned over and touched her hand gently,

"I'm sorry."

Betty continued, her train of thought seemingly unbroken, "He left my mom with eight children. Actually, nine. She was pregnant when he passed away. The baby went too when he was two and a half years old. Our relatives had to chip in for the funeral. There was a tiny, white casket."

"Poor little angel. He's with Jesus and Mary now," Emma had to interrupt. Tears hung on the edge of her lashes.

The others were silent. Their unspoken empathy prompted the speaker to press on,

"Back then, when we were all still together, my mother a widow, we moved to the big town so mom could find work. Sewing. For another tailor.

"Some of us older ones decided to leave at that point. There was no room in the tiny house. So four of us traveled to Los Angeles.

"Now my mom and the other four are living in this shack back there. Well, in reality these homes are cardboard sheds. You know, the big appliances you buy here in the US that come in those huge boxes. Made of corrugated cardboard. You see, the Guatemalan housing companies buy them and build so-called apartments on the outskirts of towns. Low-income housing.

"When we were all one big happy family, minus Dad, we had a bigger box since there were nine children, that's counting the baby until he died, and my mother. Three rooms with cardboard dividers, a kitchen and two bedrooms."

Betty looked at each of them.

161

Deal Me a Card

"The big problem is that this row of dwellings is near the river. You'll say, well that's convenient for washing clothes and bathing and drawing water for cooking. But when there are heavy rains, forget it. The river overflows its banks and the flood came into the rooms. Thank goodness the floor is just bare ground or it would be terribly soggy. Twice it has happened.

"My mom was desperate. So she went to this priest, some kind of missionary from here. She asked if maybe he could get her some concrete blocks to pile up above the flood level and then they could place the house on top and stay dry. He promised he would return to the U.S. and seek help."

Betty sighed, "We think the baby got a fever from the water that first time it flooded, and that's why he passed away. He couldn't hold anything in his system. All the family lights candles to Lord Jesus every day we can get to church, to answer our prayers."

Betty grabbed her half-empty glass of wine and took a big sip. Her eyes were downcast. She bit her lower lip, knowing that she had allowed too much emotion to overflow, and attempted to stanch any more words that might pour out.

Guillermo glanced over quickly at Emma. Her eyes were wide. He shook his head slightly, saying silently, 'No, not now. Don't raise hopes.'

He picked up the thread of conversation, and filled the empathic silence, "We'll light candles at Church also this Sunday."

He realized how hollow that sounded, and swiftly segued, "Meanwhile, I'm so happy that Daniel invited you for dinner today. Where did you two meet?"

This time Daniel responded,

"I was driving over to Topanga Mall, about three weeks ago. Going through Chatsworth. I love to cruise by those hills on the way there. Makes me think perhaps I'm far away, in Sedona. I see this Mazda Protégé on the side of the road

162

Deal Me a Card

with a flat tire. Betty is standing there looking forlorn with her hair blowing in the wind."

"So Sir Galahad stops to help. Way to go, little brother," Richard snickered.

His sibling, used to such interruptions, kept right on,

"She's has to get some air into her spare so I drive her to that place near Salerno High School."

"Of course I can't shut up about my problems. Like now," a nervous tiny giggle escaped from Betty.

"No, no, I asked about you family first," Daniel demurred.

Betty was determined to add to the story, "Yeah. So I tell him all about my nephew who just transferred from LA because of the gangs. And it's not too much better out here in the Valley since his English is so bad. I couldn't baby-sit him all day, so he was skipping school. I told him, 'Miguelito, you're going to die young, if you don't stop this cholo stuff.'

"He says, 'Tia, Aunty, what do I do? I have to belong somewhere.'

"What about friends in school," I asked him.

'They're a bunch of fools' only he used a dirty word.

"He thinks if he speaks to his teacher, the others will think he wants to be her pet. So he sits there, understanding nothing. Then he comes home, with incomprehensible homework, bored, looking for trouble. He's living with me, you see. Goes back to East LA to spend the weekends with his mom and dad."

Betty's words flew out in a rush from her anxiety, making her breathless.

Sir Galahad picked up the narrative,

"And voila! I insisted we stop at the school. We went in and talked to a counselor about classes, English for Speakers of Other Languages, bus transportation."

"You did too much, Daniel. You were there two hours."

Deal Me a Card

Daniel smiled at her. "You needed a little boost, that's all. The school district is really confusing and cold if you don't know the questions to ask."

The proud aunt continued her tale,

"Miguel is doing better already. He wants to go to school. He brought home some sort of application form about playing soccer in the second semester. He's excited. So thank you. And to think I was cursing that tire."

"You curse and swear? Really? Better watch your mouth around the kid!" Guillermo teased

"I'm trying to inspire him."

The beleaguered surrogate parent spoke, earnestly. Seeing the confused faces, she explained,

"Since I finish all my houses ... I clean houses in Agoura and some in Woodland Hills every day ... by five o'clock, I can go to school. So this semester I enrolled at the Woodland Hills community college. In the Home Health Care Certificate program. While I'm in class, Miguel has started bringing his homework to study in the library where I know he's safe. Thank God. Next semester, maybe he can dual enroll. Take Spanish and impress everyone with his fluency. Make the teacher sit up!"

Betty looked at her watch,

"Ay! I hate to break up the party but I have to leave. One of my clients had a big family dinner today and I have to clean up tomorrow. Early."

As Betty stood up, looking toward Daniel quizzically, Guillermo arose and gave her a hug,

"It's been fun and enlightening."

He stood back and took her hand.

"I'm so glad we know you now. Thanks for sharing your story with us. I know it must be stressful. But you're not alone any longer. You know where we are, and you have our phone numbers.

Deal Me a Card

"Daniel, you walk Betty to the car. We'll see you later this weekend, I suspect. Oh, Sarita, Richard, you two're leaving also?"

The young people's voices were singing their thanks.

Guillermo was expansive, his arms spread wide.

"No, no this was no trouble. Anyway, Emma did all the work.

"By the way, we'll have to talk about the Christmas event very soon. If it's anything like the bash you had last year, we're chaperoning."

"Dad, we've got it under control. Sarita and I have been working on the details. She wasn't here last year if you recall," Richard said.

"I remember. Each and every second of the back-breaking clean-up."

"I promise there won't be a body in the hills after this one. That was not a happy summer surprise!"

"Ouch! That hurt! You can't imagine the flak I'm getting from that episode.

"Emma, remind me to call Doc. We need to talk. He, and Big M and I. Apparently Big M is a suspect. Some of those officers from Foothill division have their heads up their arses," Guillermo muttered.

"And to think that mouth kisses babies … and babes," Richard remarked in mock horror.

"Talk to you soon, Dad," he called over his shoulder with a laugh, as he and Sarita walked to the car.

The hosts waved to the young people as they drove off. Then turned and strolled up the driveway hand-in-hand.

****

Five minutes later, Emma's arms encircled Guillermo's neck as he unbuttoned her turquoise silk blouse in the bedroom. Dim lamp light softened its sharp corners. A cluster of late sunflowers waved knowingly from the silver globe on the dresser. The movement from a favorite opus

165

Deal Me a Card

matched the lovers' heartbeat as they swayed chest to breasts.

She toyed with him, giggled as he unhooked her bra while licking one of his most precious spots behind her left lobe.

"I love your sons so much. And I do believe they love me too."

"You'd better love me as much especially since I'm about to give my babe a full body massage. This bottle of warm oil says right here, see, it's reserved for the most beloved in my life. Especially after a day of cooking and cleaning."

"I've got to feel it to believe it," she sang, slipping everything off. Then she scrambled, burrowing into the sheets.

A little later Emma lay on her stomach sleekly pampered. Every inch of her body tingled from the touch of kneading fingertips. Guillermo nuzzled at her ear,

"The naked masseur rides again."

"I rearing to go," she murmured rising to her knees and opening her body to take him in.

Her man's hands were almost large enough to encircle the roundness of her buttocks. His lips were petals drifting in the breeze across smooth flesh.

"My rosy cheeks," his guttural tone heavy with desire.

Then he plunged deep, withdrew, and plunged again and again. They coupled in unison until the rhythm of their lovemaking echoed in the crescendo of Ravel's Bolero pounding the room awash in their passion.

Deal Me a Card

CHAPTER 25

ALL AFTERNOON OF THANKSGIVING DAY, Eva Munoz sat guard. The lone sentry. She had insisted that all other family and friends celebrate Thanksgiving, joining together at church and table to praise the Lord for Ralphie's life.

The mother allowed herself only one comfort, leaning back in the recliner nursing staff had wheeled into the room on the second day of her twenty-four hour vigils.

Now two hundred and sixty hours has gone by.

One small part of her brain processed her activities. It knew she ate, drank, urinated, had bowel movements. Or perhaps it was the autonomous intelligence recording those processes. Some article she had read explained all that stuff.

Because she had transformed into a robot, who moved its stiff limbs each hour to stimulate blood circulation, who swiveled its head from the monitors on the wall to the body that lay immobile under the blanket and powder-blue chenille hospital bedspread. Occasionally, the cyborg would lift its slender claws to arrange the bedclothes, which needed no smoothing, since the body beneath them never moved. The unfeeling mechanical being would press a hidden button in its head to switch on a smile for the nurses who entered the room every three hours to check for the body's vital signs. Press another knob to jettison a series of inconsequential questions about prognosis, for which its ears received only one set of data.

"How is he?"

"He's looking quite good."

"Will he live?"

"Yes."

"What's going on now?"

"He's in stable condition."

Deal Me a Card

"How long before he opens his eyes?"

"Ten days. Ten weeks. The brain is a mysterious organ. We can never tell."

Finished, the nurse withdrew.

Occasionally, a screw would loosen suddenly and a torrent of bilious emotion would escape in an eruption without warning. She was like a coiled spring unwound. Tears would pour from the anxiety. Little sobs would hiccough from the despair. Violent head shakes would shudder from her rage. Words of supplication would drone from her soul to God.

Then the automaton would return to calm her. Otherwise she would have dissolved into a roiling puddle of nothingness.

Ralphie was going to make it. She willed herself to believe. Besides Doctor Robinson the surgeon and Doctor Bellamy, and the other medical staff, all the family had assured her constantly of this miracle, during every visit.

She sensed other comings and goings through a hazy weariness. Patty brought her homework every evening, silently gave her support from the corner of the room, kissed her mother good night at nine o'clock and left with an aunt at whose house she was staying. They assured each other that she would not meet the same fate as Ralphie because she would be very careful, prayed to God and His Blessed Mother, before her precious daughter walked out of the hospital room, to protect her, and half believed their plea was heard. Friends from work brought her sandwiches, and sometimes even fancy food, pasta salads and chicken a la king and from places like the Cheesecake Factory and Randy's kitchen. It all tasted like sawdust, but she shoved it down to survive. To show her gratitude.

Mr. Guerrero said she could have all the time off she needed. Emma would hold the fort and cover for her. That was so kind. After all she was Emma's assistant. She had only started working at his business about six weeks ago.

168

And she had insurance through them. God, what would she have done if not.

People, strangers, came forward to donate blood, since Ralphie's type was not so common. That second surgery had gone on and on, and on for seven hours and they needed all the blood they could get. What a nightmare. *Switch to auto pilot! Quick!*

Then the day after, even Ralph Senior had appeared. She would have turned her back on her ex if she had known he was coming. But he caught her at a weak moment. Her head was buried in her hands, she was moaning, "Please God, please sweet Jesus, please blessed Virgin, I'll do anything so that he lives." She had felt his hand on her shoulder and she had fallen into his arms.

All thoughts of his infidelity, of Rosa who stole him away and who made her weep a million tears, and he walking out on them three years ago, fell away. She found comfort and hope in his arms. They stood there looking at their boy, their only son wrapped like a mummy. They wept together, and prayed.

Two LAPD officers from the Devonshire division and a detective came by to interview, and took copious notes. Like as if they hadn't heard it all before.

"Nine o'clock in the evening, two weeks after Halloween, a car had cruised by on their street,' she repeated as rote.

"They had not seen it, absorbed as they were in waving goodbye to her sister and her family who had come to visit on Thursday, since it was Ralphie's birthday that weekend and the cousins couldn't make the party, because they were going to the UC Santa Barbara campus with their oldest. A tour for honors students. Perhaps they could return in time but don't count on it.

'My sister and her husband and their children had just driven off, and I was opening the front door, when I heard the buzz of bees accompanied by the crackle of fireworks

169

advancing on my back. And a strangled gurgle. And the thud of a body on the concrete behind me.'

She twisted around.

Her son lay face down with a bullet in his back and three in his upper body.

No, she had not seen anyone with a gun, or the make of the car. Had not heard voices, had not smelled a particular aftershave. How could she when their yard was thirty feet from the street?

Again she told the detective all she saw and smelled was blood spurting from pulsing holes. All she heard was silence as her son stretched dying in front of her eyes. Until a siren's wail sounded close to her ears. *How did they get there so fast? Did they have one of those at every street corner for the next killing when it happened.*

Then she realized that her own mouth was open as she screamed and screamed."

"Ma....Ma...a...Ma!"

The robot shot out of her seat, a yo-yo slung wildly by an inexperienced child. She grasped the buzzer. Red-rimmed eyes jerked wide-awake, stared transfixed at the bandaged being.

"Mama."

A nurse sauntered in.

"He called my name. He's alive. He's awake."

Deal Me a Card

CHAPTER 26

SOFIA AND ALFIE SAT in companionable silence at the small dining table in Sofia's one bedroom apartment. In honor of the holiday, a golden rayon tablecloth edged with green ruffles adorned the glass top, accentuated by a silk poinsettia for a centerpiece. As it trapped the candlelight, glitter sparkled on the white and red bracts.

To celebrate, the hostess wore a cream blouse, hand-embroidered with exotic mythical birds whose multi-colored plumage contrasted with the black of her full skirt. Her cheeks were pink from more than the heat of the oven as she felt her guest's appreciative glances.

The two budding chefs had just finished a hearty dinner of chicken cooked *nica* style,' that's the cuisine of Nicaragua if anybody asks," explained Sofie, grilled and topped with a mango-tomato sauce, and served with rice and beans and plantains.

After dining, Alfie had stacked the ceramic dishes, newly purchased, blue with a delicate hand painted design of lilies, and the silverware on the counter. They would wash them together later.

Now they were sipping Colombian coffee, and giving thanks.

Alfie began his reminiscing.

"Three years ago, no, about two and a half years ago, I was lying in the guest bedroom of my rescuers, cursing God and man.

"You know, Sofie, at that time, you could have sliced me open and all that would have oozed out would be yellow bile. I was so bitter, so angry. My throat felt like it was choked with thick vomit.

"All I did was pray to be dead.

171

"Oh, when that woman came in to see me, I would pretend. Give her a smile with curled lips, like this, moan like I was in pain, mutter "Oh … Oh Oh … Oh", twitch my arms so she would go away.

"She did go out of the room, always so silently, on tiptoe, crying and whispering, 'Poor man, oh, poor, poor man', like she really cared."

"But she did care, didn't she? I mean, she saved your life, right? Hospital care, sitting beside you for hours, days, and then taking you home?" Sofie interjected.

"Yeah, yeah. But why? So I could be a cripple for the rest of my life? You have to understand, Sofie. My leg was gone. My right leg was disappeared, like your son and husband in the middle of the night. Gone forever. And I was left behind, useless. Mother of God, I felt castrated!"

"Alfredo, it was just a leg!"

"Yeah right. If you lost a limb, you'd appreciate someone saying, it's only an arm!"

"Okay, okay, I'm sorry. Sorry. So how did you manage to get here from there?"

"Well, it was the man of the ranch. He got tired of seeing me moping around.

"Oh, I got out of bed after awhile, hobbled about on crutches. When I could not stand the inside of the house any longer, I'd limp outside to find a hole where I could curl up and die. Some days he would find me hiding behind the barn, smoking, drinking beer, singing crazy tarascan songs."

"What are tarascan songs? Maybe he had a right to be scared. Maybe he thought you were casting a spell on him?"

"As if! Tarascan means of the Indian language, tarasco. Got it?"

"Got it! Want another cup?"

"Sure. Anyway, he didn't like me too much. Was suspicious 'cause I was an alien. Like I dropped from a spaceship."

"A singing alien."

"It was his trap that almost killed me, so how could he talk? Also, his old lady is half Mexican, so I think he figured he owed me something.

"One day, when I threw up on his boots, man, those were shit-shiny boots before the vomit got on them."

"Okay, okay skip the details. We just had dinner."

"Excuse the language, sorry!" Alfie grimaced regret.

"While he was screaming and stamping his feet as if he was dancing the Mexican hat dance, I dragged myself over to his truck, pulled his rifle from the rack and put it to my head. For sure I was going to shoot myself. All the time I'm singing to some Indian gods. I think. I just liked the tune, and the words were comforting. My mother taught me.

"The guy, same fella, Pete, rushes over, boots smelly and stinky, shouting, 'No, No!' grabs the gun from my hands, throws it twenty feet away from us as if it's a live snake. Then he snatches the back of my neck, drags me to the faucet and washes me off.

"Doesn't care that I'm screaming about my missing part. Sits me down right there in the dirt. I'm trembling from the dunking and bawling like a new-born calf in his field. Tells me to shut up. He promises he would pay me for my work if I cleaned up and stopped giving his wife bad dreams and making her frigid."

"He said that?'

"Actually he said more stuff about that, but I don't want to embarrass you. But, yeah right, he blamed me for his limp dick. Sorry again!

"I remember I collapsed when he said that. I laughed, I cried, I rolled around in the dirt and vomit. What was I to do? I couldn't work on his ranch. Ride a horse? Brand a steer? Build a barn? What a joke. So I'm sulking, and crying like a silly woman.

"And he orders me, 'Go work in the kitchen!' So I did."

"So that's where you found your talent!"

173

Deal Me a Card

"Well, yes. I had a wheelchair and the cook taught me a lot. But I think I was threatening her, because she couldn't complain to the woman of the house how tired she was, and how her feet hurt. Not with Alfie the cripple hanging around, humming cheerfully, while chopping onions and stirring the *sopa*. This was not the magic kingdom or anything like that, you know. I still wanted to die. I tried but failed, so that made it worse."

"You didn't try to shoot yourself again, did you? What was it, pills?"

"No. Just continued to go on drinking binges every two weeks till I blacked out. Or I would sing eerie sounds while staring at the wall in my room. I had bad times when I thought I had my leg back in place. Weird stuff. Mr. Pete, he said I was catatonic. The others, and Ms. Elizabeth, they said I was in a depressed state. They wanted to give me medicine to be happy. I said 'Give me a new leg. That's what I need. That'll make me healthy again.'"

"And they did.

"There was this group, they call themselves the Sanctuary Movement. They helped me a lot."

"Really?" Sofie gasped. "Wow! Mother of God, bless them. They're still around. They were there for me when I crossed over. You want to hear about it?"

"Sure. They got me this prosthetic, and then helped me come to Los Angeles. Here I am!

"But what about you?"

Preparing to listen Alfie leaned back in his chair as he took another sip of coffee. Sofie hunched forward, her hands clenching on the table as she remembered.

"It was nineteen eighty-three, maybe eighty-four. I can't even remember what month.

"After I knew I could never find my son and husband, never, *nunca, nunca, nunca*, I stumbled from one country to another. I would keen crazily so children and even grown men would hide behind trees to avoid me as I wove from one

174

side of the path to the other. Walking alone, *nadie, nadie, nadie,* nobody wished to pick me up when I fell on my face. Then one day I jumped on a bus, going from San Salvador to Guatemala. I think. I didn't know where I was going. All I knew to do was move forward, walking or being taken somewhere by somebody. Far, far away, from the misery. I was *triste, triste, triste.* Always sad."

"Sounds like my favorite song," Alfie muttered dolefully.

"Next memory, I'm sitting in the bushes waiting for the freight train. We were at the Mexican border by then, after days on our feet. I don't recall when or how the bus trip ended. Some men enticed me, told me they knew the way, they would be my guides. So I paid them off, for the train ride and peace. I gave those filthy robbers three rings, gold with diamonds which I had hidden in my underwear. I sewed them in there.

"After the pay-off they left me alone because they knew I was a lunatic and I would tear their eyes out if they tried anything. Or I would cut off their balls before I went down. I had waved my butcher knife at them a few times. Slashed one in the left thigh when he grabbed me. Missed his cock by inches. That man is thanking God to this day, or he's rotting in hell! Meanwhile I screamed and screamed so everyone around knew what was happening. Those *pendejos* sons-of-bitches backed off."

"And all I did was throw up on Mr. Peter's shoes!" Alfie casually crossed his left knee across his prosthetic, cautiously, just in case.

But Sofie Perez was too lost in her reminiscing to overhear or notice.

"There were some others, nice people, from my country, a few farmers, seven young girls already raped and beaten but, my God, so brave, and we lay together in the bushes, waiting."

"Did they make it across with you?"

Deal Me a Card

"I don't know, Alfie. I honestly do not know. We were like flakes of skin that either the army or the rebels had flayed off, drifting light and mindless in the wind, and the air would howl through the pores, and sometimes the pieces would soar high like they knew something, recognized the place ahead. Sometimes they would fall and disappear into the bloody earth. So who knows?"

"Go on with your travels. What then?"

"Miles and miles, hundreds of miles, the train chugged along, passing many towns. One I remember because I was choking on some drops of water and the name sounded like me about to die, Coatzacoalcos. But you see, I recovered."

"Thank the Blessed Mother and her Son!"

"Yeah. I think they must have been there also in that other place I remember. Tierra Blanca. I was delirious. The sun was right in my eyes, white all around me, throbbing in my ears. And I was ready to pass out. We had stopped to buy some food, those of us who had any money left. I lolled against a wall in the corner near the train. This old woman walks up to me. She stares into my face and takes out this bleach-smelly rag and wiped my cheeks and lips and eyelids, all the time muttering some prayer, or maybe some incantation. Maybe she was a witch, and sticks a plastic bottle of tepid water in my hand, and two slices of bread with cheese inside into the other. That was the Mother of God, all right. I was in paradise. Well for at least a few hours."

"How did you get here?"

"It wasn't over yet.

"There was all this talk, frantic rumors going up and down the roof of the train. You know, that's where we lay, hiding. We never actually got to travel in the train. We paid for the view, not for the comfort," Sofie smiled sardonically. "We gave our money to be vulnerable, not to be secure. We were the mongrel border crossers, the *desechables,* those who were expendable, disposable like dirt. Who knew or cared if we lived or vanished. Word was the mafia was in

176

charge in some place called Saltillo. So we better go to Monterrey instead if we wanted to live. Right. After all this struggle and agony, we should ask ourselves, 'Do you, Sofie Perez, really want to live?' I answered, 'Yeah, I do'."

So we jumped off one train, or other people hurled us off if we were too weak to force ourselves, and scrambled onto a freight train that stopped in Matamoros."

"And?"

"I got to take a shower with fifteen other women. After three weeks riding the rails."

"Ah."

"Two small women, brown like me with veils on their heads, with strong arms, they reached out to us as we walked out of the railway station. Led us to a house of hospitality, that's what they called it. They gave me clothes to make me look like a human being again. Mad eyes, a limping skeleton with straggly hair and broken fingernails, jagged toenails.

"But human, smelling of lavender soap. And clothed. A skirt, with blue grassy designs, down to my ankles so my skinny legs were invisible. A white blouse, sleeves to the elbows, with navy buttons down the front. I looked in the mirror. Yes, there was a mirror on the wall near the front door. So we could check and make sure we were all dressed, and pretty, and ready for society before we walked out the front door. And I was! Well, dressed and ready for something to happen. I still had one gold bracelet in the hem of my panties.

"So I bounce down the three steps, I'm all full of energy now. Looking for fresh air. See a bus that says "Houston, Texas." Has a big dog on the side, running. Leaping. Makes me think of my Missie back at home, dead now probably, shot, eaten. I don't know. I start to cry. All the oomph flew out of me. I'm so lonely, every bone aches now as I creak along, my sandals slapping, slapping on the ground that's so hot the sun's rays quiver and dance with the dust. Made my head go round and round, and I wanted to

177

Deal Me a Card

throw up. And I'm thirsty but I don't want to go, can't go back to that place, to El Salvador."

"Here's a Kleenex."

"Thanks.

"There's a newspaper stand with a headline about Salvadoran guerrillas being defeated and twenty-one killed by the army the past weekend. I lean against the wall of a store that sells children's toys and clothing, and I break down. I'm sobbing, sobbing, swallowing big gulps of air. Trying not to make a sound 'cause who knows where the *migra* or its spies lurk. I can't go back!

"And then, this woman stops and speaks to me. Another angel, she takes me by the hand very gently, talks my language so softly and my tears can't stop flowing. But it's strange, I'm not scared anymore.

"I let her lead me to safety. And to food. We had this meal, not much, tacos with meat and cheese and onions, chiles. The juice was dripping down my chin. I swiped it with my fingers and sucked the liquid. Nothing would escape my mouth. was so hungry and every crumb and drop tasted like something from Randy's stove.

"*Entonces*, later, I'm in another small office on a back street. This woman, my savior, she's tall and thin and has blond hair and rimless glasses sitting on the end of her nose. Eleanor is her name. She's the leader, knows whom to call. All the time she's giving orders to her helpers. I'm wondering how she can breathe.

"The two young men, your age, both have beards, *gringos* speaking Spanish, one on the phone, the other with paper all over his desk. They're listening to five other travelers. People like me. One man, two women and their *ninos,* kids. Maybe they helped them get clean. Gave them lunch and medicine. The two children looked like they were sick with fever.

Deal Me a Card

"By five that same evening, one of the guys walks me to the bus. He puts a ticket in my hand. Three days later I'm in Los Angeles."

"There are many angels around.

"Tell me about it!"

"I'll tell you. That woman, Eleanor, as she kissed me 'adios' put a card in my hand. I read it later as we ride North. It says El Rescate and there's an address in the City of Los Angeles. When the bus arrives in LA, it's late so I had to sleep one night in the bus station. Only that one night. So I set out in the morning. I'm all eager and refreshed once more. I show the card to some people I meet on the street. And they tell me about a new place. They call it a clinic named after Archbishop Romero....Well, you know what I did."

"You started to cry again. No. I'm just joking. Don't pull that knife on me!"

"You're such an idiot! But you're right.

"I started to weep. Here I was in the United States and the first place I find welcome is in the arms of the martyr. I practically run there. Up and down streets. Got lost a couple of times. But those people who pointed me in the right direction, they saw I needed help. Some kind of stepped back. I was in my madwoman frenzy mode again. Calmer, but my eyes must have given them nightmares for a year! Man, I was sick. But here I am."

"And you look alright now."

"There's a man at that clinic place. He's another saint. He healed my wounds. A doctor, Alberto Hernandez saved my life. If I could kiss the ground he walks on, I would. But I'm going to send him a Christmas card instead."

"We can go to the bookstore tomorrow. I want to send one to Ms. Evanson. Ms. Elizabeth Evanson and her husband. We two have friends everywhere. We're the lucky ones," Alfie smiled.

179

Deal Me a Card

The couple were reluctant to break the affinity the evening had created.

Sofie picked her deck of cards off the shelf.

"Let's play poker for an hour or so, before I take you home,"

"You love to gamble, don't you? I see you with the other students playing before class. They invite me over here sometimes to join you all. But I'm too busy. Why do you play so much?" Alfie asked, curious about her past-time.

"For peanuts maybe, or pretzels, or candy. No high stakes. I don't play to win or lose." Sofie, holding the pack of cards vertical, tapped them gently on the table.

"*La verdad?* The truth? These games give me a chance to hold reality in my fingers. *Realidad en las manos*! I have the whole world in my hands."

She gave a little laugh, then continued,

"I never know what hand I will hold. It's a risk, a gamble, but in friendly circumstances.

"Life, that's different. Once you put your two feet on the ground in the morning…"

"I put my one foot on the ground," Alfie interrupted, smiling.

"I love your sense of humor," Sofie smiled back, then went on,

"When we get out of bed each morning, we have to gamble every waking minute. *Tenemos que arriesgarnos cada minuto!*

"We take risks. Jump forward. Even when we fold, we're already preparing for the next game.

"Look at all we experienced to get here. The stakes were high. Sometimes we lost, but we never quit the game. We kept moving forward.

"Poker brings my life into perspective. *Vamos a jugar!* Let's play!"

****

Deal Me a Card

What's this Thanksgiving Day thing all about, anyway, Eddy wondered to himself.

Five-thirty that morning he had slammed the alarm shut. Plumped his pillow and rolled over on his left side towards the window. No need to struggle out in the dark this morning. He could sleep all day. No work and no school beckoned to him.

He drifted off, slept until ten, surrounded by an uncommon lull. The usual traffic bombardment of rattling trucks, revving engines and irate beep-beep-beeping horns was in a temporary cease-fire. Determined to move slowly to savor the respite, he stretched himself erect, then slumped on the sofa, slurped a cup of instant Folgers's as he watched CNN.

At noon or thereabouts President George H. Bush appeared on a replay all dressed in his Sunday best, the way presidents dressed all the time even on holidays. *Who would want that job, encouraging every citizen to recognize the true meaning of the holiday and to try to serve someone less fortunate than himself or herself.* Talked about the winds of change blowing through the Americas except for Panama, Nicaragua and Cuba.

The United States was at war with Panama. Because Senor Noriega was the main man over there. The US wanted someone else to be in charge. They used to support Noriega. Even trained him in the United States. *Wonder if he got a Ph.D or just a certificate for most improved in English and Perfect Attendance.*

As Eddy sipped his second cup of coffee, no cream, no sugar, another white man, also in a suit, was explaining with a very serious face that Manolo was a marked man now. Wanted for drug trafficking, aiding and abetting the Colombia cartel, refusing to comply with American dictates, consorting with Cuba. A whole laundry list of crimes. Looking like he had one helping of turkey too many, the newsman mentioned the words 'CIA' and "assassination."

181

Deal Me a Card

You might love the USA, but don't ever, ever, cross its path. It sure went after traitors with a vengeance. Bam, bam. You're dead. No more Mr. Nice Guy. Only the American GI staring at you down the barrel of a gun. Poor Manny!

Eddy sank back on the beer-soaked-and-dried couch. He shifted his ass until the broken spring poked his gluts less painfully. As he dug his teeth into the beefy burrito he had nuked for lunch; they didn't have frozen turkey burritos in the supermarket or he would have bought some in honor of the celebration; some juice dribbled down his chin. Juggling the paper plate on his chest, he reached for a roll of paper towels. He couldn't complain.

He virtually patted himself on the back for watching gringo TV and reading gringo newspapers. His teacher told him this was a great way to learn. Of course it wasn't easy, but he forced himself and it was becoming much clearer. Plus he was keeping up with current events. That's what Ms. Bustamante at the Center called it. Knowing what was going on in the world.

She had giggled, hiding her mouth with her hand in that cute way that she had, *so cute he wanted to grab it in his fingers, raise it to his lips and plant a kiss in her palm,* and said "it would impress your date to be able to talk about world affairs, severe weather, and film critiques." And she might be right, once he got the words down and found another woman to have a real affair with.

Boy, I had really blew it with Emma. What was I thinking, to be able to attain a lady like her? Me with only seven years of education in that little village of Agua Blanca.

Though he had been a pretty good fisherman, number one in the village, and when he hunted rabbits he caught a lot of them. His family had not gone hungry many, many nights because of his skills. But here in this cosmopolitan place, nobody hunted and fished. Just roasted turkey or microwaved burritos.

Emma was so brilliant, with all those years of studying at the university, and traveling, and not even American, the only thing they had in common, and so smart.

Eddy mused, *We were pretty good together when we were making out, though.* He got a hard-on just whispering her name in his half-sleep. Better stop it. If she could stab him to death with a look he'd be six feet under right this minute. Best to forget her.

He had a long ways to go. But he was getting there.

In a way he felt cleansed. Maybe only a little bit purer, but a whole bunch better than a month ago when he and Irene broke up. He had not touched a drop for twenty-five days, thirteen hours and fifteen minutes. His breath was sweet, his gut tauter. He could see clearly, no more crimson zig-zags behind his eyeballs.

Even better, there had been an announcement on the center bulletin board and he responded. Carmelita, the clerk, *she had lovely eyes, and lips and her hair was so soft and wavy he wanted to run his fingers through it, maybe he should ask her for a date,* had told him all about the eleven-year old boy on the verge of death. He had never given blood before, but if he could walk three weeks through a desert chased by wolves and pumas and survive, he could live through a nurse poking him in the arm. So he donated.

That must be what the president meant.

CHAPTER 27

"YOU'RE SENDING INVITATIONS to all these people? That's kinda formal. Like the wedding."

"No, silly," Sarita laughed, "we just want to keep track of all the friends we're inviting to this holiday party. You know how it gets. You talk to one person, they tell all their friends if you don't specify that they only bring their dates. We can all have fun, there can be lots of bonhomie. But we don't want it to get messy and crowded. Also have to think of food and drink."

"I see," Daniel said, as he and Richard continued to pore over a computer-generated guest list on the round glass-topped dining table.

The three were sitting in Sarita's studio apartment in Winnetka, one week after Thanksgiving.

"Good idea to be organized. Takes a woman, right Richard?" he added digging his elbow into his brother's ribs.

"We may be college students but we're not beer-guzzling frat boys tripping and slipping on each other's throw-up. Sure, beer, wine, hard stuff, but civilized. No cops coming out because of some idiot's hellacious behavior. We're far away here, in the hills. But after that body and all …" Richard asserted.

"Since when did you become all hi-society and straitlaced? Bro, I've been there when you put it away like there'd be a drought tomorrow, and had to carry you home," Daniel taunted.

"Well, people grow up," Sarita lilted, clasping Richard's hand in hers.

"Ah, ha, got it!"

Daniel smiled, glanced around the dining-living room as the couple gave each other a more-than-affectionate smooch. He got up to admire the Machu Picchu abstract watercolor on the wall and to scan the bookshelf. Some aromatic incense perfumed the air. He changed the subject,

"I don't see Patrick Henderson on the list."

Richard gave Sarita one last, lasting kiss and retorted,

"You've got to be kidding. He and his twin move in a different stratosphere. You know, someone said they've spent over a million since it happened. Sarita, you know what '*it*' is?

"Of course. Who wouldn't? About that million. One of the women in my Econ class said she saw him on Rodeo Drive, driving a Jeep Wrangler. Then later, when she and her mother were having lunch at Michel's, he walks in, stops at their table to say 'Hi.'

Richard queried on a voice of awe, "Your classmates hang out on Rodeo Drive? At Michel's. You could drop a hundred and fifty for lunch at that joint."

"Not exactly a joint. Sandy's parents run with the Hollywood crowd, are part of that crowd. The 'let's do lunch so we can dream up ways to make millions more' cult. Her Dad's a television sit-com producer. So naturally, they schmoozed with James and Meredith. Sandy noticed Patrick was wearing a new Rolex. What really distressed Sandy's mom, she's rich but practical, was when he said he had dropped out of UCLA and was going professional."

Richard broke in,

"That's what I've heard also. I played a few matches against Jeff before all these troubles. But Patrick has the real strength on the course. Ron, my partner, when I played this weekend, practicing at the Northridge university campus, told me the rumor is Patrick's paying his golf coach sixty grand a year. Now that's ambition."

Sarita picked up the train of thought,

"Be that as it may, Sandy was not enthralled. She said he was, has always been, a grenade. Pull that pin and all hell will break loose. Her mother would not allow her to date either of the brothers.

Deal Me a Card

"Last year, there were some other hush-hush whispers at parties that those guys stole thousands of dollars from their friends. For God's sake! And complicit granddaddy got the best lawyers to smooth things out. Because his grandsons are too young to know any better!

"Then there were more nasty tales spread about a girlfriend and an abortion, for heaven's sake! Sarita smirked. "So Sandy's mom is thanking her lucky stars that she put her foot down. She knew all along the gang of seven - there's a sister who remained back east with her parents - and attends Harvard, was way too dysfunctional a family to get close to. Those twins are spoiled rotten weird. Rich, but not holiday season party material. You're spot on, Richard, my love. They're not in our league."

"A whole heap of funny stuff surrounded those homicides. I was assisting one of the clients, Suzanna, about two weeks ago. Suzanna's daughter had brought her to the center to enroll in classes," Daniel interjected.

Richard looked intently at his brother

"The daughter's name is Miranda, right?"

Daniel nodded. His brother continued,

"Emma told us about Miranda's graduation day last spring. Boy, she had every administrator sitting upright and uptight in their seats. Except the bishop. Apparently, he didn't have a clue."

"Tell us, tell us, Richard!" Sarita begged, all agog.

"Yeah, go ahead. I'll tell you about the other situation afterwards," Daniel urged his brother.

All three enjoyed stories from the community and its residents. Richard began,

"Well she said Brother Keith's account of the event was hilarious. He described it something like this. 'We'd decided unanimously that Miranda was going to process with her class. What an example!

"You know how the V.I.P.s, the so very, very important people, sit on the stage, yes including the guidance folk, for

186

the annual pomp and circumstance. All of us decked out in our Sunday best. Nodding, graciously, smiling toothily. But underneath the brassy exterior, the whole team was pretty nervous. Nobody had informed the bishop of course. We all agreed it was easier to apologize later!

"So we watched with bated breath, white-knuckled, clutching the arms of our chairs. Then as one, the whole illustrious band leaned forward, at least a dozen pairs of eyes, glued to Miranda, eight and a half months pregnant, standing in line with her peers, inching along under the morning sun, then laboriously climbing the four steps to the stage.

"Finally as we exhaled our collective breath, she waddled up to His Excellency, shook his hand politely, accepted his congratulations, and took hold of her diploma with an enigmatic, serene smile.

"Then she, the first one in her family to graduate from high school, plodded off the stage and down the four stairs without faltering or missing a beat. Her gown hid her swollen belly quite nicely thank you … and you'll be pleased to know the baby was sweet enough to wait two more weeks before entering the world.'

"Another success story from St Anselmo High. They believe in doing good. Walk the Christian talk," Daniel remarked then added, "I had the pleasure of holding the baby. It's a boy, really cute. Breast fed, you can always tell. Don't know how Miranda does it. She's taking two courses at the college too. Of course they have childcare on campus. Still, she's got spunk.

"Anyway, that's what has inspired Suzanna to begin classes there. Apparently, if her daughter can do it, so can she. And now she has an American grandson. She'll have to speak English with him.

"Now, back to my other story. We were reviewing her, that's Suzanna's, skills chart. She explained how she's been

187

Deal Me a Card

housecleaning for years. In Las Estrellitas, among the Hollywood Hills. On Acorn Street no less."

"No kidding," Richard said.

"I swear to God. Described how she worked for movie stars, some other *ricos*. She said sometime ago she scrubbed the toilets in the home of a very funny comedian. She's seen him on TV. She told me, 'Like a clown, Mr. Daniel, he's crazy, loco.'"

"That's cute," Sarita laughed.

Daniel continued, "Of course she doesn't have a clue about who's who. She told me she was sad about the old senor and poor old *senora* that got beaten and then dragged off from that house, because that was where she had worked for the clown. What she had seen on the news was terrible. She couldn't understand all the words but the pictures were gruesome, God rest their souls.

"She got really excited telling me all about what she had watched on TV and what she knew in reality about the crime scene.

"Imagine all that blood, Mr. Daniel," she said. "Very difficult to clean blood for the carpets and those fancy rugs. And it's not only blood, but there's vomit and food, all stepped in and smeared across the parquet floors after a party, and in the bedrooms sometimes, my heavens all those beautiful gowns thrown around without a thought, and dirty underwear mixed in with shoes. And these are rich people, Mr. Daniel. You'd think they would know better. But who am I to talk?"

"So she's got the inside scoop, so to speak," Richard said.

"But it's more than that, Richard, Sarita. She went on and on.

"She told me how that night, in June sometime, she had to work very late at one of the houses, helping with a party. She'd started at noon."

"My God, Mr. Danny, I went non-stop until eleven, eleven twenty-five. I was too tired. My feet were like lead. But I had to stay to clean up, around the pool too, all those dripping cold towels.

"I was hoping to catch the last bus. Otherwise, I would have to call my son or daughter. So inconvenient especially she's with the baby now. So I'm walking really quickly down the road. And I pass by the *payaso*'s home. Not his anymore, but you know what I mean, and there are these two boys in the yard with policemen. I'm thinking people in this neighborhood aren't going to be happy. Very rich people you know. Fancy cars, houses like castles. They're going to think the gangs from East LA have come to rob someone. Them next.

"One of the young men is screaming. Very loudly, Ohmigo! Ohmigo! Canbelieve. Canbelieveit. Ohmigo! And the other young man, he's running up and down. Straight at a tree. Then staggering backwards, almost falling, then forward one more time. I couldn't understand why's he's hitting his head on the tree trunk. Like a madman. The police are grabbing at his shirt. He shakes them off. Runs at the tree again. The other man tried to stop him. His head must have hurt the next morning.

"I slowed down to watch. Thank goodness nobody saw me or maybe they would take me in, arrest me for trespassing. I've never been arrested, ever, Mr. Daniel. Not even a ticket for jaywalking. I can't drive. So of course I missed my bus. But Miranda came for me. Her husband, he works the early shift. He stayed at home to look after the baby."

Richard added in a thoughtful voice, "Yeah, the reporters, on TV and in the Times, said they were distraught that night, blaming the mob."

Daniel's thought process was unbroken,

"That's not all. You'd think I wore a Roman collar that way women flock to me with their little stories and secrets."

189

"It's your chubby cheeks and kissy-kissy lips, and sad eyes. Gets them every time," Richard retorted.

"You know I can't help feeling others' pain."

"Oh gag me with a spoon, Daniel. What else have you heard?"

"Well, this other lady, Anabel, works the same gig. The same street.

"Lots of money. Lots of help. The dough flow, down to the great unwashed-but-willing-to- wash masses."

"The same Saturday night, she finished work a little earlier, about ten o'clock, and walked down the same route, along Acorn Street.

"She kept talking, giving me one strange detail after another.

'Mr. Dan as I passed by one of the homes, huge like the rest of them, I saw two figures walk from their car to the house. They each carried something, looked like sticks Like when people back home, in the small little towns go out in the forest to collect wood They come back with a small branch or bunch of twigs. Like that. But I kept on walking by.

'When I was about a two hundred steps down the street, I heard popping sounds, firecrackers. I'm from El Salvador, you know that, right, so I didn't want even to think it was gunfire. Then I started to move really quickly, half-run, half-walk. Scared to run, since somebody might come after me, thinking I did a bad thing and was escaping. That I fired a gun. Or maybe someone might shoot me in the back. Or, Mother of God have mercy, some evil persons might kidnap me. I have no money, you know, for ransom.'

"She said she was terrified the last two months, scared the police would come after her. For information. Or maybe the kidnappers-killers saw her and wanted her dead too. She was shaking as she choked all this up to me.

"'Leave one war, jump into another,' tears running down her cheeks. 'All I want is to live in peace.'

190

Deal Me a Card

"Even so, she still asked whether she should go to the police and report what she saw. I told her no.

"The cops can be really mean when somebody is nervous and I don't want any insults and roughness. Especially since she'd be trying to do the right thing and speak carefully. Then she'll stutter and hum and haw. They'll throttle her. She doesn't need that!"

Sarita broke her silence, insisting, "But she should tell someone in authority."

"Well, she told me. This thing is too high profile. Almost as notorious as that other double murder case in the news. That other pair of brothers. Almost seems like a copy cat. You know what the press will do if they get a hold of her. Those damn reporters. They'll accuse her of being an attention-seeking wetback whacko. No way. What did she witness anyway?"

Sarita spoke firmly, almost shrilly. She was adamant.

"Two males with 'sticks', substitute 'shotguns', entering the Henderson home at approximately ten o'clock to brutally beat, kidnap, and then murder the grandparents of Patrick and Jeff?"

Richard interrupted the discussion that was heating up, to lower the rising volume of words. He was not willing go down the righteous road the two were cruising.

"Come on, come on, we're not detectives assigned to the case. We've merrier times ahead than those guys. And no matter what, their grandparents are dead. Have a little compassion! What a lousy Christmas season for the brothers. Unlike us, Daniel. We have everything."

He paused to give his girlfriend a squeeze around her waist. She was still troubled, too distracted to respond. So Richard continued,

"Let's get back to the list. The numbers are looking manageable if we keep the guests to about seventy-five or eighty-five. Remember to include Maribel and George."

As he sensed the tension still hovering over the three of them, frozen sleet about to descend, he added,

"I mentioned to Sofie I'd like her and Alfredo, you know the two students from Randolfo's culinary arts classes, to prepare the food. They'll give us a good price, and we'll have Central American food, tamales of course, and the eternal honey-baked ham for the *gringo* die-hards."

He had hit the right note. Always the diplomat, Richard knew that the mention of food never failed to lead to happier channels.

****

"The additional truck-load of building materials will be here by Monday. I spoke to the Boise warehouse this morning first thing," Emma explained.

She listened as Vern Johnson, foreman of the building site, expressed his frustration over the delivery delay. The two were standing in the hallway outside Emma's office at Jones and Guerrero Company.

"So the materials will arrive late, and the workers will stand around idle? And they get paid for doing nothing! " queried Mr. Johnson.

"No," Emma replied patiently. "The men can start at eight, regular hours. They can prepare the area. You can review the plans and strategy for the day and the week ahead. Go over the changes the developer talked about."

Her smile became more fixed as she continued to listen to the animated voice. She looked at his jowly face but her eyes focused on a painting of the snow-capped Sierras over his shoulder.

"Sounds like I need a classroom for instruction." Johnson grumbled, frowning vexedly.

"No, it won't be like a classroom. You can walk around and discuss each townhouse unit and the modifications," Emma said, placating him. "Mr. Guerrero said he'd have our truck ready so the materials can be loaded immediately

Deal Me a Card

without being stored beforehand. I'll be there, checking the serial numbers on the invoice and the warehouse people can help me. Two of us should be able to handle the inventory."

Johnson asked, "The lumber is arriving, Saturday or Sunday?"

She was nodding as the man asked the question.

"Yes, the semi with the lumber will arrive over the weekend. So it'll be waiting for us in the parking lot on Monday. We plan on getting here by six-thirty, so your crew can count on starting the framing at nine."

"Ms. Emma, thanks for the heads-up and information. You know how delays cost all of us money. You're a patient woman to take my griping."

She put her hand lightly on his shoulder. "Sure, no problem. That's my job. I'll see you later. Have a great weekend. Get some Christmas shopping done, okay. Say hello to Rita and the kids. Bye Vern."

As soon as she entered her office, the phone rang.

"Jones and Guerrero Construction. Good afternoon, Brother. How are things at St. Anselmo's?"

As the school counselor spoke, Emma pulled a blank piece of paper and took notes.

"Does Martin needs a helping hand again?" she asked.

"Not this time. In fact he came to me with a serious request for his girlfriend," Brother Keith responded.

"Oh, his girlfriend. That's Emerald, sorry, sorry Esmeralda. Is she all right?"

"Yes, healthy, in her fifth month," the brother confirmed.

"Good. Good. So Martin is being the responsible Daddy and making sure she goes to the clinic for check-ups and pre-natal classes. But what seems to be the problem?"

"She's failed her pre-tests for the GED a couple of times, and refused to take the science section. Martin's frustrated since she has all day to study, at home or at the center."

Deal Me a Card

"You're right, Brother, she has no excuse not to pass."

Emma sighed. As Brother Keith spoke, she twirled a strand of her hair around her index finger.

"She claims she's depressed because her best friend is so sad and inconsolable."

"Right, she and Brenda are close. Yes, I know all about Brenda. The girlfriend of the young man who was murdered. I was there the day they found the body. Out there at the Guillermo Guerrero Ranch. And we were all at the funeral."

Emma's next sigh was even heavier, as she remembered the cemetery sodden with the tears of so many doomed youth.

"You think they'll call a truce for Jesus' birthday? Or is it wishful thinking. Something to ask for, in my letter to Santa. You're never too old, Brother. But it would be ironic if some gangbanger called Jesus gets nailed in the next two weeks by a rival called Roman," Emma muttered

"It's well within the realm of possibility, unfortunately," Brother Keith replied. But the man of God could not keep the smile out of his voice.

Emma tried to sound contrite,

"I know, I know, thanks for indulging me and laughing at my sophomoric blasphemy. My dark humor is rearing its ugly head. You're probably shocked. But the abominations these kids inflict on each other and their families is enough to make anyone lose faith."

Emma doodled on the sheet of paper in front of her as Brother Keith continued,

"It's gotten so Brenda can't stop crying and will not be comforted. Martin told me Esmeralda confided in him. Brenda knows exactly who killed her boyfriend."

Emma leaned back in her chair and massaged her forehead above her brows. Her head throbbed. Discomfort had taken root with the foreman's agitated discourse. And now this.

194

Deal Me a Card

"Look, I'll talk this over with Guillermo. We're meeting with Doc Velasquez and one of his employees. Actually they're all longtime friends. You might know of him. A man they call 'Big M.' He was in prison for thirty years. Can you believe it? In at fifteen, out at forty-five. They did things differently back then. Now he's a suspect! The police are fingering him. But he's mellow, calm. Thirty years inside and finding God will do that to you, I guess. Live each day by the motto, Keep your cool and place everything in His hands. They'll be very interested in what you and Martin or Brenda has to tell them.

"One of them, or I, will probably call you next week. Oops, no, not me. I'm leaving town for Christmas. Visiting family in Florida. I'll be away for ten days.

"Brother, have a blessed holiday. One of the men will definitely be in touch. Bye."

CHAPTER 28

FIVE PEOPLE GREETED EACH OTHER. They stood in the archway in front of the entrance to the pastor's inner sanctum. Three days after Christmas, the rectory and church were quiet, in a peaceful lull. The parish was taking a breather after the gloriously hectic weeks leading up to December twenty-fifth.

The modest church parking lot was empty except for four cars. One belonged to a recent widow who was inside lighting a candle, for her spouse departed after forty-seven years. Father Reilly owned the black Mazda. The four visitors had arrived in the Volkswagen and Toyota pick-up.

"Well, hello everyone. Merry Christmas to you. Hope you all had a blessed day with your families. Let's go inside."

From the faces looking back at him, he realized serious business lay ahead, so with this brief greeting, the priest unlocked the door and ushered his guests into the secretary's empty office. He continued,

"It was good to see you at Midnight Mass, Martin, Esmeralda."

The pastor and the pregnant young woman embraced. The priest shook the teenage father's hand. After this warmer welcome, they stepped back, all smiles.

Esmeralda's face glowed. Her lips were lightly touched with a rose lipstick that matched the pink healthy shine of her cheeks. A mop of sparkling black shoulder-length curls surrounded her Madonna face. Five foot eight Martin, slim, broad-shouldered from exercising on the football field, gazed down adoringly at the diminutive mother of his child.

"Yes, Father, it was beautiful. And I loved the choir and the guitars and trumpets. I'm such a wuss. Always cry when the Baby Jesus is born with all those angels around Him.

Deal Me a Card

"My mom and Dad and my two sisters ... you know them, Caterina and Lucia, one's in the fourth and the other's in fifth grade ....You baptized them. They were with us. I persuaded Martin to come along. He's part of the family now. Actually gets along with my Dad," she added, her eyes twinkling.

"Yes, I can see that. And who's this young lady?"

The older man turned his face to the other female in the circle. Her demeanor lacked a similar joy of the season. Her eyes were downcast when they were not darting, frenzied black marbles come-alive, from person to person in the small cluster of five. In contrast to Esmeralda's shimmering green dress that seemed to gently stroke her rounded belly in rhythm with her movements, the young woman's black dress hung slack from her thin shoulders.

Too late, Father Reilly realized his slip.

Tears flooded the teenager's eyes, threatening to overflow onto her sallow cheeks, whose pallor was accentuated by daubs of rouge. Strangled words,

"Don't you remember Felipe?"

Esmeralda stepped in as smoothly as possible, "This is Brenda, my very best friend. We've known each other from the cradle. Well, our moms used to live in the same apartment complex so they went shopping together. And they'd take us along in the strollers."

The priest's words rushed into the fray, a faucet sputtering compassion, "I'm very pleased to meet you again. And of course I remember Felipe. Rest his soul. It's just that, to be very honest, you've lost so much weight, my child, and …"

"It's been very hard, Father. I can't get over it. Nothing seems to matter. I'm living with it every second."

The words were stumbling out of Brenda's heart. But Esmeralda knew it was another good time to interrupt.

"But what is truly wonderful is that, she's going to be the baby's godmother."

197

Deal Me a Card

"I'm so pleased to hear that. It's good you've all come to meet with me now. There's always so much to prepare for a new baby, and sometimes we forget the most important things."

Father Reilly struggled to address his platitudes to Brenda. His inner shepherd's voice urged him to take her in his arms in a paternal hug and comfort her. But her stiff stance forbade any such gesture.

So he turned to the fourth visitor. He wore a fuzzy-azure, ribbed cashmere sweater, over an open-necked striped shirt and neat designer jeans. A lock of his black, wavy hair bounced on his forehead. His pouting lips were accustomed to drawing back in a warm smile. Now a slight involuntary twitch marred them. The young man, peering through black-rimmed glasses, was listening to the priest with a furrowed brow.

"And, Mr. Guerrero, Daniel. Will you be the godfather?"

"Yes, Padre. Martin and Esmeralda and I have become good friends. So I'm quite honored."

Now Daniel shook his head emphatically. He leaned forward. Placed a firm hand on Brenda's bony shoulder. His tone was sharp, urgent, "But there's something else we must talk about. This murder, homicide, killing, whatever anyone wants to call it for political or legal or judicious reasons, is eating away at all our lives. Look at us now, this minute. It's hanging over our heads like the sword of Damocles. We've tiptoed round and round like a bunch of cowardly, hand-wringing Indians trotting around a wagon train. If we don't act, another shot will be fired and there's another dead Indian.

"A couple of things happened in the last two days. So we put our heads together, decided to come to you. We thought this is neutral ground where we can talk and make some decisions."

Martin broke in,

Deal Me a Card

"I called Daniel last night. Esmeralda and Brenda had lunch yesterday. And when Esmeralda got home, she was almost hysterical."

"But I didn't throw things. I just cried when I was telling you about it,"Esmerelda protested.

"No, baby, you were pretty far gone. And we can't have you all worked up when you're having our baby. I read in the library how the mother's peace of mind is of primary importance so that baby develops a calm spirit."

The two other men silently showered their much younger acquaintance with openly admiring looks as he continued unruffled,

"So Father we really need your support with this problem. May we sit in your office and talk? Tell you all about Brenda's sorrow?"

The priest ushered the preoccupied group further into the sanctum. When they were all seated in the priest's room, with the door closed, Martin continued,

"It's not just that she's sad. Besides the grief, she's had to carry the burden of knowing, of seeing."

"Father," interjected Daniel, "Brenda witnessed the killing of her boyfriend. And she's in mortal fear of her own life and the lives of her family, if she tells."

"Oh, my children, my children," the priest shook his head slowly.

There was a long forbearing pause as Brenda, the subject of their earnest discussion, after a new outburst of sobbing, now finished blowing and wiping her nose. She had deliberately taken the narrow armchair in the corner where her face was in the shadows. Over her head hung a hand-carved wooden Nativity scene from Guatemala in honor of the season. Her glance went up to the Mother and Child. Perhaps their warmth, as they sat cradled in silver stars as a golden crescent moon shone above them, gave her consolation. She wiped her eyes, blew her nose discreetly once more, twisted the sodden disintegrating tissue in her

199

fingers. Daniel handed her another from the box on the desk. When she spoke, Brenda's voice was tremulous, the lump in her throat making her tone raspy.

"I think, I know I should be the one talking. But I cry so much, it seems hopeless. All of you were, are so good to me, coming here. And Father, I know this is like confession, right? You won't tell anyone else."

"Of course not, Brenda. You may speak in confidence. Why don't you tell us like you told Esmeralda. And if you cry, so what. Would you like a glass of water? Would anyone else like some water or a soda? I think I have a bottle of orange or cherry soda in the refrigerator from the altar boys' party last week. I'll bring in some paper cups and the bottles."

After the five had helped themselves and settled back in their seats, Brenda began.

"It seems like a life time ago last September, when we decided to go see that spy thriller movie. We could have, should have done something else. In fact, Felipe wanted to take me to the Topanga Mall for dinner. But I argued with him that there were too many gang bangers hanging out there. They're always so rude."

Brenda paused once more to swallow her renewed sobs and blow her nose.

Esmeralda summarized for her, "So they go to the movie at the Panorama Mall and they run into Mauricio, Brenda's cousin. He hates Felipe on sight!"

"Yeah. He warned us to go home fast.

"Then he and his homies followed us.

"It was late, already dark. And of course like a fool, I wanted to stop for a hamburger. This was only the second time I went on a date with anyone. Esmeralda had Martin, all the other girls had boys, and here I was finally with a man all my own. So we stopped at Tommie's Dogs. Then we walked back to the car.

Deal Me a Card

"Felipe had this old beat-up Corolla, minus a fender. But it's a car, right? And he's so proud of it. So, he opens the door for me. He's a real gentleman, so sweet. Shuts the door.

"I look out the driver's window at a car pulling up beside us. I see Mauricio's grinning face. Not a friendly grin. Like a devil's sneer.

"Then I hear a shot. And another. I know the sound. I, we, hear them all the time. Right, you guys?" Brenda swept her hand to include all of them.

The querulous voice stopped.

Silence poked its index finger into each of the eight listening ears, prodded the cheeks of two listeners so that they let out a tiny whoosh of air, punched all five diaphragms into painful knots.

Brenda's tone was a low, quavering trill as she continued.

"Then the car parked in front of us. I dared not move. I knew they were coming for me next. I had broken a rule. I had gone with a boy from the other side. I knew I was dead.

"He came up to my window. Mauricio. He opened the car door. He took my hand and lifted me out. I was like a corpse anyway. I should have been lying next to Felipe, dead also. My heart was bleeding so bad. Like his. Mauricio pushes my shoulder, grabs the back of my neck, presses hard on the back of my head, hurting me bad, but I did not dare make a sound.

"Mauricio said, 'See this scum lying there. Garbage on the street. No dirt bag messes with my family or the women in my family. Anybody touches our women, they pay the price.' Then he twists my head around so he's staring right into my eyes, one, inch away, 'You say a word and you will pay also. Because you're a marked woman. You're dirty, filthy with his hand marks on you. Go home and wash him off. Then forget about him. Remember, I'm watching. And my homies are watching.'

201

"He flung me across the hood of Felipe's car. My back hurt so bad, but I was paralyzed. The he walked over and kicked Felipe, lying there dead. Two, three times, as if he wanted to hurt him more. Nobody kicks a dog like that even. Three other *cholos* dragged Felipe's body. By the arms. Lifted him into the trunk of his car.

"Now I'm screaming, No, no! Without realizing it. Mauricio slaps my mouth so I shut up. I just cry, and cry. I don't dare make another sound. He flings me into his car. Drove me home. Opened the car door for me and led me to the front door. Watched as I unlocked it. Gave me a shove into the house. Slammed the door behind me.

"I hate him, I hate him. I say his name only as a curse."

Brenda was a ghost, flesh sheet-white, and her words were ashes in a crematorium drifting to the floor. Only here, in this room they embedded themselves in the hearts and minds of her four companions. Clung to their unmoving bodies like germs from a free-falling sick man's cough.

The obscenity of a car passing by, blaring *God Rest Ye, Merry Gentlemen* through its throbbing speakers, jerked the group out of the nightmare scenario.

Father Reilly, either desperately, or from habits born out of frequent spiritually trite gestures pastors accumulate, spouted, "Oh, you poor child, you poor child. God loves you. He loves those who suffer."

Daniel's barely-suppressed grimace were almost missed by his companions.

"Well and good, Father, but there's more. Brenda, I know it's really difficult, but tell us about the party at your aunt's house on Christmas night. Like you told me."

"Okay. But let me drink something drink first."

Recovering his verbal balance somewhat, Father Reilly asked, his voice rising,

"Why hasn't she gone to the police? This cannot continue. Felipe's not the only one. He won't be the last. And the intimidation!"

Deal Me a Card

Brenda reinforced, dove in again,

"You know how we all go to someone's house for dinner on Christmas day. Well, my family has that tradition. I wasn't in the mood for any type of festivity, but my mother insisted.

"Then in the midst of dinner, in walks Mauricio. And he's high as a kite. Drunk, pissed. Sorry, Father. He's like a yo-yo when a child first starts playing with it. Going every way. Wild. Laughing. Howling. Slapping his knee and his forehead. Nobody joins his fake joviality. Everyone's scared shitless of him."

Brenda's tone was sharper, her story emerging in staccato sounds. Daniel wondered if the recklessness and new energy came from the sugared soda or from the depths of a long-buried, suddenly uprooted anger, from a rage just now excavated.

"Here is my aunt pretending like nothing is wrong. She's the hostess of this year's party so she's trying very hard. Makes like all this shit is hunky-dory. 'Mauricio, settle down, honey, enjoy the day with us. How do you like your walkman? And the watch?' He pushes her away. Looks at the gifts, mutters something like, 'This is so much crap.'

"He looks around. Catches my nephew by the hand and gives him these slobbering kisses. 'I'm Santa Claus. Ho, ho, ho.' Makes the kid shriek and throw a fit, he's only four years old but he knows when the devil touched him. So Mauricio lets him loose. He's still laughing, an escaped maniac when he comes over and sits beside me on the couch near the tree. I've hidden behind it all evening. But now he's putting his lips on my cheek. 'See, I can kiss you like your boy friend cannot. Not any more. And I'm better.' Disgusting, fucking *cholo*." Brenda hung her head, looking from lowered eyes at the priest to see his reaction.

"He puts his hand on my chest. He's worse than crazy. So I slap him. Hard. If it was a pistol it would have blown half his head off. Pity not!"

Deal Me a Card

Though her friends and confessor cringed, she did not blink.

"And he turns to the whole family, my five-year old and three-year old niece and nephew, the cousins only in elementary school, and my aunts and uncles. And he says, in a cold voice, he's sober by now, while rubbing his cheek, 'I saved this girl's life. Better look at her real good. She slapped the man who saved her from a fate worse than death.'

'And you know how I did it? I, the brave cousin that she just slapped. I shot that dirt bag. Once and for all, took the bastard Felipe out of her life. No more disgrace to our name. She was going to bring us down with her stupidity. She was behaving like a bitch. A whore. And I shot him before she made us the laughing stock.

'And now she slaps me.'

'Then he slowly whirled and pointed at my mom, likes he has a *pistola* in his hand, and said, 'You better watch her. She's trouble.'"

Brenda dropped her face into her hands. The listeners heard her muffled words, "Now I'm in trouble. I'm dead."

Father Reilly looked at the four faces encircling him.

Briefly, he envisioned them all elsewhere, standing on a beach looking out to a wide expanse of ocean. Relentlessly, the pounding waves of Brenda's story thundered towards the shore. Licked at their defenseless toes. Then receded. Advanced and retreated. Luring them, enticing them away from all innocence. Underfoot, the sand ebbed with the current. The drag loosened their balance on terra firma, threatening to destabilize their equilibrium, undermining their grip on certainty. Powerless, immobilized, they were about to fall. Backwards, arms flailing, to be dragged into the depths of the bloody miasma that had become their life in this Valley.

Deal Me a Card

The priest took a deep breath. Brought his mind back to the reality confronting them. Thought, *'We are not impotent. We will not be servile.'*

Father Reilly spoke, quietly and deliberately,

"There are things I must do now.

"First, let me assure you that the only people with whom I will communicate will have the power to ameliorate the situation."

He focused his look primarily on Brenda as he made the statement. He glanced around. He jumped up,

"Now, for the other, holier business. The Lord's work. I have some materials that will instruct you on the roles of god-parents and parents. We also have meetings closer to the time of the child's birth and baptism."

He strode to the filing cabinet filling a corner of his office, opened a drawer, selected two booklets and four brochures.

"Here. Read them at your leisure."

As he handed out the information, he paused before each of the two women and murmured a prayer, placing a gentle hand on their heads.

"Let's go pray at the crèche, that the Child will bring peace to our world."

Afterwards, the two women and two men left, drained but clinging to a slight vestige of trust. Perhaps the Blessed Mother and her Baby listened and heard. They had to place their faith somewhere. Whose arms were better? Since, as Father Reilly mused as he watched them drive away, *youth must dream and keep hope alive.*

He went back to his office.

Five minutes later as he sat at his desk, deep in thought and struggling with his daily prayer, the phone rang. He picked it up, dispirited. Another broken heart or shattered body.

"Hello, a blessed Christmas to you. Father Reilly speaking."

Deal Me a Card

"Merry Christmas to you, Father. *Padre*, I've got to talk to you really bad. Urgently. There's something on my mind. It's been haunting me for three months. Ever since that young man was shot. Remember?"

Father Reilly's silent prayer could have been either a petition or a plea. He himself was uncertain.

"You sound very troubled, my son. Perhaps we should meet…somewhere?"

"Yes, yes. We must. I'll come right over. My name is Marco. I'll be there in ten minutes."

Father checked his trusty old rolodex, found what he was looking for. But he decided to wait until later, after his meeting, before he dialed Lieutenant Yow's number.

Deal Me a Card

CHAPTER 29

SOFIE BRUSHED THE BACK OF HER LEFT HAND, then her right hand alternately over her brimming eyes. If she wasn't careful the soap would penetrate her lids and scorch her irises. Her vision would become all blurry and her nose would start to run. She would have to stop the washing, rinse her hands, and clean her face before resuming.

This had happened earlier too, when she was chopping the onions for the salads and guacamole and sauces. Then it had been a nuisance. Now she didn't care.

She was so happy.

So the tears overflowed and mixed with the sudsy water in the sink where a flotilla of pots and pans bobbed, a cast-iron and Teflon armada lost in a sea of bubbles.

She actually hummed *Joy to the World* as she wept.

Between scrubbing the inside of a frying pan, and the outside of a pot they had used to boil the rice, or mopping at her eyes and sniffing deeply, she paused without breaking her rhythm to glance over her shoulder every thirty seconds or so, at the two men. She was as animated as a sparkling tree, ornamented and surrounded with piles of multi-colored gifts in the Christmas morning flurry.

The day of the Nativity was past, five days ago.

But today, before, during and after the Guerrero sons' holiday gala, two friends had received another gift. And she had the pleasure and blessing of being a witness to the reunion.

She could not stop, could not help crying these tears of elation.

****

Deal Me a Card

Sofia and Alfredo arrived at the Guerrero ranch house that morning at nine o'clock prepared for a long, exhilarating day. Richard, his girlfriend Sarita, and Daniel had commissioned them to cater the party for one hundred guests. As they unloaded the cooking implements and lugged packages of food from their van to the kitchen, they called out to each other.

"I know Richard said that they had all types of pots and pans, but I thought we should bring extra just in case."

"Sarita told me over the phone that she had purchased pretty much all the meat and vegetables and fruit, even spices. But she couldn't find the zucchini so I grabbed that yesterday and some other ingredients for the seafood recipe they wanted."

His fellow chef watched as he shouldered the door open, balancing on his false leg,

"Look, Alfie, take it easy. Sit for a few minutes while I bring in the last load. Take the weight off that leg. You'll be standing on your feet all day."

"Okay, thanks. I'll get busy laying out the stuff on the butcher table."

As Sofie gathered the last armload, a figure walked up the driveway with hands outstretched.

"Hey, senora, let me help you with that. I've been watching from over there by the pool, and you've been pretty busy going back and forth. You don't want to wear yourself out either."

"Oh, thanks, I appreciate your concern. Um, now, who are you? You look familiar. Maybe I've seen you over at the college? Or at the Center? I'm Sofia Perez. Today, I'm the chef with my colleague, Alfredo."

"That was Alfredo, with the limp? Uh, uh! I'm Eduardo Lopez. You probably see me at the Center for English classes."

"*Mucho gusto.* Good to meet you. So what are you doing here today? An overnight guest? Family friend?"

208

Deal Me a Card

"No way! I do landscaping out in Santa Clarita. Guerrero and Jones Construction are working on a new development out there.

"I was at McDonald's last week, and some of their workers came in. One of them mentioned how there was to be this party, *una fiesta grande,* and they needed someone to beautify the yard. To me that meant clean up, water the plants, little weeding, mowing, tidy up the pool. No sweat! I asked about it, got a phone number. And here I am!"

"Well, thanks again," Sofie said as she retrieved the packages from his hands and set them on the counter, "Look, if you finish early out there, maybe you can come in and help us. We'll tell Richard or Daniel and I'm sure they'll be happy to spare a few extra bucks for another able body. See you. *Hasta luego.*"

His query delayed her, "You said your companion's name is Alfredo. What happened that he limps?"

"Long story. Look, no time to talk. See you later, okay?"

"See ya!

They went back to their separate chores.

****

By two in the afternoon, pots were bubbling merrily, meats were sizzling in the ovens, salad bowls effused greenery. Sofie and Alfredo congratulated each other on their adeptness. They thanked their stars for a homeowner who believed the kitchen was the hub of any home, then furnished it with every conceivable appliance for the production of a gourmet feast. They sat now, folding festive red and green napkins festooned with angel-blown trumpets. Next they would lay out the silverware.

"Knock, knock, may I enter?"

"*Entre,* come on in, come in Eduardo. We were just taking a load off our feet and doing the easy chores. Want to help?"

209

"Well, I was thinking of what you said earlier. Since I can't cook, I can serve maybe. You know, walk around grinning, with those little trays of food. 'Would you like another glass of wine, *Senorita*?' '*Senor*, another canapé?' Like on TV. And I could wear an apron and one of those chef's hats!"

"You're a card. I don't think so. But sure, you can help later. First rule, *lave las manos,* go wash your hands. Use scalding water, recite the alphabet twice while soaping and rinsing. You've been mucking in the dirt."

"Is she always like this? Bossing you around?"

Eduardo smiled at Alfredo as he showed him the washroom around the corner from the kitchen.

While Eduardo and Sofie chatted, Alfredo had scrutinized the former from the corner of his eye. He had continued to fold the elegant shapes. Distracted, his fingers fumbled. A couple of the creases were not straight, and he had to unfold the paper and refold. Unconsciously, his hand reached down to his right thigh. His brows nearly met in a tiny furrow. His lips quivered visibly.

Eduardo returned from his requisite ablutions. He pulled out the chair facing Alfredo and sat down. Alfredo ceased his origami. Eduardo placed both hands on the table. The two men scanned each other's faces.

"We were lost and…"

"We were found."

"Alfredo, Alfie, *mi primo*, my cousin, *mi amigo*, my friend, no different, so thin."

"Eduardo, Eddie, my cousin, my friend. A little more weight on you, man, but, you're…"

"Alive! We're alive and now we're together. *Estamos vivos y juntos.*"

Hands reached across the narrow width of the kitchen table and grasped tightly. Tears started in their eyes. There was no need for words as both remembered the last time they saw each other. That early morning, between two worlds,

Deal Me a Card

when they made a decision to separate. A decision that had torn them apart for the last three years.

"*Lo siento! Lo siento mucho*, I'm sorry I abandoned you. I left you behind. But I lost my way. Then nobody would tell me anything. *Nadie no me dijo nada!*"

"It all worked out. It hurt really bad. I almost died. But it all happened for the best. And here I am. Here we are."

As the two cousins reunited, Sofie, all agog, realized the traveling companions of long ago had a lot of ground to cover. But this was not the time. One hundred people were right now advancing from all corners of the Valley, maybe even from across the county, to this destination. In about two hours they would flock in, hungry for an evening of titillating conversation, tongue-loosening drink, and delectable food. The three bore the responsibility to satisfy their desire for party cuisine. Reluctantly, she dragged them back to the present.

"Okay, okay. I hate to be the wet blanket but there's work to do. First, *abrazos*, let me hug you, both of you."

So they embraced, one at a time, then all together. Arms around waists, they whirled in a waltz of ecstatic thanksgiving for friendship amazingly reunited.

Alfie limping gamely, joy almost overcoming discomfort, panted,

"Hey, we gotta stop this," as they sung out "Merry Christmas! Happy New Year! And many, many happy years more to come!"

Without touching a drop of alcohol, they were drunk with excitement, their animation contagiously spreading from one to the other.

Then back in the kitchen, the trio drew apart to get serious. But not before they bent over laughing, carefree, child-like.

Still as Sofie let her tongue run across her lips, she tasted bitter sweet, felt intensely, painfully, the depth of the cousins' emotional reunion. She had many months ago, years

211

now, given up all hope of any such meeting with her loved ones. But that meant she could celebrate so much more exuberantly in others' delight. This was her consolation.

****

The three servers spent the next few hours in the usual whirlwind created by such festivities. They all vowed to thank the owner of the house. Mr. Guerrero had thoughtfully instructed his housekeeper, Gloria and her eleven-year old daughter, to assist the trio. The young girl, Luz Maria, very grown-up and serious for her age, dressed in a long red velvet skirt, white long-sleeved blouse, both protected by an apron, glided among the guests graciously picking up after them and conveying their every need to the waiting adults.

The mingled whiffs, from expensive perfumes and after-shaves that exuded from the pampered pores of twenty and thirty-somethings, swirled above their heads. Ladies were a rainbow coalition dotted with the more somber navy and grey attire of their gallant consorts. They danced and sang, wagged fingers and slapped shoulders, laughed aloud, and gossiped, mouths behind raised palms.

"Maribel is pregnant!"

"Already?"

"Why not?"

"Stevie's getting a promotion at the bank. Means he'll be travelling a lot more down south."

"Richard can't play in the tournament in February. Any suggestions for a substitute partner for me?"

"No problem taking fourteen units. You just have to plan your time. Organize your life. Yes, some of the units will be for practicums. I'll continue to counsel at the Center."

"Anybody thought about Spring Break. Maybe Cancun?"

"Egad, the holiday season's not even over."

"I have to move. Landlord problems. Any ideas? Know anyone who wants a roommate. Some cute lady?"

"Yeah, right. Some cute lady who'll pick up after you?'

"I say old chap, how were the Brits? We missed you, man, gone the whole semester."

"The London School of Economics was quite brilliant. So were the women, by the way!"

"Got to have more of that seafood dish. Forget the weight. January's around the corner. The nineties are almost upon us. Time to eat, drink and be merry now. Diet next week. Yo, Alfredo!"

"Here, have another glass of this chardonnay. No problem. I'm driving home. And I finished my prescribed one glass hours ago."

"Shall we dance?"

Repartee flowed like gushing rivulets. For five hours the hillside home reverberated in time with the throb of music and spirits pulsating with goodwill and conviviality. Then quiet descended as the guests gradually took their leave. By midnight, the lights on the tree were alone.

The housekeeper and her daughter left with the others.

****

After the hectic preparation and delivery, the three could afford a leisurely clean-up. Actually a slow down in movement was imperative. Sofie, Alfredo, Eduardo were weary to the bone.

Alfredo had massaged his right thigh more often as the evening had worn on. Sofie's calves ached. Eduardo's smile, well-pasted on earlier in the evening, had become unglued at approximately ten o'clock. Only a crooked curl of his left lip remained. The *toque blanche* he had perched so cockily on his head had deflated crookedly to the right. As he flung it off his head and discarded it on the counter, he called out,

"First of all, coffee. Coffee, everybody?"

Deal Me a Card

"*Si, si*! Yessss. *Por favor*. But I want mine with sugar and that thick cream. Strong, sweet, and milky. Hmmm. Then I'll attack those pots and pans," Sofie responded, basking in the knowledge that they could now relax a little.

They were not on a schedule any longer. The Guerrero sons had instructed them to do the minimum and return the next morning to do an ultra-thorough clean-up job when they were refreshed. This was included in the fee. The young hosts wanted the kitchen, in fact the whole house, to be so spotless that their father would not believe they had had a fling. They had made some kind of a bet with him.

Ah, to have sons, a son, any son again. Un hijo! Sofie thought ruefully, as she sipped her steaming *café au lait* and remembered their light-hearted banter.

Earnest discussion between her two friends drifted across the room from the table. She listened as she finished her drink, then moved over to pursue her kitchen chores at the overflowing sink.

"So while I was lying there fighting for my life, *luchando por mi vida, muriendo* in Phoenix, you were fighting for yours in Nogales?"

"I don't think my situation had quite the same drama. After I slept for about twenty hours nonstop, and those nice people from the sanctuary movement gave me clothes, a bed, water, meals for four straight days, I became human again. Began looking around the town. All day I would walk, *caminando, caminando,* then return to my haven for the night."

"Hadn't anyone heard about me?"

"Alfie, *eschuchame*, listen to me. That town was like nothing you or I had ever known. Crowded, *concurrido*. People, people everywhere. It was scary.

Remember Agua Blanca, what, with maybe two thousand residents? We knew practically everyone. We could stop, shoot the breeze, get born, get married, get old and die all on one street. *Tio, Uncle Matias* tells the parents

Deal Me a Card

about us fighting in the corral outside town, *abuelo* grandpapi is waiting with his switch when we return, and our asses hurt for two days."

"My little town too," Sofie heard herself murmur aloud.

"Mrs. Evanson was very secretive about me. She wouldn't tell anyone at first so no wonder nobody knew," Alfie interjected.

Eduardo continued, engrossed in his story,

"And in the other Nogales, across the border, the people were, like, building a factory, a day. *Las maquiladoras*, the assembly plants were shooting up like corn stalks. So the constant shuffle of bodies never stopped. Most of the people spoke Spanish, those whom I walked among. But they were always in a hurry, some place to go. More money to earn. *Mas dinero, mas dinero.* Not like home, where enough is enough. Where knowing your neighbor and worrying about your friend's welfare mattered."

"You live side by side, you develop habits, some good, some not so good," Sofie's wistful voice muttered from the kitchen.

"I got lost. I was confused. *Perdido. Confundido.* I was filled with fear, being alone in a strange land. *Tuve miedo, solo!*

"You had vanished like deer swallowed by a giant anaconda. You were always the brave one who made the decisions, and you were gone. *Te fuiste*! I hardly said a word to anyone, except to say *Por favor* and *Gracias*. Besides as I said, everyone was always busy, running around. *Siempre, todo el mundo estuvo preoccupado.* By the time I'd plucked up courage to ask a question, the person had pfft! vanished. *Desaparecido*! Even the staff at the shelter was constantly on the move, solving another problem, protecting another fugitive.

"Then I found this park. Ah, *el parque tiene unos arboles,* some trees so I could hide among them, close my eyes, and imagine I was at home. Before going there every

Deal Me a Card

day, I would leave the shelter, wander down some streets searching for a hand that would help me. *Buscando ayuda. Pero nada, nadie* nothing, nobody. Only people pushing by with unseeing eyes, *como los ciegos.* Every day, *todos los dias, dos horas, mas* for two hours maybe more I searched for work.

"Then I'd reverse my steps to the park, lean up against a tree and dream. *Memorias, cuando tuvimos trece anos y pescamos en el rio.* How you and I, remember when we were thirteen would go down to the river and fish all afternoon. When your mom wouldn't ask us about homework or what we did in school, because there was trout for dinner that night. Ah, *trucha por cena*! Or looking at the tires painted yellow in the little kiddies' area, I thought about how Salvador had made that swing for us when we were *ninos*, with the tire and the rope in that huge oak tree. *Que divertido*! What fun!

"All that thinking and longing. *Pensando. Anhelando. Malo!* Not good. It shut me down from reality, trapped me like I was in a time warp. The people at the shelter never asked me for anything. But I have my pride, you know. I' m a grown man, and I'm useless. *Hombre orgulloso pero inutil*! This goes on one week, two weeks, *muchas semanas.*

"Then one day, about eight thirty in the morning, I'm entering the park. Just then a pick-up, *un camion pasa*, one of those Toyotas. It's overloaded, bulging with plants, *muchas plantas,* some small shrubs, coupla half-grown trees. Everything tied together with this wimpy length of rope, beginning to fray from the strain. And the fool is driving too fast. *Como loco!* Well, right there on the street, it snaps and what looks like a small forest blowing in the wind, is rolling here and there, *aqui alla*, all over the road."

"Could've hurt somebody!" Alfie broke in.

"Caused me no pain! I start shouting. *Gritando*, Hey, hey! Didn't know if the guy realized what was going on. Maybe he had a bad night. Hung over. Luckily there's a Stop

216

sign. I managed to catch up. Grab his arm, it's sticking out the window. You know what? You guessed it! He speaks Spanish, *es Mexicano*."

"More Latinos working in gardens here in the U.S. than bees sucking honey from flowers," a sing-song chortle emanated above the splash of flowing faucets.

"So we reload the bed of the pick-up. The man is so grateful, *muy agradecido* because the owner of the house where the plants are headed, ordered them from Phoenix and there would be hell to pay! And *voila*, that's how the French would say it, right? Now I have a job for as long as I want."

"Nothing happens by chance," echoed from the direction of the kitchen sink.

"Mr. Nelson likes everything he owns to be super-sized and super-nice. He's the owner of the mansion. Between Nogales and Rancho Rico. On ten acres of land about a mile and a half mile outside town. So we have our work cut out for us, easily ten hours a day, sometimes six days a week. Mansion, villa, whatever, it's a castle. *Castillo con una piscina muy grande,* swimming pool stretched for a mile."

"No way, Jose!"

"Hey, I'm not kidding. Well, it sure felt like a mile when we had to haul those plants and mow the lawn from one end to the other. ... Garage holds five cars, from six different countries!"

"Huh?"

"Okay, okay, maybe I'm exaggerating."

"Could be his other name is Rockefeller," Sofie's voice came from near the sink.

"Maybe. Anyway, this house is so huge seven families from Agua Blanca could live in it. Easily. With no cramming five people into one room. Guess how many lived there."

"Nobody," was the firm response from the listening woman.

"Good estimate. All the six months I worked there, and I went to the property every day, *todos los dias los sabados*

Deal Me a Card

tambien even Saturday mornings, I saw a total of three people who lived in the house for more that a week.

"They'd come down to party sometimes. A huge crowd would descend like honking geese. But not to stay. Man, those galas were a small town's fiestas. A coupla hundred guests would arrive, way bigger than this party. Some of them would zoom in on those little two-engine planes. *Senores y sus novias*, young guys and gals, older people like *abuelos* and *abuelitas*. All dolled up.

"I remember the Fourth of July. Wow, that was awesome.

"But who were the people who lived there?" Alfie wanted to know.

"Oh, yeah. I'll tell you about the Fourth later. My first time celebrating in the United States."

"Much later. Tell about Mr. Nelson. Did he have a wife?" Alfie persisted.

"I'm not sure. There were these two women. *Dos mujeres, differentes ocasiones*. They were something special. I have to admit I wasn't entirely right about the *senor's preferencia* for the super-big.

"You mean they didn't have those huge, plastic…"

"Nope! These gals were luscious, lovely petite blonds. He bore them, each of them, very well on his arm."

"Not at the same time, I hope!"

"Nah, no kinky stuff! Bet he's quite a lover though! Among the nude statues around the pool there were some pretty frivolous naked goings-on in the water and on the deck. "

"Hey! *Un poquito respeto, por favor*! Watch your mouth. These rich folk know people. Next thing you know you're a marked man for insulting their women," the female admonished over her shoulder.

"You're paranoid. Who can hear us here? Anyway, I'm just admiring their beauty. No harm done. They were like dolls, *como munecas*," Eduardo gestured, making an hour-

Deal Me a Card

glass shape with his hands. "Shapely, tanned. One of them was making out with his highness on one of those rubber raft thingies. Shaped like a Viking ship. They do some weird stuff when they're rich and playing. She looks over his shoulder and winks at me, twiddles her fingers. And they're kissing and hugging and doing it right there like I'm one of the statues. Not my type at all. Too fast."

"What is your type?" Alfie asked, grinning.

"I'm not going there. I don't think my type has discovered me yet, and I have searched hard and long."

"So you were getting paid some pretty good money?"

"Alfie, I must say God was good. *Si*! Well, you know, a lot of money by our standards. More than I ever hoped for. So I started sending some home every week like we had promised. Remember?"

"I do. But did you speak to anyone at home? About me?"

"*Cierto, si*! On the phone. Told them you were always working so hard, that's why we could send so much money home, you had no time to talk. But you were well."

"*Gracias.*"

"*De nada.*"

"Really, though I was feeling as guilty as hell. Lying. Sometimes, I'd cry. Sniffing, so they could hear me at the other end. *Su madre* would ask me if I was sick, and I'd say '*Si, hace mucho frio*, the nights get very cold near the desert,' or 'My chest is congested. Lotta dust here *mucho polvo aqui*.' And she would get this worried tone in her voice, warn me to be careful, *cuidado, cuidado* and to make sure you stayed healthy also. Made me feel even worse.

"*Mentira!* I'd make up stories like that. Not wanting to tell the truth. That you were dead."

Edward leaned over to his cousin and gripped his shoulder.

Deal Me a Card

"That's what I believed. It kept eating at my insides. Nothing eased the pain. I drank a lot, picked up women. The stress went from bad to worse."

"Works every time. Ladies and liquor," a voice sighed resignedly in the background.

"Well, here goes. Confession time.

"You see, I like my women brown, black-eyed, black-haired, with flesh on their bodies. You know, rounded breasts and thighs I can sink into when…"

"Hey. Hey. There's a lady present, remember?" Sofie's and Alfie's voices protested together.

"Sorry. But you asked! It wasn't all sex, you know. Me and the ladies we'd dance on Friday and Saturday nights. Wild things in the dark, the salsa and the merengue taking us home. We all craved those hours to lose ourselves. Work hard, play hard."

"So where did you find these ladies of yours?"

"Those factories I mentioned. They were bringing in women by the hundreds from all over Mexico. Cheap labor. Unskilled and skilled, they just pulled them in like the profits that the rich folk, who lived in the big houses, were making.

"Only the workers didn't rake in anything. The pay was terrible. But, better than any salary they'd make back home. So they kept pouring across, a flood of cheap foreign labor."

Alfie was interested in other things, "What happened with you and these ladies?"

"Sometimes beer and beauty just don't mix.

"There was this one woman. Aah, *una senorita,* who made my skin turn inside out. She was such a dancer and a lover. Our bodies would cling together in perfect rhythm. When she sang, my head would want to burst while my heart was melting."

"But why did you have to get drunk. Sounds like you hit it big?" said Sofie joining in the discussion.

Deal Me a Card

"I didn't get drunk. Well, I did. But so did she. And man, was she a mean drunk. And when Gloria had a few, she got cruel and violent.

"One evening she throws her glass of Dos Equis into my face. Fancy beer for a fancy gal, I thought when I ordered it for her. And what happens? She's laughing like a female hyena after four bottles. An empty bottle in her hand. And my crazed dripping face in front of her.

"My head's reeling, buzzing from the booze, so I grab her hands and drag her out of the bar to knock some sense into her."

"You hit her?"

The question was gasped out, spewed like a snake's hiss.

"No, no, no, Sofie. After I saw what my Dad used to do to my mom, bruises, black eyes, one time a broken arm, I swore never. When I turned seventeen, I beat him up good almost kicked his teeth out. But *mi madre* pulled me off. I'll never understand women.

"Anyway, back to Gloria, she, who was the love of my life. Usually I wrapped my arms around her waist and caught her fingers tight in mine, to calm her down. '*Calmate, calmate*' I would whisper in her ear. Then we'd kiss and make up in a few minutes. Happened before. I was getting used to it. Don't get me wrong, I was planning to work on both of us quitting the alcoholic bingeing in the near future. The bouts were too energy-draining." Shaking his head, Eduardo looked up at the ceiling, remembering.

His listeners kept silent, waiting for the worst.

"This time, she kept up her abusive words. Really hurtful. She's sneering at my tears, calling me a no good wetback, loser. *Fracasado!* Don't I know it? But coming from her, I can't stand it any longer. So I walk away, leave her behind spitting her venom. She's a Sonoran desert viper, *vibora de desierto* no good for me. Maybe the next day or two we could make up, get close again. Find forgiveness for

221

Deal Me a Card

each other. Right then, though, the air zinged with hate. *Mucho, mucho odio.* Our blended ranting reeked with revulsion.

"I went my way home, fell asleep, dead to the anguish.

"I really loved that woman."

"I sense a tragic ending to this *amorous* liaison!" A rueful chuckle accompanied Alfie's remark.

Eduardo furrowed his brows. *"No te rias!* It's not a laughing matter! That was Saturday night. Sunday, I slept off my bellyful of beer and bitterness. In the evening, Pedro, the man who gave me the job, comes banging on my door. Gloria is his wife's sister-in-law. Pedro *me dijo que un borracho*, some drunken asshole found her and took advantage of her after I left the scene of our fight, and they were blaming me."

"They accused you of raping her?" Alfie gasped incredulously.

"No the police got the guy. Son of a bitch, *hijo de puta* bastard.

"From me, the family wanted vengeance for leaving her to take care of herself in a dangerous environment. *Venganza*!"

"They were not wrong!" Sofie's voice was hard.

"I swear, alcohol for me is a hose fully turned on. Pours into my mouth, spurts up in my brain, waters the idiot in me and makes it flower into total stupidity. *Que tonto soy, estupido, siempre estupido!* Talk about being a marked man. That Saturday night, the moment I turned my back on her when I couldn't take her poisonous mouth…,"

"Or hold your liquor!"

Without missing a beat, Eduardo continued, "Because she was breaking my heart again. That moment I drew the target on my back and chest. The family was out for blood."

"*Dios mio*, God in heaven help you, how does this all end?" Sofie spoke softly, relenting a little.

Deal Me a Card

"Pedro! Pedro saved my life, rescued my sorry butt. He knew of Gloria's craziness. We had become friends. So he's actually tipping me off when he knocked on my door.

"Next morning, Monday, my bag is packed. Only a few belongings in that hole. No feelings, no time to cry. Left it empty like I found it. Hey, it served me. For two hundred a month, my own room with bathroom and window looking out into a garden of cactus and bougainvillea. I rented it two weeks after I started working with Pedro. That was my first American home. Lived there for six months. Some memories of tenderness, but nothing more. *Nada*. Just dust left behind on the vinyl floor. *Polvo en el piso*. I had a serape hanging on the wall to make it cozy like home. Took that with me when I left. It's hanging in my apartment now.

"Anyway, I slink over to the shelter. Five o'clock. It's a dark and scary morning. *Como la primera vez,* like that first time I walked into this town of Nogales. This time Brother Arnulfo is there. *Esta siempre alla*, meditating, watching, waiting, as he prays with the beads in his fingers. All the men, who spent the night, are coughing and farting and shuffling toes but still in bed. Breakfast isn't until seven.

"I'm happy it's quiet. In the corner, there's a hollow space for the *Virgen* of Guadalupe statue and candles glowing for the dead are giving off a sweet scent. I give the sanctuary group a donation. *Un milagro, por favor*. I kneel, truly praying for a miracle once more, while ulterior motive oozes out of every pore mingling with my coward's sweat. Make a showy sign of the cross to end my prayer, then after some meaningless chit-chat, I ask Brother for an address in Los Angeles to escape to.

"He looks me in the eye. Hands me a card with directions. I'm a cockroach under his sandal, *como cucaracha* I'm squirming so much, because the look in his eyes and his last embrace and blessing are full of love.

"We part.

223

Deal Me a Card

"He returns to the *Virgen*, and to minister to other desperate men. I jump on the Greyhound bus to search for a new life.

"We haven't seen or heard from each other since!"

"My days of glory in Arizona were over!"

"How did you find you're your way to this part of the Valley?" Alfie wanted to know.

"Brother Arnulfo's friends in Los Angeles advised me that the *oportunidades* for work in landscaping and construction are better in the San Fernando Valley. With their help, three days after I arrive in the *Pueblo de la Reina de Los Angeles*, I found an apartment in Van Nuys and a gardening job at a nursery in Reseda. Two months later, one of the workers tells me the Guerrero construction company needs some laborers. *Soy el hombre!*"

Sofie, who had listened avidly, picked up the conversation,

"You're the man all right. You've played your cards right!"

She changed the subject,

"We must admit, it was the sanctuary group helped all three of us get to this place. What a coincidence. *Madre de Dios*, they are saintly people. If I was not *cristiana*, I would say they do magic. *Son magos.*" She crossed herself.

"They do perform miracles making something out of nothing. The nothing that is our lives. *Dios los bendiga!*" Eduardo insisted, his happiness unquenchable.

"Amen!" echoed Sofie.

****

The three friends spent the next day together since Eduardo wanted to hear their stories. The two cousins especially were reluctant to lose sight of each other.

Sofie invited the cousins to her apartment.

"Come on over, eleven thirty is fine," she told Alfie when he called at ten.

Deal Me a Card

"*Almorzamos*, we can eat lunch. Share memories while I'm preparing the one hundred and fifty *pupusas con carne, queso y pollos,* tortillas pork cheese and chicken fillings. *La madre de Rosie,* Rosie's mother is paying. She's having a New Year's Eve party. You can help me. *Pueden ayudarme.*"

CHAPTER 30

"I LOVE YOU, EMMA. I want to be with you too. See you soon. Happy 1990, my darling. Wish everyone a Happy New Year for me. Your sister Evelyn, Adam, Shirley his wife.

"Bye, sweetheart."

The phone started ringing a second after Guillermo hung up. He answered it,

"Hey! Hi, Isadora! Happy New Year! Well, we're *almost* there. I just finished wishing Emma in Florida. They've already popped the champagne and set off the firecrackers back east. What's up?"

He smiled as the voice at the other end extended an invitation.

"You're having a get together. You want me to come?"

He nodded at her reply.

"Thanks for thinking of me. Well, you know how guests are. You invite them for ten o'clock and they'll begin to drift in at about ten thirty. Why don't I come over now and help you. Entertain you with all the news from back east. We'll have about an hour or so to chat. See you soon."

Twenty minutes later Isadora greeted Guillermo at her front door. As her lips smacked his cheeks in a greeting, the scent of commingled wine and Dior perfume heralded the hostess' preparedness for the evening's celebration. The *faux* diamonds in her eardrops, around her neck and encircling her right wrist were alternately sparkling tears shed for the outgoing year, then blazing stars welcoming the nineties. Pleasantries complete, the two friends flitted around Isadora's kitchen and living room setting trays of hors d'oeuvres in strategic places within reach of hungry fingers. Big Band music played. They sashayed a little. They discussed Emma.

226

Deal Me a Card

"I wanted to tease her for having such a good time away from me. Told her it was nine o'clock here, and I was sitting at home all alone thinking about how much I loved her. That, boo-hoo, I was so lonely because the boys are on the way to the party at some friend's house. Richard with Sarita, and Daniel's with a new girl of course. Oh, and I told her their party was a hit. People keep calling me to thank me. Emma loves it when I praise the boys, so I heaped it on about how the house was in absolutely perfect condition, as if there never was a party, it was so neat and tidy.

"Should I open some of the wine to breathe? Two bottles, one merlot and one chardonnay?"

"Good idea."

"I went on and told her I'd sit quietly and marvel at the past year, how we met and how good we are together, and how there's more ahead in our lives. Said mournfully I'd pop a bottle of champagne and drink a glass to our future. Alone."

"You are such an actor, even across those thousands of mile. You should be ashamed." Isadora grinned

"No, really, I meant every word. Can we sit and talk now?"

"Sure. Everything's ready. Anyway, it's mostly the gang from the Center. They know their way around this little place."

More music, instrumental fifties rock hummed from the speakers. Isadora took a comfortable spot next to Guillermo, just so their shoulders brushed. Hers were bare. The sequin-glittery spaghetti straps of her black-and-grey striped evening gown strained to uplift her unrestrained breasts. The cleavage bespoke a battle almost won. The form-hugging sheath flaunted a slit up to where her left thigh bone nestled into her hip bone. Her guest could not help but luxuriate for a brief five seconds as warm, bare flesh pressed his upper leg through its woolen covering. Inching to his right further wedged his buttocks tight into the corner of the two-person

227

Deal Me a Card

loveseat. He sat, stuck. Isadora, laying her left hand casually on his knee, started to count off her guests with her fingers on either hand. He spoke when she paused,

"Sounds like the Center staff will be crawling all over your furniture. Joke! This will be a blast. I'd love to celebrate with them."

"Good. Now continue the tales of Emma and her family."

Isadora leaned over, picked up her glass of wine from the coffee table. Then, with her left arm over the back of the sofa, she leaned towards Guillermo to listen.

"It's a real family reunion back East. Her sister, Evelyn, she's older than Emma, is there from New York. She has a boyfriend with her, so she's glowing. You remember Emma told us Eve's a widow. It's been five years since the husband passed away. And then she lost her son quite soon afterwards, about two years ago. So everyone is relieved that she's found someone. Emma said Evelyn seems mellower, calmer, and happier. She's bounced back. I told her a good man will do that! My sweetheart giggled."

"I'm laughing too. Those are few and far between."

"What about me? No, don't say a word. Let's get back to other good news from Florida.

"Apparently, her sister-in-law's cousins are free at last! There is much rejoicing. That segment of the family has lived in East Germany even before World War II. It's been years since there was any communication, or it was extremely sporadic."

Isadora interjected, after a sip from her purple-red vintage,

"And now the wall is down. It came down about six weeks ago, right? Yeah, I remember November ninth. I was watching the whole phenomenon on TV, with the students. We got all emotional and teary-eyed. They know about separation from loved ones, and could relate to the excitement.

Deal Me a Card

"When will they be able to travel? To be with their American relatives? My God, imagine what it'll be like after all these years!"

Guillermo nodded, "The cousins and Emma's brother figured there's a long waiting list to cross over. They'll probably go through Checkpoint Charlie, though there were lots of openings between East and West Berlin after the first gate opened. But think of the crowds, the literally hundreds of thousands of people all jostling for the same thing. There'll be a logjam."

His listener broke his train of thought, "Well, you know how efficient those Germans are. What's the bet, her cousins will be visiting Tallahassee next summer. But no matter how soon, it'll seem like a lifetime to them. Ooh, this is a joyful thing!"

"Yeah, I told Emma to tell them congratulations. Or thanks be to God. Whatever is appropriate for such a reunion.

"We didn't talk about too much more. I told her I'd met with you a couple of times about those legal shenanigans with your ex. The one and only Mr. Pig. Where did you get that name, for heaven's sake! So typical Isadora."

Typical Isadora socked his arm playfully,

"Don't you start picking on me. This year is a fresh start and no man will be my master!"

"Well, my lady is landing at LAX at four o'clock on Tuesday. Not soon enough!

"By the way, remind me later to tell you Brenda's story. She's the student studying fro her GED, the teenager whose boyfriend was killed last fall. I remember like it was yesterday. They dumped his body in the hills behind my house. Detective Yow called me yesterday, told me they arrested Mauricio, her cousin.

"I hear somebody at the door. Time to party!"

****

229

Deal Me a Card

Alfie, Eduardo and Sofie were attending a smaller get-together at Carmelita's house. Isadora had invited her to welcome the New Year with the rest of the Center staff, but Carmelita wanted to be at home with her two *ninas*.

Others cooked dinner. The two men brought sodas, and a bottle of champagne. Sofie brought only her deck of cards. As the night progressed, people expressed nostalgia for the years gone by. Settling into the card games, the mood changed to exuberance, the players full of hope and laughter as they talked of the decade before them.

Together, at the stroke of midnight, the guests loudly drank a toast to 1990. *Feliz Ano Nuevo!*

****

At 12:30 a.m. Marco Ayala leaned back in his recliner. His eyes were closed but behind them he was wide awake. *Already one half hour into the nineties,* he thought to himself. *It's gonna be good. The new decade already looks brighter*, he asserted to himself.

Marco had every reason to feel hopeful.

For the first time in fifteen years, he would be sober on New Year's Day. Here he was at home. The family spent the evening together, playing Chutes and Ladders quietly, and hide-and-seek around their little house with shrieks of laughter. By nine o'clock *los tres ninos* huddled peacefully in their room. Right after the couple had lovingly kissed and hugged and wished each other a Happy New Year with big sips of diet cola, his wife Dulce retired. She was asleep in five minutes. The night was full of joy, unlike the last four years when he had been in jail, isolated from his loved ones.

Relaxed, mind drifting to childhood, the advice his *abuelo* had given him when he was fourteen rose in his memory. *Ten responsibilidad mijo, ten responsibilidad.* Take responsibility for your actions. That had been a long time ago. Only now he felt he could look his grandfather in the

Deal Me a Card

eye and say, *Yo lo hizo, yo lo hace. Grandpa, I did it.* I'm doing that!

Life was not easy. *La vida nunca es facile.* The difficulties would continue. Staying away from the cerveza and dope, finding a secure job, raising *los ninos* in a community where bullets did not discriminate against age. His fists clenched on the arms of the chair.

He thought of what he had done. His hands unclenched.

The streets of La Coloma and San Benitez were safer, maybe just a little, but less dangerous because a murderer had been removed.

Marco relived the minutes two days when, with a sweaty hand he picked up the phone and dialed the rectory number. His voice was hoarse. *Father Reilly must have thought he was a weirdo!* He asked him to hear his confession. *Que miedo!* How scared he was. Like at his first confession when he had to tell the *padre* he spit on his baby sister because he was jealous. Worse, when the judge sentenced him to the three years in jail.

Tuve que informar! For months the knowledge haunted him. In his sleep, while walking down a dark street, while playing with the children in the park, he heard the shots that killed that young man, Felipe,

I must tell! He read the newspapers back in September. The police sought information. The autos, the license number, the exact time it happened. Only he knew those details. *Detalles esenciales!*

He must tell, *tengo que informar,* but he was scared. Shit scared! These were gang-bangers. They would surely kill Dulce and *los ninos. Dios mio,* he couldn't lose them again. *Por siempre!*

"Father forgive me, I have sinned and caused pain. I did not tell," he murmured while kneeling in the confessional. "You must go to the police. *Tiene que ir a la policia. Por favor!* You don't know me. I have to keep my family alive. *Por favor!*"

Deal Me a Card

"I understand, my son. I will do the right thing. Go in peace.

'*Dios, Dios, ten piedad de nosotros.*' He heard Father whisper, as he blessed him. "God have mercy on us all!"

12:55 a.m. early New Year's Day, Marco pushed the recliner upright. It was time for bed. His heart was light.

Tuve responsibilidad, abuelo. I'm a responsible man.

Deal Me a Card

CHAPTER 31

EMMA PULLED THE SILKY CREAM SHEET UP over her damp breasts. The fabric settled, cool brush strokes slicking at hot flesh from neck to toe and the tangled hair between her legs. The momentary swipes of material soothed nipples raw from her lover's hungry nibbling.

Guillermo had just treated Emma to a belated New Year's Eve celebration, five days after the world had welcomed the new decade. The fireworks exploding over Marina del Rey could not have matched the fervor of their fondling hands, as each one's fingers rediscovered the other's pleasure, could not equal the ardor of lips that slipped and sucked in mutual giving. Could only be dimmed and muted, in awe of their brain-ripping climax as they came together.

"Can we make love now?" Guillermo murmured. "I just went to heaven. Now I'm back and rested, we can dance a slow tango."

"Give me five minutes."

"Really?"

Guillermo sounded like a little boy whose mom had just given him permission to have two more cookies and stay up ten minutes after his bedtime.

"Yes, my love. I missed you so much.

"I was walking through Gayfer's, shopping at the Tallahassee Mall. I turned around to take your hand, and you were not there.

"When it snowed those two days before Christmas, right there in the panhandle of Florida for the first time in seventeen years, it was a wonderland out there in the woods where my brother lives. I stood on the deck watching as deer tiptoed through, foraging, heads down, then suddenly straining their necks alert to some peril, noses twitching. But

Deal Me a Card

I had to enjoy it alone. I felt the gentle flakes touch my cheeks and my lips and my tongue…"

"Like this," whispered her man, dropping tiny kisses on her softly shut lids, delicate arched brows, and soft lobes.

Then, as he felt her body stirring, his mouth opened to swallow the buds atop her breasts, and his fingers traced a line from her belly button to her fluffy mons.

"I'll have to tell you how it tasted later."

"Not at all as sweet as what I'm tasting right now," Guillermo's voice was hoarse, muffled as he burrowed his tongue in her.

Emma's hands grasped her dear one's dense mop of hair, dug her fingers into his scalp, massaging.

"I want you my love, I want all of you."

Then they ascended, leisurely, so that they might sink, lost infinitely, each into the other's being.

****

The two were sitting in her cozy dining niche the morning after. She took another sip of tea.

"Um, that feels good. Wakes me up. Is that hazelnut coffee satisfactory for you, my lord and master?"

"Hey, no need to go overboard with the submission thing."

Guillermo's tap on the tip of her nose was a caress. Emma turned in her chair and put her arms around his neck, buried her nose in his shoulder. Suddenly she was shy, thinking of the night's intimacies. Shaking off lascivious thoughts, she leaned back and said firmly,

"Now it's back to reality. What are you fixing for breakfast? There're eggs, and bacon, fresh tomatoes and mushrooms. I picked them up at the market yesterday. Also scallions and green peppers. Wheat bread."

"Chef Willie will be most honored to prepare a most delectable omelet for his adored goddess. May it please the lady that she first sit on the lap of the cook to give him a kiss of inspiration."

Guillermo raised her to her feet. Slipping his arms into her partly-open chenille robe he kneaded her shoulder blades.

Emma insisted,

"I'm famished. Let's eat first. Then we can spend what's left of this Saturday being creative and inspiring with each other."

"If you don't have any body paint lying around, I'll run out and get some."

He bent and took a nipple in his mouth, worked it with his tongue.

"I see a budding red rose right here."

"You're my silly Willie!"

"We should get married. We have so much fun. And I won't let you get away again."

"Soon enough."

****

At eleven thirty-five on Monday, two days later, Emma set the receiver firmly back in its cradle and stared straight ahead. Her head was filled with the buzz of a thousand threatening houseflies.

Lupe, Guillermo's secretary had called. After wishing each other a good year, the conversation was businesslike. The educational program had a new schedule for the Spring sessions, lists of students were ready for the first day of classes.

Then Lupe mentioned the meetings between Guillermo and Isadora during the holiday break. She described with gusto the New Year's party the staff had enjoyed, how Guillermo and Isadora had danced until four on the first morning of January. The words she had spoken over the phone ground to sawdust any joy Emma might ever have felt

235

in the last eight months. Grated to raw edges her nerves that she thought her new-found love had soothed.

As suddenly as her mood had dimmed, the walls around her lost their luster. A clouded sky outside blocked the entry of any sun's ray. The miniature palm on the bookshelf drooped, looking like it truly could not survive those three weeks of neglect during her absence. The orchid was in dormant mode. The surface of her desk felt moist and slippery, but her arms adhered, refusing to slide beneath the weight of her bowed shoulders and slumped torso. It was as if they were trying desperately to cling on to the life she had started to rebuild, but which had evaporated as she listened to the secretary's insidious purring on the phone.

Lupe was the taciturn guard, the burly bulwark stationed stolidly in front of Guillermo's inner sanctum. She was the sentry who scrutinized every intruder and bounced any individual whose passport she disapproved.

Rumor had it that, back home in Vera Cruz, Lupe had tired of her husband's abuse. Her temper had simmered, a boiling pot of vengeance. She bided her time. On a Friday night five years ago, her soused spouse landed one too many punches in her gut. She snatched a kitchen knife as he took a breather between assaults and she plunged it into his kidney.

The finale to this tragic relationship was comedic. Guillermo's aunt, Lupe's neighbor, had contacted him to arrange a border crossing. As circumstance would have it, he was expanding his business and needed extra assistance in his facility. With a few pulled strings, her rotund form was soon ensconced in his vestibule. Forever grateful, Lupe morphed into his mostly silent, ever-watchful watchdog. Her husband recovered. Chastened and contrite, he attempted to reunite with his beloved wife. Met by spousal rebuff and her employer's firewall, he returned to plowing corn fields instead, between bouts of heavy drinking and singing slurred verses of unrequited love dousing his phony heartbreak.

Deal Me a Card

Lupe swiftly entered into the social life of the Center. Other women, students and staff, her countrymen, *paisanos* folded her warmly into their midst. With Emma however, Lupe was more aloof, though she always left the door open for Emma, at Guillermo's direction.

The two women had first circled each other gingerly, feral cats guarding their territory and prey. Gradually the waiting room's atmosphere's warmed. Now they lingered over desultory, sometimes animated female chit-chat. They shared lunches, brown bags and even a couple of meals in the company of their mutual beloved. Helpful feminine beauty tips thrown out tactfully at random moments from Emma, about color coordination and lipstick shades which lightened Lupe's mien, drew them ever closer.

But Emma could never shake off the suspicion that Lupe regarded her as an outsider, the stranger who did not quite belong.

In Emma's subconscious the energized alarm flashed its message, "Different, different, you're not like them, you're not white. You're not brown. You're mestiza, you're a mixed blood." She thought she saw the wariness towards a mongrel in the eyes of Lupe and her new-found *amigas*, their disdain in the involuntary twitch of lips, the unspoken question, and the halted conversation when she walked up to join them. As if they thought she would not understand,

"Indian, white. You're a strange phenomenon. You're something and you're nothing. Do not be so sure of Guillermo's attraction to you." Lupe's unspoken message had come through subtly as they talked on the phone.

Now sitting rigid in her office chair, Emma dredged a quote from the sole non-seething recess of her memory. *This day, as a great statesman had once growled, will live in infamy.*

Guillermo had been seeing another woman while she was on her winter break.

Deal Me a Card

Well, melodrama aside, her thumping brain reasoned, *the tumult raging in her whole being easily matched any country's bombardment by an enemy.*

Having betrayed her, he then had the audacity to strip her down to nothing upon her return. Seduced her once more all weekend long, and painted her into a frenzy of rainbow stripes, enveloped them both in the darkness and light of a passion that only the dawn, this early morning, had been able to loosen. Slightly. They had stood under the scalding water spurting from the shower head, their flesh still hungering, responding to each other's touch and glance. They needed no words to express the niceties of their affection.

What was she thinking?

What was he thinking, the bastard.

That she was some throwaway half-breed, a piece of nothing. Cheap flesh.

Emma sank into a swamp of self-chastisement, throwing everything that she had felt for Guillermo into a murky pool. Struggling with her anger and jealousy, she let herself feel like a toy used and quickly discarded by a fickle man.

Forcing aside the drama once more, she dragged herself out of the quagmire. Allowed Reason to usurp the throne where a thousand emotions squabbled.

She had no right to demand his undivided attention. She had been out of town for the whole holiday season. How could a male help being lonely when all around him people hugged and embraced as they tossed away one, and welcomed in another decade.

There were many women to fill the void. She had met some of them.

Ramona worked at his tax accounting office. The twenty-eight-year-old, slim, oval face, green-aqua eyes and shiny-red glossed lips had dallied with her employer in the past. They had gone on vacations together, weekends in Santa Barbara and once a whole week in Mazatlan. For

Deal Me a Card

whatever reason, he still maintained her services at the office.

Before that, Tamara. She taught Physical Education at the community college. Guillermo still had a photo of himself with Tammy, as he affectionately called her, astride horses at some dude ranch they visited two years ago. It hung on the wall in his den. He saw her at least three times a week during the semester and at faculty meetings.

And who knows, who else?

Now, Isadora.

So what? She and Guillermo had made no agreement. Their affinity, blossoming over eight months, was too good to be true. The lovers' closeness had been too fragile to sustain a separation. Apparently, he was a man of too many needs that defied prolonged compatibility.

Reason got the boot.

When she walked stiffly into Raoul's office to say she needed the afternoon off to see her doctor, he nodded without a word. Her clipped words and quick hooded look stanched any solicitous inquiry.

"Must be her monthly. Poor little one. We guys are so lucky!" he thought to himself, as the front door to the office slammed shut behind her.

He picked up the phone and called his brother, left a message on his machine,

"Hey, Guillermo, you're to be nice to Ms. Emma this evening. Bring her roses or a box of that Turkish delight that she consumes by the pound. You know, the kind dipped in dark chocolate.

"She's feeling the cramps today, looks very pale and down. Surprise her at work. Spoil her. You know how women love that.

"I know, I know. Like I have to tell you. Talk to you later."

****

Deal Me a Card

Emma drove home, somber, on autopilot.

Mamasan's purring machine revved loudly with pleasure as she happily partook of an early feast. But except for a few absentminded pats on the head, it was all her loving mistress offered. So she retired to her throne in the sunlit window.

Emma in turn retired to her bedroom. Carefully doffing her suit, she hung it up. Stripped to nothing. Went into the bathroom and brushed her teeth.

Then Emma did what she knew best. She escaped to a different time, an idyllic place. Pulling down the bed covers, she buried herself in its folds and softness and let her mind drift unfettered.

Midmorning, silence on the dry river-bed. Nothing moves the sand, not even a breath of wind. Feet leave deep prints. Swish, crunch, swish, crunch, swish. The air pulses, throbs in the intense heat beating down on the ground searing the already dry weeds.

I step on rocks that at once boil, scorch and send fire shooting deep into my toes and soles. Ouch, ouch, ouch.

Trees line the riverbank tall and still, sentinels of this hot summer day. Slender branches will wave a warning to the sun if a breeze advances. But the air is windless. So the boughs stand uneasily, at ease.

Scan the ground. No snakes. A defiant lizard or two dare to dart across the rocks, pause to ogle the nearby water, then make a zigzag reptilian line for their cool underworld.

Splash, lap, lap, splash, splash, lap. I step on the small rock half-submerged in water, and survey the land.

I look around. Upstream, this section of the river is slow and shallow. It trickles lazily around a bend, cool, fresh and confident, shaded by the overhang of

Deal Me a Card

stunted scrubs rooted in the low riverbank. I watch the water first sparkle with intermittent stars bursting from the sun's rays, then reflecting the shadowy images of dangling leaves. Ripples hold these images, wavering, swaying, never still. Listen to the stream murmur its certainty, its forward thrust, knowing its power. Hundreds and hundreds of little rocks respond to the impetus, shift imperceptibly, gently, determinedly. Catch a bubbling tune. Rumble of drums from countless small stones rubbing against each other, inching millimeter by millimeter along the riverbed.

Flash of blue, a jay dives, plunges in for a swig of cool liquid, ruffles its damp feathers, dips for another gulp, gone, soaring. Two dragonflies buzz by, translucent wings reflecting the black, green, blue of the water, sky and stones. They hover, land on a rock, freeze for a long minute savoring the glory of their existence in the sun, move on.

Burble, burble, burble.

Downstream the water gathers speed. Quickens first along a gentle slope, flows faster and faster over piles of great rocks, over stony layers that become steeper and steeper, then slows again as the incline flattens once more

Where the stream is swift, midstream, I end my meandering and take my seat in a rocky jacuzzi.

Icy water roughly slaps my back, my shoulders, my arms. A waterfall pounds on my hips smacking my fleshiness there. A persistent cascade repeatedly whacks at my reverberating stomach. Eddies massage my thighs and lick my toes. Little waves stroke my breasts, my buttocks, caress my inner thighs, soften the hard rock beneath me. Some drops splash my face, sting.

Deal Me a Card

At the mercy of the river, I loll, naked but for a hat to shield my head. I look up. The sky is agonizingly blue. Clean, clear, cerulean with a satin sheen, sends its crackle and crispness down on the water. Invisible jolts of energy lay siege on cold liquid and warm my flesh. The sky's heat embraces me. Minutes of ecstasy pass.

Minutes, add to minutes, to minutes, until perhaps an hour goes by.

I sense movement. Flash of brown flickers at the periphery of my vision. Lift my head following the rhythm of the water flowing around me, and swivel it, millimeter by millimeter. Eyes barely move. A blink could break the spell.

Inch by inch without a splash to disturb the water, a spotted fawn is crossing the stream behind me.

Emerging from the shady woods on the left bank, he is crossing to the dry riverbed on the right bank. Focused, intent, unaware of the presence of another creature, or if aware, very cautious, quiveringly audacious. Treads so lightly, soundlessly, no splash, on the long, long slender legs of a yearling. White spots on his coat, white nubby tail, his fur a mix of burnt sienna and alizarin crimson. Little nose wiggles as some rocks shift under his tiny hoofs. Daintily he steps onto the bank, pokes through the shrubs silently, barely disturbing the leaves. Self-possessed, he walks across the burning sand, pauses to shake a hoof stung by the heat, glances furtively over his shoulder, crosses the dry riverbed, meanders up the slope, and into the shady trees.

Gone. No hello, no goodbye.

Afternoon, nothing changed.

The sun scalds the sand. Leaves rustle slightly. I perch on my rock midstream. Behind, the ceaseless

242

Deal Me a Card

river meanders around the bend bubbling. Gathering speed the cold water still pummels my body, flows by. Ahead, it swirls, rolls, thunders, roars in a cascade down to the next bend in the river. Slowing down, quiet lapping eddies once more drift into the dappled shade.

Purified, I seek blessings on a mountain top church, then drive home, refreshed.

Once upon a time, many months ago in the mountains where we first loved.

Emma returned to the present. Unaccustomed to napping in the middle of the workday and with uneasy thoughts pounding at her temples, she could not rest. She flipped on her back, then flipped on her stomach. Then rolling over once again, she pressed her pillow over her head, turned her face to the side and stretched her neck for air. She needed to sleep, to take a nap before the evening classes.

The phone rang out for a long fifteen times, but she let the call go unanswered.

Deal Me a Card

CHAPTER 32

ISADORA POWER-LOCKED THE WINDOWS of her Miata, secured the auto, and turned towards the building. Guillermo set his materials on the hood of his Acura as he locked the car. Grasping his armful of baggage in a clumsy embrace he started towards the Center.

The two came face to face in the darkening parking lot.

"Hi there, Guillermo. Let me take some of that load before you drop it."

"Thanks. Here, grab the flowers. I thought I could manage this box and my briefcase in one hand, and the bouquet in the other."

"Just like a man. The cellophane will crush. The flowers will break. You want to give Emma a nice fresh-looking bunch, not something that looks like it's from the jiffy-sale, fifty-percent-off rack."

"When we go in, hide it behind your back if she's around. I want to present it to her after class over coffee and dessert."

"No problem.

"By the way, all the paperwork went through fine. Mr. Pig's lawyer in Miami got it from the attorney's office in Van Nuys. I'm really grateful that you looked over everything. The divorce should go without too much of a hitch. Three more months. I think that's how long Mr. Scott said it would take to finalize the settlement. Thank goodness I don't have to speak to him, or see his face ever again. Mr. Pig, not Mr. Scott."

"These are difficult times for you, I can see that."

"How's Christopher holding up?" Guillermo changed the subject. "He looked a little ticked-off at lunch last week."

"Well you know how much he loves his father. He's the younger of the two. And misses him more. Adela is taking it

244

Deal Me a Card

so much better. It was nice of you to include him in lunch, since his sister was down in La Jolla with friends. She left the day after Christmas. Though he would never admit it, he misses her. He was moping around the townhouse like a stray puppy."

The concerned mother sighed heavily,

"Not a very merry season for the three of us this year."

"I can't ever be his Dad. But boys in their teens need a father figure, so I can try to fill in the void in a small way," Guillermo said as he pushed open the Center's front door.

"Having you there these past few days has been very comforting. When you came over that other night…"

"Quick, hide it" he whispered.

Isadora was coming up through the door behind Guillermo. Peeking over his shoulder, she saw Emma standing in the reception area. Swiftly she stuck her hand behind her back.

As the two were entering, Emma looked up from her conversation with Carmelita at the front desk. She nodded abruptly, stared at the couple. The furtive movements did not escape her. Their low conversation was not completely indistinct, although Isadora's lips were practically glued to Guillermo's ear. She caught a glimpse of Isadora trying vainly to hide the flowers behind her. And she saw him smile into her eyes. His mouth appeared to brush Isadora's cheek as he spoke.

Emma turned on her heel, and strode down the narrow hallway to her classroom. She didn't hear Isadora's exchange with Guillermo,

"…I'm sorry we only had pizza. Chris's comfort food.

"Once again, thanks a million for the advice and line-by-line scanning of those documents. It took a long time that night. Wow, you didn't get home till two in the morning? I just didn't want to make a single error and have Mr. Scott send it back for revision.

"Now, when Pepe gets back from Colombia, I'll be as fresh as a daisy and ready for a new romance."

The two were walking down the short hallway that led to Guillermo's office as they discussed their mutual friend.

Guillermo laughing and shaking his head, responded,

"He's ready for daisies. That's the truth! Working in landfill management can't be the most pleasant work in the world. Slogging up to his thighs in human detritus. Did he tell you about that ghoulish experience he had that last time in Las Vegas? His team was surveying a site and they came upon a leg, with an attached foot."

Isadora made a gagging sound.

"Eeyew. A leg. A disembodied leg! With toes? Was there blood? Whose was it?"

"Who knows? We both agreed it had to be some mafia killing. But the county health department identified it as a horse's leg."

They both stopped at the open door of Guillermo's office. Isadora retorted,

"Yeah, right. A coroner can't tell a horse's hoof from ten toes. You ask me, they're all in cahoots with each other out there where the big money is. Or maybe the doc didn't want to be chopped up for shipment on the next Las Vegas garbage truck."

Isadora was looking around Guillermo's office as she spoke. The ghoulish tattle drifted away.

"Should I put the flowers in this vase? I'll get some water. That'll keep them lovely and fresh. They're beautiful. What do we have? Red roses, lilies, freesias, sprigs of eucalyptus. Heavenly scents. You've got very good taste. In women also. She's going to love them and give you a huge kiss!"

She left, then returned in two minutes from the ladies room with the water.

"I better hurry. Only five minutes till class starts."

Deal Me a Card

After arranging the flowers with little ceremony, Isadora set the crystal vase of blooms in the middle of Guillermo's desk and walked out of his office.

****

When classes were over, Guillermo returned to his office.

"Lupe, where's Emma?"

"She hurried out right after the students. Said she had to take care of some business, Mr. Guerrero. Those flowers on your desk are gorgeous. Who's celebrating?"

"She didn't tell you where she was going? It's late for any kind of business. Hope everything's okay."

Guillermo threw a casual comment over his shoulder as he walked into his office,

"Who's celebrating?" Isadora and I are celebrating. The two of us really got it together this past week. It's all falling into place."

He came out of his office and stopped in front of his secretary's desk.

"Maybe if I call her at home now? No. She won't have arrived yet. I'll call her tomorrow at work. She'll be feeling better, rested. We'll have more time to talk.

"Well, goodnight, Lupe. See you tomorrow."

As Lupe turned off the light in her boss's office, the flower petals drooped, their luster dimmed.

****

On Thursday evening in the therapist's office, Emma sat with her knees locked primly together in front of her, toes pointing forward. Her arms rested on the cushioned rests. She looked down at her lap as Doctor Schwarzman addressed her.

"So, you won't be returning. This is your last session."

247

Deal Me a Card

"Yes, Doctor. I've made up my mind. Two nights ago, I sat down to analyze what's happened. I'd like to share something I wrote.

So I theorize on men's eternal struggle. They want to feel, think, believe that they're in charge, in control of something, somebody. They cling desperately to the hope that they exercise some power and allure even as the wily, wild, unwieldy penis goes its own way, dominating, distracting. Yet I play along, loving them, hating them, they unknowing thinking me oblivious, naïve, a softie, willing, an easy lay, loving me as I grasp their weapon."

Neither she nor her listener winced. Emma continued,

"But in the end, Doctor Schwarzman, I will not, cannot face deception and lies."

"Have you spoken with Guillermo?'

"What's there to talk about? I was gone. Isadora was here. She's the sensuous Cuban who's been waiting on the sidelines for months. Everyone's been watching, gossiping.

"They were made for each other. She's a lying bitch who looks at every male with those bedroom eyes. No wonder her husband left her. And those men, they run panting to stroke her ego and other parts! So now her parts are available, and mine are not."

"Decisions made in anger or haste should be given more thought, Emma."

"I've thought about a life in Florida. My brother works for the Department of Juvenile Justice. He was telling me over the holidays they need teachers at the facilities. There's one located quite near to his home with a vacancy for a teaching position.

"He actually invited me to live with them. There's a mother-in-law apartment, detached, down the driveway. His wife's mother is dead, so it's vacant. I could live there for awhile until I find a place of my own. They have nice homes in the Tallahassee area, very inexpensive."

Deal Me a Card

"You were working on a more lasting, as you called it, mature relationship, Emma."

Doctor Schwarzman in vain tried to return her patient to the crux. In vain.

"Well, I can do that just as well in Florida. I expect I'll meet a Jimbo or Bubba, or Chuck or who knows. Don't you love those names? I kinda like Bubba myself. I should have no problem connecting with someone who has that name. Or perhaps there's an eligible state worker. Being the capital city, Tallahassee teems with them. Or even a professor at one of the universities. There's no lack of fine Southern gentlemen.

"I could buy a gun and learn to shoot to prove how well I fit in. God help those men. They're very enamored of their weapons down in the South. See them as extended penises. Hunting and fishing are their favorite pastimes. They keep harping on something they call the war of Northern Aggression, when they talk about the Civil War. They're still aggrieved, felt the South should never have lost, that they got a rotten deal. So they keep fighting it over and over. Manly men!

"And of course, there's football.

"My time's up, isn't it?"

"I am going to ask you to consider returning for one more session next week. You're obviously very distraught, and angry.

"Will you call me? Or will we block out your usual time?"

Emma glared at the therapist, her lips tightly locked. Then she decided,

"Oh all right, I'll be here.

"Yes. Good. Next week, the same time is fine. I'll call if things evolve differently."

****

Deal Me a Card

Monday morning bright and early, Isadora breezed in the Center at nine o'clock. She peeked around the door at Guillermo. He looked up from the letter he was writing, smiled,

"Good morning, young lady."

"Hi. I told Lupe I had something very special for you, so she let me in."

Isadora drew a package, gift-wrapped in silver and tied with a red-and-gold bow, from her faux-patent leather purse.

"A present from the three kings. A little late, by about ten days," Guillermo laughed.

"Perhaps you could say that. But it's from me to you because you have been so kind and generous with your time. Why don't you open it?"

"Yes, Lupe," Guillermo looked over Isadora's shoulder at his secretary standing in the doorway, "what is it?"

You have a phone call. Do you want me to transfer it? It's Emma. Or should I tell her you're busy?"

"No, put her through, please."

He was tearing through the wrapping paper as he picked up the receiver.

"Hello, good morning. I apologize that this weekend was so busy and we couldn't get together. I had another meeting with Doc and Big M. A follow-up of the one before Christmas. Things are heating up with those young punks...

"Isadora, this is truly special....

"Oh, sorry, Emma, Isadora just delivered a gift from the Three Kings. It's one of those ink-filled pens. A Parker, the old-fashioned type that writes script so beautifully.

"How did you know I coveted one like this, Isadora? And gold-plated too....

"Sorry, Emma. Emma?"

Guillermo stared at the receiver,

"She hung up! Must have gotten another call. I'll have to call her back later.

"But thanks so much, senora. You're very thoughtful.

Deal Me a Card

"Isn't it something, Lupe? This woman spoils me."

Lupe and Isadora flashed toothy grins at each other.

****

At the five thirty staff meeting that evening, Emma announced her departure when it was her turn to report on any business.

"My brother Adam has offered me an excellent position, teaching juveniles in a residential facility for young criminals.

"It's an ideal situation. I'll be near to all my family. And my son can visit me from Europe. I think I told a couple of you about Thomas who's studying at Cambridge. He'll have no excuse now not to fly over.

"The big adventure starts in mid-February, so it's hurry, hurry, hurry."

"But, Emma, what about the students here. The ones you were helping me with. You're so good with them. And Brother Keith really communicates best with you. And what about ..."

"Nobody's indispensable, Daniel. That's what a nice holy Sister of the Holy Spirit told me on my very first job. I've never forgotten it.

"Besides, you've developed a great rapport with Brother Keith and the kids, Daniel.

"With the New Year, the birth of the nineties, we're all into fresh relationships and ventures.

"Right, Isadora?"

"Right, I tell you, it's a relief that Mr. Pig is out of my life once and for all, and new doors have opened. Mr. Guerrero here knows all about it."

Emma gave Isadora a steady look, pausing for ten seconds before she continued, cocking her head and smiling sardonically,

"That's for certain."

She dismissed the other woman with those three short words, then turned to Carmelita,

"I'll need to talk with you tomorrow, Carmelita, so we can have all the students' paperwork ready for the new teacher."

Then to Guillermo,

"Now if it's all right with you, Mr. Guerrero, I'll go to my classroom. I'm still here for about two weeks, but the business at hand doesn't really concern me."

"Emma, I want to speak to you after class about this move."

"I'm sorry, Mr. Guerrero,' Emma interrupted, "but Adam is calling from Tallahassee at ten o'clock tonight regarding some application forms I have to fill and return as soon as possible. And that's a priority right now. I'll have to leave right after class ends this evening. Just tell Carmelita what needs to be done."

Her nod swept across the room. Then she turned and walked away. The group watched as she slipped out the door.

A pin fell off the bulletin board, and they all heard it drop. The liberated memo offering child care services fluttered to the floor soundlessly. Robin's pencil, trapped bird-like in his fingers and performing its arrhythmic tap dance on the table, was the only other sound in the room.

****

Three days later, Emma shut the front door and entered, shoulders hunched, into the living room of her townhouse. Exhaustion from her Thursday session, earlier that evening with Doctor Schwarzman, had slowed her every move since she stepped out of her car.

Sash untied, she slipped off her brown suede coat, and hung it on the back of the armchair. She hit the Select and Play buttons on her stereo. Then massaged the nape of her neck as the first notes of Sibelius' Second Symphony bounced its glacial drops off the ceiling.

She flung herself onto the sofa. Reaching down, she languidly unzipped first one and then the other calf-high boot. Eased them off her legs. Wriggling her bottom into the soft cushion, she leaned back. Then stretched her feet atop the coffee table.

She let her lids droop over her swollen eyeballs. Yes, she had wept. But the tears had been cleansing. Now she let her mind wander, pick through her unfocused thoughts, selecting the details of her last outpouring a couple of hours ago.

Well, that was that. She had terminated her therapy sessions. During the last few months, Doctor Schwarzman had served as an empathic listener, a gentle sponge absorbing her narrative, helping her sift through her lifelong foray into the realm of relationships. She had been the gracious recipient of Emma's tentative insights, opening the way for her client to probe deeply hidden memories.

Some of her relationships had been hardly liaisons, being ever so little, of hardly any consequence, yet persistent. Others were good for a laugh, for cheer and for warmth. Some, when and if resurrected, once again wielded blows of excruciating pain to the psyche and stirred emotions that would continue to bruise and draw blood throughout her life.

She knew she had to uncover these wounds. Including her marriage of nearly twenty years. It could not hide, a raw carcass suspended in a deep freeze, an intricate image woven in the fabric of her emotional and spiritual tapestry. Unraveling the knots could bring closure. She had used almost every minute of her final session to untangle the bonds.

Now, as she sat there on her couch, she rewound the mental tape of the words she had spoken during that last hour with her confidante.

Deal Me a Card

"Finally, Doctor. Schwarzman, you must hear about my last relationship of any significance. It brought me to where I am.

"Each person has one monkey on his back probably. The man who was my husband has three.

"In the beginning they were invisible, silent. Then they started their chatter, and never shut up. Fresh Love, blind, deaf and dumb, ignored them balanced on his shoulder.

"Devoted to his parents, the man was forever filled with remorse on the one hand because he could not live up to their expectations, and rage on the other because they gave him so little tangible nurturing and no pocket money at all.

"Always broke, always borrowing like his family, the man has no financial savvy. Our joke, cute at first, then as years went by making the mouth pucker from the bitterness of reality, he married me because he could not repay or pay his debts. For rent, for food, for car payments, then over the years for our mutual indulgences, fripperies, mortgages, fine art, second mortgages, vacations, our son's teeth.

"Master's degrees, teacher certification, mine. Salary growing, spend, spend. Refinanced the home, spend, spend, spend. Worked two jobs sometimes three, to pay the bills. I saved for the boy's future, for retirement. We bought real estate, raised a child. Save, spent, over and over.

"Addictions stifled, strangled, and stunted the man. Their treachery pulsed through the family's blood, their seductiveness curled around our ankles. They swept over our heads. I waited, patiently. Promises, promises.

"Night after shattered night, a decade, then two decades of nights he spent in the garage drinking, smoking. And in our bed an empty space beside me. Watch his eyes, observe his stance, follow his footsteps. Walks lightly when he's had a few, when he's high or drunk, speaks softly, shoulders squared, eyes steely, cold piercing icicles penetrating, intent, focused on empty dreams and promises. But he can't disguise the breath.

Deal Me a Card

"Insanity, desperation. Once I actually had a loaded gun in my mouth, one shot would end it all. Wound my tongue around the barrel, caressed its seductive swollen roundness. Inviting metallic coldness slowly, lovingly penetrated my palate, my throat. Yanked it out before pulling the trigger, before I swallowed its exploding, life-ending, numbing spurting ejaculate. Considered wistfully many times more, but never tried again. There was work to do, a child to raise, money to earn, an image to maintain.

"Quiescence.

"'It's only cocaine. Harmless, they say it's milder than pot if you're careful. They're using it in the bathroom at the office. We stood on Santa Monica beach, just a little snort, it was cool. No harm,' he said.

"When the boy is grown up, I will leave.

"Watch his eyes, watch him walk, shoulders squared, he's drinking again after a six-week hiatus. Stares at me intently, furrowed brow, red eyes, cold as steel, looking for approval, disapproval, forgiveness, any reaction to jump at, criticize, blame for our problems.

"'Look at me. I've gotten up every morning for the last nineteen years no matter what, to go to work. Grow up.'

"Night after lonely night, a sliver of light under the garage door, an empty space in our bed. Weeks of nights, months of nights. His pain drowned in alcohol. My pain, my problem.

"Once during a vacation in Zihuatanejo, I entered the room excitedly, to tell of the dolphins leaping in farewell at sunset, and he was sitting, drink in hand. Hilo, balmy Hawaiian nights on the lanai of the Wild Ginger Inn, cruise liners glinting on the Bay, scent of frangipani, silhouettes of coconut palms. Endless cicada shrilling of a tropical night. Even the air swayed with unspoken sea mysteries. Kilauea erupting silently, glowing in the distance. He found a low-dive bar, and drank.

Deal Me a Card

"Our son went off to college. Left me behind with the father he loves, the model hardworking stiff, the lovable Dad, the sot.

"Weeks of lonely nights, empty space in my bed, and a sliver of light under the garage door as he drank, and drank.

"Then souring Love stifled for twenty years, choked, slowly died.

"After two years of a long-distance, online affair, a handful of discreet cross-country trysts concocted as business trips, I was ready to leave.

"The man and I discussed the move one morning on a carefully selected deserted beach, slightly windswept, mild spring weather, sunny, steady beating of waves on the sand, whispering swishing breezes. Very calculated.

"One night, our last week in the same house, the man, my husband asked for a final act of love. Showed me some porn on the computer, Asian woman fellating some white guy. Asked for the same, our modus amandi for the last fifteen years or so. Blind, deaf, dumb, I succumbed. A mouthful of remorse, regret, no, remembrance, goodbye.

"So now you know my angst, Doctor Schwarzman. I need and don't need men. I can take them or leave them. I'd mostly leave them - but, I remind myself they really are a mere one chromosome distance from me. It's a matter of jiggling genes and juggling hormones after all. That's the fascination. But for now, I'm writing the end of another chapter."

Emma's eyes jerked open as a sudden weight landed with a thud on her midriff. She gasped. Pulled herself back from the psychologist's couch to the present moment. Smiled, giggled as Mamasan's loud purr tickled her right ear-lobe, and raccoon-bushy tail swept up and down her left arm. The kitty endured her mistress's strokes, patiently waiting until the symphony began to wend to its finale. Then both listeners rose. One to fill the cat's water bowl and daub two teaspoons of her favorite tuna in her dish, the other to

Deal Me a Card

delve into the food. As the pet lapped daintily at her dinner, Emma looked down at her with affection.

"Mamasan, you're going to love your new home in Florida. But we'll have to watch out for the hawks. Or they'll swoop down and snatch you up, carry you far, far away!"

The cat ignored her, continued munching stolidly as her tail snapped back and forth. Back and forth like a metronome, marking time as the symphony climaxed.

* * * * * * * * * *

The following day, Friday, Guillermo sat waiting at the corner table. A vase overflowing with a cascade of hothouse blooms accented the perky checkered cloth cover. The open bottle held their favored wine. It had begun here at *Joie de Vivre*.

Promptly at seven thirty, Emma walked through the door. His eyes absorbed her every move as she made her way towards him. She wore deep blue, her favorite color. The knit dress lovingly hugged her form. Its flared skirt graciously parted the way for her steps, stroking her hips as she, the woman he adored, gracefully swayed across the room. The hollow of her neck his lips had so often owned, were now under siege from the luster of her pearl collar. Light from a myriad candles flickering in wall crevices and on the twelve tables, shot sparks from her undulating cobalt-black hair, recently styled, the last trim before her departure. Ah, how often he had stroked those thick tresses when she lay in his arms.

Guillermo rose to take her hand. Turned it over and kissed her palm. Let his lips linger. Emma withdrew her fingers from his caress. Her eyes and a sharp swish of her head signaled no, to any further signs of endearment.

"I'm glad you chose this place. It's genteel, and the menu is so fine. A nice memory to take away with me."

"I thank you for agreeing to dine with me. We need to talk."

257

"Yes, away from the rest of the crowd we'll be able to tie up some loose ends."

She sipped from her glass, "This wine is good. Shall we order?"

The attentive waiter leaned forward.

"Madam, the soup du jour is a crème of asparagus, and for entrees tonight, we have salmon served with an herb sauce or chicken *en croute*. The vegetables? Baby carrots or sautéed squash *aux oignons*, and mashed potatoes or saffron rice. Would you like a few minutes to decide?"

"No, I'll have the salmon, squash and potatoes. Thanks."

"The same for me."

He waited till the server had walked off with their order.

"Emma, what's happened?"

"Guillermo, we have both made decisions and it's time to act on them."

"I've decided nothing." His voice had a hint of desperation and confusion.

"Exactly. But I have. And I must move on."

Emma selected a crispy roll of French bread from the basket. She broke it apart, added a daub of butter to a morsel. She chewed silently, listening.

Seconds before, plaintive notes of *How Am I Supposed To Live Without You* piped through the dining room.

"You can't do this to me. I don't understand. We have so much going for us. I won't let you go. I can't let you go."

"The only contracts I know of, are with Jones and Guerrero Construction and with the Educational Center. And each has received my notice as required. I don't recall any other formal business between us."

She broke off another brittle fragment, buttered and ate it.

"What do you want? Just ask me. Please."

Deal Me a Card

"Nothing. Just dinner right now. I'm hungry. And here it is. *Bon appétit!*"

Guillermo strained to keep his voice low. "How can you eat at a time like this? There's so much going on. We need you. We've had two meetings about the gang situation and you're an integral part of the next stage of the community plan."

"As I said at the meeting on Monday, nobody's indispensable. You have a whole bevy of ladies to step into my shoes. I'm glad to be shedding them anyway. They were getting awfully tight. Pinching my toes. Isadora should do a splendid job. She's just the right fit with her background and culture and personality."

"She's the problem, isn't she? Well, let me tell you exactly what …"

"That's quite unnecessary. Lupe explained it all. I understand completely." Emma's voice was icy.

She smoothly changed the topic to concerns she had about some students' progress, giving suggestions about which teachers should best meet their needs. She reminded her date to have any of her belongings that lingered in his home ready for her pick-up the next day, Saturday, in the morning.

They finished their entrée. Neither could have described its finer points, let alone its taste, for a million dollars.

"Let's look at the dessert list, shall we? The chocolate mousse is quite superb, "to die for", as Stanley, the chef at the college would say. I'm going to miss some of the characters around here."

"I'll miss you terribly. You've become part of my life. Emma. Please, can we talk some more?"

"The void is always swiftly filled. We both know that very well. I give you two weeks, and you'll be on to bigger and better things."

The only sound as they ate their dessert was the tinkle of spoons on china. An observer might have been puzzled,

259

the dessert usually relished in slow motion by diners, was scooped up like loam to fill a flowerpot. From the look on the couple's faces, the mousse might have tasted like dirt.

Emma reached out and raised Guillermo's wrist. His heart somersaulted. She checked the dial of his watch.

"It's almost ten o'clock. We must go. Time to call it a day." she said.

His arm dropped back on the table, as his heart sank to his toes.

Then the waiter was hovering over them smiling, benevolent and politic as he returned Guillermo's credit card. Unlike the agitated angel flapping its desperate wings as it fluttered uncomfortably, then finally lost its balance and fell off Guillermo's shoulder. It ended. There at *Joie de Vivre*.

Deal Me a Card

CHAPTER 33

TWO DAYS LATER at eight o'clock it was already dark as midnight. *Normal for the end of January since winter was still upon them,* he mused as he stood on his porch and stared into the nothingness of his backyard. The density of the evening air was laden with foreboding echoing in the coyote's howl from a nearby slope.

Guillermo's shoulder blades ached as if burdened with those sacks of tomatoes or cantaloupes, or onions or whatever the hell he used to lug from field to truck those many years ago. *Ah, those were the good old days. What was so wonderful about them? No heartbreak. Only back breaking.*

I should stop being so emotional, so melodramatic, he thought as he took another large sip of his third vodka over ice. On the rocks, like his life.

He should forget the last thirty-six hours. But relentlessly, as he stood in the pitch dark, his mind drifted back, a shipwreck of battered thoughts through storm-tossed waves.

****

Saturday morning, Emma had dropped by as promised to pick up her clothes, shorts and tee-shirt from last summer, a pair of thigh-high suede boots, panty hose and the strappy midnight blue gown she had worn when they attended *Madame Butterfly* at the Dorothy Chandler Center last November, and three sticks of lipstick.

After a stilted search around the house, he muttered,

"I think that's all. If I find anything else, I bring it to the Center on Monday."

Deal Me a Card

She uttered blithely, "Or you can give them to Goodwill or the Salvation Army. That's all they're good for," twisting the dagger a little deeper.

She turned away from Guillermo and smiled brightly, too brightly, at Richard and Daniel standing silently in the kitchen. The former looked as though he might burst into tears. The latter wore a frown and a sulky pout on his face.

"One of you could help your dad deliver my discards. Cheer up, guys! I'll send you postcards."

"Emma, are you sure about this move? You're a part of our family. You must know that. You were to be our mom," Daniel pleaded.

His voice choking, Richard added,

"You know you're the best thing that happened to our family since our mother died. We need you. No, it's more than that, we all three love you, Emma!"

Emma pursed her lips and swallowed. After a minute, she spoke,

"No more sentimentality, okay? I love you also, Daniel, Richard, but I must leave this place. Let the cards fall where they may."

She turned back to face Guillermo,

"I'll see you Monday. My last week."

Her eyes met those of all three men.

"Isn't that exciting?"

Nobody had a response.

One last look in the closets, one farewell touch of her cold lips on his cheek, as the couple stood in the open doorway. Then, shutting the car door for her after she had secured her seat-belt, he watched as she drove off leaving him alone.

He stood there motionless, steeling himself to grapple with the blood that spurted from his broken heart, seeped through his shirt, and dripped onto the gravel path. *Well it should have.*

Deal Me a Card

When the Jetta disappeared around the bend in the road for the last time, he went indoors. His sons had disappeared into their rooms. This was no time to have a heart-to-heart conversation.

He grabbed his lined corduroy jacket, threw it on and wandered off in the hills behind the house. The strenuous eight-mile hike wearied every bone in his body to a welcome numbness. But his mind refused to shut down.

Back home, following a long hot shower, Guillermo had sunk into a restless sleep. Dreams, of standing on the deck of a ship shouting farewell into a dense mist, or calling out Emma's name and only hearing her infectious laughter echoing disembodied in a vast empty room, shook him awake a dozen times.

Six glasses of spring water and four trips to the toilet helped not at all.

He woke on the Sabbath to relentless unholy agitation. Missed church services, sulked all morning long. Paced the living room.

After Mass, his sons had made a quick visit to their aunt Juanita at noon, then driven home bringing Sunday brunch with them. Guillermo had passed up her customary invitation pleading a suspicion of flu symptoms. His restless all-night tossing in bed over the last week, the tightness in his heart, and yes, though he would kill before he admitted this to anyone, his weeping were not details that he had any inclination to share. Though he intuited from his sister-in-law's soothing words that she had heard the news.

The thick chicken and vegetable soup and chiles stuffed with Monterey jack and spicy meat raised his spirits somewhat. But his dogged tilting of the Stoli, clinking of ice cubes, raising of crystal to his lips, and gradual slurred words fulfilled their function.

He succeeded. The young men fled, early, at four thirty. Slowly at first, edging towards the front door. Surely in fear of being trampled underfoot by the twenty-ton elephant in

Deal Me a Card

the room refusing to stop trumpeting the absence of Emma or eulogizing her imminent departure. And she a mere size ten.

Avoiding the issue. Promising to return early, in a couple of hours. Talking about research for a paper, studying for a test, an early appointment scheduled for Monday at the Center.

Then they were gone,

"Hope you feel better tomorrow, Dad!"

"Try to get to bed early, sleep it off."

Out the door. Where most things seemed to be headed.

CHAPTER 34

"ARE THERE LATINOS in Florida?"

"My three cousins and their parents live in Miami. Some place called Homestead."

"When I first to the US, I lived in Central Florida for five months. We worked in the fields down there in Immokalee, harvesting the tomatoes. Man, that was hard work. Almost broke my back, day after day. The bossmen, they treated us like we were slaves, like the blacks way back when.

"Hey, I lived like that in Moultrie, in Georgia, not so far from you. All the single men together in these camps with trailers. Families with children in a different section.

"My brother is still down there. He just travels in a circle, following the fruit and vegetable harvests all year round.

"If I give you a letter, Miss Emma, can you give it to him? His name is Samuel. He's in a place in Florida now. Called Havana.

"How about that? Like Cuba? That's not Cuba, no?

"It's Florida. Don't you remember the map she showed us with all our countries?"

****

The classroom conversation, on this Thursday, her last evening at the Center, echoed in Emma's head as she walked slowly to her car. Her students had brought a *tres leches cake*, the favorite delicacy made with three kinds of milk, to bid her farewell. They would miss her, they said, but they were accustomed to transience, to saying "*adios*." Even as they murmured their goodbyes and tried to hug away her tearful smiles, they were already asking at the front desk about who would replace her the following Monday.

Deal Me a Card

"Emma, Emma, slow down, I have to speak to you. We have to talk. It's urgent."

Emma quickened her pace as she heard Isadora's voice behind her. Up to now she had deftly avoided her. Indeed, she had evaded everyone.

The faculty farewell dinner the evening before, had been stilted and swift.

Instead of the usual lavish spread of multi flavors, scents and tastes of chicken, chile, rice and legumes, a circular row of sandwiches, *a la* nondescript fillings, had decorated the table, fringed with liter bottles of soda. Emma thought she might as well have eaten the plastic tray for the satisfaction the few nibbles and hasty gulps gave her. Especially after she had taken a fleeting upward glance at the fluttering *Good luck We'll Miss U* banner.

She had choked something down, and then hurriedly excused herself to finish some last-minute scheduled post-tests. Nobody had stopped her as she left the room, coughing, with shoulders hunched.

Last night and this evening, the hours had passed by rapidly, with her attention totally focused on the students to the exclusion of all Center personnel. Her exits on both nights, Wednesday and Thursday, were swift and silent.

In her mind's eye she saw herself moving determinedly and rapidly through the past week, as she trashed discarded memories and firmly cast away any lingering doubts while reaching toward the future. Tomorrow's lunch hosted by Jones and Guerrero was the last appearance she had to endure. She had saved one fixated smile for that event.

The hand on her shoulder now brought her back to the present moment. Isadora had caught up with her, dragging along the overpowering smells of her perfume.

Emma half-turned to avoid the grasp. Her mouth opened in reprimand. She stepped back a pace.

A crack in the sidewalk caught and held the heel of her shoe. Off balance, she stumbled backwards. There was no

Deal Me a Card

way she could catch herself. She kept falling. Her head smashed on the sidewalk, hard. The skull connected so violently with the concrete that the contents of her head oscillated. With the impact, her brain felt as though it dislocated. Eyeballs vibrated, almost jerked out of their sockets.

Emma wanted so much to pass out, but she willed herself not to. She knew if she shut her eyes, she would lose consciousness and be gone for a great while. This was not the time. She lay there, unable to move. Hurting. Her tailbone had also bashed harshly against the unyielding ground and the pain was nearly unbearable. Numbness in her head. Agony in her body.

A few students had stopped, responding to Isadora's screaming,

"Get over here. Quick, quickly. Something's happened!"

One knelt down by her. She recognized Ignacio who had worked in the fields of Immokalee. He asked urgently, "Should we call an ambulance?"

Emma answered from very far away,

"No."

She slurred, "I'm sorry."

He muttered, "There's nothing to be sorry for, teacher. You're hurt."

For some reason, those words comforted and reassured her, gave her permission to be vulnerable and wounded, but strong.

Then there was blackness.

267

CHAPTER 35

ON THAT PRISTINE SUNDAY NIGHT THREE DAYS LATER, Guillermo lay prone. Once more alone. In his deserted backyard.

An hour ago, he had surrendered with much resistance his vigil at Emma's side.

Juanita quietly murmured,

"She's breathing peacefully and sleeping soundly. Go home, get some rest for a few hours." Her admonition was to no avail.

Stubbornly he remained standing by the bed, looking down at Emma's face.

Arriving at eight o'clock to offer him some respite, Daniel and Richard were able to guide him firmly by the arms out of Emma's room, down the hallway and to the car only because they had threatened him.

"Dad, you're a ghost. Your eyes are bloodshot, your hair disheveled as if you've not bathed for a month," Richard chided him.

"Look at his lips, Daniel. They're chapped and twitching every other minute. His breath smells awful! He's about to break down just when Emma needs him most!"

"He's right, you know, *Papi*. When she opens her eyes, Emma will want to see you. Alive. Now, go home, get some rest. We'll stay here, and *Tia* Juanita won't leave her side either. If anything changes, we'll call you. I promise. You can be here is ten minutes." Daniel urged.

He drove home, parked, and headed to the backyard.

Spread like a blanket in the universe above him, the Milky Way strove in vain to reassure him that some things are eternal. Though the woolen serape hugged him tightly, it afforded little warmth and no consolation. He shuddered, his fetal shape cradled in a hillside rock. The wind's lullaby was

Deal Me a Card

not soothing. Though he hoped it would keep away any pestilential creepy-crawlies.

Just seven days ago, a wild beast had crouched here in this hollow stone. In his numbed state, he remembered that ominous sound. Then, he, wretched drunk, had welcomed the sound as a sympathetic echo of his misery. Now he knew, that should he open his mouth, sounds would spew from his lungs, far outperforming any hyena's lamentation. So he forced his lips shut.

He steeled his mind, shuffled his thoughts into some sense of order so they would not dissolve into a chaos of utter disbelief and despair. His reason forced him to recall, to retrace, so as to create some meaning out of the pandemonium hammering on the door to his sanity. He willed himself to nail down every detail of the past week leading to the meltdown of the last seventy-two hours, the heart-wrenching events now threatening to annihilate his world.

****

Seven days ago, before the accident, he had believed that nothing more could devastate his life. No event could further wreck the bleak future that lay ahead without Emma.

When he finally turned off the lights at ten o'clock, on the debacle of Sunday fun with his sons, his imbibing had not numbed his heartache or filled the emptiness. But he had to quit, since neither his head nor his digestive track could take any further abuse, and sober reality faced him in the morning.

His stomach bulged from the excesses of the day and from the thirty-two ounces of water that he had poured down his gullet, despite the imminent urge to heave up his insides. So what if he had to rouse himself to piss at two in the morning. All the better to cleanse the system of toxic wastes.

His left brain was elbowing his right brain out of the way. Tomorrow was going to be different. He tossed about

269

under the covers for what seemed like hours, then fell into a deep sleep. Once he jumped up, emptied his bladder. A cascade of purifying urine.

****

Refreshed the next day, he awoke at six. He had plunged into the demands of Monday morning, clear-eyed, with sharpened focus, his stomach lining only slightly fragile.

First he tackled a meeting with his team of earnest accountants. The two men and three women, bespectacled, suited and shiny-shod, were gearing up for the onslaught of nervy taxpayers. These they would combat valiantly during the days and evenings of the next three months.

The brochures his secretary had mailed, and the e-mail reminders, were already reaping results. He assigned two of the group to review the previous year's records and contact the company's permanent business accounts. Methodically, he spent an hour on the phone with four of his reliable customers.

During the course of the morning Raoul had called, concerned about him. Guillermo responded, joked about his capacity for liquid consolation.

Then Raoul had explained that the construction company needed certified security guards nightly, to watch over its projects,

"One for Lakeview Hills and one in the Santa Clarita Valley. There've been break-ins. They steal the materials, tools. What they can't take with them, they vandalize. Gang graffiti sprayed on some lumber, probably ruined the quality permanently. They're monsters.

"It's getting out of hand, *hermano*.

"You and Garcia and Velasquez are coming up with any innovative strategies at those meetings?" Raoul had queried.

270

Deal Me a Card

"One thing we all know. We've pretty much lost the war against the proliferation of gangs. They're here to stay, Raoul. How the communities are able to control them, is now the million-dollar question," Guillermo had responded, sighing. Felt himself slipping into despondency again.

"By the way, how's Eva doing? Settling into her new position okay?"

Raoul guessed where the question was coming from.

"She's working out well. Emma is only coming in each morning this week for a couple of hours. To answer any last questions, iron out the glitches.

"Friday will be Emma's last day. Really, on that day, she's just joining us at Sierra's for a good-bye lunch. The office wants to present her with a going-away gift.

"No need to assume that you'll be there. I know you won't. Sorry, *hermano*.

"Call me if some prospects show up for those positions. Eva can schedule the interviews.

"And, you know I'm here if you need me." Raoul hung up.

At the staff meeting that evening, Guillermo reminded the teachers that starting the next day he would be visiting classes to deliver the usual pep talk he delivered during the first weeks of classes. They discussed the food for the farewell party.

Emma was, of course, not present.

****

Tuesday before the calamity, he had met with his team again to review changes in the tax laws and new computer software. The college had called to ask if some of his accountants could provide pro bono services, tax preparation workshops and appointments with students. He set up a calendar for the next three months, lined up volunteers.

That evening he dropped in on two classes. One of them was Emma's. She sat, silent with a glued-on smile, at

271

the back of the room. Somehow he managed to deliver his usual light-hearted speech sprinkled with self-deprecating asides. Without looking at her once.

"You went back and forth each year from Queretaro to the San Joaquin Valley for five years?" one fascinated student asked

"Yes, when I was thirteen until I was eighteen.

"You know how it is. The work is seasonal. When the harvest was complete I'd take back what I earned to the family. I'd pick the fruit and vegetables here, and then return to Mexico and go to school if I could. But education was sporadic because my parents needed me to plough and plant the fields at home. I being the youngest and strongest. You wouldn't know it now, what with all this flab. Too much good living."

He laughed as he rubbed his firm belly and massaged his muscular upper arm.

"And you were all alone with no family when you worked in those fields?" a listener asked.

"Well, Raoul, my older brother, some of you know him, he's half-owner of Jones and Guerrero Construction, was here in the valley. He got connected with the builders and never looked back.

"By the way, the company needs two security guards urgently, so see Carmelita or Leticia if you think you qualify, or if you know somebody who does. These are excellent opportunities to enter the workforce.

"Back to those early days of my life in California. I stayed up there in the Central Valley. There was an uncle and his family, near Stockton. I visited them a couple of times. But mostly, we young guys hung out together."

Another student interjected,

"Not a bad life. Freedom."

Guillermo asked the speaker,

"Have you ever worked in the fields for a day. Or even an hour?

Deal Me a Card

The student who had made the remark looked shamefaced. "Nah ha. No way. My father and my grandfather but not me. They brought me over here, to this region, when I was twelve. I stayed with my aunt."

Guillermo got into it. "Well, let's say that a burro has it better. At least he has four legs to support his load. We were bent over for hours and hours, limited breaks for a drink of water. A half hour for lunch and using the toilets. No, let's not get into that. Enough about the fields of hell.

"Let me tell you the happy part, when my life changed.

"I tell as many of you folk about this as I can, because I want you to realize that anything is possible. Grab at every chance. Don't be scared. Take a risk. I'm not talking about anything illegal. Okay? None of this drug dealing. What I mean is that you must grab at it when someone suggests an opportunity."

"What? Some young white lady falls off her bicycle on the street and you help her up and she takes you home and marries you?" joked a slim young man, dressed in a starched white shirt and jeans sporting sharply-ironed creases. The class laughed politely, and Guillermo continued,

"Hey, that could happen. But that was not my ticket to salvation. Would you believe it was because I did not speak English?"

"So why are we here?" someone sassed back.

"No, no, that's not the point.

"Listen. I'm talking about being in the right place at the right time.

"I remember that morning so clearly. So let me tell you the story of how I got here.

"It's February, about twenty-five years ago, a Monday, still quite dark at dawn. All weekend we had been celebrating the Candelaria feast. Two nights of carousing. Innocent fun. Eight young men from our group, dressed in homemade costumes, ponchos, masks and raffia wigs, dancing endlessly to a throbbing rhythm, in honor of *El Nino*

273

Deal Me a Card

de Dios and His Mother. One of the guys even sported a straggly white beard, false of course, representing the prophet who welcomed the Child to the temple. What better reason to rejoice? Needless to say there had been a steady flow of beer. The music was loud. Feet and hands were tapping. Gradually the party grew raucous as we ate, drank and made merry. Ephraim, my trailer-mate, had roasted a pig. We all had pitched in for the expenses. Yeah, good food, beans, zucchini squash, rice, tortillas. Some of the wives traveled with their husbands. So they sustained us, cooked for us on many occasions like this."

Guillermo walked back and forth between the desks and the students, taking each of them in.

"Those were the good times, when we had community spirit.

"Next morning we're standing there, with unwilling bodies but needy pockets. Still drowsy, not looking forward to the drudgery and aching muscles. Like we always did, the group assembled so the foreman could tell us which trucks to take to which fields.

"At least that's what I thought he was telling us, this time. You know how it is when you maybe understand a couple or three words someone is saying. You nod, and nod, smile, bob your head, smile. He's pointing this way and that. I was all eager to do his bidding, whatever it was. So I kept on nodding."

Someone interrupted the storyteller,

"We don't do that anymore. We understand. We ask questions."

"Exactly. And more power to you, and thanks to your teacher sitting back there." He gestured toward Emma who merely acknowledged with a slight smile. He resumed,

"Anyway, there I was, bobbing and smiling. And he beckons to me to follow him. Me. I couldn't believe it, so I looked behind. To my horror, everyone else had taken two steps backwards. I was standing there in front of the whole

274

crowd, about forty of us. All alone. So it appeared like I'd volunteered for the job."

Another voice interjected, breaking the narrative,

"You think some of them understood what was going on?"

"Of course. But they were not willing to take the risk.

"Me, I was simply ignorant of what was happening. Besides I was the youngest, and they figured I could take the beating, or stress."

A woman spoke up from among the rapt students, her question squeaky with fear,

"God, they weren't going to hurt you or punish you for something, were they?"

"No, no, no.

"Turns out they needed a driver. One of the usual workers had called in sick."

The same person sounding relieved, asked

"And of course just by chance, you knew how to drive?"

"No way. Always too poor to own wheels. But I had watched my uncle at home in Mexico, and the other drivers when they trucked us to work in the fields. So I put on the big pretense. Apologized. Said with my broken words that I needed a little practice since I had not driven for so long. So the bossman Mr. McClellan, showed me. Twenty minutes later I was on the way, at my new job. I had become the leader of the McClellan farm workers."

Three men spoke together,

"You helped him out."

"Exactly. His whole perspective of me changed. He'd send me on errands in the truck. I began to work on shifts with the other drivers.

"Actually, the truth of the matter was that he could pay me less. But I didn't care. I had new skills. Wider horizons stretched out before me.

Deal Me a Card

"And the day he asked me, 'Hey, Guerrero, why aren't you speaking English after all these years? There's the school where you can go to learn in the evenings.' That day was another ten steps up the ladder. That very night I enrolled. And my first teacher, Mrs. Ellison was my guardian angel personified. She never gave up on me."

"Like Ms. Emma!"

"Yes. All teachers like them are sent from heaven. No doubt about that. Ms. Ellison guided me all the way through college. I had many other instructors but she was the one, outstanding, always there. And, now, here I am!"

Standing up, Emma stated,

"Excuse me, Mr. Guerrero, but I think it's almost time for our break. And Ms. Isadora and her class are eagerly waiting for you."

The pre-selected class spokesperson declared,

"Mr. Guerrero, I want to thank you for inspiring us. Maybe some of us will make you proud too. One day!"

The same speaker seemed to pluck up courage,

"But before you go could you tell me one thing?'

"Sure!"

"If Ms. Emma is such an angel and great teacher, why are you letting her go?"

He had fled from the room without another word.

* * * * * * * * * *

Velasquez, Garcia and Guillermo had sat hunched at the table in the meeting room. That was Wednesday before the disaster. Occasionally, during a pregnant or convenient break in the discussion, one of them would scrape back the metal chair, push their palms against the edge of the table, and stand up. Loosen their hip bones. Shake the numbness out of their bums.

The other men and women, there were ten, would nod, sympathizing with the need to change position. Especially as each half-hour rolled by. *Though*, Guillermo thought

Deal Me a Card

irreverently, *their collective butts appeared to be made of tougher steel than his.* They seemed to have no desire to ease the pressure on their gluts, not even a wriggle.

None of the group had changed their position on the direction of their agenda either. A deepening concern and rising community hysteria about the gang activity in their neighborhoods had drawn them together. They had convened in the Victors' Gym to confront life and death issues. The agenda was laborious, but necessary.

Brother Keith described ponderously the new discipline code and counseling sessions that St Anselmo had implemented. Cold comfort, since it was a private institution with its own philosophy and timetable. Sister Nuala from the Family Services agency she had opened last October, with her crisp Irish brogue, recited a litany of individuals, young, middle-aged, old, lost or found, who arrived at her door, weeping their tales of intimidation and fear of death. Detective Yow and his partner reported on their expanded data base of gang member action. The pastor in his roman collar, Father Reilly, from the La Coloma Church, and a City council person in a pin-striped navy two piece suit, were mostly silent as they wrote copious notes on yellow, dog-eared legal pads.

The tenth, a youth named Smiley Perez, also listened, his eyes fixed almost unblinkingly on the table's crayon-scribbled surface. When he entered the room earlier, he ignored their muttered greetings and invitation, had taken the thirteenth seat that placed him two empty chairs frigidly apart from the rest. Fully aware of his role, the object of all attention brushed his hood off his head, unzipped his sweat-jacket. Eighteen eyes scanned him surreptitiously from under lowered lashes.

His shaven head, sinewy neck, and naked arms bore extravagant tattoos. Some expert with the needle had emblazoned him with the red-and-blue badge of his turf and

Deal Me a Card

his soul's identity. He wore them so proudly, as he did the zircon stud that pierced his left earlobe.

Guillermo had intuited a mixture of dread, curiosity and caution exuding from the more-adult section of the gathering. *They're probably wondering about his moniker. Smiley?* he thought to himself.

Smiley was not about to enlighten them. He was here because the priest at La Coloma Church, the guy sitting across from him, had thrown him a casual invitation at the *Super Mercado* three days ago, and his mother, who had been shopping with him added about a million entreaties besides. He was doing this meeting to get her off his back already. He had nothing else to do all day, anyway. He sat taciturn.

The other attendees took turns around the room.

"I'm sensing a willingness to talk. An opening seems to be taking shape, so we can all come out alive and safer at the other end."

"We have to establish neutral territory, a place where we literally can stand on ground sacred to all, owned by none."

"If there's no trust, there'll be weapons. Then looks exchanged. Some words taken wrongly, and any semblance of a truce is kaput!"

"Mr. Velasquez must be a key player. There's not a young person who doesn't know about this gym, or might have even worked out here, and doesn't appreciate the commitment he and his wife have made."

"Representatives from at least the following gangs should be there, Pacoima Flats, San Fer, Blythe Street, Treces, Vaughan Street. Can you add to the list, any others who should be invited?"

"Administrators, and maybe some faculty and students from the other schools need to be here too. A couple of the principals are simply throwing their hands in the air. Sorry officers, they say they get very little response from the

Deal Me a Card

juvenile division of law enforcement when they call. Who would be the most open? Suggestions?"

"The inmates are sleeping in the hallways at Juvenile Hall. They're stacked like packs of tarot cards. We book at least ten every day, and the judge has a backlog of at least two weeks for hearings."

"The convocation, I like to give it some sort of solemn name like that, so everyone understands this is serious business, life and death, the convocation should be just for the gang leaders and their look-outs. No crowding. There's too much risk of trouble."

"I hear you."

The discussion continued building hope and visions of peace. Even Smiley's countenance reflected his nickname, as he nodded in agreement with the plans. Though he was not able to force the smile into his eyes.

Finally the meeting had ended on a positive note. Yow, Sister Nuala and the councilperson promised personal contact with local schools' personnel.

Hovering in the air over the boxing ring, the punching bags and the weights, was a wavering mirage of a truce meeting in the near future. At least they resolved to set a late spring, or early summer date.

Doc Velasquez, catching up with Detective Yow and Father Reilly as they exited the meeting, expressed his hope,

"I'll breathe a sigh of relief when we make this happen. We need those safe streets. For the kids. Every last one of them. My boy too, Israel. He's just now spreading his wings. Got a girlfriend, Araceli Manolo. A cute little senorita. Her mother is raising her right. Israel's learning to drive and Araceli is giving him lessons. All the joys of youth, and who am I to say 'no' when he wants to venture out. He's such a good boy. Apple of his mother's eye. Excelling in school, thinking about college in two years. But with crack so accessible, it's volatile out there."

Deal Me a Card

Guillermo had overheard the men's exchange as he said his goodbyes, and nodded his agreement.

"See you next week."

Then he had turned to his car, and headed toward that evening with dread in his heart.

With a heavy step he strode towards kismet.

The Center was staging its final pathetic one-act play for Emma. The drama opened and closed that night, a flop as he had morosely expected. Bad food. Sad attitudes. Mad longing. The last stemming from his secret desperation.

It was worse than he had feared. Inedible refreshments. Robin teary-eyed and blowing his nose ostentatiously. Isadora spouting unintelligible, irrelevant anecdotes, cackling, refusing to be crushed by the surrounding gloom.

When the guest of honor had taken her bow and walked stiffly away from the doleful festivities, he slunk to his office. The solitary rose, grim remaining reminder of the misbegotten bouquet from two weeks ago, gave one last dying sigh as he crushed it in the wastebasket.

The Parker pen almost met the same fate. But as he turned it over from palm to palm, pondering its fate, he randomly thought *some man, woman or child would doubtless glean much pleasure from it*. So he hid it for another day. It fit snugly behind a row of Tax Code and Psychology tomes that rubbed shoulders with the set of Britannica's.

Lupe had left early, pleading a headache.

Desolate, abandoned, he had slumped in his leather armchair, empty-handed, light-headed from stifled emotion. The usually noisy hallway leading from the classrooms to the parking lot were uncharacteristically hushed. No perky students peeked in to say 'Good Night' or 'See you tomorrow.' He locked up the school, then drove mindlessly home.

****

Deal Me a Card

He welcomed Thursday and the all-day droning of state and federal specialists at a downtown Los Angeles Comfort Hotel conference. One after another they preached ad nauseam. First, the perky young woman provided an overview on the oft-narrated history of immigration. Then a doughy middle-aged man offered the *raison d'etre* for laws, amnesty and evaluation. Later, a silver-haired lady reviewed the revised testing materials, the purpose of the meeting.

Staring aimlessly at each presenter, Guillermo had let his mind wonder. Slipped into a fantasy.

He visualized the male presenter loosening his tie, unbuttoning his striped shirt, unzipping his dark mustard-brown trousers crumpled and tightening around the crotch. Meanwhile Presenter Blondie unhooked her bra, slipped off her kelly-green midi skirt. They had hurtled up the elevator during the twenty-minute break. And now were in the throes of pre-coital gyrations. Just as they were about to do the deed sprawled across heatedly ripped-off sheets, grunting throaty sighs, Ms. Senior Tight Curls brought him back to the doings of the conference hall,

"Well, ladies and gentleman, they've signaled lunch is ready in the dining room. We have forty-five minutes. Each of the presenters will be seated at one of your tables so take the opportunity to discuss any questions you might have. We're making good time, and should be finished by 3:30, including the panel discussion and completion of the conference survey. Plenty of time to get you on the road before the worst traffic."

What was he thinking!

On the 405 freeway heading back to the Northeast Valley at 3:48, he had forced his evening schedule into focus.

Lupe had called three candidates. He would interview them and would choose one to assume Emma's classes. Never her place. Nobody could, ever, would, replace her. Anywhere.

Deal Me a Card

He was emoting. *Here, alone in his car, he was making a fool of himself. Well, what better place.* He continued to sink deeper into self-derision and remonstration. *Whoa!* He slewed back into his lane, nodded apologetically to the middle finger gesticulating wildly from the car alongside him.

His pointless resolve to stay alive despite all odds, and the resulting will-power, carried him home. The half-pound hamburger, with lettuce and tomatoes, but minus the onions this time since he did not want to offend the interviewees, those wannabe substitutes, and a large black coffee, ignited his energy but hardly his desire for the task.

Doggedly, back behind his desk at six thirty, he sat down to the chore that he would gladly have wished away.

Warmth,

"Tell me about your experience in the classroom when a student was obviously distraught?"

Smiles,

"You note in your resume that your travels are an asset to your career? Why?"

Charm,

"Why do you want to work here, in this particular setting?"

His eyes watched the words twittering from between their lips. His fingers grasped a ball-point pen making hieroglyphics on the paper under his fist. His ears resounded with the chirp-cheep-chirp responses. The two and one half hours crept by.

Then he had shaken the last hand and mouthed the ultimate, "We'll call you tomorrow with a decision."

Exhausted by the forced amiability, drained from gushing enthusiasm, Guillermo limped past Lupe's desk. They muttered vague words of discomfort and mental fatigue at each other, grumbling about the late hour.

Back in the recesses of his chilly sanctum, he had leaned back against the soft leather of his commodious chair.

282

Deal Me a Card

Far away he heard the students chatter, some subdued, others animated. Classes were over for the night, for the week. For Emma, they were over forever.

The last door slammed shut. The Center shook, a dog-tired Saint Bernard settling down for the night after a long day succoring the needy.

Guillermo picked up the telephone. Though his heart hung stone-like in his breast, his reason clamored for him to fill the next day to capacity with action.

He had begun to dial Daniel's, or was it Richard's, number when he heard the scream.

The ambulance arrived seven minutes later. Guillermo knew because he had looked at the clock above the Center's front door as he ran out.

The small crowd that had formed a circle spilled onto the street. The mixture of fear, consternation, confusion, and the cautionary arms of a few kept any Good Samaritan at bay. Its collective voices were low murmurs, hushed whispers. Even the close-by traffic kept a muted tone.

Except for the damned hysterical sobbing somewhere on its periphery. Guillermo wished whoever it was would control herself. Apparently others felt the same way. From what seemed like a great distance he heard,

"Come, come with me, Miss Isadora. You cannot do anything. Be calm now, quiet down."

In the ensuing quiet, Guillermo had scrutinized his lover's prone body. There was no blood. No gunshot wound. Her legs and arms were loosely on the sidewalk. A discarded rag doll. Except that her eyes were shut.

The doors of the emergency van shot open as he continued his desperate, futile visual dissection of Emma's still frame. Two paramedics leapt out, moving rapidly. One examined the motionless figure, eliciting no response, from his touch or his questions. With deft movements coming from endless on-the-job practice, four skilled hands lifted the

Deal Me a Card

body off the ground. They placed her on a gurney, rolled her into the vehicle.

Guillermo saw the oxygen mask put in place, the vital signs check. He answered the EMT's questions giving the patient's personal information. Then they drove off. For some reason the technician's name, Jesus, gave him a slight reassurance.

He raced to his car and followed them to the Holy Redeemer Medical Center.

****

Early Friday morning, seven and a half hours after the fall. Guillermo wondered, as he dialed the number, if the trembling of his hand, of his whole body, was the result of the multiple cups of wide-eyed strong, high acidity black coffee coursing through his blood, or the anxiety finally overtaking his self-control. He ground his index finger into his right temple as he counted the rings. On the seventh, someone picked up.

"Hello. Hello, Adam? It's Guillermo, yes, Emma's friend. I'm afraid I have some bad news. Your sister had an accident last night."

Adam cut in.

"What? When last night? Why didn't you call when it happened? What's going on?"

Guillermo shook his head, hoping to drive out the fuzziness. But the headache persisted, as he answered,

"What? I'm sorry I didn't call earlier. It would have been after midnight in Florida, your time. It's four-thirty now in California, so I figured you or your wife had to be up and about."

"This was an emergency. Life or death. We sleep next to a phone."

The caller swallowed sour bile of nervousness.

"Yes. I know. But I wanted to have some information for you from the doctors."

Deal Me a Card

"So! What are they saying?"

"Well, it's not good. The next few hours, days are critical."

Guillermo held the phone three inches from his ear as the blustering expletives blasted from the other end.

"Damn it to hell, is there any fucking medical assistance available to her?"

"Pardon me?"

"Doctors? Specialists?"

"Of course. She's getting the best care possible, the attention of the best medical specialists at the hospital and the area."

"I do not want her anywhere but at UCLA Medical Center. Get her moved. I insist."

"No, this is a trauma center, so they don't need to fly her out to UCLA."

Guillermo wearily pulled some vestiges of rage out of his gut,

"Look, Adam, calm down, man. We've already marshaled every resource, human and technological. As far as is possible, she's stabilized."

"Okay, okay, I'm sorry. But she's my little sister. Where's she now?"

Emma's lover heard the quavery break in Emma's brother's desperate voice. His own tone softened,

"She's already in the intensive care unit. She needed x-rays, an MRI. That's all done."

"Shirley wants to speak to you. I'm going to call Thomas on the other phone."

"Thanks, Adam. Hello? Oh, that's you. Shirley, right?"

"Yes, yes. This is dreadful. How did it happen? Poor Emma!"

"She's in a coma. Massive head injury. She fell backwards hard on the concrete sidewalk. The contact must have shaken up her brain very severely. The tumble was at a critical angle."

285

"I see you've done all you can. So we'll wait and pray. How're you doing?"

Guillermo shook his head and wiped his eyes.

"I'm okay. Holding up, but nervous about the prognosis."

"What are they saying?"

"Well, the neurologist did a GCS, the Glasgow Coma Scan. "

"You sound like you know all about the problem."

"Yeah, how quickly we learn, Shirley. And the result fell between an eight and a nine. Means she's comatose."

Emma's sister-in-law interjected, sounding worried,

"What do those numbers mean?"

"That's the average range. Most patients in that state come out of it. But there's always a chance …but I'm hopeful. I have to think positive for her sake. But I have to steel myself also against the worst."

Shirley insisted,

"She's strong, healthy. Has taken care of herself. She's a fighter."

"Yes." That was the only response Guillermo could muster.

"Adam and I will check plane schedules and rearrange our work schedules, so we'll be there as soon as possible. Soon."

"You're coming out? Good, absolutely. You're welcome to stay at my place."

"Thanks. Adam had just gotten off the phone with Thomas. He's coming too."

"Good. He must be with his mother at a time like this."

Now Adam was back on the line. He picked up the conversation,

"Thomas is very close to Emma emotionally, though they live so far apart. He said that he would never forgive himself …"

Deal Me a Card

Guillermo heard the crack in her voice, stepped in with words of comfort that he scarcely understood,

"That's right. We don't know and we don't want any regrets. I hope you realize, and please tell Thomas I love his mother very much. I will be at her side. I or my family will be there every minute. We love her. She's a part of our life. I love her."

"We know. She told us all about you. She loves you too."

At no time during their worried exchange had there been any mention of Emma's leaving California to live in Florida. Guillermo was grateful.

He wanted to burst into tears. Instead, he ended the call.

"Yes, call me about your flights."

The rest of Friday went by in a series of jerky scenarios. Daniel and Richard replaced him as sentries at the fortress of Emma's dilemma. Guillermo remembered glowering at his older son, who arrived for the first shift, for daring to have the slightest inclination to be light-hearted. Richard had the decency to hang his head in shame and to hide his tiny smile.

His father stomped off to clean himself up at home and to breeze, a spiraling tornado, through his two offices to maintain an external show of management, and control that inwardly had long ago collapsed in the face of his lover's fall. Obediently Guillermo ate something Lupe served, wondering, as he chewed the steamy lunch, if she intended to finish him off, with poisoned mud soaked in dishwater and sprinkled with grass blades. Reluctantly, he accepted Isadora's tearful offer to hold vigil at Emma's bedside. So long as, he made her promise - if there had been a Bible in the room she would have had to swear on it - she would desist from all speech. He stumbled away from the encounter, her protestations battening on his bowed frame. Before he left the Center, a poster on the bulletin boards in the front office and all the classrooms announced Daniel

287

Guerrero would provide interim leadership, in case for Guillermo's unavailability.

Back at the hospital, Daniel and Richard reported nothing new. Sarita and Betty had spelled them. The three men discussed hotel reservations and airport pick-up of Emma's kin, as the need arose. Guillermo returned to Emma's side for the night.

When Father MacGregor, the chaplain stopped in, their exchange was brief and prayerful. God was once again invited into the room. But Guillermo sensed that He was elsewhere preoccupied with other momentous happenings. Guillermo felt very alone.

"Dad, Dad!"

Guillermo unfolded out of a dream in which he and Emma were swaying in a slow dance, when suddenly his fingers lost their grip on hers, and she began to float away, lifting off the ground. She was smiling at first. Then her face crumpled. Her arms moved frantically, the wings of a scared bird. Up and down she bobbed. Now she was screaming. And even as he tried to grab her skirt, it billowed out of his reach.

"Dad, wake up. He's dead."

Guillermo's eyes popped open,

"No, no, no. She was breathing steadily."

He leaped up from his chair that the nurse had thoughtfully provided. The clock on the wall thrust its face into his blurred vision. Its hands pointed to eleven forty-three. Taste buds bled stale institution-grade coffee, almost forcing a gag. He stumbled over to Emma's side, stared in dread at her pale cheeks, barely visible under the oxygen mask that ensnared her nose. The white hospital gown, dotted with miniscule red and blue flowers, visible from her neck to her chest, could have been a funereal robe clothing a lifeless doll. He went down on one knee, clutched the pink thermal blanket that hugged tight the rest of her body.

Deal Me a Card

"No, Emma, my darling, you can't die. No, we have too much to live for. We love each other. I'm sorry that I hurt you."

"Dad!"

Daniel tugged at his father's arm, holding on tight as the distraught older man tried to shake it off,

"It's Israel. Doc's son is dead. They've killed him."

****

Thus, thirty-two hours later on that Sunday night, scrunched under the stars at the base of the foothills edging his home, Guillermo rewound and scanned the tapes of the last week's turmoil whirring deliriously in his head.

The serape had once again failed its test. When grabbing it off the rack he'd been too distracted to recall other past experiences with the sorry garment that never afforded a single fold of solace. So he huddled, hugging his body tight to capture any scrap of warmth the shawl would afford him. To no avail. Coldness penetrated, a numbing sting permeating his entire being.

The excruciating recollections of Emma's accident and Israel's murder wreaked their havoc. Slowly he descended into the lowest point of despair he had felt since Emma's decision to leave. He wriggled into the unforgiving earth, wishing to disintegrate and disappear.

He ruminated. He could lie there and die. That was one option. Not a bad choice. But in every way, manner, shape and form a weakling's decision. His dead wife, Mary Lou would fall off her heavenly cloud of glory in total amazement. Why, he had never ever left her alone, to just slip away into oblivion. Richard and Daniel would grab him and hurl him into the icy pool to shock him out of his stupor if they had an inkling of this cowardice. 'That's the example you want to set, right Dad?' Splash, big splash.

Deal Me a Card

And Emma. Oh heavens. If she wasn't lying there as still as an alabaster effigy, he wouldn't be here. No. Don't go there.

He shook himself, shedding morbid ideation like a surgeon stripping off bloody scrubs. Hands and knees raised him to his feet, out of his stony cot. Engulfed mummy-like in the useless blanket, he stumbled, stiff-legged but quite sure-footed, into the warmth of his home. He shut his ears to the insistent crickets' chirp. His sliding door clicked firmly shut on the lonesome summons of the coyote.

As Guillermo drank water to dilute the deleterious effects of caffeine flowing through his veins and munched slowly on the two slices of pepperoni pizza, remnants of a meal he, Daniel and Richard had shared earlier in the day, he felt a quieting in his brain. The vast immutability of nighttime darkness must have lent an iota of its stoicism on his being.

Finished with sustenance, he crawled under his blanket with new resolve to be stronger the next day. He had to be. Doc Velasquez and his family needed him. He had been selfish and centered on his own well-being and Emma's dilemma for too long, to the exclusion of all details surrounding the death of a fine young man. He yanked his mind back to the concept of sleep and rest. He slept and rested.

Deal Me a Card

CHAPTER 36

WHILE GUILLERMO'S THOUGHTS AND PASSIONS were floundering in another reality, Israel Velasquez had died. Emma's accident and his fatal shooting were unrelated, except for proximity. His murder wore the mark of the evil genie that reared her ugly head once more, wringing blood out of her tresses and demanding an additional cupful, rising from the undertow of unease and violence winding through the twin communities of La Coloma and San Benitez.

****

At 9:30 p.m. that first Friday in February, Detective Yow's phone rang as he sat watching television in his home. He had just popped his first of three cans of Yeungling beer that he allowed himself each week. The night officer on duty read from his all-points bulletin,

"We just received an anonymous call. I've dispatched it to the lieutenant on duty, and he advised me to call you. There's a body in the northwest end of El Dorado Park, next to the bathrooms. The caller did not state what had occurred. The caller sounded like a young male. The call could not be traced. No other information."

****

Father MacGregor glanced over the top of his bi-focals at the clock on the wall. He leaned back in his recliner. His little niche to the left of the Holy Redeemer Medical Center chapel was lit only by a table lamp. The glow was set at its lowest level to sustain the aura of peace. The door, with a stained glass panel of Easter lilies, was closed. It led to the place of prayer. Flickering shadows, from candles that made

Deal Me a Card

the colors on the vitrine shiver, emitted hope and despair, elicited thoughts of both beginnings and ends.

The priest was meditating on the fifth Sorrowful mystery of the rosary, the crucifixion of Jesus. Brown wooden beads slid easily through his fingers, his practiced thumb moving them along his index finger to the rhythm of his *Ave Maria*s, Hail Marys.

He thought the family he had comforted two hours ago. A grandfather had passed away. A nonagenarian, he had, until two weeks ago, been driving his car and smoking foul-smelling cigars. Then the systems had crashed. And he went to the Lord.

Earlier in the night, he heard the confession of a twenty-nine year old woman who would undergo ovarian cancer surgery in the morning. The doctors had expressed very little hope, been frank with her about her chances of survival. She made her peace and her pleas to the Almighty that He keep her children in His care when she was gone.

In ICU, coiled tubes rudely probing her body silently sucked in and expelled air and water and waste through Emma Hazelton's slumbering body. Father MacGregor exchanged comforting grunts and tsk-tsks with Guillermo, a stoic sentinel. Guillermo's smile was fixed, his responses at once positive and hesitant. The priest and the anxious man had prayed together. The chaplain bestowed encouraging words on the unconscious patient's guardian, urging him to pray aloud and talk to his beloved.

Otherwise, this had been an uneventful Friday night.

The twelve strokes of midnight were a trumpet's summons for the gates of hell to open and disgorge its detritus into the emergency room. A victim of a bar brawl, broken jaw, bloody brow split perhaps, or a wife, arms bruised, eyes swollen shut from the belligerent abuse of a husband home after a night out with the boys. Maybe a suddenly vulnerable teen-ager, ankle cracked from its

Deal Me a Card

encounter with the edge of the sidewalk in the dark. Others. A steady stream dependent on medical rescue.

The phone's jangle broke into his musings. The familiar voice of the medical examiner spoke at the other end,

"Father, we need you down here. The police have identified the body of the young man, Israel Velasquez. Detective Yow asked if you would accompany him to notify his parents."

"I'll be right down."

Father MacGregor looked at the clock. It read 11:45.

Half and hour later he met Israel's parents in the ER. Together they walked to the morgue where their boy lay dead.

CHAPTER 37

BY EARLY AFTERNOON ON SUNDAY, news of Israel's murder landed a vicious punch in the collective gut of the communities of La Coloma and San Benitez, and blown out every flicker of hope. Four people stood facing each other uneasily, perhaps searching for strength in others' gaze. None was forthcoming.

Raoul and Juanita Guerrero greeted Cora Manolo and her daughter, Araceli, at their front door. Their welcome was subdued. Unintelligible sounds issued from their lips, sympathetic grunts and sighs hissing like deflating tires.

Araceli Manolo spoke not a word. Her only sounds were spasmodic sobs and gulps of air she inhaled between the sniffling. The hood of her denim jacket engulfed most of her face. Wrestling despondency, Mrs. Manolo, standing by her side, attempted a start as she took a step into the house,

"Thank you for being here for us. We're desperate for your help. Araceli and I decided it was best to come to you. Juanita, ever since the day my husband, Narciso, collapsed from a heart attack at the machine shop and never recovered, you have been good to me. Now, to my shame, I must come pleading for help again. I could not talk on the phone. Israel's death has overwhelmed both of us."

As if the utterance drained her of strength, her body sagged. The rest of her words disappeared into the wide comfort of her friend's shoulder. She began to shiver violently. Juanita grasped her tightly around the waist and led her into the dim calmness of the living room.

Raoul put his arm around Araceli's bowed shoulders and they followed the two women.

Once they were seated only sorrow broke the silence. Words are not created for times like this. Compassionate sighs let them know that they were among friends who

Deal Me a Card

understood their pain. Grieving Israel's loss united the couple, and the mother and her daughter. Minutes passed.

Then Araceli burst out,

"I must speak of it. Help me, mom, so I leave nothing out. Help us, Mr. Guerrero, Mrs. Guerrero, to know what to do now. Israel is gone, gone forever. They took him away with their guns as he sat there harmless…"

She reached back into the darkest part of her soul. Sobbed, took a long intake of air, and began to speak,

"I will tell you all every detail as it is stamped on my memory. Last Friday afternoon we were together …

'Look Araceli, it's still light. Won't be dark for at least another hour. Heck, maybe two hours. It's just four o'clock. We can get out to the park, you know the small one out there, beyond the college. There're some good roads winding this way and that way. I can practice.'

Israel and I were standing in the junior section of the La Coloma High School parking lot. School was out. It was Friday. He was negotiating a driving lesson from me, since I'm…was five months older than him and have a driver's license."

The three adults listened intently as Araceli's narration continued.

****

"Okay, Israel, no problem. But we have to get back by five thirty so I can get ready for this evening. You're taking me, right? Second semester back-to-school hop."

"Yes. Whether I want to or not!" Israel nudged her.

"What'd you just say?"

"No, no, I didn't mean it that way! I just meant that I'm obligated to go there this evening. I couldn't take you to a movie or somewhere else?"

"That's right. Your Dad got this thing organized. 'Friday nights', I overheard him tell the principal, 'let's keep the kids safe, off the streets, sober'. I think it's great. So do

Deal Me a Card

the other kids in my classes. A whole crowd of us will be there!"

Israel looked dubious. "Well, he's not going to be there, so that's good. Imagine if he was. Man, that would be so embarrassing. 'Hey, Izzy, you checking in with Daddy every fifteen minutes so he knows you're not high?' 'Israel, here, take a sip. I promise I won't tell your Daddy.' You know how those guys are!"

"But they're just joking."

As Israel grimaced, the two pals jumped into the Ford Escort. Israel, confident behind the wheel, strapped himself in, fixed the mirror, and started the engine. As they rode along, Araceli enumerated the couples who would be dancing around them that night.

In ten minutes, while the young driver-in-training was obeying all rules to a T, they reached their destination. Araceli poked a finger at the windshield,

"Hey, we're almost there. Just go past the No Fishing sign, take a right down this path. I've been here before. Used to come here when I was learning to drive. You can practice three-point parking, backing up, avoiding the trees."

"Watch it, I'm not that much of a rookie.

As Israel deftly turned into a curve, he saw a figure leaping out of the shadows of the trees. Its arm was raised, gesturing him to halt. Since it now stood stationary in his car's path, he stepped hard on the brakes.

A little too hard. Both he and Araceli jerked forward despite the restraining seat belts.

"Don't do that, Israel! Just press on the brakes lightly! You scared me. What's that person doing out there?"

"That's why I stopped. I didn't want to kill him."

Israel rolled the window down and smiled a greeting,

"Hi, can I help you? Need a ride to some place?"

The form had a mouth that uttered a slurry command,

"Step out of the car slowly and raise your hands above your head."

Deal Me a Card

"Sir, we were just out here to practice driving. My name is Israel. I just turned sixteen and I'm going to get my license in two or three weeks. My girlfriend has hers already."

A voice from behind the figure yelled, urgently,

"Hey, Nosey, let them go. They're harmless."

The swaying creature gestured a hushing wave. Araceli and Israel could now see that his arms shimmered in the late afternoon light, alive with tattoos. He called back without taking his eyes off the couple,

"Yeah, that's right. He's clean. But, boy, you've gotta learn sometime. Some places you don't go."

"This is a public park, sir. We're leaving right now anyway."

Israel's tone was assertive, but conciliatory. The talker leaned closer, belligerent,

"Why you calling me 'sir'. You dissing me? Who do you claim?"

"I don't know what you're talking about, sir. I told you …"

"You call me 'sir' one more time and I'll shoot you like this. Pow. Pow."

The aggressor fumbled under his tee-shirt and pulled out his .38. Pointing it at Israel, he giggled as he drew back the trigger,

"Like this…Pow, pow!"

Araceli heard the gunfire and the bullets penetrate her boyfriend's chest. She was that near, she heard their blunt heads stab the flesh.

Someone was laughing hysterically. She could not understand why. Her hand went to her mouth to check if perhaps it was coming from her throat, the laugh of a person gone instantly insane in the face of death. No.

The click of the car door opening at her side swiveled her head away from the sight of the gunman opening the driver's door and tugging at her lifeless friend. Then she felt

297

Deal Me a Card

the weight of another across her chest. A male who was not Nosey the killer, but who wore an earring. He stretched over and twisted the keys out of the ignition. Then he turned and hurled them into the nearby undergrowth.

As if in slow motion she watched as he ran around the car, grabbed the murderer and another *cholo* companion by the arms. He pulled them back to the Chevy that was parked behind the bathrooms. The man wearing the earring drove away. The other two men were in the back seat.

When they were out of sight, she jumped out of the car then, and stumbled over to where Israel lay, his body on the dirty ground, his knees and legs bending into the car, one on the seat, the other on the floor. She listened to the last gasps of the boy she loved. She watched, eyes wide with horror, terror-stricken, faced with this image of hell. She witnessed, with a close-up, in-her-face vision, her science-lab buddy's blood oozing from his mouth and his lungs and his back. She inhaled with wrenching, anguished breaths, the last agonized death gasps of her lunch-time companion and keeper of teenage love secrets.

Araceli made the sign of the Cross as she stared at Israel's face.

She tried to stand up. Her knees buckled under her, and she sank to the dirt. Pushing hard with her hands she attempted to rise again. Her shoe slipped on the sandy soil and her hip hit the ground.

"Take it easy. Slow down. Now stand up," she muttered to herself.

"*Gotta to get help. Gotta save him. Israel has to live. God let him live. He's so young. He's too young. We're too young. He's my friend. We were going to USC together. Stand up, you can do it.*"

Now her hand was shaking Israel's shoulder, first slowly, then violently.

"Quit fooling, Izzy. It's not funny. We'll be late for the dance. Come on. Open your eyes. Let me see them so I know

Deal Me a Card

you're okay! Israel. Israel, you're my best friend ever. You just can't leave me like this! Open your eyes. Breathe! Please!"

Her voice faded, wafted away. Nothing happened. Gulps of air heaved out of her lungs. She wanted to vomit. Shriek at heaven and against God! But instead she made herself go cold. Colder than the winter blast that had begun its attack as soon as the sun retracted its saving light.

Her mutter was a delirious woman's,

"Better to go get help. I saw a phone at the entrance. Go. Walk. Run."

Araceli stood at the phone booth. Sobbing. The receiver dangled destroyed, the telephone gaped off its perch, pulled out of the wall by some enraged maniac, or some gang-banger, imbecilic on weed or blow, intent on killing his neighbor.

She turned away and started walking, almost running, in the direction of the main road that bordered the park. A drizzle of raindrops quickened their pace on her bowed shoulders. As she reached the park entrance, a woman in a pick-up slowed down behind her. Stopped, and called out through the open passenger window,

"Hello there, young lady, can I help you?"

The driver leaned across the passenger seat to peer more closely at Araceli through the dimness. She spoke,

"It's too dark for a young person to be wandering around alone at this hour. What were you thinking? It's almost seven-thirty and getting wetter by the second. You don't know what's lurking out there. Crazies. More and more every day. Your mother's going to be worried."

The speaker by now had a closer look at the girl. Araceli could feel her eyes scrutinizing her disheveled appearance. She sensed the woman's stare pierce through the bloodstains on her blouse.

Deal Me a Card

"Goodness, what happened. You're all messy. And, hey, there's blood on your hands and your shirt," said the voice from within the car. It now sounded less friendly.

Araceli heard the slight revving of the engine as the driver put her foot slowly on the accelerator and turned her face towards the windshield. She realized her only means of immediate assistance was about to drive off, scared that this dirty young girl was just another trouble-making teenager. The window slowly rolled up and shut her out.

Araceli leaned against the passenger door. She pressed her mouth against the glass and yelled out. Her own ears heard the pleading tone in her words,

"Please, please, wait. Don't leave me here. Please give me a ride. Please?"

She clutched at the door handle.

The older woman pressed on the brake. Against her chest, Araceli could feel the car halt.

The window rolled down again.

"You really need help don't you?"

The driver leaned over and opened the car door.

"Jump in!"

Araceli gazed at her for a second, relief and stifled sobs keeping her silent. Then she scrambled into the seat before the other woman changed her mind. While the teenager clicked her seatbelt, the woman scrutinized Araceli up close,

"You are not at all okay, are you?"

Her miserable passenger babbled,

"I was in the park and I tripped and fell. We were there hanging around after school. You know how it is when it's Friday and someone has a car. But my friends left me behind. I was running after them and I slipped. They're really mean. I'm going to get them back tomorrow."

Araceli heard herself rambling, lying. But she could not stop the falsehoods from bursting forth.

Deal Me a Card

The woman slipped the car into gear and drove. Wearily Araceli gave her directions, then leaned back in the seat.

Images blurred, on a death march behind her blank, staring eyes. Among them, three shark-eyed men, the gun exploding, Israel's pale face, his blood coursing out of the hole in his chest. *Oh God. What would happen if she told, and they came after her? Was she going to die the same way?* She saw Israel's falling body, his eyes go blank, stare up at nothing. He had been warm one minute and the next, there was no life. *Or was there?* She had to get home and call someone to go find him. Give him help so he would live.

Her driver's tone was gentler as she picked up on Araceli's remarks,

"Well, that was very thoughtless of your companions. Sometimes we need to think of how we pick our friends.

"Is this the street? Great, I'll drop you off here."

"Thank you," Araceli said flatly as she exited the little truck.

Neither waved good-bye, their minds in different realities.

Thirty minutes after she had collapsed onto the living room sofa, her mother walked in.

"Araceli, Honey, it's eight-thirty! I thought you'd be at the dance." She chatted as she hung up her coat.

"I stopped at the hospital to visit that nice woman, Emma. Remember, I sent your *Tia* Lilian to her to start enrollment in English classes. She had a terrible accident last night. They wouldn't let me see her. She's still in a coma.

"Your cousin, Elena, she's one of the nurses in ICU was on the night shift. I got to speak to her up there. She says it's an only fifty-fifty chance of recovery.

"Mr. Guerrero was there. Gave me a hug. He's so good-looking, but boy, were his eyes red from not sleeping. Said he's been up the whole night, and with her all day.

301

Deal Me a Card

"Anyway, I figured you'd be long gone. What's the matter? You didn't have a quarrel with Israel, did you?"

"No, no. I didn't feel well. Started throwing up at school. Maybe it's the flu. Or you know how I get when I'm starting my period. So I thought I'd just stay at home and watch TV."

"Oh, honey. I'm sorry. It would have been fun with Israel. Why are you crying? It's got to be your monthly. You always get so emotional.

"Let me change into my house robe, and we can watch a movie together. Cozy mother and daughter night. Who needs men anyway?"

She paused and looked back at her daughter, and glimpsed Araceli's face.

"Araceli, what's wrong?"

"Mom, mom. I saw something awful. Israel's dead. They killed him. I'm so scared." The words spilled out of her like a bursting dam.

"*Madre de Dios*, Mother of God, Blessed Virgin of Guadalupe! *Mija, mija*! My child, my daughter! Tell me what happened?"

Cora Manolo looked at the girl's face and stifled the moan of anguish that rose in her throat.

"Mom. I had to leave the car. He threw away the keys in the bushes, so I couldn't find them in the dark."

"Forget about the damn car. What about Israel?"

"I didn't want to leave Israel. Only after a while, he wasn't moving or breathing. So I ran away from him. Jesus forgive me. I didn't know what to do. I was so scared, I just ran and ran. And a nice woman gave me a ride home…. Mom, what'll I do?"

"Cora enveloped her offspring in her arms, hugged her *nina*, her *carina hija*, her beloved daughter in an effort to absorb her grief. She gathered her wits,

"Don't you move!

"First I'm going to call Juanita. She and Raoul will guide me about what to do. If they ask why I didn't call the police yet, I'll tell them I want to be sure what to say."

She did not voice her horror and alarm at Araceli's involvement. Through her mind flashed the dangers in which her family now found itself. Perils of threats, death warnings. She disentangled herself from the clinging child-woman.

Crossing herself and touching her fingers to the bleeding feet on the crucifix that stood on the *retablo*, she reached for the phone.

****

Araceli stopped, slumped in her chair. Telling her story had drained her. She was as pale as the ghosts that spun around her head. When the listeners' silence broke, Mr. Guerrero's questions sounded very far away. Her responses seemed too loud. They reverberated in her ears.

"Yes, I'm sure the one who flung the car keys into the bushes wore a stud earring."

"They were all covered with tattoos, all over their bodies. At least the two that I saw close up."

"No, no, only one man shot the gun."

"Yes, he was high. He slurred his words when he spoke to Israel."

Hearing herself say his name, after she had forced her heart to become coldly brave and objective while she told the story, destroyed her resolve. She collapsed in sorrow like a wounded animal.

Mother and daughter drove home. Sunday dinner was not an option. Each woman crept to their beds, but sleep was not an option either. At seven o'clock, Araceli nestled into her mama's bed and moved close to her. Still neither slept but fitfully.

Deal Me a Card

CHAPTER 38

SIX O'CLOCK ON THE SAME SUNDAY EVENING, Smiley, whose given name was Julian, shoved his dinner plate away, as if repelled by the odor of the steaming chicken *mole,* rice and beans that his mother had lovingly prepared. She did it just that way every Sunday for her family, *todos los domingos por la familia* for as long as he could remember. He did not raise his eyes, knowing that she would be gazing at him reproachfully. She would not utter a word, since she had learned a few years ago that keeping her peace was the best way.

She, Senora Perez was the mother of four sons - one lying in the cemetery, a victim of drive-by shooting, another in jail for dealing drugs, a third, Willie, a junior taking honors courses at La Coloma High School, and this stranger - but she was not bitter, only resigned to God's Will. *Es la voluntad de Dios.* So she prayed to Him and the Virgen, lit candles, and seldom spoke.

Though the woman was silent, she was actually looking across the table at Evelinda, Smiley's girlfriend, searching for a clue. Her raised eyebrows were met by the same from the teenager. So she made a stab at conversation. This local tragedy that was so close to home drove her to speak,

"*Es tan triste*, this is sad, but both of you have heard about Israel Velasquez, right? *Murio*, he's dead. *Como el varon*, my first-born. *Es triste.* Willie is very upset. That's why he's not here as usual. He went over to be with some friends from school. I think they are at Pasquale's home.

"You know Israel was Willie's buddy, *eran muy buenos amigos, como hermanos.* Like brothers. *En clases juntos, cienca, historia. Jugando futbol, peleando de boxeo* They were in science and US History classes together. Played soccer, boxed at the gym.

Deal Me a Card

"*Anoche lloro, no pudo creer*. Last night, he was weeping, unable to believe it, wanting to deny it. But reality kept hitting him, *realidad le golpeo*. He looked like a baseball bat had stunned him. Another one dead, *otro muerto!*"

Before she could continue, Smiley pushed backwards so violently that his chair screamed rage into all ears present. It almost overturned, as he leaped up and rushed from the small dining room. His mother and girlfriend remained seated, stunned by the vehemence. Mouth-watering steam from the chicken evaporated as dinner grew cold.

The disturbed young man sped to his room and crashed on his bed. Thirty-six hours without crack, his head was fairly clear. He forced his mind to return to Friday. *Nosey and Chico were long gone, escaped into the depths of East Los Angeles where they could hide out forever. But he had this family, his natural family, who he lived with and who he owed plenty. And he had a girlfriend.*

He closed his eyes, seeking respite. Remembering each blood-chilling detail from two days ago in the park.

****

Smiley heard his cap scrape back and forth on the rough surface as he leaned up against the park's lavatory facilities. His blue jeans, red tank top, black-and-white tennis shoes blended with the graffiti scrawled on the wall. Euphoric from crack, he lolled, his bobble-doll head nodding as he watched his two comrades continue to binge.

They were safe in this location. For now. The three young men had reconnoitered the area earlier on arrival, to ensure security. Picked up the clues. They could not be too careful. Not one, not two, but who knows, probably five rival gangs had laid claim. The mutilated calligraphy, scribbled-over crosses, hearts, fields of flowers, Virgin of Guadalupe faces, swastikas and monikers rubbed shoulders in a hodge-podge of hostile gang takeover and turf domination. To the

Deal Me a Card

unpracticed eye the images were random, purposeless. But their fellow warriors who had passed by in the days before had sprayed messages of reassurance for the family. Right now Homies ruled.

Smiley's eyes slewed from one of the men to the other. Chico's head was nodding. His given name was Edgar, last name Nunez. He was so out of it. If he wasn't careful he was going to fall flat, wallowing, swallowing dirt and leaves. Nosey, though, he was volatile. His real name was Juvenal, last name Navarro. Got his nickname because he couldn't take his nose out of the white powder. He attempted to get it any way he could. He'd kill for it. And when he was high, you'd better walk softly around him.

Another thing, that bro' always had his piece sticking out like a deformed hip under his knee-length shirt. He'd had the number six-six-six silk-screened on the back. And he'd laugh about how he had a dozen of those shirts, made especially for him, customized he proudly bragged, because he had a six-shooter, and he was a devil with a weapon. Shot someone six different ways that time in Los Angeles. Smiley privately thought he was full of shit. But he nodded, bowed his head in mock awe, went along since he himself didn't own a gun. Yet.

Simultaneously all three heard the purring of a vehicle driving slowly into their territory. Across the few feet that separated them, dilated eyes met, gathered focus. Without a word each drug-addled boy-man staggered towards the other two. They had to defend their lair. As one, they staggered out from behind the building. The tall pines and eucalyptus cast a deeper shadow on the day already darkening. Nosey's shoe caught on a stone. He said a dirty word, maybe two. Lurched forward, tripping for three steps.

"Fuck, fuck, fuck this damn place!"

Then he regained his balance. Standing erect, trying to keep his swaying in check, he turned to the other men,

Deal Me a Card

"Let's get them. They came to the wrong place at the wrong time. They gonna be at the wrong end of the law. My law."

"Hey, no need to do anything if they're just passing through. Could be a couple from the school coming to make out."

Smiley spoke soothingly, slowly, aware that Nosey was breaking bad. When he was dusted he could go ballistic. The white stuff did that to him sometimes. Actually more and more often now. At least he had not drawn his persuader. That was what he liked to call it, when he wanted to threaten or worse.

"Let's see. They're circling back around. Musta seen us. Coming to check us out. I'll check them out all right."

Chico was alert now. His face twitched as he threw nervous sidelong glances at Smiley.

"Nah, we don't have to follow them. Let 'em go back. They haven't seen us."

"Well, I want them to see us. Want to let them know who owns this place. Show them it's ours. Okay? Scare the shit out of them with this."

Now he pulled out the weapon.

Smiley dreaded this moment. But his head hurt when he tried to form some words of admonition. He heard himself, fuzzily dull,

"No, man. Let it be."

Nosey, pretending to obey, stuck his .38 back under his shirt, but he was already tottering rapidly towards the center of the road. As the car drove up, he stepped in front of it. About ten feet from the hood.

To some, Nosey might have resembled a dancing clown. To Smiley, Nosey's hand looked like a palm branch waving gently in the breeze.

A teenage boy, Smiley estimated he was as old as his brother, Willie, rolled the window down and smiled a greeting,

307

"Hi, can I help you? Need a ride to some place?"

"Step out of the car slowly and raise your hands above your head."

"Sir, we were just out here to practice driving. My name is Israel. I just turned sixteen and I'm going to get my license in two or three weeks. My girlfriend has hers already."

Smiley heard the boy's name, and his heart missed a beat. He called out,

"Hey, Nosey, let them go. They're harmless."

"Yeah, that's right. He's clean," Nosey threw over his shoulder. The he turned back and thrust his face through the car window.

Smiley heard his earth screeching on its axis. Or was it the sound of the girl's ear-splitting shriek, that infiltrated deep into his cranium, as she heard the gunfire and the bullets penetrate her boyfriend's chest. Or was it Nosey's lunatic high-pitched hiccoughs as he opened the car door and shook the wounded body loose from the safety strap so that the torso hung halfway out of the vehicle.

The cocaine slushing through his body did not slow him, did not cause him to pause. Smiley's tennis shoes scrunched across the five yards of sand in a millisecond. He yanked open the passenger door, dived over the girl and Israel's skewed body parts, and wrenched the Escort's keys out of the ignition. Struggling backwards, toppling on his heels, he whirled and with a spasmodic jerk he hurled the keys into the nearby undergrowth.

Then he descended on his homeboys. Vise-like, his fingers grabbed the still-chortling Nosey and gaping-mouthed Chico by the arms. With an adrenalin-powered force, he dragged them back to the Chevy that squatted in one of the spaces behind the bathrooms. Like limp rags he hurled them into the back seat where they sprawled an idiotic pose of stupefaction.

Deal Me a Card

In seconds the car snarled to life. He revved the engine. The wheels spun forward, crunched towards the exit. Then Smiley screeched the Chevy's brakes, raising dirt like a maddened bat escaping hell.

Somehow he wove his way through a maze of streets without hitting something or some body. With his head still in the drug cloud, pounding from the reverberation of gunshots recently fired, his hands scarcely acted from any sense of perception. But he managed to drop the two other crack-heads off at the bus station, leaving them to their own devices. He reached home and threw himself, stunned, onto his bed.

The drugs Smiley had smoked prohibited any tranquility. He lay wide awake, his heart clambering so that he thought he might pass out cold, forever. The image of the dead boy and of the girl kneeling over the corpse blocked out any other. Wandering round and around that picture were random thoughts of his own inevitable destiny, of Smiley's mother and Evelinda crying over Smiley's motionless, bloody body and looking into Smiley's lifeless eyes.

Smiley writhed and whimpered.

After awhile, he reached for the phone and called 911. It was not right that the body should lie there alone.

Even so, Smiley could not calm his agitated state of mind.

****

Now, still in that prone position, Smiley opened his eyes and pulled himself back to the present. His mother's words, as he and Evelinda were sitting down to Sunday dinner, had galvanized him, but only to relive the nightmare. *He was truly fucked!* The mood would not leave him. Like during the prior forty-eight hours, Smiley could not eat, or sleep, or act. He feared this would continue for many days. *Damn, damn, damn.*

Deal Me a Card

CHAPTER 39

EMMA HEARD THEIR VOICES as they came through the door. She breathed a sigh of relief. Daddy was talking, telling the others that he had come as soon as he could.

Maybe he could save her.

As she crouched in the middle of the room, she sensed their footfalls. But they seemed so out of reach of her outstretched arms. Too far away to get to her on time before the walls closed in again.

Her mouth opened but no sound issued. Muscles in her throat were in the grip of a strangling force, choking off the screams. Paralysis grasped her appendages, locked her body from neck to toe, and stilled her being.

As the ceiling descended lower and lower, and the walls inched nearer on every side, her tightly-shut eyes mercifully sealed off the menacing squeeze.

Air suddenly filled the room. She sensed the pressure recede. Light tickled at her lashes, but before it could thrust open her sight, the onerous crush swooshed down, deflated her.

It happened again. She buckled under the tightening clutch of the room.

Just as she breathed her last, the air seeped into her lungs once more.

Respite.

Then again came the embracing vacuum that sucked her whole body into stillness.

She struggled vainly to move. Not even the tip of her finger responded. She slipped to the edge, nearly expired.

Deal Me a Card

From a bright hole high in the ceiling a whooshing wind spiraled down, entered her. She revived again.

Now her flesh sensed tentacles stroking her thighs and calves, running up and down her lower and upper arms. She stiffened. One sinuous limb licked her neck. She winced. Quieted her tingling nerves. She could not silence the desperate words that shrieked from her stomach,

"Daddy, no, Daddy."

Then the walls and the ceiling caved in once more on her immobilized body.

"She moved, she moved when I touched her. She did. Emma, it's me, Adam. And Thomas is right here, also. Can you see us? Did you hear her? She said something. Is that good?"

This would be a good trip. Emma leaned back in Seat C, a window seat. Her favorite. Shut her eyes, prepared to take a nap. Relaxed her tired back and shoulders. It hurt right there in the middle and straight up to her neck. If she relaxed, the pain would ease. When she arrived at the other end she'd feel so much better. She'd be ready for work.

The shift in her posture was not good.

The weather changed suddenly. A giant demonic hand had laid siege on the little plane. It was smacking her, back and forth, flipping her up and down. Her head throbbed from the shaking. Battered babies floated in front of her glazed-over eyes. All the pain in her back had returned with a vengeance.

But even the slightest move was not an option. Petrified, she sat trapped by a seatbelt. Transfixed.

The plane shuddered and swooped, rattled.

"I don't want to die," she moaned, feeling like a coward though all the faces around her were sympathetic. They stared hard at her, some were

311

smiling, some had tears on their cheeks. *Were they afraid to die too?*

She began to feel queasy. But there was no recourse. Eyes closed, she allowed the plane to carry her where it would.

She sat, a bone shard, an undigested ort, a lump of indigestible lead rocking in the belly of the bird. It lurched, she jerked forward. It dipped, she sank backwards. Giving in to its sway and swoop. But the grasp of the storm refused to free her from this eternity of beating and pummeling. Then as suddenly as the storm had engulfed the plane, it now spewed the aircraft into a calm.

Descent into the dark night was paradisiacal.

The night shift nurse consulted with Guillermo.

"Mr. Guerrero, I had to move her. This ensures her comfort, prevents bed sores. It's routine for all comatose patients. Did she feel pain? We can never be sure. But what is certain, is that she has said a few words. Ms. Hazelton has also grimaced. And she senses pressure. All good signs. The doctor will be very pleased when he comes on his rounds this afternoon."

****

Guillermo enfolded Emma's right hand between his long fingers. He clasped it firmly, almost tightly, willing energy to surge from his power source into her quiescent body.

He was alone in the hospital room. If anyone came in behind him, he was oblivious, indifferent.

It was Friday. Again. Events of the past few days, since Emma's fall on that fateful Thursday one week earlier, nudged at his deflated spirit, acted as an urgent prod.

"Emma, death is too much with us. Today, I had to leave you for a while. I stood among the mourners, the bereaved and the sobbing kids that packed the cemetery this

312

Deal Me a Card

afternoon to say farewell to a young man who should be living. Breathing. Dancing.

"Just six days ago that's what he was doing. Life picked him up off the floor. Encircled him in her arms, swirled him around, light as a feather so that breezes of the past, the present and the future could caress him. He embraced every moment.

"This afternoon he lies six feet underground."

"Emma, Death is too much with us. But we can fend him off for a while. You and I. Together.

"So live for me, my sweet Emma. Open your eyes. Please reenter our world. I know you're there. Somewhere.

"Think of our love. We had love. We have love. It never went away. Just sagged from doubt. But I love you, my dearest one, and I know you love me.

"Listen to me. Deep, deep in the recesses of your soul, rekindle your desire to live when you hear me.

"That time you sat by my son, Daniel, and soothe his anguished heart, I loved you.

"When you danced with the college president at that fundraiser, he surprisingly twinkle-toed, and you so glamorous, and I winked because we know that you are not at all shy when you're in my arms. You stuck out your tongue at me over his shoulder. I loved you.

"And right afterwards we waltzed to the *Tales of the Vienna Woods*. As you and I danced our way to the stars and into the heavens, and still remained wrapped in each other's arms when we landed back on earth, I loved you.

"When you were so enraged that Richard called you Ms. Limp Wrist because you could bat the tennis ball ten feet over the fence but couldn't get it over the net, and you threw your racquet to the ground in a snit, I loved you.

"Remember the woman you brought to my office, jobless, husbandless, with a school-aged daughter, and you told me I needed a housekeeper, so I took her in, I loved you then, too.

Deal Me a Card

"As you piled the shopping cart with toys and made me fill up another for the Church collection, one week before Christmas, the day before you went away, and you heard me mutter money doesn't grow on trees and too much of a good thing is a bad thing. Then you gave me "The Look" so I kept on throwing toys into my cart and wrote the check to pay for all of it. I loved you."

Guillermo continued conversing as though Emma would answer.

"How we hooted at your Dirty Old Man Halloween costume and my Miss Piggy finery at the Halloween party. In the midst of our silliness, I loved you.

"Remember the sunflowers, the bunches of daisies and bouquets of lilies and baby's breath we found at the farmers' market in Santa Monica? As you stood there before me with that armful of blooms, I loved you."

He paused, then said, "That night at *Joie de Vivre* when you told me we had nothing left between us, when you cut me out of your life and declared you had no need for me, ever. You broke my heart. I forced myself to believe I hated you. But every scream from each miniscule fragment of my broken heart drowned out my cry. I loved you, I love you, I will always love you.

"Open your eyes, now, so that the first words you hear spoken will be I love you.

"When you are well again and we grow old together, you can never be embarrassed of your wrinkles because I will tell you that I saw you stuck with tubes in every orifice and your pee in a plastic bag. And I loved you."

Guillermo's hands shook from the urgency of his entreaties. Perhaps that was why he did not detect the tiny quiver in Emma's palm as his thumb rubbed against the sensitive flesh.

He kissed her forehead and lips lightly. Seated back on the recliner that had become a fixture in the room, he opened

Deal Me a Card

a book and continued to read aloud from the poems of Keats and Wordsworth that Emma cherished,

"Though nothing can bring back the hour of splendor in the grass, of glory in the flower, we will grieve not, rather find, strength in what remains behind."

He closed the book, set it on the seat of the chair as he arose and went to her side again.

"I love you. Marry me, Emma."

Deal Me a Card

CHAPTER 40

ON THE SATURDAY EVENING AFTER ISRAEL VELASQUEZ'S FUNERAL, Guillermo stepped out of the shower. The steaming water had pounded his brain back into high gear. He felt the blood likewise throb through the length of his arms and legs and torso. Tension had seeped through his pores and disappeared down the drain. His head was light, though, from lack of sleep. Tonight, perhaps he would catch a nap for a few hours if Emma rested easy.

As he toweled his hair, the phone rang. Heart in his mouth he reached out, picked up the receiver with a shaky hand. The strength that he thought he had regained ebbed.

"Guerrero!"

The voice at the other end eased a sigh of relief from between his lips.

"Hi, Raoul. What's up?"

He inserted a smile in his response to his brother's query,

"How's Emma doing? No news yet. Very little change."

He hated that a tremor was evident in his tone. Changed the subject,

"The relatives are leaving on Tuesday. They decided to stay at that motel, you know the one at the bottom of the hill just off the freeway. They wanted to be closer to the hospital. In fact, Adam is there right now replacing me. He's a decent *hombre*. He and I get along. Not a great talker like his wife, Shirley. But you know women, *tu sabes*. Anyway, what's up?"

He listened.

As Raoul unraveled the news and details which Araceli and her mother had uncovered, his tone rising and falling,

316

Deal Me a Card

mostly rising as emotion took hold, Guillermo's smile was replaced with a frown that morphed to a scowl.

"I know that son of a bitch. Bastard. Araceli said he was wearing an earring?"

He paused as the caller described the adornment.

"Yeah, I know, a stud. No, I'm not talking about the man's sexual prowess. This one's a murderous son of a bitch."

As Raoul detected the rage rising in his sibling, he took a stab at placating him.

"Hey, Guillermo relax, okay. Let's talk about this sanely."

Guillermo interrupted,

"No, I will not calm down. But I'm in perfect control of the situation."

"Fine, fine, Guillermo. But don't go jumping the gun. Excuse the pun. No rough stuff."

The man's fury obliterated any humor in his brother's words. He punched back,

"Why would I hurt myself? Emma needs me. But there's some justice to be done! My friend's son is dead."

Raoul's shocked question hissed, "You're not going to go after him and, and kill him or anything?"

He responded,

"What? Of course I'm not going to kill him. Maim him, maybe. But not kill him."

The older brother's voice sharpened, tried to take on an assertive tone, demanded,

"I think I have a right to know your game, your plan. As your older brother. You have your sons. I'll be left to clean up the mess if anything happens to you. It's only fair."

Guillermo flung back,

"No, I'm not going to give you any details."

Silence at both ends for ten seconds. Then Guillermo broke the silence,

"I need you to help me out tomorrow?"

317

Deal Me a Card

He drummed his fingertips on the table as he heard his brother's muffled voice speak to his wife at the other end. Raoul came back.

"Just wanted to check with Juana about dinner plans for Sunday. You know how things are. Can we let you know tomorrow morning?"

"Yes, I know. Sure I'll be at Church. I need you to sit with Emma in the evening for a few hours, probably from about three to six."

"That's fine. I'll be there."

Guillermo heaved a little sigh of relief,

"*Gracias, hermano*. I know I can always count on you. See you at church in the morning."

Raoul had the last word,

"Seven thirty. And do some serious thinking in the meantime. Please."

Guillermo's blood was still pounding as he took his time grooming and dressing. So he donned a loose tee-shirt and his baggy linen gauchos.

Settling in yogic stance on the four-by-four Turkish prayer rug in the bedroom, he inhaled and exhaled deeply. The way Emma had taught him. Centered himself to his core. He sensed a calming warmth spread through his body. To reassure himself equilibrium suffused his aura, that reason not rage, would guide his actions, he remained in lotus position for fifteen minutes more. Then he unwound.

Stepping lightly to his desk, he rifled through the pads of paper and found the notes from the community meeting held at the gym two weeks before. Murmuring a phone number, he dialed.

"Hello, is this Smiley? Hey, see, I recognized your voice!"

The voice at the other end was cautious. The young man sounded subdued. The response was whispery,

"Yeah, it's me. Mr. Guerrero, right? I'm sorry for …"

Deal Me a Card

Guillermo broke in, "Yeah, yeah it's been a pretty bad time, this last week."

A pause of two seconds, and Smiley answered, still speaking slowly, "These times are evil. I prayed for the dead."

The older man swallowed hard, choking down the expletives, hoping that the sound resembled a sob. The he uttered,

"Sure, I saw you there at Israel's memorial event! At the graveside too!"

In his head, he heard the words pound soundlessly, *You little bastard. You dirty hypocritical gangbanger idiot!*

Smiley seemed to be gaining confidence. His words were almost a lilt,

"He was my little brother, Willie's friend. You do what you gotta do. But why're you calling, what can I do for you? *Que pasa?* What's going on?"

"Hey, man, with all this happening, I need to meet with you. *Un reunion.*"

The gangster seemed to take a mental, or physical step backward. His voice was back to a hoarse whisper,

"Why, *porque?*"

"Why? Well, because his father, Mr. Velasquez asked me. You heard how he was talking about forgiveness, and loving your enemy, no matter what."

Smiley interrupted. Now Guillermo thought he heard a sob. Smiley muttered,

"That man, Senor Velasquez , he made me shed tears. I couldn't help it. I wept, *llore.*"

The caller bit back the snarl that rose in his gullet, swallowed the obscenities,

Yeah I bet you cried like everyone else.
You filthy pig, weeping shit instead of tears!

Aloud, he spoke firmly after clearing his throat as if commiserating,

"We have to continue. He is very adamant."

319

Deal Me a Card

The listener broke in,

"I thought his name was Doc, not Adam."

Guillermo bit his lip, continued,

"That means he insists …"

'*You uneducated moron*,' almost slipped out his mouth.

The unschooled youth made a nervous sound,

"Sorry, I'm a dropout. Don't know them big words. But what do you want me to do? *Que quiere*?"

"We have to plan that convocation. Some preliminary schedules."

The swagger had returned to Smiley's words when he replied,

"Wow, that's great, man. *Muy bien, muy bien*! That you want to include me. When will we meet?"

"Tomorrow's a good day."

"On a Sunday? *Mi madre cocina.* My mom usually invites me for dinner. Why tomorrow?"

"Because Sunday is my day off from work."

Which you would never know anything about, you sick cholo slacker, banged at the inner walls of his temples.

"And I was able to get someone to care for Miss Emma from four to six tomorrow."

"Oh, yeah, how is Miss Emma. I heard about the accident. Is she going to be okay?"

Say her name once more and I'll shove my boot down your throat slammed inside his forehead. But he swallowed hard again,

"Thanks, she's stabilized."

The words snapped out tersely. He took a deep breath and pushed,

"So how about tomorrow?"

"Okay, okay. I'll tell my mom I have to see you. She thinks you're Mr. Wonderful, teaching her English. You know, she went to the classes for six months and got a job after."

Deal Me a Card

If he was not feeling such animosity, Guillermo might have considered he was addressing a human. He quelled his emotion.

"Great. I'll pick you up at the corner of MacAdam and San Fernando and we'll confer at the gym."

"Thanks, Mr. Guerrero. This is an honor."

"Yup, you're a real important part of this effort. See you tomorrow."

Smiley's *adios* held warmth, but the older man was not impressed.

You dumb jerk scumbag! *Adios, you motherfucker*! was his silent farewell.

That settled, Guillermo dressed, slipped on his black suede jacket, to match his mood. Then he drove over to the hospital. There, Adam and Shirley willingly assented to keeping watch from seven until eleven in the morning the next day. They each kissed Emma's pale cheeks before leaving. Guillermo settled down in the recliner, and began to read aloud a Carlos Fuentes short story to boost his dear one's spirits. If only she could hear!

****

All through Mass the next morning, Guillermo's mind focused on the twenty-third psalm. *Though I walk through the valley of death, I fear no evil for you are at my side* drummed in his head like a rap song thumping through the earphones of an adolescent music lover. Only the last blessing and the celebrant's cheery sending-forth brought him back to earth.

He strode, still meditative, out of the holy place.

Daniel and Richard greeted him as he walked to the car, on their way in to the next service. He hugged them both,

"Guys, I need both of you to cover my back this afternoon. Scrap all other activities. This is a priority. Be at the gym at four o'clock precisely."

His sons nodded. They noted the stiffness of his jaw.

321

Deal Me a Card

Richard looked into his father's eyes, an intense stare. Younger eyes were the first to look away. The cold iciness he espied in the older man's hooded glance, had sparked Richard's one frightening memory of his parent.

When Richard was thirteen, he had cut school to go to the movies with his buddies. Harmless enough, he conjectured, since all his pals had gotten away with it a few times already. He was sick of them calling him a chicken. Unfortunately, he missed his ride home and his aunt Juana, had raised hell about him being lost or kidnapped, or some craziness like that. It had just been a silly caper, for cripe sake. Kids' stuff. He supposed it would blow over by the weekend. All was forgotten, he thought, until he saw his father's face.

He remembered the words so clearly. "Your uncle told me about your little escapade this week. Didn't need to attend algebra class on Wednesday, huh? Since you're so good at math, you can go count to one hundred in the garage. I'll join you there."

He wasn't certain to this day which was the worst, the anticipation of the punishment, the ten agonizing whacks with the belt that left his buttocks raw for days, or when his Dad grabbed his shoulders, stared in his eyes and reproached him for his behavior. Every word was another lash. "Do you know how much you have disappointed your mother and me? How you have disgraced us? Don't you ever hurt her again!"

That was the first and the last time.

Now he nodded at his father, "We'll be there."

Guillermo returned home. He fixed a breakfast heavy in carbohydrates and proteins, eggs, bacon, pancakes.

Then he went back to Emma's side. He held her hand, stroking it from time to time. Her fingers, her palms, both her tiny hands were warm. That was good, comforting to him. He chose a book from the tomes neatly lined up on the built-in dresser. This time he read Lao Tzu's *Tao de Ching*.

322

Deal Me a Card

He was not enamored of the ancient Chinese verse. But in another happier time, Emma had lapped it up. Perhaps the words would excite her to consciousness now. Or soon.

Raoul and Juana arrived promptly at three o'clock. They looked anxiously at their brother, but their visible concern elicited no response. He said nothing except for "thanks" and "See you later. Not too much later, I hope."

The last remark caused Raoul instant heartburn. His sphincter clenched in trepidation. His preoccupied sibling ignored his quick intake of breath.

Stiff-backed, Guillermo turned and left the room.

****

Two men stood in a boxing ring. The younger male sported a white tee-shirt and baggy scarlet boxing shorts borrowed from the closet where spare clothing was available to the athletes. He had opted to retain his own combat boots. Otherwise, he reasoned within himself, he would be totally devoid of any weapons, since the two idiots had forced him to stow his blade in the locker with his spiked armband. What a couple of assholes, like their fucking Dad. The older man was attired in similar fashion. His shorts were navy, shoes were white, the running kind.

Half an hour earlier the youth had slid into the front seat of the man's car as previously designated. Neither spoke on the ride to the Victors' Gym. Smiley had watched cautiously as Guillermo unlocked the front door of the facility. Just as they entered, another vehicle pulled up and parked alongside the other. Two well-dressed men exited and joined them in the vestibule.

"We have to change. Go wait by the ring," the father told his sons.

He turned to Smiley.

"We have a score to settle. I have a death to avenge," the aggressor told the captive.

Deal Me a Card

"I didn't do nothin'. He was crazy. He had a gun. It happened so quick. What was I to do?"

"Guilt by association."

Smiley was too petrified to ask what that meant.

Now the two would-be pugilists stood face-to-face. Both were bare-fisted. Neither appeared to know what steps to take. Then Smiley sneered,

"So, you old fart, want to punish me? C'mon, try me. I'm going to kill you, you fool, mother-fucker. My fists are going to prove that I didn't touch that guy."

He bounced up to Guillermo and struck him in the chest with an open hand.

It was as if the seventeen-year-old had pressed a button in the forty-seven-year-old. The latter's arms flew up, springs jettisoned from shoulder sockets, one first, then the other. Fists connected with opposing mouth and cheek, hammer blows that jiggled teeth and split blood vessels.

The hostile collision of body parts jarred the skeletons of both fighters. The two staggered backwards from the impact. Limbs dangled, arms momentarily at their sides, their knees near to buckling. One sobbed from acute physical distress. The other panted hard from adrenaline and wrath.

Smiley dashed a hand over his lips to wipe away the gore. Then suddenly invigorated, he lowered his head. Propelled it towards his opponent. He lifted the cannon ball at the last second and everyone present heard bone meet bone.

As a brilliance of stars spun a myriad eclipses in his head from the contact, Guillermo pulled back his right hand and brought its full force against his foe's stomach. Then he did the same with his left. Smiley oofed and arfed, turned away from his assailant. He gagged. But held down his vomit.

Guillermo's world was still revolving around him. He swayed for a moment regaining his balance. Fingers of his right hand moved his lower face from side-to-side. Then he

Deal Me a Card

shook his head impatiently. His eyes pulled into focus. Spied a target.

The fighter saw the ass in front of him, open to attack. His foot rose straight. He kicked hard, hefting the full weight of his body. The defenseless butt, borne up by two wobbling legs, quivered. Guillermo launched another full-blown jab. The laces of one combat boot tangled under the sole of the other. Smiley went down.

The chastisement persisted. He who had been so frequently the aggressor surrendered powerless to the retaliator. Now that Smiley was laid prostrate, Guillermo shoved him on his back, and knelt beside his foe. Slapped his face, four, five, six times.

"This is for Israel, for Araceli, for his mother, his father, his grandmother and grandfather, his family and friends! His unborn children!"

One tooth already loose, dislodged from the impetus. It rolled off Smiley's face dragging along a red smear.

On the sidelines, Daniel's felt his bile rise. He sublimated. Began to compose a song in his head that went something like,

China, bloody China …
Valley, bloody Valley …
Pathetic bloody Earth ….

From the floor of the ring, Smiley attempted a comeback. He reached up. Leaning on his elbow he raked at Guillermo with his talons and scratched at his spiller's eye. Nails gouged his attacker's forehead leaving a slit above his left eyebrow that oozed thick red liquid. Guillermo spasmed, jerked, almost toppling backward. He caught his tumble and straightened. Even though ruby droplets blinded his right eye he resumed his assault on the weaker man. Husky utterances erupting from a fathom of rage, were barely human.

"Take that, you bastard! So, how you like being the victim?"

Until his sons yelled for him to quit. And their voices brought him back to sanity.

He struggled to his feet.

Richard and Daniel kept their distance, warned away by the stink of ferocity that oozed unstoppable out of their father's pores.

Guillermo panted,

"Pick up that loser. Throw him in the shower. Don't let him drown."

They did as they were told.

Clean of sweat but still bleeding, Smiley limped out from under the stinging, cleansing needles. His bruised and broken visage belied his moniker. Red, puffed cheeks and split lips forbade any utterance of agony or protest. He cringed and gingerly struggled into his clothes.

Richard and Daniel had followed him. Now they watched him.

"You know, Richard, when I was a sophomore, we watched two guys fighting on campus. They beat each other to a pulp. Father Terry separated them. I heard him tell the coaches, 'You can take the man out of the street, but you can't take the street out of the man.'"

"Damn right!"

Guillermo's growl came up behind them. The two brothers swung around to see him walking towards them, toweling his hair. A deep-red splotch was seeping through a cotton wad over his left eye. A pair of band-aids precariously held it in place. Every few seconds his fingers involuntarily wiggled his chin cautiously where a red-blue bruise lasered electrifying jolts up his jawbone.

Shaking off the discomfort, he lumbered over to the man he had almost killed. He gripped Smiley by the left bicep and thumped his butt on the locker-room bench. Glared deep in the cowered coward's eyes.

Deal Me a Card

"My sons are taking you to Foothill Division. They are your good Samaritans. Remember that. Always. They saved you from me."

No gratitude shone from the wounded eyes. A different emotion filled them, from which the other two men shrank as from a viper's venom.

Seemingly immune to the hatred, Guillermo growled,

"You will sit down with Detective Yow. You will give him a written confession providing every detail of Friday evening last week. From the moment you and your pals arrived at the park until the moment you fled. Understand?"

Smiley moved his head up and down. A throaty croak or two reflected the harrowing effects of the motion.

"I will talk to the officer tomorrow morning. And if you omitted a single item, we will meet again. And then you will not walk out of this gym on two feet."

Smiley's testicles shrank further up into his abdomen.

The father commanded his sons, his voice firm,

"Richard, Dan, you take him to Foothill. Make sure he's in Yow's hands. Tell anyone who asks that I sent him. Refer all other questions to me. You two don't need to say a word. Just deliver this package."

Guillermo gestured to Smiley, and added finally,

"If you don't mind, my sons, I'd appreciate you spending the night at Emma's side. I need to bind up some wounds at home."

Richard's tone was not sarcastic.

"Of course, dad, anything."

The two autos exited the parking lot. One turned right, taking a man to face the music. The other took a man home, who felt a kind of music in his heart that comes from a job well done.

Deal Me a Card

CHAPTER 41

THEY WERE ALONE AT THE LAST WATCH. Aunty and Emma.

The room was quiet. The summer dusk stretched, light lingered for a long time.

Aunty and Emma held hands and led each other along that last journey. Neither of them pulled back or hesitated. They moved forward steadily, though sometimes Emma stumbled, falling behind.

Now all around was brightness, whiteness. The sky and the path merged, dazzled and shone. Crowds of people robed in white lined the way. Their cheering roared in Emma's ears. She added her voice, urging her aunt forward. Her lips whispered the whole litany of saints and angels and cherubim and seraphim, the names of those who had died, of all those whom her aunt had served in her lifetime. Now they stood along the path arms outstretched, welcoming her, waving, singing and calling out her name joyously, triumphantly. A jubilant chant rang out.

Come, come, welcome, join us, come.

Yes, yes, go, go, you must go now, join them, join my father, and your father, and your mother, and your brother, your sisters, and your brothers. See them, take their hands.

Emma's palms pushed her aunt forward gently from behind. But she herself hung back, remained on the threshold.

The rhythm, the crescendo of the cheers and roaring welcome gathered momentum, resounding on and on.

Deal Me a Card

But there on the bed, the body lay. Breath labored in her aunt's chest, and death rattled in her lungs. The hollow rasping was a primitive, ancient drumbeat. A steady rustle of air caused her sinking chest to rise then fall tortuously.

Slowly, gradually, minute by minute, hour by hour, her systems failed, shut down, even as the welcome roar rose higher, and a heavenly chorus resounded with triumphant *Glorias*.

Then the music stopped. Her body stilled.

Emma stood alone at Auntie's bedside, looked down at her.

A death mask, her remains, lay on the bed. Dark eyebrows etched on white parchment arched over veined eyelids that shielded sightless, bulging eyeballs. Her high cheekbones were sharp, jutting, stretching the paper-thin skin. Spare bloodless flesh stretched over the body's bones. A corpse reposed.

Emma's composure broke. Her chest heaved as if ripping apart the chains that had restrained her anguish.

"That's not me! I'm not ready. I can't die yet."

"Guillermo, I think we see light at the end of the proverbial tunnel. There will be many difficult days ahead. But the difference from three weeks ago is most encouraging. We'll gradually remove the life-support devices as Emma regains her awareness. Then I'll refer her to the rehab center next door.

"Now don't get your hopes up like those soap opera characters. This is not *The Daze of Our Wives* or *As They Whirl and Churn*. Recovery will occur as it must. Slowly. Or as fast as her body regains its strength and capabilities. She'll need physical therapy. And occupational therapy. Key phrase, 'Easy does it'. And don't kid yourself that it'll be easy."

329

Doctor Sullivan stared hard at his patient's lover's lower face. Then frowning, remarked,

"Looks like you took a hard left in the chin recently?"

"Yes. Felt like a sledgehammer when it connected. But it's mending."

"Get it checked anyway. Have a good afternoon."

"You too. And thanks."

CHAPTER 42

ISRAEL HAD BEEN DEAD SIX WEEKS.

Brenda, Esmeralda and Araceli stood in a circle looking at each other in silence. They checked each other's simple attire for the occasion. Nodded in satisfaction. Brenda and Araceli wore blue jeans, scoop-necked blouses, one rose, the other tangerine and denim jackets. The seven-month pregnant Esmeralda wore dark-grey maternity pants; her turtleneck sweater hung loose from her shoulders to her hips but did not hide the ripe bulge of her stomach. None of the girls wore make-up. Their hair shone with health, their eyes with zeal, their minds were forged in steel.

In two minutes they would walk out onto the make-shift stage erected in the Victors' Gym. The little team had a message to deliver based on what life had recently either handed to them, or snatched from them. The blood of their murdered male friends had baptized Araceli and Brenda, soaked into their psyche and penetrated their flesh and souls. The young men's premature demise destroyed forever the possibility of a future with them. Esmeralda carried new life, the future generation who would inherit the environment wrought by their parents. The three were determined to present themselves as the newest young women of the *barrio*. The female voice must be heard, had to call for change.

Equal numbers of teenagers and adults filled every one of the two hundred chairs in the hall. If an Impressionist was painting the scene, the artist would have included a chiara-oscuro mix of colors, ranging from black to golden, to reflect the mixture of dark and bright emotions which throbbed in the low chatter of many who were present.

A grandmother and grandfather sat side by side. The old woman stared straight ahead, with her silver hair perfectly coiffed, and lips pursed in grim resolve. He sat ramrod upright, smelling of cigarette smoke under his broad-brimmed sombrero, emitting side-long looks through layers of wrinkles at the young, gum-chewing whippersnappers all around them.

A mother, not a day over sixteen, nursed her three-month-old *nina* while chatting to her friend, glamorous in sparkly mascara and star-spangled barrettes. At the edge of row five, Eva sat next to Ralphie's wheelchair. The intensity of his dark-brown eyes made the boy's bleached brown face look whiter. Every other minute, the mothers' loving hand would stroke the child's thick hair as she and her son spoke earnestly, not looking around.

Two middle-school youngsters, wearing baggy, low-slung jeans, tartan shirts and spiked hairdos, preened for their admiring girlfriends. Two others sat in the last row peering through their glasses at algebra homework as they awaited the start of the performance.

The facility's acoustics sent the crowd's loud murmuring reverberating in an echoing swell to every corner. The hubbub switched off as the three presenters and the evening's host, Mr. Garcia, the gym's manager climbed onto the raised section of the floor. A young man wearing a garnet tee-shirt with *Security* emblazoned on the back, offered his muscular arm and vigilant hands to the very pregnant Esmeralda. She smiled. The pair exchanged some words, spoke just loudly enough so that people in the first two rows heard,

"Thanks, Martin. Keep your fingers crossed so it'll … I'll be good."

"You'll be great, baby. You're doing this for our son!"

"*Buenas tardes, madres, padres, abuelas, abuelos, hermanos y hermanas, bebes.* Good evening, everyone. Mothers, fathers, grandmothers, grandfathers, brothers and sisters, babies. *Mi nombre es Brenda.* My name is Brenda

Deal Me a Card

and I'm here this evening to ask for an end to hatred between families. *No mas odio, no mas!*"

"*Hola a todos.* Hi, all of you out there. Once again, like Mr. Garcia, I welcome you all here. *Como Senor Garcia, bienvenido a todos. Mi nombre es Araceli.* My name is Araceli and I am here to plead for a rejection of violence. *Rechaza la violencia!*"

"Hello. My name is Esmeralda, and in the name of my unborn son I urge you all to work together for a new time of peace. *Hola. Mi nombre es Esmeralda y en el nombre de mi hijo no nacido, pido la paz en la comunidad.*"

Then they began to speak in earnest.

Daniel stood listening to the young women's impassioned speeches. Each story gushed, a river of tears and fears. Two of them reminisced on the joys of a past life, the sickening and abrupt end to the existence of their boyfriends, and the bleakness that ensued.

Araceli recalled her nightmare,

"One minute he was smiling at me as he steered the car to the right. The next minute his blood was dripping through my fingers and smearing the front of my shirt. I told him over and over as I sat there with his head in my lap I was sorry I could not save him. For one second, his eyes were open and they forgave me. But I cannot forgive myself for not trying harder."

Brenda spoke of her life in the absence of Felipe,

"On Friday evening I dress up, buy a bunch of flowers from Prieto's, then I meet my date at a four foot by seven foot plot of earth. Sometimes I give him news about school and our friends. I wonder if he hears my stories and my prayers. But I don't think so, because he can't answer me. When his mom is there, it's worse. We two cry together. It's hard to be strong."

The third, Esmeralda, struck a note of hope but dampened the vision with references to the fear and terror

Deal Me a Card

that gripped her at all times as she visualized her son growing up in a war zone.

"I sing to my baby. He can hear me. He moves in my belly when he listens to how an angel will watch over him all his life, and that Jesus loves him. Will that happen? How will I protect him? How will his Dad shield him from harm? How long is his designated time on earth?

"I want him forever. To see him crawl, and say, 'Dada', and play catch with his father. We three will go to the beach for a picnic. Then one day he will graduate when he's twenty-four, from law school, and soon after my hair will be black-and-white as I hold *mis nietos* my grandchildren in my arms... Martin and I want that with all our souls.

"But what will happen if one night the phone rings and there's a message from the hospital?"

Daniel could sense the emotional reaction of the audience. Even from the rear of the hall he could distinguish sobs and whispers of assent as other listeners responded to the pain and identified with their sorrow.

Daniel was participating as a member of a small crowd from the surrounding communities and schools of la Coloma and San Benitez. They were playing a low key, by-standers' role in the back of the gym, giving the public a chance to hear and to air their concerns on the ravages of local gang strife. They realized their responsibility now was to listen and learn. Later, they resolved to act.

Another cursory glance alongside, behind and around him, swelled the feelings of hope and elation in his heart and muted his discomfort. Earlier he had gestured his welcome to Brother Keith, his uncle Raoul Guerrero, principals and vice-principals from the local high schools and middle schools, the two Council representatives from the districts, and Detective Yow, and nodded, bobbed his head to others whom he could not name. All were offering support with their presence. They were listening intently to the collective yearning for safety and an ease of tension.

Deal Me a Card

This was the third gathering and the numbers had increased.

****

Right after the burial of Israel Velasquez, a cohort of almost one hundred and ten like-minded youths had spontaneously coalesced to search for solutions.

That was the first meeting, a time to weep and vent when hearts were in the fateful grip of vengeance and retaliation. A dangerous time. Much aimless milling around, a herd of young wildebeests uneasy, seething, but powerless. Chafing at perceived encirclement. Feeling trapped. Mourning too many brothers and sisters no longer among them, gunned down by predators. A volatile two hours with a shaky nebulous outcome. The only result was a written promise from the leaders of local gangs sent by messenger to shed no more blood for the duration, before the next gathering.

Another call to peaceful arms had brought out some parents and more young people. Cliques formed. Suspicions lurked, occasionally striking out with a serpent's venomous tongue. One group intimidated another, preventing it from entering the skating rink on Young People's night. Girls in rival factions had met to brawl on a Friday night. But a yen for survival prevailed. A clarion called for order and organization.

Leaders had emerged.

The three young ladies, tonight's prime presenters, were in the forefront. Araceli, Brenda and Esmeralda had come to him to strategize after the first successful convocation. The girls, all seventeen years old but ageless in their determination and fury of purpose, had a decidedly militant quality in their planning. The glint in their steely eyes was more than businesslike.

"Mr. Guerrero…"

"Just call me Dan."

Deal Me a Card

Right from the first moment of their meeting they amazed and humbled him with their faith and resilience. Brought him close to tears. Almost in unison, as if speaking a prayer or a poem, they pressed the urgency on him. Araceli spoke first,

"It's our responsibility to make the right choice."

Esmerelda added her thought,

"You know there's some story in the gospel or the Bible somewhere. I heard it one Sunday at church. It says there is a reason for bad things happening, like the fall of a sparrow."

Brenda interjected,

"But Israel wasn't a bird and neither was Felipe!"

Esmerelda apologized,

"I know, I know, I'm sorry. But there's a reason you guys got this tragedy. You gotta believe."

Brenda agreed,

"Yeah, you know, one day I was in Church and it was so embarrassing 'cuz it was during Mass and all the people were around me listening. All quiet and holy. But I thought, Fuck them, I'm going to cry, I don't care what they think…"

"Did you really say the 'F' word in church?"

"No, I thought it. But that's still a sin, uh, Mr. Dan? To cuss at them in my head?"

"Well, you were kinda stressed out."

"Anyway, I don't care. I was thinking of the reading. Some words. A sentence. 'A father would hardly give his son a scorpion instead of a loaf of bread."

Esmeralda voiced her thought,

"Right, what Dad would do that? Though I know some Dads who give you the back of their hand."

Brenda pushed her perspective,

"Well that's not God. And they're talking about Him. See?"

Araceli joined in,

"What do you mean?"

Deal Me a Card

"Well, my cousin, Mauricio, and all his *cholo* buddy gang-banger pals are the scorpions."

"No doubt about that!"

"And we have to see how we can change them into positive things. Like guide them to stop killing for fun."

Araceli heard Brenda out, but could not help her retort,

"What you're saying is really, really hard for me. First I just said to God, 'Forget it, like you're history letting Israel die like that, and not even giving me the strength to help him.' I'd scream into my pillow. So loud. My mom thought I was having nightmares. Which I was."

Brenda agreed,

"Me too. Only I was so scared of Mauricio and what he would do to me, I was hiding from everyone. And my mom would force me. 'Eat, my child, you must eat or you'll get sick and die also.' And I would scream that I wanted to kill myself. That's why she called you that one time. Remember, Mr. Dan? But I refused to keep the appointment."

Daniel nodded. "That's okay. Sometimes you have to wait for the right moment, like now."

Araceli spoke once more, excited,

"And this is it. Now is the time. We gotta do this thing. Now.

"Sometimes the guys have this macho attitude, try-to-kill-me-and-see-what-happens-to-you bullshit talk. All talk, and then all the wrong action. Pow, they're six feet under. And we all cry and scream, and hug their moms and get angry and want revenge.

"Then, more killing.

What's even worse is that Israel was not even a gangbanger. He was so kind, he wouldn't hurt a fly. Loved everyone. I looked at his mom and Dad in the cemetery at the graveside, and I said to myself, 'No more, no way!' And …" Araceli paused. Her serious face lit up at what she saw next to her.

Esmeralda pointed to her watermelon-shaped belly, patted, and rubbed the bulge lovingly. The three listeners watched, mesmerized, as the unborn child squirmed as if in ecstasy under the caress.

"See this baby here? His papa and I are raising him right. He's the reason why we have to get this movement going, and keep it alive."

They went on to include Daniel in their vision. They outlined the details of what they required from him and all the people he knew who had power and money.

"Okay, Dan. We have this list of names from that meeting. Now we need your help at the schools and at the Center, and at the Boys' and Girls' Club, churches, places like that."

"Yeah, we have to recruit more kids. We got to keep the momentum going."

"Then," Brenda piped in, sounding more mature than her seventeen years, "we must enlist the adults, the grown-ups so they see it's not just their children who need help. It's the parents and families working. Struggling together.

"Then when they get all fired up about it, they can round up their neighbors, friends, of all ages. Everybody looking out for the others. A Neighborhood Gang Watch here in the *barrio*."

"Absolutely, we need some gang members who are kinda like sitting on the fence. The younger ones who are really afraid or are just losers. Or need a papa. Because their fathers are inside, in jail for a long, long time perhaps. We gotta get those guys involved. So they feel accepted. Not let them skulk in their corners all furious because they think they're outcasts."

"Please, Dan, could you help us get some materials together. So we can spread the word about other meetings, the dates and times and places," Araceli pleaded.

Deal Me a Card

"Do you think some of the businesses will help? Like your Dad and your uncle? I know Sister Nuala said she would let us use her copy machine," added Esmeralda.

The members of the new corps made commitments to organize and train. These soldiers would fan out to others, to educate them on the ways of living side by side in harmony, the lion lying beside the lamb, the hunter hanging up his weapon.

Daniel Guerrero fell right in line behind them.

The communities and schools were beginning to respond.

CHAPTER 43

SHE STIRRED, UNSETTLED, anxious, yearning. Another image rose, haunting.

A stack of skulls stretched. A barrier, a hedge, six or seven hollow-heads high, arranged in long, neat, organized rows. Death-pale, chalky, bones clean of flesh, grinning in anonymous vacuity, empty eye-sockets widened in amazement, shocked that anyone would want them to pose after torture, ignominy, and slaughter immortalized their nothingness. Their jaws drawn, stretched, yanked backwards to where their ears once jutted, teeth clenched, in the last, eternal, everlasting, defiant refusal to reveal their identities. Bereft of ownership, the skulls squatted forever unmatched, unmatchable, interlocked, to form a silent, macabre wall of stubborn silence.

The image turned to dust.

Warmth of slightly tangled bedclothes, sheet and blanket twisted under and over her toes and thighs, disturbed her body. She shifted, adjusted her spine, straightening her backbone into better alignment. Lying very still, she took a deep breath. Hospital antiseptic odors were missing. The room smelled of roses and lilacs. The quilt strewn across her, of lavender. Somehow, the lightest perfume from the orange tree blossoming outside her window had wafted in through the louvered windows. A cellist played Brahms on the bookcase. She was home after five weeks. The doctor had discharged her three days ago from the rehabilitation center.

Opening her right eye a mere slit, she saw Guillermo leaning over her.

He saw that she was awake. His fingers caressed her cheek, traced the arch of her eyebrow. Like the kiss of a butterfly. A smile flickered across her lips.

Deal Me a Card

"Good morning, my darling. How are you, my sweet Emma?"

Her eyes blinked wider.

"I heard you shuffling and snuffling from my bedroom. Said to myself, 'Ta da, it's Saturday, I have Emma all to myself. We'll jump up, exercise on the treadmill, eat a huge breakfast!'"

Emma hand reached up and touched her beloved's cheek, assuring herself of life and the living.

"I was d.d.dr.dreaming of dead things. Then you made me alive again."

Her protector kissed her on the lips.

"I love you. But these morbid thoughts have got to go. We're going to immerse you in a zestful pursuit of all things joyful and gay.

"Talking about gay, I have something to tell you about your townhouse."

The newly-roused patient, quite alert now, leaned up from her pile of pillows and wriggled over to the right side of the bed. She moved gingerly but confidently. Lakshimi, her physical therapist of two weeks, would have been proud of her. She patted the warm, empty space she had vacated.

"C.c.come cuddle down here b.beside me. I want to hear all about this. Wh .Wha What exactly has happened to my townhouse?"

"When your accident occurred, Adam and Thomas asked me to handle your affairs. Along as you were in the hospital, I put everything on hold. Put aside all thoughts of leasing or selling the place. Too much on the balance, too many unknowns. I just didn't need the stress of renters' and realtors' calls."

"Th.tha.thanks. Then?"

"Then things started to improve, when we knew you were going to be hale and hearty quite soon after intensive therapy. We could think beyond your problem…"

341

Emma felt a wave of self-pity. *Or was it remorse. Or guilt.*

"That's true. I am the st.stum.stumbling b.bl .block ...."

Guillermo, who was now lying on his back by her side, rolled halfway over and glared at her. Straight into her eyes. His were not laughing.

"Before I start kissing away your silliness, I'm going to tell you to cut this out, this 'poor me, isn't it awful it happened to defenseless little Emma, please tell me you're sorry that I had such a horrible experience,' bullshit!

"You're recuperating, well on the way to full muscle recovery in your legs. The speech person told me yesterday that your larynx is strengthening and the stuttering and slurring will diminish day by day. You have to practice those tongue exercises as much as you can."

"I'm tr.try. trying, I truly am. See?"

Emma proceeded to demonstrate with her mouth open and her tongue wagging. Which sent them both into fits of giggles. Which led to Guillermo exercising his tongue to full strength all over her body.

He showed remarkable restraint, considering how long they had been apart.

First he unbuttoned the five pearls to open up her nightie. Spread the silky folds. Then he settled down to the task. Reawakening Emma.

After a few minutes, when childlike laughter had morphed to amorous sighs, Guillermo continued,

"Lakshimi and your nutritionist, what's her name?"

"Doris."

"We are going to have a chat about your diet and body-building. See how we can bring back those bouncing breasts and some flesh to those ribs."

As her attentive, observant lover planted more kisses on her rosy buds, Emma reached down and cupped his testicles in her hand.

Deal Me a Card

"If we're not careful, the cops will be around to arrest me for causing too much joy," he murmured, his tongue still lively on her.

"I promise I won't tell," she whispered, guiding him into her.

"While I, my sweet one, am ready to shout it from the rooftops."

As he aroused her from her long sleep.

Some time later, after purring and stretching, not unlike Mamasan the cat when she had had her every desire met, Emma snuggled more closely under her man's musky armpit. She lazily circled her fingertips amidst the damp curly hairs on his chest. He growled.

"Tell me about my tenant!"

"Oh yes, Damon. You made me forget."

He grinned. 'Well, I decided it would be safest to have the place occupied. Also I was looking ahead to this time and beyond. You'd be here."

He paused,

"Maybe permanently?"

Another pause. Hearing silence, he resigned himself to patience. Continued,

"I told the boys first. You know how these students network. Turns out Daniel had met this fella in his tap dancing class. What's with that look?"

"Daniel t. ta. tap dancing?"

"One of the General Ed requirements is a humanities course. Or maybe it was a Fine Arts requirement. Who knows! Daniel thought it would be a kick to learn some different physical moves. And he did. And he is. Practicing. You'll see tomorrow. He met Damon."

"So, does he like my place?"

"He's settled right in. To the point where I've had to restrain him. The day after he moved in he called me to discuss décor. Insisted that I come over. So of course I

Deal Me a Card

hightailed it over there, afraid there might be termites or roaches."

Emma pinched the inside of his arm.

"Ouch. Okay, all right, there're never roaches in your place!

He'd found a 'divine divan', his words. 'Emma's couch has got to go,' he told me in a hushed, reproachful tone. 'It disturbs the feng shui. If not, he backed off when he saw my smirk, he thought perhaps some of the walls in the salon…"

"You mean my living room?"

"Yeah, the living area to you. The salon, he effused, should have a bolder eye-catching aura. That, or a white paint job in every room, even your boudoir, with an ebony contrast."

Emma quit her circling. She leaned up on her elbow. Tickled her protector softly.

"Wha.What did you d.do? Say?"

"You'll be so proud when I explain. First I did not laugh or sneer. I listened. Nodded a lot, grunting from the pain of biting my lip and choking. I think he imagined I was having some sort of aesthetic orgasm."

"That wasn't polite to lead him on!"

"Well, then I cut him off at the pass. Told him there were restrictions in that particular condo development about changing the décor."

"Yeah, right!"

"Hey, he's young, he's gullible. He believed me. Sort of. And here's the hook."

"What? You p.pr.promised to go to his first dance performance?"

"No way, that's small potatoes. He is going to accompany you to I. Magnin, or to whatever grand boutique you lovely heart desires. To help you select your spring and summer wardrobe."

"You, beast, you. But such a creative, cunning b.b.beast."

344

Deal Me a Card

Guillermo glanced fondly at his dear one who, as of late had done little else but mope and moan. Doubtless, some of it had been justified. But his heart burst into an alleluia as he sensed her upbeat demeanor.

"He became quite excited. Spoke in that breathy voice of his about the exquisite lingerie. Mentioned that he had seen the catalog with their latest in lacy drawers and *chemises de soie*. He was hoping that he could help your with your choices from top to bottom! His words."

"W.W.Will he follow me into the dressing rooms, do you think?"

"My first instinct would be to crush him like a flea if he ever broached the subject. On second thoughts, I'd never find a safer bodyguard. You will be in the delicate hands of a man with impeccable finesse. His words."

"I want to meet him. Is he cute?"

"When you step out with that dandy, you will be put to shame. Manicure every week. Sassoon boutique 'do, also weekly. Has a personal trainer every other week."

"As if you don't indulge!" Emma teased.

"Right, I get my nails done when I go to the barber's once a month."

"Obviously Damon's not a m.manly man," the amused listener mused.

"But he smells real good. You should try walking into your bathroom. I tried. Almost tripped and keeled over the array of lotions and balms and men's scents."

"Yummy!"

"Comely is the two-syllable GQ description I choose, with a buff bod. Five eleven, brunette with a slight wave in his thick hair. Blue-green eyes, sometimes behind rimless Versace shades. And the outfits! 'Ensembles,' to use his word. Before I entered the walk-in closet, at his invitation of course, I had thought yours was an oversized collection."

"Well, you like your women p.p. pretty!" she needled him and smirked at his hurt grimace. Hurried to recapture the

345

Deal Me a Card

hilarity. "N.N.Next you'll be telling me his underwear and socks m.match!" Emma challenged.

"They do! He showed me. And shoes. He's put Imelda to shame!"

Their light-hearted banter had resumed.

"If I didn't know better, I'd think this young man has taken a shine to you!"

"Daniel has told him all about you and me," her love spoke gently.

"I believe Damon will su.suit m.me like a p.pai.pair of this season's Prada's."

Emma's stutter was at that instant more from amusement than from impediment. Nevertheless it sobered her listener, whose smile faded,

"But first, you must be back on your own two feet, laughing and talking again. You'll lose the cane. You'll be our Emma of old."

Emma wriggled back into prone position. Stared at the ceiling as she mulled over his words. She spoke more slowly, pensively,

"Well, I hope it's not just a switch in fashion that you'll see. I believe I'll call Dr Schwarzman and resume my sessions. I just hope she can fit me into her schedule after my dramatic exit."

Seeing her rueful grimace, Guillermo took her into his embrace. As they lay close, he stroked her hair. Its healthy scent drew him in. He inhaled deeply.

"My sweet Emma, 'We are such stuff dreams are made of, and our little life is rounded with a sleep.' I read that in the *Unshakeable Shakespear*e book of quotes your son brought to the hospital.

"Emma, shed your dream of the past. Let's dream of our future together. And we'll not sleep for a long, long time yet."

Emma hugged Guillermo tightly, "My Elizabethan lover! How I love you! I'm hungry, let's eat."

346

****

The next afternoon, Emma relaxed on the couch in the living room of Guillermo's house, basking in every one of her lover's proprietary gestures. As he had promised, Richard and Daniel and a few other intimates were gathered for a party to celebrate Emma's renewed mobility.

They had much to rejoice over. The guest of honor was upright again. Though to calm her sentinel's ever-watchful mother-hen fidgets and to settle his nerves, she rested frequently. Even now with the soiree in full swing, he paced back and forth attentive to her teeniest wish. Uncannily, he read her mind. In a response to unspoken desires, Guillermo would send a smile and a wink across the room, or would pause and brush his lips on the crown of her head as he walked by behind the sofa.

"You're so beautiful, my lovely one!" he'd whisper.

Emma felt delectable, svelte in her turquoise silk *ao dai,* the traditional dress of Vietnamese women, embroidered with pearly-pink chrysanthemums, and a touch of Shalimar behind her ears.

Wine flowed, loosening tongues and dancing feet. The refreshments were light, like the banter. Blithe hearts matched the nimble-footed. Within an hour Daniel felt constrained. After some chardonnay and very little urging from sibling, Dad, uncle, cousins and buddies, he picked up the ornamental cane that Emma used. His dance was a mime that wished away *el baston. Magico, desaparecido,* magic gone*!* Maybe the dance would cast a spell, and make it vanish. So he tried his best with a flourish of dirty dancing. His adaptation.

"Hey, *hermano,* I'm impressed. You've got some moves there! Sort of a Fred Astaire-Michael Jackson combo. *Mon Dieu,* are those ballerina's thighs you're developing? Love your shoes too."

The dancer, grinning as he wiped the perspiration off his neck, socked his brother, Richard, lightly on his upper arm.

"You get yours from the tennis court. I get mine from the dance floor!"

Then the mating of violin and guitar in Schubert's *Fifteen Dances* insinuated themselves into the two men's awareness. They turned from their good humored teasing.

Damon and his friend, Joshua had taken the floor.

The music played. The men danced. Their bodies merged, hand in hand, eyes in eyes, elbow to elbow, hip to hip.

The music stopped.

Guests around the couple stood speechless. Silence was applause enough.

The duo kissed gently, on the lips. Smiled, nodded into each others' eyes. Then they turned and walked off to separate bathrooms to freshen up. The backs of their Abboud silk shirts, straw and winter birch respectively, were soaking. Their double-pleated llama-silk slacks, Joshua's indigo and Damon's faded burgundy, hung gracefully from their slim hips.

Emma's unspoken memo to Guillermo was dulcet in the midst of otherwise frivolous party badinage. Her gracious host and attendant bowed graciously, bussed her fingers. Made a mental note to further pursue the therapeutic quirks of dancing.

****

Later that night, the house was still. Though some forgotten peals of laughter tip-toed along the baseboards, bumping into giggles that jumped back in surprise then burst into guffaws at the corners of the room. Happiness was regaining a foothold.

Orleans' lyrics entwined themselves through and between the lovers' clasped hands and near-touching lips.

Deal Me a Card

The two murmured, disjointedly making the words their own as they swayed.

"Dance with me … I'll take you wherever you want to go."

Deal Me a Card

CHAPTER 44

DOCTOR SCHWARZMAN HAD FOUND a slot for her. Amazingly, it was on Thursday evenings. Initially Emma had felt pressed. She had so much more work to do, picking up where she had left off. Quickly though she felt at ease. Her therapist had kept her demeanor of warmth and kindly objectivity. Even her psychologist's uniform - as Emma privately labeled Doctor Schwarzman's white blouses, A-line dark-colored over-the-knee skirts, ecru nylons and navy or black pumps - was comforting to note.

At the first appointment, Doctor Schwarzman was wearing a pleated Prussian blue skirt, an ivory shirt with elbow-length sleeves and an antique cameo at the throat. As always, her all-natural silver hair with its brunette streaks was only slightly disheveled from the occasional movement of her fingers through its thick strands.

All was as it should be in Emma's mentor's office. Even the flowering orchid.

Emma began,

"Doctor Schwarzman, I'm glad to be back. I'm relieved!"

"I'm pleased that you made the decision. You're taking the reins. That's what you said over the phone. It's a brand new start."

"Well, yes and no. There's another element. I'm looking at life differently."

"What's changed?"

"I'm still in the making. I'm not finished yet. And there's more to that thought than this recent brush with disaster."

Her therapist interjected,

"You're not finished yet …"

Deal Me a Card

"Not with therapy. That's true. I'm continuing with you, so that's one part of it! But that's not what I mean. Am I confusing you?"

"You're doing your best. But let's continue. Clarify?"

"All right. I'll do my best. What you said a few seconds ago. About taking the reins. It's a very delicate balance. I'm sure to flounder and fumble with my thoughts and words."

"Take it slowly. Take your time explaining. You might have had many hours and days to meditate on things, but you still have to sort out your thoughts."

"You are so right.

"Looking back over the last few weeks, I seem to have spent a lot of time swimming around in the murky pool of my psyche.

"It's like this. Before the accident, I could never shed the self-recrimination. I believed I was powerless to allay the guilt nagging at me. But I suppose since all my defenses were down as I lay immobile, as I slowly recuperated, it was safe to go into the water. To submerge myself in self-analysis. Many times. Surprisingly, I didn't drown, and no jaws opened to swallow me. I just gave in to the memories. Thoughts of my infidelity and the man's alcoholism that led to our divorce, struggled to the surface. I confronted them.

"Perhaps this analogy will work.

"Last autumn, Guillermo and I went to the mountains for a quick break over Veterans' Day weekend. You remember last fall, even late October, was quite dry. We thought the river and solitude would be refreshing.

"Early on the second day, Sunday morning, it rained. From inside our pup-tent, I sat, trapped and pleasantly indolent, and watched a dead rock come alive. The surface was splotched black, spread with grey smudges and speckles of white. Parasitic mosses clung to the niches, reduced to a silver-grey thirsty weariness. The drought was killing them.

"Then droplets of moisture sank into the rough sere vegetation. Wide-eyed, I watched. It was as if the strokes of

351

an invisible paintbrush had splashed a swath of vivid green across the small boulder. Moss sprang to life.

"In the same way my soul's eye recently became a giant CAT scan. It swept over my inner being and reignited my life.

"Now I'd like to lean back, Doctor Schwarzman, and let my stream of consciousness flow. Is that okay? We have time?"

"Of course, Emma! Please continue."

Her patient settled into one of her most favorite chairs. She closed her eyes.

"For the last two and one half years of my failed marriage, I lived a staged existence. My shadow self, too strong, too proud would lead me astray over and over again. I was weak, weak, weak, blinded, surging forward supposedly liberated, but instead a slave to my lust and longings, urges. Faustian in my needs for Mephistopheles' magic to work in every nerve-ending, in every drop of blood throbbing through my veins, in every fiber of my body.

"When I lay in the arms of an illicit lover, far from home, the whole continent-span away, I was fulfilled. I was a sensual, sensuous female again. I loved his loving, demonstrating his appreciation for my femininity and sexuality with a tenderness I had not experienced for a long, long time.

"I felt whole.

"But looking back, I can only shake my head in wonder and amazement at my adroit juggling. I was an actor in a medieval morality play, the one who represents a dizzying series of characters, wearing a different mask each time he comes on stage. I stood on a revolving lazy-susan with four parts depicting the worlds where I lived, worked, loved and lied. Loving mother, devoted wife, dedicated career woman, adulteress. As days, weeks, months passed by, I moved from scene to scene playing each role as befit the moment.

Deal Me a Card

"Outwardly I was myself, it seems, since there were no remarks, queries, whispers behind hands, voices hushed when I drew near, no pointed fingers. But I knew my inner epithelium bore the tattoo. The scarlet letter, splayed on every inch of my cheating body, was branded on my soul.

"All the time I kept knocking at the door, begging for respite from Heaven, pleading for a change of heart. And God is my witness. I looked down at my outstretched hand. To my horror, to my dismay I saw an asp instead of a loaf of bread.

"I let myself down. I had all the tools at my disposal but somehow I could get none of them to work the way I had been taught since babyhood. I was in control in so many ways except in the things that mattered. I forsook the social and religious mores of my family, my culture, my age, my community.

"Now much, much later, in spite of all the grief, that coma gave me back to myself. The bible says something like 'O happy fault.' I suppose I could say, 'O happy fall?'"

Emma opened wide her half-closed eyes. She leaned forward, reached out her hand to her listener. The she leaned back, and resumed,

"I know I am getting there, dealing with the guilt and the anger. Putting in perspective the distrust I feel and urge to control everything and everybody.

"I now have a different perspective and will strive to act accordingly.

"I'm very adept at bringing people, creative ideas, strategies together. I'll continue to do that.

"Then, I'll let them go their way, come what may. Perhaps not in my vision, but according to some other's dream about where the daily bread will be delivered. I will relinquish my control, my grasp, my grip on the realities that I believed were, are mine alone to construct, to mold.

Deal Me a Card

"I used to behave with such insurmountable pride, really believing I could shape the future, of things, people, of the world. My future!

"No more!

"And, you know, I am submitting with a joy, a relief, an-almost ecstasy, a leaping of my heart, a hiccup of happy laughter, a giggle of glee.

"I know that I can help maneuver, but never absolutely set anything in place or in motion."

"But I need not know. I need only trust. I have come this far. My bruises are fading. I am not cowed. Just humble as I wait for the next affirming challenge."

She stopped. Fell silent. A tiny gulp combined with a sob escaped through her lips and nose.

"There, Doctor Scharzman, I've verbalized it. Gave the words flesh. You're the first to know."

"And others will see, Emma, as time goes by.

"But our time is up now. And you look exhausted."

Emma answered, fatigue in her tone,

"Surrendering the rest of a life is wearying."

"You are growing in wisdom, certainly. I'll see you next week."

"Thanks."

****

On another Thursday, Emma settled into her chair, looked straight at her therapist,

"I've never broached the subject of my father with you. And you were kind enough never to ask."

"All in good time. Is that time now?'

"Yes. I've been thinking much about my parents' married time together. And how brief it was. And how it affected my mother. That's what we lived with, I lived with, longest. Her devastation.

"My Dad was gone. He abandoned me, when I was nine, dying suddenly of a perforated stomach ulcer. For three

Deal Me a Card

days, a week-end of excruciating pain, he suffered. Then Mom rushed him to the hospital. Too late. He was dead before they could operate.

"They brought his body home in an ambulance van. The four children rushed to the door. 'Daddy's home.' 'He's well.' 'He's alive.'

'No, he's dead.'

"Doctor, I don't want loneliness to wrest at my heart strings, tear at my soul. I never want to echo my mother's desolation. I remember her grieving, day after day, week after week, month after month. She even lay immobilized in a hospital for awhile.

"My mother was always fair skinned. Now she metamorphosed, mutated to a ghost, Lalique-like. And still so young. He was only forty-five and she was just thirty-eight when he died. After that, it was as if those transparent fragile phyllo-like layers of flesh shrouded an essence, a spirit shredded, when she lost her spouse. That ghost, who was my mother wept, mouthing words, as she mourned unceasingly. As a thoughtless child I would watch her in dismay. As a grown woman I shook my head behind her back. How could one creature hold so much moisture to feed that never-ending flow? She did.

"Then she died. Too young at sixty-two. My mother vanished. A shrunken mind in a skeletal, sere-skinned, tiny body, lying in an enormous bed, attached to morphine-delivering, pain-killing fluids. The specter slipped away."

"Love can annihilate."

CHAPTER 45

THE FOUR WOMEN SLOWLY FINISHED their after-lunch drinks. Emma sipped her wine, white zinfandel. Brenda and Araceli slurped their sodas. Esmeralda was content with her glass of fruit juice. Their dresses melded in an ode of jubilation for the season. Emma's flowing deep-purple and white stripes, and the pastels of the younger ladies.

Warm sun's rays had prompted to action both the wafting of perfume from the overhanging jasmine and the lazy buzz of busy bees. These served only to further mellow this Saturday afternoon, in the last days of March.

Spontaneously luxuriating, the group surrendered to every subtle tickle of breeze caressing their flesh. Now and again the little troupe of females stretched their bare legs and arms in a sensuous reflex.

The jovial Emilio of Pastamore's pranced over to check their drinks. They requested another round. What the heck! Winter was past. Easter was a few weeks away.

But their meeting looked beyond, to the summer months. So they got down to brass tacks.

Emma smiled and asked, "Esmeralda, the baby's due on May 11. Right?"

"Absolutely. Got my suitcase packed. The baby's room is almost decorated. Very cute. Blue and white. My mom is going crazy with the crocheting, blankets, booties, sweaters, bonnets. Knitting too."

"I thought nobody knitted anymore!" Emma was surprised. *She remembered her mother and her aunt knitting for her son years and years ago.*

"Well, come over some evening and watch her with those clicking needles."

"That baby's going to be a handsome hunk! *Un gran varon!*" Brenda said, with admiration.

"From the size of him now, he is," Esmeralda chortled, stroking her distended stomach.

"And you're nursing him, so Martin Junior is destined to be Mr. Bouncy Baby!"

"Well, since I'm starting at the college in the fall I want to give him a running start. He'll be in day care right on campus. But I'm concerned that the breastfeeding is going to be a challenge."

"Don't worry. The nurse will tell you how the ta-tas work. That's great about your college career." Emma sounded pleased.

"Yeah. After Daniel gave us that talking-to last fall, I figured I better get my act together. I got my GED results last week. So I'm eligible to enroll."

Emma announced, "Speaking about college and courses. Guillermo was offered a full-time instructor's position and he accepted. I'm so proud."

"Mr. Guerrero's a really smart man, isn't he, Miss Emma? When are you two getting married?" Araceli asked.

Emma lowered her eyes and smiled, "I was waiting for someone to ask that question. Well, he hasn't proposed formally but I think he's on the verge. So we'll probably have a quiet wedding. Then a big reception in the summer sometime so everyone besides his brother and sister-in-law can give us a blessing."

Brenda segued,

"Well, Araceli and I are taking the PSAT right after the Spring break. And she's going to take the SAT in June."

Emma, relieved of the scrutiny and easily catching her breath, complimented them,

"Wow, good for you, girls! With all this stress, you've just hung in there. You're pretty hot stuff. And I'm not talking about how you look! Israel and Felipe would be so proud of you!"

Deal Me a Card

Araceli responded, "I'm doing this for me and also in his memory. We used to talk about our futures. Studying hard, getting the grades for scholarships and being admitted to the university. He'd be the big-mouth attorney. I'd be the Hollywood plastic surgeon. We were going to do it all together. In a way we are. Only Israel's like the wind beneath my wings now."

Brenda spoke, "You know, I was thinking about law also. But Dan has really inspired me to go into social work. He says I have the personality. I'm a good listener and I'm pushy."

"Great choice, Brenda. But keep your options open. And I mean all three of you. Speaking of being pushy, how're the events shaping up for the summer youth program? I have some info, but you all go first."

Brenda started, "Dan and I met with Mr. Velasquez and Mr. Garcia. The Victors' Gym is reserved for all three months mid-June through the end of August, all day and all night. They will work around anything we plan."

"Nice work, Brenda."

"You've got a crush on Mr. Dan, huh?" Araceli teased.

"No way! He's older. A sophisticated dude!" Brenda denied emphatically.

Her friend persisted,

"Doesn't matter. Your blush cannot lie. Every time you mention his name, you stammer, your eyes flutter, and your cheeks go all pink."

Brenda gasped in mock horror,

"Oh my God, you think he notices when I'm around him?

"Actually what I dream and pray for, is one day, when my heart stops aching so much, I'll find a guy with Felipe's smile and Dan's wisdom. But that'll be a miracle. Hey we're off the subject. What have you been up to, Araceli?"

"I bet you find that guy. He's waiting for you somewhere."

Deal Me a Card

Araceli pulled herself back to the main topic.

"Okay, okay… Back to serious business. All the committees from the middle schools and high schools have met. The representatives pressed for commitments from the administrators. In May, they'll start signing up students for events and workshops. We didn't want to start any lists until we knew what kinds of activities would be available."

Esmerelda, whose eyelids were growing heavy, spoke up,

"While Araceli has been busy with the schools, I've been talking to the adult students at the Center and the college. I worked with Carmelita and the teachers let us visit the classrooms. They're scheduling a series of breakfasts, lunches and dinners for the students. Some of them are soliciting donations from the stores and agencies in La Coloma and San Benitez even as we speak.

"It goes without saying that the women will do the cooking. And Randy has offered his expertise and help from the college kitchen. They'll bake a few hundred pies. He'll give credit hours to those who help with the food preparation."

Emma added.

"Dan and Richard and their father have mostly done the footwork for me, but I've offered suggestions. They're getting volunteers from the Hispanic student organizations and professional groups to provide the workshops and presentations. Richard has already lined up a dance performance by some men and women from Theatre Arts departments at UC and Cal State campuses for August. I believe it won't be solely performances by the college students. The kids who sign up will have the opportunity to learn some dance moves, the history of dance. Act out some skits. They'll develop body awareness, broaden their minds, we hope."

Araceli told the group,

359

Deal Me a Card

"The father of one of the La Coloma High students is a member of the Chamber of Commerce. He's conferred with its Young People's Education department. They're putting together a workshop for resume writing and job interviewing practice. They said they could offer that a number of times. Maybe some of the college students could be trained and could work with small groups."

"Great idea."

Esmeralda shook herself out of the catnap she was snatching. Since she was so close to giving birth, the others were indulging her. She stifled a yawn,

"Oh, excuse me. The sun and the bees and the lovely scent over us were kinda like a lullaby. Really, I'm not bored at all. And I've been busy with my idea. Listen!"

Her grinning companions assured her of their forgiveness and understanding. She went on,

"Junior will be two months old. Some of the other girls, with whom I've met in pre-natal sessions, and I want to offer a workshop on the realities of motherhood."

"And include the realities of fatherhood also, please!"

"Of course! Martin and I are working with Sister Nuala on a workbook to use in the class. Actually, she's the adult in charge so we can stay organized."

Almost as one, the group paused. They took a deep breath in concert. Emma began to sum up,

"It looks like we have many things in motion. I want to offer you my office at the Center. Guillermo had very kindly freed up a room for me, and we can use it to centralize all our youth summer activities. We have use of a phone, copy machine, computer. Though if Sister at her clinic and the schools give you materials and offer the use of equipment, take them up on their offers. Every bit helps to lower the cost and it shows their willingness to buy into the cause."

Araceli interjected,

"It's the end of March now. How about we set up a date in mid-April when we firm up dates, fill slots for workshops and events. Put everything, or as much as we can, on paper. Then we'll be coordinated."

"Thanks, Araceli. Let's meet on the Monday after Easter. By then, I'll have some sample press releases drafted, and also letters for our sponsors. You know, the college, the police department, the Chambers, businesses. We need to get those out so they can respond by May.

"This is going to make a huge splash!

"And I don't know about any of you, but all this talking and planning have made me thirsty. Let's have large glasses of cold spring water. Emilio, can you help us?"

A little later the gang of four walked out of the restaurant and stood for some moments saying goodbye, giving each other half-hugs. Araceli spoke, thoughtfully,

"The plan is going to work. I pledged to make it work. To my dying day I will remember Israel's mother and father giving the eulogy for their son. They said they forgave his murderers. At that moment I made a promise to myself that Israel did not die in vain."

Deal Me a Card

CHAPTER 46

EMMA LAY STILL in the king-sized bed. Alone, since she had the room to herself for as long as she wanted. She overheard Guillermo rattling pans in the kitchen. The dream ebbed and flowed in and out of her consciousness. For some odd reason, her sweet man had punched the button on the cassette player before he headed to the kitchen. Beethoven's Moonlight Sonata lulled her back into her reverie. She dreamed.

On the water, kayaking, a perfect morning, cool, with warming sunbeams, an eagle-eyed guide spoke gently, gestured.

An ibis, white wings undulating in rhythm with the stream. Water snakes, one camouflaged, coiled around the branch of an oak tree. An alligator eyes-only unblinkingly peering through the hydrilla. Mullets, momentary silver show-off I-can-fly flashes.

Banks overloaded with dense, deep-set vegetation. A sprawling metropolis of cypress, maple, hickory, and willows. Tangled mosses. Exuberant life sprouting from the murky odor of decay.

She lolled, dragging her fingertips in the tickling wavelets, as breezes and the leader's words stroked her cheeks. Sweat beads trickled down her neck, while her shirt glued to her back and to her armpits with damp, sun-scented perspiration.

Then she roused herself to sit upright and paddle steadily for a few yards. Observed, listened,

Shrills of random birds, an osprey shriek.

One turtle sunbathed on a half-sunken post with five others,

The guide motioned. Worrisome heavy, dark, grayish-black clouds hovered low overhead, ready to drop a storm.

He kept her company since she had fallen behind.

Then the rain fell.

She rowed midstream completely drenched by a tempest pelting unrelenting heavy explosions in watery circles. A storm firing, hurled grauples, crackling lightning bolts, stabbing the river's ripples, lashing them into writhing waves that vaporized around her little vessel.

While above rumbled applause, thunder claps urging encore after encore.

In those few minutes she felt no fear or panic, only exhilaration, excitement of being at one with primal elements of nature. She felt blessed, as she rowed doggedly and steadily with aching hands and arms, as around her the beauty and wildness, the unrestrained wind whipping the sweet bays, rocking the palms, shook the riverbanks into a green frenzy.

She exalted in the raw warm wetness, even laughed a little as her ever-watchful guide glanced at her frequently, nervously, lips twitching.

They made it together at last to the bank, rain still pouring, she and the guide with Guillermo's face.

Emma's eyes blinked rapidly, alert. The stirring third movement of the sonata was trilling to a close.

Wide awake, she rolled over, and jumped out of bed. Running into the kitchen she threw herself into Guillermo's arms. Obligingly he wrapped them around her, careful to hold the buttery knife and slice of wheat toast away from her swishing silk nightdress.

"You saved me, you saved me from certain death. The lightning storm would have burned us to a crisp!"

Deal Me a Card

She nuzzled her lips at his earlobes.

"You're very welcome, my darling."

He would admit to anything to encourage the renewed vigor, and the ardent kisses.

"There's toast and marmalade. We could poach eggs. Sit down and tell me all about the daring rescue. But kiss me again. Like the first time."

Emma indulged him. It was the least she could do.

****

"That was very special and wildly entertaining! Thanks for the lovely evening."

"We haven't had Greek food before, together. I thought you'd enjoy it."

It was later, much later that same day, a Friday. evening, Guillermo clasped Emma's waist as they sashayed through the front door. Strains of Hellenic rhythms echoed in their heads.

Dinner at *The Great Grecian* restaurant had been a kick. Besides feasting on the lavish spread especially prepared for them, the two had spent a little time on their feet with other exuberant customers gyrating and linking arms to the beat of drums, flutes and guitars. Listened rapt to a plaintive lyre.

"You didn't overdo it, did you?"

Guillermo, ever solicitous, settled his beloved, slightly tipsy from ouzo, in the soft luxury of the leather couch in the living room. She sank back with a sigh. Her gossamer blouse showed off the roundness of her breasts, the slit of her wrap-around skirt gaped just enough to divulge a tanned thigh.

"Well, maybe ever so slightly. But I don't regret a single second."

"Here's a glass of water. Good for you before bedtime."

He handed her the water, then turned on the stereo. They were silent in their closeness as Johnny Mathis once again insinuated his lyrics into their souls. As one, they rose at the end of the song

"Will you love me to the Twelfth of Never? It's a long, long time."

Emma looked directly into her love's eyes.

"Emma, Emma. I need you, I need you. Like roses need their perfume."

Despite the intensity, they leaned away from each other and burst out laughing. At themselves.

"In the midst of our passion and fervor we are just a couple of plagiarists!"

"Nah! I give Johnny full credit for getting me all stirred up and fervent."

"Me too."

As they stood in an embrace, Emma mused,

"Do you think, Guillermo, when we've been married ten thousand days, we'll still be just as soppy?"

Her man, usually never at a loss for words, could only mutter hoarsely,

"When will we start?"

"Ask me again, nicely."

****

"Doctor Schwarzman, look, look!"

Emma held out her left hand to display the solitaire nestled in a circle of five diamonds.

The therapist took Emma's hand in her hand and looked delightedly at the engagement ring.

"Yes, I noticed when you walked in. Who could miss this rock? Congratulations!"

"It wasn't easy. You know. After all that's happened. Me being such a fool, and the accident. I was so ashamed. And so afraid. Kept asking myself, 'Was he just pitying me?'"

"Emma, he loves you."

"Yes. I know. I went for a long walk up into the hills behind his, our home. Alone. Last Sunday. We were going to

365

Deal Me a Card

pick this out on Monday, and I needed time to collect my last thoughts. To reflect on this decision."

She flickered the fingers of her left hand.

"Some of the hiking trails are quite easy, for beginners. The therapist said it would be fine to go for about half a mile. No strain, not too much sweat."

"You decided to go alone? Isn't it a little dangerous?"

"No. On Sundays, hikers are up there all the time. Especially on such a lovely early spring day. Cacti blooming. Anyway, I told Guillermo where I was headed."

"Good."

"And as I trudged I thought about whom I was, leading up to my meeting this man. And all the time after."

"I was paralyzed. My feet were glued to a crevice here, stuck to a tiny niche there, in the wall of perpendicular rock that was my life.

Then he was above me, looked down and saw my plight.

'Emma. Emma you can do it. Here, give me your hand.'

Fingers reached out and down to touch mine, grasp mine. He held my hand, warm, tightly. His was reassuring, linked to mine, twining, intertwining.

'Emma! Lean into the rock. Lean toward me, hold my hand. Here, tight. Now.

I have your hand. Don't worry,

I won't let you fall.

There.'

He never let me fall."

Deal Me a Card

CHAPTER 47

"THANKS FOR DINNER. *Joie de Vivre* never lets us down!"

"It'll always be our favorite place. And the place is never really too crowded."

Emma and Guillermo glanced around the half-empty parking lot as they clicked their safety belts. The fragrance of jasmine perfumed the mild air. Emma unfastened the second button on her off-white linen blouse to savor the cool evening breeze caressing her ever so lightly.

"It's Memorial Day weekend, everyone's out of town."

"True. It's been a good week, exciting, really exhilarating. Kind of emotional, but satisfying. Now we can all take a breather."

Emma remarked, "Esmeralda and Martin's baby boy came right on time. He is just the cutest little fella. Sucking at his mother's breast right off. Cute and hungry."

"You've obviously visited the family already. Will they be home next week?'

She answered, "Certainly by Monday. Perhaps we can drop by their place on Tuesday. I'll call first. Probably after work for you is the best time. Okay?"

"Great.

"The pomp and circumstance at the Center. Wasn't that something? All you women decorating the place made the room look palatial."

Emma nodded, agreeing. "That's for sure. They deserve the recognition. Earnest, hardworking students graduating. Clutching those certificates of completion."

Emma stretched her hand across to her beloved who was driving the car, stroked his cheek.

"I love you," both said in the same breath. And they laughed softly in unison.

Deal Me a Card

"The president of the college taking the time to present the certificates was a really nice touch. Very thoughtful gentleman," Emma returned to the recent event.

"I loved what he said," she smiled. A trifle grandiose. Something about the Center being 'the pillar in the community against which the worried, downcast, hopeless, and destitute trainees could lean, and from which they would invariably draw a measure of renewed hope and belief in themselves. That every person was a treasure newly discovered for the world to embrace and value.' On and on…"

"He didn't say that, did he?" Guillermo asked, sounding pleased.

"He surely did. Robin video-taped the whole ceremony and I saw it. Well, parts of it."

Guillermo's smile could be heard in his words,

"Makes us seem like some kind of grand institution, with real brick walls and a statue in the front gardens."

Emma said seriously, "In a very real sense, those students own the Center. It's their place of empowerment. Take Hector for example. He's the computer whiz kid, self-taught, with barely a high school education and the biggest heart in the world."

"He's the one who had the twenty-first birthday party, right? On Thursday, yesterday?" Guillermo asked.

"Exactly. Do you realize that was the first birthday celebration he had ever experienced in his life?"

Guillermo raise his eyebrows. "So that's why all you women were teary-eyed, and your man Robin too. Hey, even Randy was sniffling and harrumphing a little when the birthday boy blew out the candles. I walked in on that one. Didn't know what to think. Randy, with tears in his eyes? I didn't dare ask. You know how touchy he can be!"

"All the tears were tears of joy," Emma retorted.

Guillermo changed the subject.

Deal Me a Card

"On the other hand, Monday should be a whole lotta laughs. I invited dozens of people over for a barbeque. Richard and Daniel and their girlfriends will help out, and of course Raoul and Juana will want to take over. Maybe I'll let them. You're fixing dinner for all of us Sunday, right?"

Emma replied, excited. "Oh yes! Paella. Juana picked up the seafood, and I'll be hard at it tomorrow morning. I guess we'll have to get to bed early tonight so I'll be alert and ready. Do you mind?"

"My sweetest one. We have our whole lives ahead of us. And it's only eight thirty now…. So we can jump in the spa, and then drift off leisurely."

"Oh, oh!"

"What's the matter?"

"One of my all-time favorite songs. Johnny Nash. Can I turn up the volume a little?"

Emma spoke as the tune played softly in the background. Her words matched the tempo,

"He wrote that song for us." She listened for a few seconds, humming along then spoke again, "Last Sunday when I took a walk along the ridge, the rain was gone. All I saw was an expanse of blue sky curving down to meet the brown earth. I stumbled a little on some rocks, but there was no pain. You've taken it all away. I thought then that if I feel sad sometimes, the sun changes my tears to a rainbow. You make my days sparkle."

She giggled,

"I'm such a silly sentimental fool."

Then she sang along, interjecting her very own creative lyrics. The way Guillermo loved.

He reached over and touched her cheek gently, as he smiled,

"You make every song yours, don't you?"

"You bet. Ours."

"A trifle late in the day for blue skies," Guillermo murmured.

Deal Me a Card

"There's always tomorrow, and the day after, and the day after that, with you. Us together," Emma sang, making up her own tune.

Guillermo muttered distractedly as he glanced to the left. He was turning down his driveway.

"Boy, was I relieved when the county installed that metal gate up there. After that body dump, I was uneasy. The hikers can still walk on the path. But the barrier keeps the crazies out. I hope."

Emma continued to sing and hum as she exited the car and closed the door behind her. The song still on her lips and in her heart, she reached up into the air with both hands, her fingers pointed to the Milky Way and the rest of the universe. Guillermo picked up a recent train of thought.

"You know, you can't get too involved with the people at the Center. Emotionally involved, that is. They are there for just awhile. Then they leave. Bye-bye. A week later, there's a new group."

They were almost at the front door.

Emma stretched her hands out wide, now shoulder-high, and demurred,

"It's impossible for me to remain aloof. They become a part of my tapestry. And you know, like me, they remember. They return to share their loves and lives and triumphs. And we still love them. And we have enough love for the next class, and the next."

Guillermo unlocked the door and pushed it open.

Deal Me a Card

CHAPTER 48

THE FIRST VOLLEY OF BULLETS took Guillermo down. He uttered a guttural croak. Fell on his side against the wall.

Emma had no time to scream. She saw the purple cobra emblazoned on a bare brown chest two feet in front of her. Its hood was spread. It reared its head. With a vicious leer, it spurted its forked tongue at her face. But it was her body that recoiled from the blast of the automatic weapon aimed at her waist. The force of its sputtering poison dropped her.

****

"Why are the bad guys winning?"

The anguished scream sprang forth silently from Guillermo's mind.

"I love her but I cannot save her. I've lost…"

The energy it took the dying man to form the broken thought left him with no strength for the effort needed to lower his lids over his eyes. So, unseeing, the orbs stared straight into the face of his lover. A final beat fluttered, struggled, then faded from Guillermo's shattered heart.

****

Emma tried to call out to Guillermo. He would save her. He was looking right into her eyes. Her beloved had rescued her from terrible pain before. Just three months ago. He had pulled her back from the grave. Why was he not soothing her, stroking her brow as he had done so often, so that the gnawing in her gut would quit and the throbbing in her chest would stop choking off her breath.

Her head screamed,

Doctor Schwarzman, we both agreed that my mother was wrong. I needed a man, I needed Guillermo, I need him

Deal Me a Card

now. You said it was a good thing that I found him. I thought we were safe in his house, our home.

Where am I now? Where is he?

Why I'm five years old again, a girl-child.

My stomach hurts. I'm dizzy, walking around and around, circling and mourning the death of the little yellow bird.

No more fluttering, no more soaring, like a soul freed from all pain...

Please God!

Its wings are taking it up, up

Not to the clouds, since it is impossible...

Too little to reach so high.

But the little yellow bird touched heaven, anyway,

Felt the power of a little piece of the peace,

of the élan that only love,

even forbidden love will, must give.

It lies on the concrete floor, cold now on the hard, ungiving stone,

Like a soul withdrawn, forcefully wrested, dragged away from the fruit not allowed to be tasted; but savored nevertheless.

In its eyes blank dullness sits triumphant.

Already the army of ants has taken possession of the tiny corpse, brigands, looters sucking blood, juices, the last rich vestiges of life and any kind of identity from the yellow bird.

It feels nothing, senses nothing any longer.

Death numbs like the awakening from a dream that confounds and confuses the one who just a moment ago was lost in the delicious reverie of what should not, must not ever be.

The ants will slowly diminish the life, reduce the little yellow bird to a dry skeleton, to a slack bundle of bones devoid of marrow, empty of pulsating life-generating blood.

Deal Me a Card

And leave behind, as they march to the next conquest, a few desiccated feathers lacking luster.

My stomach aches...I can't breathe. These men won't help me...

What's that sound, music of the spheres...

Why, it's daylight...The pure blue sky, sterilized by the sun, a vivid contrast to the brown earth...it's rubbing shoulders with the rounded hilltops.

That circling hawk, eyes searing the ground far below for a somnolent snake, is the only thing moving.

There, there's a player, he's an oboist, tootling under the old oak. A crowd of fellow travelers...I...follow this pied piper like bees sucked in by the pastoral lilt. Only he knows the notes, composed a hundred, a thousand eons earlier, to wrap around our hearts.

Gophers in the fallow soil dig their way out to listen.

A daring jack rabbit lopes to the shelter of a cactus bush so that he might catch the beauty of the chords.

Now the hawk merely circles forgetful of hunger. The snake escapes.

The audience...I...am serene, lulled by the rhythm.

Notes float through a haze. The blue's turning to grey, the music's fading, Orpheus walks away...

The burning...the pain's returning.

One more hour, two minutes in real time, slid by.

A tsunami, released by tremors reverberating from the crash of bullets against flesh, surged upward from the deep. A red choking vomit gushed from Emma's lips.

****

The two bodies twitched in protestation. Then they were still. Guillermo and Emma lay close enough that the fingers of the man and the woman touched. Two pairs of eyes gazed into each other, eternally expressionless.

Deal Me a Card

The killers looked down at the corpses, lying in the doorway. Pools of dark red blood, seeping from under them, were beginning to stain the marble tiles scarlet.

"You think they're dead, Nosey?"

"Dead as the raccoon we ran over on our way up.

"Here, Chico, call this number. She'll get the message to Smiley. The job's done.

"Then, we light the match, and we're out of here."

Deal Me a Card

CHAPTER 49

THE BLAZE RISING FROM THE FLAMES emitted a glow that sparked a thirty-minute pseudo-sunrise. When that light darkened, nothing remained for the wailing sirens and the gushing fire hoses to mourn.

Slowly the stars overhead blinked back their tears and disappeared.

Deal Me a Card

CHAPTER 50

THE THREE FRIENDS HAD DINNER TOGETHER. To celebrate the start of a long holiday weekend. Eduardo had brought the salad. In the spirit of the holiday, Alfredo purchased the tortillas at the corner store where the woman worked who attended classes with him. Sofie made *pupusas* and meatballs. The full-bodied scent of the entrée made the trio's mouths water.

All three drank diet sodas of some kind. It was hot enough they consumed three liter bottles. Also they kept toasting their triumphs. Sofie and Fredo both achieved the first level of culinary arts skills that opened all manner of job prospects at local restaurants. Eduardo had attained six months sobriety and work retention.

They sat around the kitchen table where they had eaten dinner. The conversation was relaxed.

"If everybody else who has it as good as we do, and appreciated it, the world would be a better place," Sofie mused.

Eduardo picked up the thought,

"Have you been following the trial of the Henderson brothers? Man. Those guys had everything and they had to go and off their grandparents. Okay, so they were being abused by their dad when they were kids. Boo hoo. Who isn't? Just you wait. They'll be in prison forever."

Alfredo added,

"Some kids got it right. Take Brenda and Araceli. Both lose their boyfriends. Violently. Murdered right in front of their eyes. If that happened to me, I think I'd lose my mind. They'd lock me away in the loony bin. What do they do? Organize the community to fight gangs. I hope they'll be at Mr. Guerrero's party on Monday. I want to ask them how I can help during the summer events."

Deal Me a Card

Sofie answered,

"I'm sure they'll be there. The Guerrero family is totally committed to stopping the violence. They want to celebrate the progress and announce the upcoming plans. But it hasn't been all treaties and truces. You heard how Mr. Guillermo took on that guy Smiley?"

Eduardo had been tracking the news on that crime and the unfolding complications.

"Sure did. The dude, Smiley, he's in jail now. The problem is with the other two, one of them did the actual killing. They're still on the loose. Foothill Division and every other police department in the state have APBs out for them. Not good news."

"You heard, didn't you?' asked Alfredo.

"About what?"

"How Father Reilly spilled the beans on Mauricio to Detective Yow for the murder of Felipe, Brenda's boyfriend."

Sofie made the sign of the cross.

"*Dios sabe,* God knows," she murmured low, "he must get to hear many, many secrets. *Muy, muy dificile por los padres.* Must be real difficult deciding how to get the information to the police. Priests are supposed to keep their mouths shut about the sins people confess to them. But I bet there are ways."

"I know somebody who's had it with this corner of this bloody Valley!" Eduardo remarked.

"Eva called me the other day. Asked if she could pay me to move the family to Santa Clarita. With Ralphie in the wheelchair, she needs a safer place. Mr. Guerrero, though I hate the old man's guts, is giving her a position at the Jones and Guerrero Construction office out there. The development is still going strong."

"So, Eduardo, when is she leaving here?" Alfie queried.

"Next weekend. It'll be the end of the month. She's renting a pretty nice place. Townhouse. Two bedrooms; den

Deal Me a Card

downstairs that Ralphie can use as his bedroom; two baths. Little garden."

Sofie stated, "I'm happy for her. It's not easy with a kid who will never be out on his own. God help them."

She stood up and stretched, curving her back to ease the twinge. She rubbed her vertebrae with the palms of both hands.

"Want some coffee, gentlemen?"

Eduardo accepted. "Sure! Is it that strong Colombian blend? Pour me a cup. I'll take it black and sweet. Could you bring it to me?"

He turned to Alfie who was still sitting at the kitchen table.

"Why don't you bring Sofie's cards over here, Fredo? The deck's on the counter near her purse. Right behind you. We can play poker."

He looked at the clock on the wall. "It's almost ten thirty. Time for the news. I'll watch TV for a few minutes."

Eduardo strolled into the tiny living area, hit the ON button. He sat down on the sofa. The late night anchor appeared on the screen.

"Breaking news tonight. A fire reported at a home in the Sylmar hills is turning out to be more than arson. Two bodies were found in the ruined residence of Guillermo Guerrero, a community activist, college instructor, and San Benitez businessman."

Sofie and Alfie rushed into the room as they caught his words. Sofie was clutching a half-cup of coffee in her hand. Alfie, two steps behind her, carried the deck of cards. He balanced heavily on his good leg. They stood aghast in front of the TV absorbing the newscaster's meaning.

The commercials flashed on. The two plumped down, one on either side of Eduardo, their bodies close to each other.

Eduardo was the first to speak. His voice was leaden.

"I think…they're dead."

Deal Me a Card

He tried to deny the truth. "Maybe not. They go out to dinner on Fridays."

Then he accepted the truth.

"If it is them, part of our world has just burned to the ground."

His knuckles kneaded his eyes, to stop the flow of tears.

Alfie's hands were shuffling the cards. His fingers belonged to a robot, going nowhere as if the assembly line which it operated had malfunctioned.

"It's them. Guillermo Guerrero. Emma Hazelton," he affirmed, his voice cracking.

"They were good people. They cared. They worked hard for this community. They wanted the best for us." Clearing his throat after each sentence as if choking.

He set the cards down on the table in front of the sofa when he finished speaking.

The TV screen continued to blare its jingles. Alfie got up, limped across the four feet and turned down the volume. Returned to his seat. Silent. Tears streaming down his cheeks, he sat numb. He covered his mouth with his fingers, stifling his protests.

Between muffled and disjointed sobs, Sofie's words were a stark contrast to the muted cacophony of the TV. Eduardo's arms were around her now. She was bent over, crouched low, her face covered in her hands.

"*Madre de Dios! Dios mio , Dios, ten piedad!*" she sobbed.

Then she raised her head, screaming to address her whole world,

"They were our friends, *nuestra familia*, our family. Why did they die, *Dios mio, por que*! *Mi familia, nuestra familia!*

Eduardo hugged her close. Alfie patted her shoulder. Neither of them said a word.

Deal Me a Card

An image returned to the TV. In hushed tones it predicted sunny weather for Memorial Day, but a good chance of some rain in the following weeks.

Sofie's weeping subsided. She brushed the back of her left hand across her runny nose. Ignored her cheeks streaked with tears. She struggled to speak. Her voice broke. She swallowed. Tried once more to talk. Succeeded.

Sofie looked back and forth at her two friends.

"In the morning we will learn more. It's too late tonight.

"Now, *por favor*, please, Alfie, deal me a card."

\# \# \# \# \# \# \# \# \# \#

WHAT JESUS DID

The Sequel To

DEAL ME A CARD

Available In Spring 2013